A
HOME
FOR THE
LOST

BOOKS BY SHARON MAAS

FICTION

Of Marriageable Age
The Lost Daughter of India
The Orphan of India
The Soldier's Girl
The Violin Maker's Daughter
Her Darkest Hour
The Far Away Girl
Those I Have Lost
A Home for the Lost

THE QUINT CHRONICLES

The Small Fortune of Dorothea Q
The Secret Life of Winnie Cox
The Sugar Planter's Daughter
The Girl from the Sugar Plantation

NON-FICTION

The Girl from Lamaha Street

A HOME FOR THE LOST

SHARON MAAS

bookouture

Published by Bookouture in 2022

An imprint of Storyfire Ltd.
Carmelite House
50 Victoria Embankment
London EC4Y 0DZ

www.bookouture.com

Copyright © Sharon Maas, 2022

Sharon Maas has asserted her right to be identified as the author of this work.

All rights reserved. No part of this publication may be reproduced, stored in any retrieval system, or transmitted, in any form or by any means, electronic, mechanical, photocopying, recording or otherwise, without the prior written permission of the publishers.

ISBN: 978-1-80314-239-5
eBook ISBN: 978-1-80314-238-8

This book is a work of fiction. Whilst some characters and circumstances portrayed by the author are based on real people and historical fact, references to real people, events, establishments, organizations or locales are intended only to provide a sense of authenticity and are used fictitiously. All other characters and all incidents and dialogue are drawn from the author's imagination and are not to be construed as real.

PART ONE
PARADISE LOST

Guyana, September–October 1978

LUCY

September 1978

When you read this, I'll be dead. We'll all be dead. The kids too. You'll be told it was suicide but that's a damn lie. It ain't no suicide if you ain't got no choice in the matter. If you was forced. It's murder in cold blood.

My name is Lucy Sparks. I write this in secret. So you can know the truth of it, the whole truth. If you get to read this, it's all over. It's about to happen. Tomorrow night. White Night. Words that chill my heart to the core: the night of death. Our death. All of us, every man jack. So I need to get this out there. He wants us all to die!

So if you read this, it's happened. We're all dead, hundreds of us. Maybe a thousand. Nobody ever counted. But now you'll count. You'll count our bodies.

You'll know now what happened, but you won't know why or how. I'll tell you. Because you won't know all of it. What went on before. The inside story. That's why I'm writing this. When we're all dead maybe someone gonna find this. I pray to God not Moira. Not HIM, that devil.

Lucy glanced up and out the window above the desk, then dug the heels of her hands into her eye sockets and rubbed as if to stimulate her brain. What next? Think. Think quickly. Where to begin? Back at the beginning, the glorious first days? Or about Alexis, and Beryl, and the horrors of now? What would they want to know, the folk who found this? It might be the only truth they'd ever know. Such precious time. Just a few minutes. So little space. Just one page, and Moira might return at any time.

Stolen time, stolen paper. Paper was so rare. This was the first she'd seen in a year, apart from the newspaper scraps they gave you for the toilet. She was so starved of the written word, she read those news snippets, sitting on the wooden latrine seat while taking a crap: half-sentences, half-words, as if they were the bestseller of the week. Reading them in the half-light.

Stop dreaming and write. Stop wasting time, wasting thoughts.

She shook her head as if to cast away the cobwebs. No time to lose in idle musing. Moira was always in the radio room these days, which meant there was time to do things like this, steal paper and write forbidden letters to people in the future, people who'd read it when she herself was dead. Now that she'd got this office job, a promotion. A chance to steal paper, write. But what?

Journal. That was it. Write it as if it were a journal. Write what's in your heart, and don't try to analyse.

She used to be good at writing. An A student in English, before it all went wrong and she hit the streets. She wrote better than she spoke. 'A promising student,' Miss Harvey had said. She could go far. And look where she'd ended up. On the streets. Stealing. In jail. And now, worse, much worse.

She was good at stealing; Big Joe had taught her well, back then, and she used those talents in this place. Yesterday she stole a tin of Father's Corned Beef, but not for herself, for

Granma. God would forgive her because Granma was hungry. But if Moira found out...

Confess. Confess everything.

She stole more than paper, she did worse than steal. She lied, she betrayed her friends; and all in the name of survival. *Write it down. Confess.*

She wrote quickly, bunching the words to save paper; an illegible scrawl. Would they be able to read it? No matter. Just write. They had those handwriting experts; they'd decipher it. *They.* The CIA, the FBI, the people who'd find this once she was dead and they found the bodies.

She stopped again; her hand trembled with the horror of her greatest sin. Worse, far worse than stealing. She couldn't begin to write *that* down. Couldn't even think it. No forgiveness for that one. She'd go to hell. *But it was just survival, Lord, I had to! I had no choice! You know I wouldn't kill! Never!*

Confess.

Beryl Hoskins did not die of cancer; she was 'put out of her misery'.

She underlined the words three times, for emphasis. Tears pricked her eyes. Poor, sweet Beryl, who never hurt a fly. Why couldn't they just send her home, to die with her own people? 'We have to get the dosage right,' Moira said, and gave her a glass of spiked Kool-Aid. Lucy'd been right there, handing Moira the glass. Moira was Father's right hand and Lucy was Moira's. She obeyed because she had to. Else she'd end up like Alexis, and what good was that to anyone?

This place, this living hell, made a devil of her. *Write it down.* One day someone would find it – when they were all dead. Who would that be? Who would read these hastily scrawled, rambling words? And what would it be like to be dead? Would she look down from heaven, or up from hell, see them reading it? What would they think of her?

Don't judge me, you who read this, because what would you have done? See, I learned to go along to get along, like they say, and to lie, even lie about others to save my own skin. I'll admit it. I did just that. You can call me an Uncle Tom if you like, but we all do it here. That's what he's turned us all into: a bunch of lying cowards. Even our own brothers and sisters are not safe from us. We throw them to the lions.

The damning words tumbled out of her, agonised words, whips of self-flagellation. She read the whole page over and longed to tear it up and start again. Dumb stuff. They'd think the worst of her. Mom would read this too, one day, when she was dead.

MOM! Help me, Mom, get me out of here! You were right and I was wrong! I don't want to die! Forgive me, Mom. You warned me. I was so stubborn. But you were right.

Stop it. Stop whining and write. Think, Lucy; think. What else to say? Just a few more lines till the page is full. Don't waste space with your own confessions. And stop scribbling. Write slowly, clearly, legibly.

Don't believe those tapes: they are lies too. This is a snakepit of back-stabbers and liars. It's a prison; the jungle is our wall, two hundred feet high and as many miles wide. The guards have guns with orders to shoot. Bruno Grimm shot a woman once, shot her dead. Her name was Jeannie Young. Her crime: she tried to run away, but he got her first. No one will ever know, outside of Jonestown, because the law can't reach us here. Tell Jeannie's mom how she died. Get us out!

Time to stop. The page was full; enough for today. Where to hide it? She had no idea as yet, but for the time being she tore it from the back of the writing pad, folded it up, and tucked it into her bra.

CHAPTER ONE

DECEMBER 1978

Zoe

At last it was all over; every last body counted and flown home. Time to collect myself, collect the facts, to write, to put it all into order. Time to go back to the beginning, to my first sighting of Moira. Back then, she was just a weird white woman on the *Witte de Roo*; nameless, to me, yet even then somehow sinister. But maybe she's only sinister in retrospect; we're all wiser with hindsight. Back then, she was nothing more than weird. Weird. A weird white woman. I certainly noticed her – who wouldn't?

I first saw her on the jam-packed Georgetown dock, that fateful day in early October. Tall, thin, blonde, suntanned and ramrod-backed, she sliced through the hot sweaty crowd, the Black and brown hoi polloi, like a swift steel blade, hurrying to board before us, the rabble. That first glimpse of my nemesis should have set all my red flags waving, but those were my sweet days of innocence. I shuffled forward with everyone else, crossed the gangplank, and sought a sufferable spot to spend the next thirty hours.

Once on deck I saw the reason for her haste. She'd bagged

one of the rare benches, a bald-faced demonstration of her privileged place in the pecking order. A whole bench for herself and her bags. Technically, anyone could have asked her to remove her luggage and make room for three more passengers, but no one did – such is the power of white skin in this country, and she knew it. And there she sat for the entire trip, sitting and reading, or lying and napping and planning devil's work, she and her bags together giving a clear message to us lesser beings of dark skin: *keep off*. A message so clear that even in her short toilet absences the bench stayed free.

No tourist, this one, in spite of the sunhat and sunglasses, both of which she removed once she'd found her luxury spot in the shade; and anyway, what would a tourist be doing on that ancient wreck? Her skin had the tanned, leathery, mosquito-bitten look of a seasoned backpacker, and the cheap flip-flops on grubby feet told me the rest. Tourists wear expensive leather sandals in the tropics; backpackers know better than to tempt the natives.

She bore that worn-out look of white nomads, people who washed their panties in rivers and slept under the stars in sleeping bags or hammocks. It's the martyred, emaciated look of a survivor, a foreigner who has learned to bear amoebae, dysentery, hepatitis and worse with patience, and even pride, so that survival itself is a badge of honour.

I'd met a couple of them on the road, and knew the type: ageing road-hippies, American, usually, and past their benign prime. They'd start off warm and fuzzy, eagerly emulating the laid-back natives, spouting their naïve back-to-nature ethos to anyone who'd listen. I know, because I'd once been one of them.

Some of us simply return home to fade into the background, happy to find a modest but secure place in the very Establishment we once disdained. Others end up edgy, weary and, occasionally, trickier than a huckster in an Istanbul bazaar. I suspected the latter of this lady.

I sat down-deck from her on my battered, trusty old suitcase. I passed the hours reading an old paperback or writing in my notebook. Sometimes I sipped at my flask of fresh water, and nibbled at the picnic Mum had packed. But mostly I just lay back, using a rolled-up towel as a pillow, and daydreamed of Paul, nursing my precious little heart-knot of grief. My favourite pastime.

Poor dead Paul.

But once, to stretch my legs, I walked the deck, and passed by she-whom-I'd-one-day-know-as-Moira. She looked up, and fleetingly, our gazes met. I smiled, because that's what we backpackers on-the-road do: we look, we smile, we stop and introduce ourselves. Networking, they'd call it today. But her cold eyes deflected mine; the *Hi!* died on my lips and I realised I was no longer abroad. My restless travelling years were over and I was back in my own country, and to her, I was just another native, invisible, whereas she stuck out like a pineapple in a crate of oranges.

I walked on and forgot her. I didn't take her indifference personally. White travellers are used to being stared at by the dark-skin-locals, and that was all I was to her. My interest, to her, was routine, my smile the ogling of a common sycophant beguiled by white skin. Perhaps I wanted to beg. To her, I supposed, we all looked alike.

Around us the *Witte de Roo,* a rickety rust-bucket dating back to the days of our Dutch colonisers, bounced and rocked to the rhythm of full-blast reggae; some young people were partying up-deck. A group of hunky Black men down-deck swigged back rum, jostled and laughed, tore off their shirts, slapped each other on the back, leered at Moira with rudely appreciative noises, bellowed insults at each other, hawked, spat: little boys begging for attention. East Indian market women, returning home from Georgetown with their baskets empty, yelled to each other to be heard above the clamour, gossiping, joking, enjoying the forced holiday. Screaming children chased each other around the decks. Babies bawled. Hobbled chickens clucked. A bent old man led a bleating nanny goat around on a string.

The *Witte de Roo* herself chugged unconcerned forward before a foaming wake of white. The Atlantic at starboard stretched away in undulating brown, muddied by the Amazon's mouth several hundred miles south. We were headed up-coast, to the North West District near the Venezuelan border.

Other districts in Guyana have magical names: Essequibo, Corentyne, Kyk-Over-Al, Rupununi, Pomeroon. The North West is so remote they haven't troubled to name it, and my future there was just as vague. I sought wholesome, clichéd things. Peace and quiet. Back to nature. A new beginning. Except – but I didn't know it then – this trip was not the beginning but the end; the end of an era, Part One of my life.

Just a few yards away from where I sat musing on my suitcase sat the woman who would usher in the Grand Finale of that first era. My life can be divided into a Before and an After, neatly axed apart by Moira.

Moira. The Angel of Death, I was to call her later, when it was all over, but that day she was of fleeting interest; only much later, with the wisdom of hindsight, did I realise I'd met my nemesis.

Peace and quiet? Back to nature? *Honey, have I got news for you*, Moira would have mocked.

CHAPTER TWO

We arrived at Port Kaituma the next day, only half an hour behind schedule. Once the last stragglers had left the boat I struggled to heave my suitcase down the deck and on to the gangway. Midway across a huge male hand closed over mine. I looked up to dismiss the porter; they can be obnoxious in their insistence on helping. But it was only Uncle Bill.

'Let me take that,' he said, and tried to lift it. 'Whew – what you got inside there, girl, gold bars?'

I smiled up at him, and let go of the handle. 'Far as I'm concerned – yes.'

We reached the dockside. Uncle Bill put down the suitcase and I flung myself into his arms. 'God, it's good to be back.'

'Let me look at you.' He pushed me away, holding me at arm's length.

'You lookin' thin, man. Edna gonna have to feed you up. Come along, the Jeep's over here.'

Uncle Bill edged the Jeep into the crowd. The *Witte de Roo*'s arrival was the big event of the week in Port Kaituma, and the atmosphere buzzed with carnival jollity. Everyone knew everyone, it seemed, for they called and whistled to each other, gathered in gossiping groups, filling the road. One or two people stuck their heads through the open window to exchange a few words with Uncle Bill; others grinned and waved to him as the Jeep crawled past. Others yet ambled, chatting down the middle of the road with their baskets and bundles as if they had all day, pointedly ignoring us creeping along behind them. Some people wheeled bicycles, others rode them at a snail's pace, wobbling and ringing their bells. The man with the nanny goat passed by, crouched on the crossbar of a bike pushed by a younger man. The goat itself, strapped to the handlebar with several lengths of rope, bleated pitifully to an indifferent God of goats. An escaped chicken bounced off the Jeep's bonnet, and a young girl lunged after it. It fluttered away over the sea of heads and disappeared. The crowd parted to swallow the girl, and she too vanished.

We passed a flatbed truck parked on my side of the road. Something caught my eye, and I looked back: it was the white woman from the *Witte de Roo,* climbing into the passenger's seat of the cab. A Black man sat at the wheel, his elbow resting on the open window.

At last the crowd thinned and the Jeep picked up speed. Port Kaituma was less a town than a straggling collection of dilapidated buildings strung along a red sand track. One little shop, as ramshackle as the rest, crouched behind a bright red Coca-Cola sign twice its size, like a beggar girl ashamed of her rags. Doll-size houses of weather-beaten wood squatted high above ground on spindly stilts, sagging with age as if longing to lay themselves down to sleep. Their corrugated iron roofs were more rust than roof, their front stairs buried in masses of tangled vines, their windows sad, glassless holes. Yet the faces framed in those windows were anything but sad: mothers and little children laughed and waved as we passed by, their faces bathed in the pure joy the very poor can derive from life's simplest gifts, in this case the gift of friends passing by. How rich they are in that ability, I thought as I waved back. I envied them.

Before long we'd left all habitation behind us. Overhanging branches whipped at the windscreen as we bounced and rattled along a tunnel carved through dense jungle, filtered sunlight tinting the air a luminous green. I closed my eyes. The dank earthy smell seeped through my being, transported me back twenty years. Uncle Bill's catching-up chatter faded into a pleasant backdrop, and the annals of my memory opened up.

When I was six, Mum broke a leg falling down the rickety staircase of our first home in Georgetown. She was laid up for several weeks, and farmed us four children out to various uncles and aunts. My two younger brothers and elder sister stayed in town, but I ended up with Aunt Edna here in the North West, and she became a second mother to me, her children my new brothers and sisters. She ushered me into a magical world where plants could speak and the earth could heal, where senses cracked open and souls broke free.

One strong image seeped up through the mental crusts laid down by the years: me, waking up one dark morning, before the crack of dawn, sitting up in bed, rubbing the sleep from my eyes; she, outlined against the silver moonlight flooding the room and veiled by the mosquito net, an angel bending down to me in her robe of white.

'Where you goin', Aunty?'

'Shhh! Don't wake Uncle! I'm going to birth a baby!'

Aunt Edna was the midwife for the whole region, like her mother and grandmother before her. Immediately, all sleepiness fled.

'Can I come too?'

She paused. I was not an easy child. I poked my nose into places it didn't belong, and up here in the tumbling abundance of nature's miracles I had at first gone berserk with curiosity. That could be dangerous; it could even be fatal. But Aunt Edna led me through these perils with an angel's patience. She taught me to open my eyes and feel into the life around me, to respect and understand nature's secrets.

'But it could take hours, and you got school!'

I pressed my palms against the net. She placed her own hands flat against them.

'Please, Aunty! Please!'

'Well...' Education, for Aunt Edna, was many things. It was school, it was books, but it was also Life itself, and sometimes Life has more to teach than words and numbers.

'Very well. But you gotta be real quiet and not say a word and don't touch anything, and if you get frightened, go outside and wait. Right?'

'Right!' I scrambled out from under the net, and ten minutes later, she and I were gliding down the creek in a two-man canoe, she paddling, I dangling my fingers in the sweet black water. Ahead of us, in a smaller canoe, was the husband of the mother-to-be, and that picture embossed itself in my mind: two canoes sliding silently down a moonlit creek, the Amerindian's broad bare back rippling with the rhythmic stroke of his paddling.

And then, later, the birth itself: after all the panting and groaning and moaning, after all the straining and struggling, the anguished cries of the new mother and Aunt Edna stroking her forehead and crooning back at her so that she stopped her crying and listened and her breathing became slow and long and rhythmic, and the whole world became a still straining everlasting moment as if holding its own breath; and then the wet, slimy thing bursting out into the open, a wriggling, squawking purple thing, and everybody laughing and the woman crying, but from joy not pain, and the entire power of the universe filling the room and my heart, too vast for me to hold so I, too, burst into tears.

Later, when the baby was washed and clean and wrapped in a sheet, they let me hold it, and awe and wonder swept through me and the majesty of that moment dug itself into my being and lodged there forever.

Right now, bouncing in the Jeep beside Uncle Bill, that morning came to me with all the immediacy of a motion picture. The memory engulfed me in an emotion so strong, tears welled up behind my closed eyelids. I bit my lip, and almost choked in sadness. Uncle Bill must have sensed something, for he glanced over.

'You OK?'

'Yep. I'm fine.'

But I wasn't. I hadn't counted on this. Coming to the North West was supposed to wash away the sorrow, soothe the wounds that refused to heal, not rip them all open again. Yet here it was. All the agony all over again, laid bare and raw and bleeding. I held my breath and willed myself to be strong and stared through the window, unseeing, so Uncle Bill would not notice. But he already had.

'Zoe.'

I turned to look at him.

'Zoe, life hasn't stopped. It goes on.'

'Unk. Please. It's OK.'

I placed my hand protectively on the gold band dangling on a chain round my neck, invisible under my T-shirt.

'But—'

'No buts. I *know* all that. I know I have to move on. Heck, what d'you think I've been doing the last three years?'

'Running away?'

'No, not running away. Getting out of my hole. Facing new

challenges. Taking life by the horns. Getting a grip on life. All the clichés. It hasn't worked, Unk. I'm right back at square one, starting all over again, and I know what I need. Peace and quiet. That's why I'm here. So my simple request is—'

'"Don't talk about it."'

'Exactly! Please! I know you care, but I have to fix this on my own.'

Uncle Bill placed a hand on mine, turned to me and smiled. The tension melted.

'Sorry. I didn't mean to patronise you. And you know, I love your writing. We read all your articles. Amazing, just amazing. We're so proud of you!'

I smiled back at him. 'Thanks.'

'You should write a book, you know.'

'Brilliant idea, Unk! It would never have occurred to me!'

Our eyes met and we both burst into laughter.

'Aha! So that's the big secr—'

'Shhh!' I put a finger on my lips; he smiled and nodded.

Then suddenly the countryside opened up, and on either side of us the jungle gave way to green fields, rolling hills, and white wooden cottages on tall thin stilts, some of them slanting at precarious angles. Uncle Bill slowed down, and I soon realised why: children ran out into the street, golden half-naked barefooted Amerindian children, laughing, shouting, running beside the Jeep. Uncle Bill smiled and waved, and looked at me, but I said nothing.

My heart constricted. The sight of children, happy laughing children, always did that to me. With older children, like these, it was just manageable. But any age under two, and the scar burst open and bled all through my being. Now, I took a deep breath. This was no good. I pushed away the sadness and waved back, my smile a mask.

The Jeep slowed further as we passed a long, low wooden building in the middle of a sandy courtyard. A weathered sign on the fence proclaimed: NORTH WEST DISTRICT HOSPITAL. I pointed to it.

'That's where you work, right?'

'Right. I'll take you to visit one day soon. You'll want to get to know my colleagues; a couple of them are your age. It can get lonely out here, so they'll be company for you.'

Right, the neighbourhood kids, for me to play with. I smiled; for Uncle Bill I was still a child, six years old, not twenty-six. I decided to indulge him.

'That'll be nice,' I said.

'In fact...' said Uncle Bill. He braked, reversed the Jeep a few yards, and turned into the compound. 'No time like the present. This won't take a minute.'

The moment he left the Jeep the children swarmed around him, laughing, crying out his name. He laughed too, and held up his arms, and the smaller ones leapt up to dangle from them. My heart lurched. This was a bit too close for comfort. I shoved my hands into my pockets, bowed my head and followed him up to the building.

A covered veranda ran all along the front, from which doors opened into the wards – all very basic. He showed me around, but there wasn't much to see, just what you'd expect in a country hospital: a few beds, a few patients, a pretty nurse or two. They all smiled and greeted him with 'Hello, Dr Turner,' and he in turn introduced me as his niece.

The last ward was the nursery, and there a tall dark man – early thirties, perhaps – in a white coat stood leaning over a child's cot. He looked up as we entered, and smiled in greeting, and he was so handsome I immediately saw right through Uncle Bill's little ruse.

Here we go again, I thought. Ever since I'd returned to Georgetown a month ago Mum had presented me with a never-ending stream of eligible – and willing – bachelors. That was one of the reasons I'd fled to the peace and seclusion of the

North West, but apparently, I wasn't safe here either; Mum was close to her brother Bill and no doubt had explained 'Zoe's little problem' to him, and asked for help.

Uncle Bill turned to me now, and gestured. 'Zoe, I'd like you to meet my colleague, Dr Andy Roper. Andy, this is my niece, Zoe.'

We shook hands; Andy smiled. His eyes, friendly and welcoming, drew mine, and in spite of my resolve I found myself smiling back. I'd learned the trick of creating inner ice, but even the coldest ice is vulnerable against the glow of a warm and genuine smile.

'Pleased to meet you. I've heard so much about you. I read your articles – fascinating!'

He tried so hard. He bent over the cot and picked up its contents, a little Amerindian girl with a bandaged head.

'...and this is Marie!' he said. 'A brave little girl. She'll be out of here in a day or two.'

Marie chortled and hugged him, raised the skirt of her little dress to coyly cover her face, lowered it slightly to peep over the top, hid again, giggled, and finally, throwing shyness to the wind, flung out her chubby arms to be taken into mine.

I froze. Instead of taking her I stood there staring, arms stiff at my sides.

Marie quickly withdrew her arms and turned her head away. Andy's smile vanished.

Uncle babbled an excuse. 'Zoe's tired,' he said. 'She's had a long trip. Zoe, go and wait in the Jeep, I won't be a minute.'

Mortified, I mumbled a goodbye and walked away. Sorrow welled up inside me, the heartbroken, soul-gutting grief only a mother who has lost a child can know.

My own child had never seen the light of the world; I'd never held her in my arms, but she'd been real, as real a being only love can create. We'd thought of her as *she*, Paul and I. Our hearts had already contained her. We'd built a golden future around that golden child, heard her laughter, gloried in her rosebud bloom. She'd completed us. Since losing her – and him – I could not bear the beauty of a living infant, could not see or smell or hear, much less touch, a baby's newly minted perfection without crumbling to pieces. And it had happened again.

As I walked back to the car I looked back, and knew they were talking about me; Uncle Bill's shrug, as if excusing me, and Andy's hand gesture that said 'It doesn't matter.' Marie was back in her cot. She watched me walk away, as if she'd just met an alien. I wanted to melt into the ground. I wanted to run back, take her in my arms, tell her it wasn't *her*, it wasn't personal, it was *me*, sick me. But I didn't. I climbed into the Jeep, slipped my inner mask back into place, the take-no-prisoners mask I presented to the world.

Uncle Bill joined me a moment later, and we drove off. As we left the hospital compound, I spoke.

'I'm sorry. I didn't think, I...'

'It's OK. You're tired.' Uncle Bill said, but I could feel he wasn't finished, that he had a whole lot more to say.

'Zoe, could we...? I mean...'

'Unk, please! I really can't talk about it. I'm going to be fine, really, I promise. I know what you want to say and it's OK. I've *got* a grip on myself.'

Uncle Bill nodded, as if to comply, but he couldn't resist one last barb: 'Just, sometimes, it slips.'

I looked away, biting my lip. He was right.

I must have fallen asleep, for the next thing I knew the Jeep was slowing down to turn into a gateway beneath a wooden sign proclaiming PARROT CREEK FARM. The paint was faded and peeling, but it was the same old sign of twenty years ago, with an open-beaked parrot flying above the words. The Jeep crunched to a halt in the white sand of a wide compound.

The main building, a many-windowed wooden house on stilts, stood to the right, just as I remembered it. The paint was now grey and peeling rather than white, and the palings in the wraparound veranda had several gaps, but it was the same old house. Another snapshot emerged from the recesses of memory: the coconut grove in the background, the latticed chicken coop beneath the house, even the barking dogs rushing out to greet us. Behind the dogs came a plump little Amerindian woman, arms held out to embrace me: Aunt Edna. I fell from the Jeep and into her arms.

I hadn't seen her for three years, not since my wedding.

Clasped in her arms just like back then, the next memory came rushing back. I heaved as if I would cry again, but didn't. Aunt Edna rubbed me gently on my back as if she knew, and no doubt she did.

Mine had been a fairy-tale perfect wedding. Flooded with joy, I floated up the aisle of St George's Cathedral in the tried-and-tested tradition of brides: in foaming white, on Dad's arm, smiling left and right to a sea of joyfully turning faces, slowly in step to 'Here Comes the Bride'. Eyes brimming with pride, Paul received me at the altar; we exchanged our vows; the priest declared us man and wife; Paul kissed me; the female guests wept appropriately.

Then it was over, and we were married. Mendelssohn's 'Wedding March' pealed out. Paul and I, hand in hand, hurried laughing to the open doors and out into the sunshine, the wedding guests pouring out behind us.

Outside the cathedral, the press photographers waited. Not much of a press, it was true; there were only three newspapers in the entire country, and no television station as yet. But I was one of their own, Zoe Quint, Women's Editor. I ran the *Sunday Chronicle* women's page, and weddings were usually my domain. Weddings, and babies; and now it was my own wedding, and, in a few months' time, my own baby. And Paul –

a pillar of society: Correia's Jewellers, the Jaycees, Georgetown Cricket Club and all that manly stuff. Ours was the wedding of the year; they'd reserved a half-page just for us.

Instead, we got a whole page – but edged in black.

Press cameras clicked, freezing those moments of perfect joy forever. Fate's little prank, considering what she had up her sleeve, and the tragic headlines that would juxtapose those same photos just two days later.

The wedding guests swarmed around us, and confetti rained down, blossoms from heaven. I hugged aunts and cousins, Grandma Quint, all the uncles, kissed babies, tossed my bouquet at the single girls (Edna's daughter Jennifer, my maid of honour, caught it, as intended). Paul shook countless hands, said countless thank-yous and, I noticed, glanced surreptitiously at his watch.

And then it rained, bringing the joyous cliché to a sodden end, one of those sudden and violent tropical downpours where you're drenched through in seconds. My wedding dress was ruined, and so was my coiffure, but both had served their purpose, and a short, sharp burst of rain at a moment of great happiness is always a blessing. Paul and I ran laughing to the waiting limousine and scrambled into the back seat, dripping with nuptial bliss.

One devastated *Graphic* reporter waxed poetic in his coverage of the tragedy two days later:

> *As the car drove off, the pounding rain tore the 'Just Married' streamer from its bonnet, lashed it to the road and whipped it into the kerb, where it squirmed beneath the torrent like a dying snake. The car turned a corner and the rain stopped as if on cue, as suddenly as it had started. The twisted streamer lay half-sunken in the roadside gutter. The rest of it lay on the road, where the departing guests trampled it to shreds.*

For some macabre reason, as if inspired by premonition, someone took a photo of that mangled streamer just before the trampling began, the mocking words still visible. It was published in the *Chronicle*, and became a symbol for the shortest marriage the country had ever known. With the wisdom of hindsight, people said later that it was an evil omen and that they'd known at once that the marriage was doomed.

All this came back to me as I gave myself into Aunt Edna's embrace, and perhaps the healing process started in that moment, for I knew: no more running away. No more adventures. No more roaming the world for a place to lay my head and forget. I had come home.

LUCY

Nobody knows the exact date around here, we have no calendars, but it must be October by now.

Moira returned from town the other day and she brought poison with her. She's been bringing it up bit by bit. I know cos I saw. She came from Georgetown on the Witte de Roo. She's been collecting it for White Night. She's got enough for us all now. I know because she told me and she showed me. It's in the hospital, right next door to Alexis's room, locked in a steel cabinet.

Lucy chewed the end of the pen, remembering.

'Up to now, it was just practice,' Moira said. 'Next time it's the real thing.'

When y'all read this, when it's all over, you'll know the real thing worked. She'll be dead by then. All of us. Dead. It'll be a real White Night.

Moira had told her that deliberately, just so she'd spread the word. They'd cried wolf so many times people had stopped caring, stopped believing, stopped being afraid. Nobody took White Night seriously any more.

We've had three trial runs up to now, and each time, we'd believed it was real. The first time was the worst, back in July. The loudspeakers on high poles at every corner, that crazy, screaming voice: 'White Night! White Night! White Night!' The sirens screeching, driving naked terror into every heart. The faces, eyes peeled open in trepidation. All of us lined up, to drink the Kool-Aid, believing it to be poisoned, our hearts thumping with suppressed panic. The goons in their combat uniforms, all with rifles, to keep us in check.

By the third time, we'd started to treat it as a tiring game.

Lucy's mission, now, was to wake them out of their lethargy. Because she knew: one day, White Night would be real. Maybe the next time. She had to tell the world. She began to write again:

She wants one more trial run, this time with Alexis. To see if it works. She wants me to kill Alexis. And I can't say no, or she'll kill me. Or lock me up in the Box.

Her hand trembled and she stopped. Alexis. Her best friend up until the betrayal. Now Alexis lay in the hospital drugged out of her mind. Alexis was the next guinea pig. Moira said Beryl was old and sick so they couldn't count her death. Alexis now: Alexis was young and healthy and strong.

That morning, Moira had sprung it on her, out of the blue. She'd looked at Lucy with those pale blue X-ray eyes of hers, and asked, innocently as if really wanting Lucy's opinion: 'What do you think, Lucy? Should we try it out again?'

What should she say to that? She hung her head and said nothing.

'What's up, Lucy? Don't you think Alexis deserves to die?'

No! Lucy's heart screamed. But, 'Yes,' she whispered, and lowered her eyes in shame.

'Lucy, look at me when you speak.'

She looked up, and saw the ice in Moira's eyes.

'Alexis was a conniving, lying bitch. She was hungry for sex with Father, and when he did her the favour, she turned on him. What do we do with vicious bitches who cry rape, Lucy?'

'Punish them,' Lucy whispered.

'Exactly. Alexis does not deserve to join us in our White Night. She's a traitor. She must go first, and alone. Do you agree?'

Well, what should she say? If she said no it would be *her* instead. She fought the tears and the desperation and looked Moira in the eyes and said yes.

'Good. We'll try that out soon. I knew I could depend on you. You're the only one I trust.'

Lucy turned her face away and nodded, loathing herself for the coward she'd become. That's what this place did to you, turned you into a coward and a traitor, denying your best friend. But it hadn't always been this way.

Once she'd hoped to save them all. She'd hoped to win so much trust she could go to Georgetown on her own, with Danny and Granma. And then run, tell the authorities, save them all. But she was never good enough for that privilege, never as good as Patsy. Patsy got to live in Georgetown with all her kids, like a normal person. The lucky, lying bitch. Because only through lying and deceiving did you get to be in town.

Still, Lucy was luckier than most. While they worked in the fields, dawn to dusk, in the broiling sun and in the rain, Lucy got office work. She did the accounts, controlled stock, bought the rice. Buying the rice was her last hope. It got her out of here. Maybe one day she'd get a chance, run away. Like Katy.

When Katy Harris defected a few months ago, ran back to

America, Lucy thought she'd tell the world and they'd all be rescued. That the US government would come and save them. But nothing of the sort happened. Obviously, Katy had just gone underground to save her own hide. People who talked got killed. Or else Katy *had* talked, and nobody believed her. Why should they? The truth was so preposterous. Mass suicide of 1,000 people? The world would laugh it off.

If she kills Alexis I'm going to kill her. And him. I swear it. With my own hands. I'll kill them both.

CHAPTER THREE

'Come, lemme show you your room,' Aunt Edna said. She took my hand and led me across the yard to a hut built against the forest's edge. Uncle Bill followed with my suitcase.

'It's very simple,' she said in apology. 'But you said you wanted...'

'It's perfect!' I said as we entered the hut. It was indeed just that: a one-room hut, the walls of thatched coconut branches nailed to a wooden frame, and reaching only up to my shoulders all around. The door was simple bamboo, the floor of rough wooden boards, the roof more coconut thatch. I remembered it vaguely; back then, Uncle Bob, Aunt Edna's father, had lived here.

I let my rucksack slide to the ground and looked around. There wasn't much to see. In a corner, a simple bed with a mosquito net balled up above it. A table and chair, some shelves. A kitchen cabinet, on top of it a one-burner kerosene cooker.

'You can cook here if you want,' said Aunt Edna, 'but you ain't got no fridge. We ain't got no current. But of course you gon' eat with us. Tuck in the net tightly, mosquitoes bad here.

And keep your feet away from the net, otherwise the bats gon' come.'

I remembered: the bats. The vampire bats that flapped through the dark, endemic to the North West; I'd been terrified of them back then. Another memory burst forth: the black shadow of a bat crawling across the mosquito net in the dark, wings spread. Memory is selective; it pushes away those things that mar the perfect image. The bats had flapped themselves into some gloomy corner of my mind, and here they were again, casting a dark stain across my picture-book recollection of a paradise of flowers and butterflies, puppies and kittens and rolling green meadows. I shuddered, and pushed them away.

'And the toilet? I'm bursting!'

Edna walked to the wall and pointed over the thatch to a small outhouse in the yard.

'It's very simple,' she apologised again, 'but we got a proper flush toilet in the house, you can use it. And outside you got water in the drum, rainwater. I'm sorry...'

I hugged her and laughed. 'No, no, this is fine. *Toilets I Have Known*: could be the title of my next book! I remember one, a rest stop on a ten-hour bus trip in South India – oh my God! Just a plate with a hole in the middle, between two footrests. You're supposed to squat down over the hole – trouble is, seemed some of the people didn't know how to aim. Little lumps of poo all over the place, swimming in a stinking brown liquid.'

Aunt Edna chuckled. 'What did you do?'

'What could I do? I was desperate. You can't be too squeamish on the road. I did my stuff.'

We laughed together, and Aunt Edna relaxed. Though a queen up here in her own country, Aunt Edna was touchy about her living standards. She'd suffered much humiliation on her rare trips to town, for Amerindians were at the very bottom of the racial hierarchy, as low as Blacks, and people can be cruel. 'Where's your grass skirt?' the Georgetown folk teased her, and explained things like electricity to her as if she were a child. They asked her if she could read and write; if she'd ever driven in a car.

In fact, Aunt Edna was a phenomenon. She'd been educated by the nuns at the Catholic Mission in an Amerindian community in the Essequibo district. She proved so bright they'd sent her to Georgetown, where she lived at the Ursuline convent as a boarder and attended St Rose's High School for Girls, one of the country's three most prestigious secondary schools. After graduating, she'd returned to the Essequibo to teach and deliver babies and develop self-help programmes for the local women about health and hygiene. There, she'd met Uncle Bill; they'd married and moved here.

Now, she said briskly: 'We gon' go shopping tomorrow... Well, I gone now. Rest youself. Supper gon' be in about an hour. Come over when you're ready. You can have a shower, too.'

'Wait,' I said. I opened my backpack and lifted a cloth bag out of it. I opened that, too, and one by one removed the little luxuries I'd bought in London, things you couldn't get up here, or even in the whole country. Guyana was in a permanent state of emergency; sometimes, all you could get in the shops was bleach and matches. I put the items into her hands, and she exclaimed over each one.

'Oh my, Palmolive soap! I ain't seen that in years! And shampoo! Ovaltine! And books, novels! You spoiling us!'

'You deserve it!'

She embraced me; we packed the items back into their bag and she left with it.

Alone at last, I stretched, yawned and took a deep, long breath. I threw myself onto the bed and closed my eyes. Home at last. I lay there for a while basking in that knowledge.

Three years. Three years on the run, never more than a month in one place, always moving on, never growing roots. Making friends and leaving them, knowing you'd never see them again. Crossing oceans and continents, sleeping in hotels and boats and in the homes of strangers, never knowing what the next day would bring. And writing, writing, writing, at every moment writing, fixing each day on paper as if the very act of living was so ephemeral it would drift away and leave me bereft and alone and empty.

Uncle Bill was right: I'd been running away and I knew it. That was why I was here, now.

I had one gift, and that was listening to people. I'd built my career on that gift. People told me their stories, and I wrote them down.

At first it had been happy stories, soaked in feminism, of contented, successful women with enviable lives, the stuff of women's pages everywhere, women who juggled careers and children and marriages with ease.

In the last three years, though, it was the tragedies I wanted to hear. I ran after misfortune as if it were the Holy Grail, as if to cover my own woes with fates much worse. The world's ills became my stock-in-trade, exposure my mission, as if I alone could free it of pain and injustice and cruelty, just by writing. My pen was the sword with which I'd conquer evil. I was the Joan of Arc of writers.

But only I knew it was all a mask, and behind that mask I was always this: bereft and alone and empty, left that way by the day, the hour, the minute that had ripped my life apart. I was just so tired of it all. It hadn't worked. I was no better now than on the day I started, but now I had come home. The exhaustion I'd been holding off overcame me and I drifted off into the sweet oblivion of sleep.

. . .

Later, after a quick shower over in the house and a change of clothing, I knelt down and opened the suitcase. It was packed full, mostly with red and blue notebooks, organised according to a simple system: red for South America, blue for Asia, subdivided into countries and labelled accordingly. India had been the last, and that's when I'd finally admitted failure, given up and come home.

Of course, I hadn't lugged this whole suitcase round the world with me. I'd sent each book home the moment it was full, and Mum had collected them, and here they were, the last three years of my life packed into a suitcase.

I arranged the notebooks on the shelves, as well as several reams of paper and other stationery. Tucked into one corner of the large suitcase, another, smaller case. I opened that and removed a portable typewriter, placed it on the table.

Finally, the backpack, now half-empty. I removed my few pieces of clothing and stacked them on a different shelf. Last of all I held up a small, framed photograph. A bridal couple: me and Paul.

I looked at the photo for a long time; touched it, and placed it too on a shelf, all on its own, in a place of honour where I could see it from the bed.

Just then I heard my name, and the door creaking open, and swung round, almost in guilt. It was Aunt Edna. She looked at the photo, then at me, and then at what she held in her hands: it was a small transistor radio.

'This is for you. We get Radio Demerara quite well.' She switched it on and fiddled with the antenna. The crackle of static gave way to a funereal dirge.

'*Deaths and Messages*,' she said with a satisfied smile. 'Every day at four. If you don't mind, I'll come over to listen to that now and then.'

The mournful announcer began, '*The death is announced of...*'

'Is how we hear who dead,' she said. 'And how we get we messages. Better and quicker than letters, nah? Lemme see that photo...'

She took the photo from my hands, looked at it, up at me, and frowned.

'I want to see you looking happy like this again,' she said. 'One year of mourning is OK. Three years is too much. Wake up, child. Andy's a good boy. Life goes on.'

'I—' The protest rose to my lips, but she wasn't finished. Her hand reached forward to touch my neck; she slipped a finger beneath my chain and lifted it, gently pulling my wedding band out of hiding. She weighed it on her forefinger, as if inspecting it for value.

'Don't chain yourself to the past,' she said, and before I could finish my protest she was at the door and out.

'See you at supper, then,' she called as she walked down the stairs.

Supper was a simple affair, just the two of us, for Uncle Bill was called out on an emergency. I struggled not to yawn the whole time, and she sent me away early to bed. I was grateful.

'You want me to come with you?' she said as she handed me the torch. 'It's a bit spooky out there at night.'

'No, it's OK. I'm not afraid of anything.'

'Not of ANYthing?'

I chuckled, and flicked the switch on the torch. 'Well... that's not quite right. One or two things scare the hell out of me but I'll be fine. Goodnight.' I hugged her.

I crossed the yard to my hut, the beam from my torch cutting a ray of light through the blackness. It was like crossing through an ocean of sound: jungle noises crashed in on me from all sides, the chirping, cheeping, beeping of a billion bugs. It was a moonless night, and the torch's light made the darkness seem even blacker, while the jungle on my right loomed up in a black wall above me. I shivered, and it wasn't from the night's chill. Indeed, the breeze that brushed my bare arms was quite warm. Not just the breeze swept past me; a flapping of wings, and a black creature swooped down, touching my cheek. A bat. I flinched, and quickened my step.

High above me, stars twinkled like sparkling pinpricks in the canopy of black, and round about me, other tiny lights flickered and swooped: fireflies, or else eyes, watching, from the jungle. I jumped as a piercing screech rent the curtain of sound, followed by a vicious yowling and snarling: animals fighting. And then a crashing of branches, and a beat of silence, as the jungle world held its breath for a moment, waiting; and then the night orchestra resumed its chirping, cheeping chorus.

With great relief, I reached my hut, and entered. Fighting off the mosquitoes, I prepared for bed. The little monsters flung themselves at me, hordes of vicious needles nosediving into my skin. My own counter-attack was terrible but futile, for the more I slapped them dead the more they came, and I hurried to tuck the mosquito net into the mattress. And then I dived inside it: I was safe.

The mosquitoes gathered outside the net, some perched on it like tiny birds of prey waiting their chance, others languidly, aimlessly winging around it, drawn by my blood. Their buzzing almost drowned the jungle noises. I wondered if I should take up Aunt Edna's offer after all, and move into the big house, but then another noise caught my attention.

A human voice, very soft as if from the far distance, hardly discernible, ethereal, as if floating over the forest canopy. A voice rising and falling in waves, like somebody giving a lecture. At times it grew louder, as if angry, then it became wheedling, placating. But I could not make out the words, or even tell if it was English.

Then suddenly, from far away, a muffled scream, and a

child crying. Behind the ghostly voice and the scream and the crying the cheeping jungle noises continued, a backdrop of natural sound to these new discordant noises. A bat flew in over the thatched wall of my hut, flew into the taut mosquito net, bounced there once, squeaked, and flew out again.

I scrunched myself into a foetal position, grabbed my pillow and pulled it down over my head, pressed it tight down over my ears. The noises stopped.

CHAPTER FOUR

The next morning, I awoke at dawn, and the sounds now seemed much friendlier. Outside my hut a kiskadee warbled from a treetop: *kisk-kisk-kiskadee!* The familiar cry conjured up happy childhood days, freedom from care, home comforts and all's-right-with-the-world serenity, wiping out last night's spook.

Aunt Edna was up before me: she was sweeping the yard as I went to the outhouse, and we waved at each other. I returned, grabbed my towel, and walked down the forest path behind the hut to the waterfall. I'd loved this place as a child: the path led through tall bushes down a steep incline to the creek the farm was named after. A smaller track led off to the waterfall pouring out of the hillside in a silver gurgling gush. This early in the morning the air was fresh and the water ice-cold, but it sliced away the last shrouds of night and travel and fatigue and left my body tingling and my mind exultant. Just one quick soap-down, a rinse, and I was ready for the day.

'What were those weird noises last night?' I asked at breakfast.

Uncle Bill, pouring me a cup of coffee, clucked his tongue.

'Ah, yes, I forgot to warn you. That's Jonestown, a settlement up the river. Some Americans have settled there.'

'Really?' I said. I raised the steaming cup to my lips and blew on it. Local coffee; better than Nescafé. The aroma curled around me as I reminisced aloud.

'They're everywhere, those Amis! All over South America – every backwater village has a commune of American hippies.'

It's then that I should have recalled Moira, but didn't. She had completely slipped my mind. But perhaps my mind was doing me a favour? Perhaps it had sensed the threat to my peace she represented, and locked her memory away? Our subconscious minds are much wiser than our conscious ones, and mine knew more than was good for me.

'No, not hippies,' Uncle Bill said. 'It's some crazy church. You'll get used to the noises. The loudspeaker is on sporadically, day and night. Some preacher giving a sermon. But at night the sounds carry better.'

I grimaced. 'Yikes! You don't say! I ran into a group like that in Peru, in the Amazon, deep in the jungle. Some American church got it into their heads to translate the Bible into the local Indian language and bring them the glories of civilisation. Teach the Indians how to wear clothes and eat with knives and forks and stuff like that. They built up a real little American town there, complete with drugstore and cinema and schools – yep, they had kids, too. Whole families living the American Way of Life deep in the Amazon. Surreal. Can't believe they've come here as well.'

Aunt Edna placed a plate of steaming hot bakes on the table, a typical Amerindian dish. I took one; it was almost too hot to touch. Uncle Bill passed me the butter. As they didn't have a fridge, it was in a jar, and almost liquid, bright yellow.

'No, it's not like that at all,' he said. 'They're not missionaries. They avoid the locals. Most of them are Black, too.'

'*Black* Americans? That's weird. What are they up to?'

'I met some of them,' Aunt Edna said. 'Couple years ago, when they first came. It was different then, only a dozen or so people. They was like pioneers – clearing the jungle, building the first houses, growing things. One of the women was pregnant and they asked me to deliver the baby, so I went in. They was nice people, young and enthusiastic. They loved it here, they said. It was kind of a back-to-nature thing.'

'Yes, back then there was no problem,' Uncle Bill said. 'Then last year they started coming in their hundreds, locking themselves away, acting strange. They fly to Georgetown then come up by boat. They got their own boat, the *Cudjoe*. Boatload after boatload came and disappeared into that place. And all those noises. God only knows what's going on in there. But apart from that, they don't bother us. The most anybody sees of them is when they come to get their supplies at Dora's shop.'

'Yes, once a week,' said Aunt Edna as she pulled back her chair to take a seat. 'Every Saturday.'

Stupid, stupid me. I'd come here for peace and quiet but all the old habits were still alive and kicking. I never could resist a good story.

'But that's today, isn't it? I've got some shopping to do anyway – maybe I'll bump into them.'

I was right back in journalist mode – bumping into people by planned accident was my modus operandi.

'What time do they usually go?' I asked casually as I poured myself a second cup of coffee.

It was the same rough jungle track I'd driven down the day before with Uncle Bill, but today I'd decided to walk. I strolled along at a leisurely pace, my empty backpack bouncing on my back. It was mid-morning, and already the sun's heat was filtering through the coolness of the jungle canopy and heating up the air. Though the track was in the shade, I could feel sunlight spreading, dissolving the dew and the last remnants of night's freshness.

The jungle was so close on either side that if I walked down the middle of the track and held out my arms I could almost touch the overhanging vines and branches. And that's exactly where I walked, down the middle on a raised and grassy platform between the two deep furrows. I'd been walking for half an hour when the faint hum of an approaching vehicle peeled away from the jungle sounds. I let it come a little closer, then moved to the side, pressed myself against a bush to let whatever it was pass by. It was a flatbed truck, bouncing along the track.

It slowed down to pass me. I stood still, my back to the jungle, to let it pass. A man and a woman sat in the cabin, the man driving, the woman a passenger, on my side. As they passed her eyes met mine. Only a grazing of glances, but in that moment my fate was sealed. Her eyes hurled a balled message at me, and mine caught it. I reeled with the impact. Never in my life, not in all the years seeking and finding the heartsick, the troubled and the downtrodden of this world, had I ever seen such desperation. Despair, tight as a coiled spring, and abject terror rolled up into a plea so pitiful it stung. Only a moment. The truck passed by, belching stinking exhaust. I quickened my pace.

Ten minutes later, I arrived in Nazareth village. The shop was easy to spot: it was the only one in a straggling collection of ramshackle buildings. The flatbed truck stood parked outside it. The driver emerged from the shop as I approached, bent by a bulging sack over his shoulder. He heaved the sack into the flatbed and re-entered the shop just before I did.

The woman with the stinging eyes stood at the counter, her back to me, talking to the shopkeeper. I walked up, removed my backpack, placed it on the counter, unzipped it, removed a shopping list, placed that too on the counter, and waited my turn. Half-turning, I saw the man lug another sack of rice onto his shoulders and leave the shop. At the entrance, though, he stopped, turned and spoke. His accent was American.

'Hurry up, Lucy, OK? I'm almost done. Just two more sacks.'

The woman was in her mid-twenties, Black, bent over a ledger into which Dora the shopkeeper was writing. At that moment she looked up, and for the second time our gazes met, and again that utter desperation. I recoiled. Thankfully, just then Dora asked a question, and called those bleeding eyes away from mine.

The man's footsteps distracted me, and I missed the woman's answer, but once he had left the shop she grabbed my arm, glanced at the door, then at Dora, then back to me.

'You gotta help me! Please!'

The words were whispered, but with an urgency that made them sound loud. She glanced at the door again, and back to me. Terror quivered in her eyes.

I stuttered: 'How? I mean... what's...'

She did not wait for me to finish. 'Call my mom for me. Please! In America!'

The man re-entered the shop. The woman had already let go of my arm. Hidden from his view, she grabbed the list I'd placed on the counter, turned it over, picked up Dora's pen and scribbled across the back.

Dora went into the back room. Immediately the woman grabbed my arm again, pulling me nearer to her. Her long fingernails dug into my flesh; it hurt, and I flinched away. As our eyes met, her grip loosened, and her hand slid down my arm. Hot sweaty fingers curled around my hand. Her eyes held mine, refusing to let go; they hooked me with raw terror. She shot a barrage of words at me in a low, raspy voice: 'You've got to get me out of there, he's gonna kill us, kill us all! He's mad, he's a monster, and *she*, she's worse, she's evil! Help me, please, get me out! Tell my mom! Don't tell the Embassy, it's full of CIA spies!

The FBI is after us! They bribed your prime minister! They'll warn her! Just get me out, please, I beg you, and don't trust the—'

The words had tumbled from her lips and fallen over each other like terrified creatures hurtling away from danger – but then she stopped mid-sentence as Dora came back. The woman immediately dropped my hand and stepped away; just in time, for footsteps behind us warned of the man's return.

'C'mon, Lucy!' he called, and she obeyed. Without a further word, not even glancing back at me, she scurried to the door and disappeared.

The truck doors slammed, the ignition coughed. I ran to the door; the truck peeled away from the kerb in a cloud of red dust, reversed into a small car park, and returned the way it had come. The woman sat at the window looking out, anguish brimming in her eyes. Back at the counter, I picked up the note she'd left and read the scrawl: *HELP!!!* Then: *Mom.* Followed by a number.

Dora took the note from me and turned it over to read my shopping list. Her movements were slow and casual, her face placid, and when she spoke her tone was chatty, as if she were totally unaffected by the little drama.

'One piece of advice, girl: don't mix with them people. She give me that number already, I tear it up.' My shopping list in one hand, she began to take items from the shelves and place them on the counter, muttering as she worked: 'Sugar, tea, washing powder...'

As if I hadn't heard, I asked: 'Where's the nearest telephone out here?'

'Telephone? Ha! You see any telephone lines out here? The nearest one's in Georgetown!'

'Well, that's the end of that, then.' Relief mingled with my disappointment; after all, if there were no telephone, I was off the hook. I did want to be off the hook, didn't I? My warning inner voice was quite clear: *Keep out of this. Don't get involved. Peace and quiet is what you're here for.*

I opened my purse and handed Dora a ten-dollar bill. She took it, opened a drawer, put the change into my open hand. I packed my shopping into my rucksack.

Her face still placid, Dora reached for the note lying on the counter. But involuntarily I grabbed it before she could, read it once more. My fingers curled around the paper, ready to scrunch it up and give it to Dora. Lucy's fate, and my own, hung in the balance. *Throw it away*, a sensible little voice inside me said. But I didn't. I smoothed it out and read it once again. Deep down inside, beyond the voice of reason, I felt a familiar nagging little itch. I folded the paper carefully, then tucked it into the front pocket of my backpack.

LUCY

She didn't get a chance to write for several days. She was clinging to a gossamer-thin lifeline. The note she'd passed to the woman in the grocery shop. Maybe she'd help, call Mom. But why would she bother? Why would she care? The shopkeeper had torn up the first note, right in front of her.

Whenever she thought about the note a spark of hope lit up within her. The woman had looked friendly; something in her eyes. Maybe she'd help. But then again, why? Probably she'd tear it up too. The tiny spark died. It was always that way. Hope flickered, only to die again. Like they were all going to die, soon. Days passed. And then, once again, she was alone in the office. She grabbed the notepad, and a pencil, and thought for a moment. Maybe it would be good to start from the beginning so that people wouldn't think they were crazy.

When they find the bodies the world will say we're a bunch of loonies. Off our heads, to drink that stuff and die. But I want you to know we're not crazy. We're just afraid. Terrified. He keeps us in terror, and that way we do as he says, because we ain't got no hope. I'm gonna start from the beginning, to let you all know we was just ordinary nice people, people with a dream.

A big dream.

I was one of the first to come to Guyana, in the first group. The first days here were wonderful. We were all filled with hope and joy. We were the blessed. He'd sent us to the Promised Land and it was going to be paradise on earth. We called him Dad, because that's what he was. A loving father, who'd save us from evil America. We came to prepare the Promised Land for all of us. We were the pioneers, the Chosen.

There was me, and Alexis, and Chuck, Ray, Laverne – about twenty of us young people, friends. We didn't mind the hardships. We loved the place. The folks here, the Amerindians, are the friendliest in the world. We were welcomed and made to feel at home. We cleared the jungle, we built our first houses.

The words came easily today; they flowed from her. She wrote and wrote, not pausing once, reliving the early days.

I had Danny, and I was pregnant again. Ray was the baby's father, and it was a mistake, a sin, but I knew Dad would forgive me, just like he forgave me for the other stuff I'd done before in my younger days – Big Joe, the whole drug thing, and the hold-up, and then even jail – but it was all behind me now. Dad had saved me and I was born again.

I loved the Indians. As we passed along the river on the Cudjoe they'd wave to us and smile, and the children were golden and beautiful, and so loving.

It wasn't all easy though. The mosquitoes, the botfly that laid its eggs under the skin and when they hatched, maggots came out. The vampire bats. There was all sorts of strange noises too. There were tigers growling in the night, and what they called howler monkeys that make a ruckus in the early morning.

And farming was hard. We fought the jungle and it fought us right back. We had to clear acres and acres of land. We battled with our machetes through razor grass tall as a man that cut right through our skin and made us look like we'd been attacked by a blind man slicing at you with a knife, covered with blood. But the cuts weren't deep and they healed up and we kept at it, and hope kept us going whenever we got the blues. This was our home. We was preparing paradise for the others, for Dad and the rest of the family, who was to come over in 1977.

But we never had a proper harvest. The rice crop never amounted to much. The vegetables we tried to grow was puny and wrinkled, and would never feed the hundreds due to arrive. One night, cutter ants came and destroyed our whole crop and all we could do was sit and watch as they marched off, each carrying a piece of leaf a hundred times its size.

But we was carried by the spirit of hope, and we felt blessed in our own way. My daughter Serena was born in 1976. She was delivered by a local Indian woman, the wife of the only American-educated doctor up here. My beautiful Serena was a miracle who made my joy complete.

When Dad came over it all went wrong. Dad, and Moira, and that lying bunch of no-accounts called the Inner Circle. That's when all hell broke loose.

CHAPTER FIVE

That night at dinner I showed Aunt Edna the note. Uncle Bill was working late again, so we were alone, sitting opposite each other at the formal purpleheart table so out of place in the otherwise simply furnished room. A single kerosene lamp flickered on a side table next to the dining table, and cast grotesque shadows on the walls: grasping monsters, winged dragons, oversized bats. Aunt Edna herself sat in the shade, but her eyes shone with a brightness that drew mine through the dark. She handed the note back to me.

'Lucy,' she said slowly, and her eyes turned dreamy. 'Lucy. That same girl name so.'

'What same girl?'

'The girl with the baby. Gap-tooth girl.'

'You mean the girl you...?'

She nodded. 'Yeh, I birth the baby, nice healthy li'l girl. The mother name Lucy, she got another child, li'l boy.' She held out her hand to show me how big the boy was. 'Lucy was so happy, she love that baby so much.'

'Well, if it was the same Lucy, she wasn't happy yesterday.'

'See, I knew that place turn bad, real bad. Since all the people come it turn bad. And that man...'

'What man?'

'The man on the loudspeaker. Since he come the air poison. A poison cloud hang over the place, and one day it gon' bust. Poison worse than bushmaster.'

A shiver ran down my spine. I had a short sharp vision of the bushmaster, the most venomous snake in the bush, curling and writhing among the shadows lunging across the candlelit room. The staccato bleeping of the night noises outside grew suddenly louder, and Aunt Edna's last words echoed through them with the power of a prophecy. I felt suddenly afraid.

Without warning, Aunt Edna scraped back her chair and stood up. I looked up, startled.

'What's the matter?'

But she'd already disappeared into the kitchen, leaving me alone with the flickering shadows and phantom snakes. I nibbled on my chicken drumstick, unnerved. I was just about to get up and follow her into the kitchen when she reappeared, bearing a plate of sliced pineapple. The darkest shadows with their hidden ghosts seemed to flee at her coming; I relaxed. Then she spoke.

'You gotta help that girl!' It was a command.

'I want to, but how? There's no telephone up here, and I'm not going down to Georgetown for a while.'

'You don't have to call the number youself. You could write you mum. Ask she to do it. And...'

She paused. The silence and the shadows closed in once more, unearthly, disquieting. I spoke, just to break the spell.

'And...?'

'Zoe, you is a writer, you does change things. You got to do something. Find out about these people, find out what evil that man doin', write about it. Get them out of here, Zoe, before is too late! Get them out of here! I can feel it! I can hear it!'

As her voice grew louder and more desperate she clamped her hands over her ears, shaking her head as if to throw off a creature clinging to her skull, her face distorted in a mask of agony.

She sprang to her feet again and ran to the kitchen. This time I ran behind her and took her in my arms. Her body quivered as if under an electric current. I held her close, and gradually she calmed down. The shaking stopped.

She pulled away from me and took both my hands in hers. Her eyes pierced into mine.

'You got to stop the madness, Zoe. You're the one. God hear me prayers and send you.'

CHAPTER SIX

I didn't see Aunt Edna at all the next morning. I rose before dawn – I hadn't slept much anyway – and lit my kerosene lamp. Its flame flickered nervously, hurling up wild sooty fingers that painted black patterns on the funnelled glass and gave off putrid smoke. I adjusted the wick and the flame calmed down. I washed myself over the enamel bowl, went outside, did my t'ai chi, and got dressed. By the time first light crept over the forest I was ready. By now the flame burned steady and blue. The lamp stood on the table next to the typewriter, inviting me to take a seat. I did so.

With great ceremony I removed the machine from its case and set it on the table next to the lamp. I stuck two sheets of paper, a carbon between them, into the carriage, advanced it until the page was centred. Across the page I typed:

The Third World on a Shoestring
By
Zoe Quint
Book One: South America

As the keys clacked and the letters clicked into place across the page I felt the familiar elation – I was back in my element! Writing by hand into notebooks just isn't the same; it's the clatter of typewriter keys that gives me the rush, but I'd had no alternative in the past few years. Travelling light is the first imperative when you're on the road, and taking my typewriter was never an option. Touching it again was ecstasy.

There on the table sat the first of those notebooks. On its cover just one word: *Brazil*. I opened the notebook, perused the first page, removed the paper from the machine, put in a new page, and began to type again.

A minute later I was lost in another world. People and places loomed into my mind, as real as they had ever been. Smells and sounds and long-forgotten incidents rose up from memory, and my fingers hammered them into tangible, readable form.

The idea for this book and its sequels had been ripening in my mind for almost a year. On my way home I had stopped off in London to visit my brother David, and there I'd found a letter from an editor at Penguin. I had written to several publishers with the idea: a series of travel books for backpackers, loaded with tips and anecdotes; written as a journal, in first person, with all the wisdom of the road, and how to do it spending peanuts. Where to sleep, where to eat, the people you'd meet, who and what to avoid, who to turn to in need. Nothing political, nothing controversial, nothing of my usual style; though I did enclose a couple of my articles as a writing sample. There were no other books like this available – I was sure I had a winner.

The letter from Penguin was enthusiastic, and suggested a meeting. Once in London I rang the editor; we met, and discussed the details. I showed her a few pages of my notebooks; she couldn't read my writing so I read them to her, and she rocked with laughter.

'Yes!' she'd said. 'Go ahead. I love it!'

Nothing concrete yet, no contract, but as soon as I'd made some headway I was to send her the first chapters.

I could think of no better way to spend the next few years. I was heartily sick of the road, exhausted, and not too healthy due to my erratic eating habits over the years, and the various bouts of amoebae, dysentery and, once, hepatitis. Writing about my experiences would kill several birds with one stone: help me to consolidate and make sense of them, record them for the amusement of my friends and family, and give me a worthwhile occupation for the next few years. And, if this turned into a proper book contract, make some money.

I didn't need much to live on, but even so the insurance money was almost at an end. Thank goodness for Paul's sense of responsibility; the moment I told him I was pregnant he'd signed a life insurance policy, with me as beneficiary, *'in case anything happens to me* (him)'. I'd been against it; it seemed so pessimistic, sort of a self-fulfilling prophecy. Life meant well with us, I was convinced; we should trust Life, trust God, and all would be fine, happily ever after.

How wrong I was; how right was Paul. The payout from that policy had, literally, saved my life, or, at least, given me something to live for, a quest to divert me. Not much, perhaps, considering what I'd lost; but a straw to cling to, a direction to take. A way of forgetting, and moving on.

I wrote all morning. I forgot time and place, forgot breakfast, lunch, forgot everything. I was back in Boa Vista, and then Manaus, playing canasta with my friends from the Peace Corps, stepping among the rubbish on the docks in search of a boat to take me up the Amazon. By the time – on paper – I tied my hammock up on that boat it was almost midday in present time, and my growling stomach told me it was time to stop. I fell back into the here and now.

I pulled the last pages from the carriage, scanned them, and laid them upside down on the growing pile next to the typewriter. I placed a stone on them as a paperweight, covered the typewriter with a cloth, stood up, stretched and rotated my head. I felt light-headed and free – a magnificent beginning.

I was hungry. Yesterday, Aunt Edna had brought me a bowl of fruit. I ate a banana, drank a glass of water, then decided to go for a swim. I pulled on my swimsuit, wrapped myself in a sarong, and left the hut.

The stone path to the waterfall led on down to the creek. At the bottom was a long wooden jetty, to which three boats were tied: a rowing boat and two canoes. The creek was black and smooth, an elongated mirror reflecting perfectly the trees and shrubs that flanked it. The blackness, I knew, was deceptive. It came not from mud or dirt but from the centuries of composting jungle; in fact, the water was as clear as glass, fresh, sweet and cool, and, most important of all, piranha-free. I walked to the end of the jetty, let the sarong drop, and plunged into the water.

My hair still wet, my skin still tingling, I arrived for lunch back at the big house. At the bottom of the outside stairs I noticed a basket of ripe pineapples, and felt a prick of conscience; I'd promised Aunt Edna to go out to the field today to help with the harvest. I thought she'd said afternoon, but obviously she'd gone without me.

I found her in the kitchen, removing a pot of rice from the stove. She smiled up at me.

'Hello, sweetheart, you had a good morning?' Without waiting for an answer she continued: 'So you started your book – good! I didn't want to disturb you so I went to the field alone.'

'I thought it was this afternoon... sorry.'

'Don't worry, I changed the plan. Remember what we talk last night?'

I shuddered at the memory. She'd really scared me. Listening in vain for Jonestown's sounds had kept me awake half the night, and I'd tossed and turned in fitful dreams haunted by Aunt Edna's words. Now, the bright sunshine made last night's phantoms seemed like a bogeyman under the bed and last night's fears the terror of a little child. I chuckled.

'Yes! Auntie, you really spooked me, you know! Don't do that again.'

She didn't smile back.

'It ain't no a joke. It's a big thing. And I promised to tell you more about Jonestown today. Remember?'

My own smile faded.

'Yes?'

'I ain't gon' tell you. I gon' *show* you. You got to see for youself.'

'But how? Uncle Bill said they're so secretive that they won't let outsiders in!'

This time she smiled, winked, and placed a finger on her lips; in jest, since we were alone in the house.

'Is a secret. And don't tell Bill. It very bad of me; if your parents knew they'd have a fit. A big, big secret.'

She was teasing me; she knew very well what that word 'secret' would do to me.

'The thing is – there's a back way into Jonestown. We Amerindians know it. The inmates don't.'

'It sounds like a prison!'

She frowned. 'Yeah, a prison, with jungle walls. That's why you got to go. Zoe, that Lucy – she in danger, big danger. Look – just thinking about it I get gooseflesh.'

She held out her arm and, indeed, her brown skin was puckered, in spite of the midday heat.

'Why? What's going on in there?'

'I don't know. None of us really know. But we see things, hear things. You know, we Amerindians is a private people, we don't tell outsiders things, but in the village everybody know.'

'In Nazareth?' I remembered Dora, her reaction to the note Lucy had given me. She'd torn up her own note, she said; that was in keeping with Aunt Edna's words.

'No – not Nazareth. Akinawa village, up the creek. You can't get there by road. Near Jonestown. They know; they see. They watch. But they don't talk; we don't talk. But I feel... I don't know. I think this time, we gotta talk. To stop it. Those people got no business here. They don't belong. That man up to something...'

She shook her head, as if words failed her.

I prompted: 'What man? And what's he up to?'

'I told you – we don't know nothing. But we can tell when things ain't right. That voice at night, it don't give you the creeps?'

I knew what she meant. The voice had made my skin crawl. I'd put it down to this being my first night in the jungle; the night sounds, the animals nearby, the bats. But that eerie, faraway voice – even the memory sent a shiver through me. I nodded.

Aunt Edna looked at me in silence, as if assessing me, then turned away and went on with her work. She dumped the steaming rice into a bowl, uncovered a pan of seasoned fish. She placed a frying pan on the flame, poured coconut oil into it.

'No. I can't get you mix up in this. I shouldn't a tell you all this. Your parents trust me.'

'I'm an adult now.'

'Yes, but they worry about you. They want you to have peace and quiet.'

'I'm an adult,' I repeated. 'And this peace and quiet stuff is driving me mad.'

'I know... when people come up here from town they can't take it. It's *too much* peace and quiet. Nothing to do all day – no entertainment. We had visitors who flee back to town after one day.'

She must have seen me open my mouth to speak, as she added in haste: 'Not you – you've got your work. But I thought... I hoped...'

She paused. I waited. She was coming to the crux of the matter.

'Go up there with Winston. Go up the back way. Listen. You'll hear that voice from close up. You'll hear what he's saying.'

She tossed one of the fish into the frying pan, where it sizzled in the hot oil, and nodded.

'People up here don't want to know. Everyone says we got to mind we own business, ignore them. Even your uncle. But I got a bad feeling, Zoe, and I can't put my finger on it. You know, like when animals feel an earthquake coming, or a hurricane? Like that. There's a gathering cloud over there, over us all. A gathering evil. But if I tell the police they gon' laugh at me, me being an Amerindian and all. I know what they gon' say: Hocus-pocus, mumbo-jumbo. But if someone came with *facts* – if someone wrote an article, someone like you, with authority, exposed them, if it all became public...'

I grinned. This was more like it. 'So, when do I go?'

'I told you – this afternoon. Winston brought me this fish this morning and I asked him to take you. He agreed.'

She turned the fish in the sizzling oil.

'I'se a bad woman,' she said. 'I should be protecting you, not send you to that snakepit. Don't tell your uncle!'

'I won't,' I said. I enjoyed the conspiracy. Aunt Edna had always been different. As a child, she'd never protected me from risks; she let me face them, but told me how. She showed me the dangers, and taught me to deal with them. Mum would have had a fit if she'd seen certain things I'd done as a six-year-old, with Aunt Edna's blessing and advice. She'd have a fit now; but she'd never know, not until it was too late.

LUCY

I was nineteen when I first met Dad. I'd just come out of jail. Granma introduced me to him and that's how it all began. Granma sang in the choir at People's Temple. At the time I was a lost soul, pregnant and all alone, and with nowhere to turn. And Big Joe was dead. Big Joe died in that dumb hold-up we tried at the gas station.

I never in my life met a man like Jim Jones. Meeting him was like walking into a big warm beating heart and knowing you was never again gonna be lonely and afraid. Never, ever again, because this love was true, it was everlasting, bigger than myself, big enough for me and all my troubles. My yoke is sweet and my burden light, we sang, sweet Jesus, and that's how it felt to us back then.

That's how I imagined God's love to be, only I never experienced it before. And here it was, shining through this man. That's the word: it shone right through him. How can I explain it? Guess you've got to be lost like I was to know the feeling. Know that song, 'Amazing Grace'? I was like that too. A poor wretch that Dad was going to save. Just like in that song.

But this is not about me. It's about HIM. I want to let you know how this could have happened. Am I a fool? Are we all fools? Why am I here, in the hands of a lunatic? Was I wrong to follow him, to believe? Were all of us wrong? How could a man of God go so far over the edge? I don't know. It'll take a wiser person than me to figure it out someday.

CHAPTER SEVEN

Guyana is an Amerindian word meaning 'land of many waters'. Wherever you go, you are not too far off from a waterway: a mighty river, with its network of tributaries, or a narrow creek like this.

We had taken the rowing boat, and to my shame I let Aunt Edna, older than me, do the rowing, but she handled the oars with ease and lightness, and when I offered to take over, she only chuckled.

'When last you row a boat?' she asked.

'Um...' I frowned, trying to remember.

'Exactly.'

In fact, the creek banks were further apart than they seemed. Mangroves had completely taken over the creek, creeping across it as if to join in the middle and growing high above our heads, their roots like spindly legs pushing into the water. High above us ranged the treetops, and a channel of vivid blue sky, perfectly reflected in the black mirror of the creek. The sun had passed, and down here in the cool greenness the gloom held me in a shroud. Beside me the mangrove's tangles seemed like tentacles reaching out for me, and behind them, jungle shadows held all manner of life.

As we progressed the mangroves thinned out on one side, and soon a grassy bank appeared on our left, and then a coconut grove, and finally, the village. An Amerindian youth ran down to greet us, and caught the rope Aunt Edna threw to him. A horde of laughing children ran down behind him, most of them half-naked, all of them barefoot.

We climbed out of the boat, Aunt Edna first. She grabbed one of the smallest children, swung him up into the air and settled him on her hip, and looked at me as if expecting me to do the same. The children were not shy; they danced around me, squealing and giggling, eager to play, but all I could do was put on a smile, hang my head and stride forward towards the village. The children turned their attention back to Aunt Edna. The youth swung the basket onto his hip, and we walked up a path of crunched shells to the village.

Now two women came out to greet us. They hooked arms with us, one on each side, and walked us up to a wooden bench in what seemed like the village square.

The village consisted of about thirty small houses and huts. The houses, as usual, were of unpainted wood and raised on stilts. None of them was bigger than one room, though a few had box-like appendages clinging to them: kitchen annexes, just big enough to hold a counter and a kerosene stove. Most of the buildings, though, were no more than huts, just like mine, with half-high walls made of thatched coconut leaves. At the village centre was a huge round community building, the *benab*.

We sat down on the bench. The youth placed the basket of pineapples before us, and Aunt Edna distributed them to some of the women, who took them with exclamations of thanks and admiration. A man walked up and the women and children peeled away.

'Winston,' Aunt Edna said, 'my niece.'

Winston was short and sturdy, and wore only a pair of khaki shorts held up by a belt of frayed string. His arms and chest muscles bulged like thick ropes beneath his leathered skin, brown and shiny from coconut oil – I could smell its sweet aroma – and free from body hair. The hair on his head, on the other hand, was thick, solid black, and shoulder-length, held in a ponytail with a piece of twine. It was hard to tell his age, for his facial skin was smooth and free of stubble, his body lithe, yet his expression was that of an older man. His eyes seemed ancient, able to assess me in one glance. And unlike the women he did not laugh, did not smile; his mouth was a thin, straight line across his face, and were it not for Aunt Edna's reassuring smile I would have thought myself a nuisance, and left again. But when he spoke his voice seemed amiable enough.

'So dis is de girl,' he said, and scanned me again, as if wondering if I was up to the rigours they'd planned for me.

Winston waved a hand, and almost immediately a woman walked up, followed by a girl; the woman held a water coconut in each hand, the girl two glasses and a cutlass. His wife and daughter, I assumed.

Winston prepared the water coconuts for us. With a quick slash he sliced the crown off one, dug a hole into it with the point of his cutlass, tipped the glass over the hole and turned it all over so that the water gurgled into the glass; he did this twice, handing the first glass to Aunt Edna and the second to me, and in silence. Meanwhile, the younger children recovered their courage and returned; they crawled all over Aunt Edna, and would have done the same to me if I had given the slightest sign. Which I hadn't.

Fifteen minutes later, I was alone with Winston, in a two-man dugout, sliding up the creek. We both held oars, but even as I dipped mine into the water I could feel his strong thrust propelling us forward. The canoe cleft the creek like a knife, silent and sure, piercing the mirror-like surface with a cut so clean it left hardly a ripple, the water opening as we came and closing as we passed.

High above us, the trees arched like the dome of a cathedral, leaving a ridge of blue through the dark green canopy. The light was green and cool, scented by creekwater and saturated with the tang of moist earth and rotting leaves, moss and marsh and mould, acrid with beetle-juice and sweet with fermentation. Sound and stillness surrounded us, stillness so deep it could not be disturbed by sound. The high-pitched chirp of insects, punctuated by the rhythmic tinkle of oars and the occasional parrot squawk, seemed merely to scratch the surface of that silence.

Soon the creek narrowed and the mangroves returned, thicker and higher than ever, reaching out from both banks and leaving just a narrow central channel to pass through. After a while Winston turned into another, even narrower creek, almost completely covered by the tangle of mangroves. Here, the trees were higher and closer and rose up on either side of us in deep, dark walls. I shuddered involuntarily, an inner trembling rather than a physical one.

The tropical rainforest is not my favourite place. I'm a sea person; I like open spaces, wide views, far horizons. There's none of that in the jungle. It's teeming with life, and not just audible, visible, discernible life. In the Peruvian Amazon I'd met Indians who claimed to know the spirits who lived in there, evil spirits and good ones.

Now as we slid up-creek between the mangroves I felt a faint inner tingling that told me we were not alone. Whether good or evil I could not tell, but I knew they were there, watching without eyes, listening without ears. I wanted to speak, to dispel the feeling – for silence is its medium – but right now, speaking seemed crude.

I was a foreign body, as tangled as the mangroves around

me, outside nature's rhythm and out of synch with time and place. Winston's sinewy back before me, rippling with the rhythmic motion of rowing, was my only anchor in an inexhaustible *now* and an overwhelming *here*. His solid presence kept me rooted in time and place.

I only know that at some point Winston stopped rowing, and turned the canoe in between the mangroves, and I realised that a small channel had been cut through them leading to the bank; and on the bank a log had been firmly lodged into the earth to form a kind of landing stage and step. Winston signalled to me to get out. He followed, and tied the canoe to a tree. He entered the jungle. I followed.

He carried a cutlass in one hand, and attached to his belt a leather sheath, from which protruded the wooden handle of a knife. I by contrast had a camera and a pair of binoculars dangling round my neck. He was barefoot; I wore jungle boots. His legs were bare; I wore old but tough jeans. Yet there was no doubt who was better equipped for this world.

The earth was black and spongy from centuries of composting leaves. At first, wild bushes blocked our way and he hacked through them to clear a path. I could see that a path had been cleared here once before, as the tangles were thinner than elsewhere, but this was jungle property and anything stolen is reclaimed in no time. *Slash, slash, slash*: Winston sliced our way forward.

After a while the undergrowth stopped and we were enclosed by tree trunks. Here, the path seemed even less distinguishable, but Winston walked on with confidence, seeing signs I could not. He still held his cutlass. I was glad of that: my imagination ran wild, and every rustling became a snake, every crooked branch a tarantula. I was ashamed. So much for my proud boast to Aunt Edna that I feared nothing.

Suddenly Winston stopped, standing stock-still as if listening, his back rigid and alert, as if coiled springs lay beneath the skin. He turned round, put a finger on his lips, and pointed – behind my back, and up. I turned and looked.

On the sturdy lateral branch of a tree, high up, lay a jaguar. Watching us. As still as a statue he lay, the only movement the twitching tip of his tail. In the shadows his eyes burned yellow and bright, unblinking and strangely serene. His face wore a still, inscrutable serenity, something archaic and penetrating and wise, as if he could see right through me and into my thoughts and mock my fear, just as a cat watches a mouse with dignified apathy. My hand flew to my mouth to stifle a gasp. I looked at Winston for my cue. Suddenly, that cutlass and that knife seemed grossly inadequate.

But Winston merely smiled, gestured to me to follow, turned and walked on. Unwillingly, I obeyed, reluctantly turning my face away from that mesmerising stare. I remembered reading somewhere that wildcats only attack from the rear, and that they can be kept at bay by wearing a mask on the back of your head. With my back to the jaguar I felt exposed, a willing prey, and as I walked, I held my breath. Only Winston's back ahead of me gave me the courage to go on, for my imagination ran amok and would have paralysed me. But nothing happened. After a few steps I looked back: the jaguar was gone. Gradually, my heart stopped its frantic racing.

A distant memory rose up then, of Aunt Edna telling me a story about jaguars. God made the jaguar the king of the jungle, she said, but gave him the command never to eat men; and the jaguar, unlike Adam and Eve, obeyed, and since then stays away from humans, eating only fish and small, weak or young animals. We had never been in danger. In fact, it's rare for a human ever to glimpse the jaguar, for it's shy and stealthy, and keeps away from us.

I had no idea how long we walked. Once again, time stopped – a second became eternity, and eternity a second. After a while I felt myself melting into the rhythm of the jungle.

It was as if nature's soul had started to seep through my own tangled spirit, dissolving fear. Winston's confidence was potent and contagious, and seemed to take me by the hand and lead me on. The jungle seemed less menacing, its sounds less threatening, more the benign song of a million souls calling out their kinship.

After what seemed like several hours, or a few seconds, Winston turned, placed a finger on his lips again and spoke his first word since we'd left the village. He pointed to the sunlight gleaming between the trees ahead of us, and whispered: 'Jonestown.'

CHAPTER EIGHT

It must have been around now, just as I was exploring the backwaters of Jonestown with Winston in early October, that the telephone rang at the American Embassy's agricultural attaché's office in Georgetown. Rex Bennett answered it. Rex, who was to become my friend and would-be lover. Rex, who tiptoed through this world of secrets and conspiracies, truths and half-truths, helping me to sort the wheat from the chaff. Things were just about to get hot, but nobody knew it yet. With the wisdom of hindsight, we later figured out that this was the moment: that telephone call is what set the ball rolling.

On the line was Congressman Leo Ryan, from California. Later, much later, Rex reconstructed the conversation for me, told me of the dynamics: Leo pushing, Rex stalling, doubting, rebutting. Could anything have been changed, had his reaction been different? But no. We cannot rewrite history, it is what it is. But Rex took notes and shared them with me.

'Rex?' Ryan said. 'It's me, Leo. Listen, there's been a couple of developments. Since Katy Harris's story broke, I've been swamped with letters from relatives, asking the government to get their folks back. They call themselves the Concerned Relatives, and they're making a lot of noise.'

A few months previously Katy Harris, a privileged member of what she described as Jonestown's Inner Circle, had escaped with a story so sinister, so outlandish, nobody she told believed her.

Rex Bennett was dismissive. 'Leo, I told you. I've been to Jonestown twice myself and not heard one single complaint from the residents themselves – people on your list. I spoke to each one of them personally. Those people are there because they WANT to be there; , I've had not a hint of evidence to the contrary.'

'Well,' said Ryan, 'Just maybe they're telling you what they have to tell you? The reports I'm getting all tell a different story. Jones has a way with people: coercive, manipulative. According to Katy—'

'You can't really take that that woman seriously. I mean, come on. She's exaggerating to get attention, and she's sure getting it. It's all dramatics.'

'Your predecessor didn't think so.'

'Dan? I know. But in hindsight, that was all a bit like a bad thriller, wasn't it, that secret escape action...? And that story of hers. Those threats. Leo, the United States government won't be held at gunpoint. We won't be blackmailed. And anyway, it's an empty threat. Mass suicide? It's ridiculous. They'll never do it.'

'I'm not so sure. Katy—'

'Well, I am. And you know why? Because of the children, and the mothers. You've got over two hundred kids up there, more if you count the teenagers, with their moms. That's the best safeguard ever. Moms protect their kids. Trust me, it's all hysteria.'

'I'm not so sure, Rex,' said Ryan. 'The way Katy tells it...

Anyway, like I said, we've had some new developments. Katy's going to the State Department next month to tell her story. We're hoping it'll lead to a formal investigation. And I've put in an application with the State Department to come and see for myself.'

Rex drummed his fingers on his desk. 'You're putting me on the spot, Leo. Jones isn't going to like that, but I'll let him know. You, and who else is coming? How many?'

'Not sure yet. A lot of folk here are asking questions, getting involved. Might be a small delegation. Journalists, concerned relatives.'

'Well, let *small* be the operative word. The smaller the better. The man's paranoid as hell, thinks the world's after him. I'll talk to Patsy about it.'

'Patsy?'

'Patsy Boyle. Their representative in Georgetown. Nice lady, very level-headed. Easy to talk to. She's a liaison officer for Jones; , we speak to him through her.'

'Well, you do that. I'll let you know as soon as the trip's approved. *If* it's approved.'

Rex walked to the bookshelf, took down the fat Jonestown folder, and made a note of the conversation.

Later, when it was all over, he showed me those notes.

'Poor Ryan!' I said. 'He walked straight into a trap. And you let him.'

'No. I did my best to stop him. It's all there, in these memos.'

'You could have done more.'

Rex turned away. The guilt in his eyes spoke volumes. I felt sorry for him; it's so easy to point the finger of blame in retrospect. But in fact, Jonestown's fate had been no secret. It was all there, broadcast to the world, shouted from the rooftop. The

Amerindians knew. Why not the Americans? Or if they did know, why didn't they act? I'd never understand.

'The loudspeakers, Rex. The loudspeakers. It was all there for anyone who had ears. Shouted from the rooftops.'

'They turned off the loudspeakers when they had visitors. You of all people know that.'

It was true. Yet it was the loudspeakers that had first announced them to the world; perhaps they did not realise how sounds carry at night in the jungle. Perhaps they did not know that the Amerindians were listening, and could hear every word.

And right now, crouched behind a bush at the forest's edge with Winston, so could I.

In fact, I'd been hearing the voice for some time, faint at first, then ever louder as we approached. The closer we came, the easier it was to understand, and my ears strained to make sense of what at first seemed a barrage of words.

> ...and the Cubans didn't give a shit about dying, and that's one thing I liked about them, it – you – it was almost like taking a glass of water or sipping on a Coca-Cola. They could give a shit less, they were not going to bow to the bombings, and they resisted, and everybody had a gun, and if Castro wasn't a good man, he'd a been killed, cos every fucker had a gun.

On and on it went, the voice rising and falling, jumping from one subject to the next, sometimes incoherent, sometimes clear, sometimes low, sometimes screaming; a rant, a senseless, disjointed rant. The CIA, the Guyana government, the FBI, Cuba. Guns, bombs, deserters, defectors, communists, spies – that was the gist of the rant.

...and they brought my wife and I, not knowing that we had been communists all of our lives, and I don't even know what the hell you – anybody else woulda killed, anybody that looked Yankee and slightly white, they pulled us over and they said, come over here. They thought we were missionaries, they said missionaries!

Suddenly, a barrage of giggles, hysterical, maniacal giggles. And then on to the next subject:

The following people did not, according to White Night Alert, report in: cottage 9, 10, 13, 19, 25, 27, 38, 40, 42, 51, 60. Apartments 2. Dorms 2, 4. 2 and 4. These cottages and apartment dorms did not report. Supervisors from each cottage and apartment was to report to Maisie Doncaster, right?

I looked at Winston, and he shrugged and raised his hand, pointing beyond the bushes. Parting the bush to see what lay beyond, I stopped listening, and looked.

In spite of the undergrowth, I had an excellent view. Jonestown looked like a large but ordinary, rather run-down village in a jungle clearing. Several wooden cabins, white-painted, cheap tin roofs and, in typical Guyanese style, on stilts. A few longer buildings; and in the centre a larger one, looking like a community hall of some kind. I could see in the distance men leaping around a field, playing some ball game. Other people walking around between the buildings. A banana orchard. The atmosphere was peaceful, orderly. Only two things were out of the ordinary: that voice over the loudspeakers. And the sentries.

Up and down they patrolled, in the space between the jungle and the buildings. They wore black clothes, and bore rifles over their shoulders. A tiny hairy creature crawled up my back. I reached behind to brush it away, thinking it real – it wasn't.

I raised my binoculars and scanned the area, picking out individuals for a closer look. A woman toiling in a garden bed, in a spotted dress. I focused on her. She was Black, and not young – late forties, I guessed. She held the handle of a fork in her hands, and was digging away, turning over the earth. I focused on her face. Her hair was covered by a tight headscarf, and she looked exhausted. In fact, as I watched, she paused in her work and ran her hands over her face, as if wiping away the sweat. She looked up, directly at me; I clearly saw the bow of her lips and the curve of her nose, and I saw her close her eyes for just five seconds before picking up her fork again and continuing with her work.

I turned the binoculars away, and caught another woman in them: this one was bearing a basket of laundry on her hips. I followed her, and saw her enter a building that was no more than a tin roof held up by pillars. Underneath was a collection of what appeared to be primitive washing machines.

I scanned several other people. There was a pattern. Most were women. And most were Black. The only men I saw were the sentries, and one official-looking white man walking down the steps of a building carrying a pile of papers. I followed him. He soon disappeared into another building.

Above the constant drone of the loudspeakers a bell rang out, and a moment later a herd of children poured out of a building: a school, I assumed. I moved on. I caught the basketball players in the viewer; more men.

And all this time on and on whined the voice over the loudspeaker.

They – they'd come with big planes, they'd come with little planes. They threw the bomb out and – but fortunately struck his own tail of the plane, blew the plane up, and the plane catapulted down and came through the house, killing children in an orphanage and killing several in the uh, refinery. But not near the damage it would've been if the bomb had dropped, because it was all tore to pieces.

I took some photos, but I knew they would be useless for publication as even the nearest building, the nearest human, was too far away for clarity. I'd need a far stronger lens for that. But I'd had enough. I signalled to Winston, and we returned the way we'd come.

CHAPTER NINE

Aunt Edna was working in the kitchen when I got back. I told her what I'd seen and heard, and she nodded.

'And that's just the start,' she said. 'A mile or two further on you get to the cane fields. They trying to grow sugar cane. They work those fields from morning to night. They burn the trash, they cut the cane, everything, just like the lowest field workers. Like slaves.'

She shook her head. In Guyana, working the sugar-cane fields was the most menial labour of all, despised work. It stank of slavery: Africans labouring under threat of the white man's whip, and later, after the slaves were freed, the East Indian indentured servants who came to replace them, they too treated like slaves. It was back-breaking, soul-destroying labour.

Guyana's legacy of sugar was bitter, not sweet. It was our history, our heritage. The Amerindians, in particular, despised the industry; they had always refused to work the cane fields. The notion of Americans, citizens of the richest and most powerful country in the world, breaking that taboo was bizarre. Nobody willingly cut cane.

'And rice?'

She shook her head. 'No. They buy their rice – you saw, in Dora's shop. Rice don't grow up here. So, you going to start writing?'

I nodded.

'I'll do it. I'll write an exposé. Something bad's going on in there and it could be a big story. A scoop. And they're Americans; I could sell it to an American newspaper. There might be some money in it...' If that happened, I'd give the money to her. Uncle Bill might be a doctor, but he earned little out here in the wilds. Their needs were few, but I knew they were saving for a motorboat.

'But I need more information, lots more. I need to speak to Lucy again.'

Aunt Edna kneaded her dough vigorously, then tore off knobs, which she rolled into soft balls, coated white with flour. She nodded.

'How?'

'Maybe, if I go back through the jungle, maybe we could meet...'

'You didn't see those sentries?'

The sentries... They carried rifles. They guarded the community, monitored the perimeter. They were admittedly a headache. Speaking to Lucy was going to be harder than I thought.

'And the note she gave you... you done anything about it?'

I hadn't. I'd decided to write to my ex-colleague in town, Donna Ramdehall, give her the number and the instructions. She'd do it. I wouldn't have to explain much. Meanwhile, I needed to investigate, and Lucy was my only contact. I planned to return to the shop next Saturday.

'I feel sorry for that girl,' Aunt Edna said as she rolled out the puris. 'I feel sorry for all of them. They work so hard, but they can't win here.'

Flour floated up around her, coating her arms, her chest with a film of white.

'I've lived in so many communes,' I said, 'all over South America. Americans trying to set up some kind of farm, dropping out of society, trying to be self-sufficient. All of them fail. They don't know the first thing about farming.'

I could have added that they had all been high on pot. We all had. Which didn't exactly foster the inclination to work.

'Is not just that,' Aunt Edna said. She tossed one of her puri circles into the air, clapped it as it fell. 'Is the place. You can't just come here from America and start farming. Is suicide. These people, they work so hard, clearing the land, burning back clearings, planting their provisions. But they fighting the jungle and the jungle always wins. If you didn't grow up here, if you don't know this land, know this earth, the plants, you can't do it. We coulda tell them from the start: go away, you wasting you time.'

'I wonder how they got permission,' I mused. Americans weren't highly thought of by our socialist government.

'You wonder? Not me. This whole country for sale. A bit of cash in some minister's back pocket, and all kinds of doors fly open.'

'They must be coming in by the planeload.'

'Well, they did. Seems to have stopped now. They've got their own boat, they bring people up from town in it. Must be hundreds there by now.'

'Somebody in town must know more,' I said, and wished I'd heard of Jonestown before coming up here. I could have interviewed the right people. Now I was dependent on Lucy. But how reliable was her story? Whenever I thought of her I saw those huge, pleading, desperate eyes, that hysterical cry for help. Lucy wasn't my best source, but she was the only one I had.

'Why don't you go yourself?' Aunt Edna asked.

'To Georgetown?' I frowned and shook my head. 'No way. I just got here.'

It wasn't as if Georgetown was a canoe ride up the river. I'd had enough of the *Witte de Roo* to last a lifetime.

LUCY

Alexis is dead. I killed her.

She was like my best friend, my soul sister and my mom all rolled up into one. She was my best friend in the whole wide world and I killed her.

Moira was the one who made me do it. She stood right next to me, watching. She's the one who made me add the poison to water, and then made me give it to Alexis. I held it to her lips myself. Poor Alexis was so thirsty that she drank it all in one big, long gulp.

'Well done, Lucy!' said Moira, and I turned away so she wouldn't see how much I hated her, and how ashamed I was for the wrong I done.

I am so sick I can't write more today. I need to tell you more about Alexis, but not now. I'm too sick. Next time. Unless I'm dead by then.

CHAPTER TEN

The siren's wail tore into my dream, yanked me upright. Faraway, floating over the canopy, it yet seemed present in the room. Gunshots, a rapid volley of them, ripped the last shreds of sleep from my mind. I sat rigid in the dark, heart pounding, exposed, alone, bound by terror. A third sound mingled with the sirens and the gunshots: the loudspeaker. That voice, louder now than ever before, screaming something I could not understand, hysterical, wild. More noises: screams, bellows, almost palpable, as if night's thinness had dissolved distance. I even heard running, a baby's cry, a child's terrified shriek. Stampeding feet, or was it the riotous hammering of my own heart?

The sirens stopped, but nothing else. Sporadic gunshots still rang out. The screams continued, and the loudspeaker, and then, gradually, the gunshots stopped, as did the screams, and all that was left was that maniacal voice. I strained to decipher it, but in vain; as near as it sounded, the actual words, floating in the night sky over the jungle's canopy, escaped me.

My heart calmed down, my breathing slowed, and I lay down again. But I could not sleep. I lay awake for hours, and for hours that voice continued. Some time in the wee hours I fell asleep.

'You heard that racket last night?' I asked at breakfast, as casually as possible. Uncle Bill lowered the *Sunday Chronicle*. It was over a week old; newspapers and post came up with the *Witte de Roo* once a week, and this one had arrived with me. Uncle Bill read the entire thing from first to last page, like a novel; the news might be stale, but up here that made no difference. The dearth of events created a hunger for the tiniest snippets of information. And yet, right under our noses, something big was happening. Something bad. By now I knew it was both big and bad. We all did. But some people didn't want to know.

'Those crazy people,' he said to me. 'Over at Jonestown. Crazy, crazy.'

He shook his head slowly to emphasise the craziness, and to dismiss it, and returned to his newspaper. Aunt Edna and I exchanged a glance; she pointed at Uncle Bill, and shook her head in warning. A promise to tell me more, later.

Later that day, the water truck drove up and parked outside the gate. We grabbed several buckets and walked out to the roadside water drums, where the driver stood beside a thick hose, holding it steady.

Drinking water sloshed into the drums, quickly filling them. We filled our buckets and, one in each hand, returned to the house. Aunt Edna carried her two buckets with ease, hardly spilling a drop. I staggered several paces behind her, the water in my buckets splashing so much I lost a quarter of it on the way. We filled the house vats and returned for more, back and forth until they were full. At times like this I longed for the ease of running water, a tap and a porcelain sink. Aunt Edna noticed my distorted face, and laughed.

'Don't worry, a few months here will toughen you up.'

'Ugh! How do those people over at Jonestown get their water?'

'Same way we do, with buckets, but theirs isn't delivered. There's a creek through the bush; they all line up with buckets, pass the buckets along, like when there's a fire. A bit easier than carrying them, but I don't know why they don't figure out some sort of pipe system.'

'You seem to know everything about them.'

'Only what Winston and a couple others tell me.'

'So... what was that commotion last night?'

We walked up the stairs to the house, entered the kitchen. She removed her apron, hung it on a peg.

'We don't know, exactly. It happens regularly – sometimes once a month, sometimes once a week. We think it's some kind of drill.'

'Some drill! It sounds like a war zone! What's that guy screaming over the loudspeaker?'

'We can't figure it all out. Only two words: *White Night.*'

White Night. Yes, I'd heard those very words. It must be some sort of a code. The hair on the back of my neck stood up.

It was Monday, the start of the workweek for Aunt Edna. I'd forgotten; one loses track of the days out in the jungle.

The first mother entered the gate: a thickset Amerindian woman, a little girl on each hand. From over the top of my thatched wall I watched as more mothers arrived, more children, about ten in all, chattering, giggling, golden Amerindian children. Aunt Edna came down to greet them. The mothers left, and Aunt Edna took two of the children by the hand and walked the whole bunch of skipping and giggling kids to the open-sided hut down towards the pineapple field – her school.

I watched all this while I tidied up my hut and prepared for my own day's work. When I was ready, I peeped again, and saw the children all sitting cross-legged on the sand under the roof, at Aunt Edna's feet. Their sweet voices raised in song: '*All things bright and beautiful...*' I felt the familiar clutch at my heart, but then I sat down, shut out the outside noises, and began my own day's work.

It went badly.

Yesterday afternoon had been so crammed full it was hard to believe that I'd written the last words less than twenty-four hours ago. I recapped. Where was I? The Amazon. I remembered it so clearly; I had my notes, my journal open beside me. I tried to type. Nothing came. I reread my notes, trying to bring myself back to the bustling Brazilian riverboat, so reminiscent of the *Witte de Roo*. Nothing came.

All morning, I wrestled with words. I typed slowly, refusing to give in to this mental insubordination. I did not believe in writer's block. My writing-self was a servant; it did what it was told. But not today: Jonestown was a parasite sucking at my soul.

As I wrote, I kept hearing those sirens. The gunshots, the screams. I saw those people in the fields, toiling in the blistering sun. I saw the sweat on their bandanas, the soaked cotton shirts clinging to their backs. I heard that voice on the loudspeaker, wheedling, coaxing, whining, goading, screaming, and the high-pitched cackles that sometimes interrupted it. I tried to see the Brazilian faces on the *Evandro*, the boat that took us up the Amazon into Peru, but all I saw was Lucy's face, Lucy's eyes bleeding desperation. I tried to hear the cacophony of Spanish and Portuguese on the dock in Leticia but all I heard were scrawled words rattling through me like a mantra: '*Get me out of here*'.

Jonestown had dug its hook into me and would not let go.

At the end of the morning I counted the words I'd written. 456. The day before it had been nearly 5,000. Jonestown had started to devour me.

LUCY

Alexis is NOT dead! Not, not, not!

It was just a test, a test of my faith. That's what She says. The stuff I put in the drink was plain water. The bitch! See, that's how she tortures us.

We had a White Night last night. Sirens blasting into our sleep. Hearts racing like crazy. We pull on our clothes in the dark. Gunshots. Panic. We run to the pavilion, run for our lives. But what do we run to? Our own deaths.

Dad says it's better to die by our own hands than at the hands of the fascists: YOU. Yes you, the American government. Because it's all YOUR fault.

I don't know who will read this. I want everyone to read it, once you find it. I want the world to know. I want journalists, yes, YOU!!! to read it and tell the world. But most of all, I want the US government to read it. You men in your black suits in Washington! You who make the rules! You in the White House! You who pretend to care for us, our welfare. It's a lie! You want to destroy us.

I don't get it. Why? What did we do to you? We're Amer-

ican citizens same as you. We never did you no harm. First, you chased us out of America and now you chase us out from here as well. Is it just cos we're Black? We never hurt nobody, all we wanted was to live in peace like one big happy family and still you had to come all this way to make our lives a hell. You want us dead like Hitler wanted them Jews dead, and I just don't know why. If you didn't do these things to us Dad would leave us alone. It's cos you're scaring him he's gonna kill us.

If you would just leave us alone we might have a chance. If you don't, he'll kill us, and say it was suicide. He's talking of moving us to Russia, or Cuba, the whole damn lot of us. But why should Russia or Cuba want us? I don't want to go to no Cuba and Russia. I'm tired, so tired. I don't want to go nowhere except home to Mom and put this all behind me, with Danny and Granma.

They're going to pay the Cuban government millions to take us. Where they got those millions from, I ask you. I know where. From us. We gave them all we had, our property, our pensions; I had nothing, but they're getting Granma's pension all right, and look at the way she's living. She don't even got her medicine, they take that away to give Dad. We're from the richest country in the world and we live like homeless tramps.

If they have millions to give the Cuban government why don't they spend it on us instead? Give us food, give us houses, clean toilets, more showers. I don't get it.

But that bitch gonna do it again, and one day it'll be for real. They have what they need to make it real. I've seen it. It will happen. I know it. You have to feel the evil to know it is gathering and one day will strike.

Whoever you are reading this: by now we're dead, so you need to check on the money. I don't know where they keep it. Probably in Swiss banks. Only Moira knows the full deal, but she'll be dead too. Make sure the money gets into the right hands. It's ours. Give it to our survivors. Make sure Mom gets her share. She sure can use it, for the farm. Please pass this message on to her:

Mom, I'm thinking of you. I'm taking good care of Granma. Her arthritis is killing her but every day I steal a painkiller and pass it on to her. See, I get to deal out his pills. He takes a ton of them each day, and I'm in charge. He stole medicine from the people who came here. They keep them in the room next to Alexis, along with the poison. I stole a whole bottle of painkillers once. For Granma. I wish I could help all the other old women in pain. Granma's friends, Amy and Kathleen. But I do what I can for her. We both should have listened to you, Mom. You were right and we were wrong. If only we could turn back the clock. I love you, Mom.

CHAPTER ELEVEN

The week crept by, one empty day after the other. The water truck came and went. The chickens scratched. The dogs barked. We chopped wood. We fetched water. We harvested pineapples. I swam in the creek. I bathed in the waterfall. I sat at my typewriter. At night I tossed restlessly beneath the mosquito net, unable to sleep. Sometimes the loudspeaker echoed through the night, mingling with the usual jungle noises. I listened, straining to catch the words, in vain.

Saturday came round. I had reached a decision: I wouldn't try to meet Lucy today. Instead, I wanted to see Jonestown, but from the front, in the open. At breakfast, I told Uncle Bill I was writing an article on Jonestown. As I expected, and as Aunt Edna had warned, he was against it. He lowered his *Chronicle* and said, predictably, 'Zoe, don't get yourself involved with those people. Leave them alone with whatever they're doing. You came here to get away from that sort of thing. I thought you were writing a travel book?'

'It's just one last article. I think I could sell it to an American paper or magazine.'

'Yes, but I know you. Leave well enough alone.'

I ignored that last advice. He was my uncle, it was his job to keep me safe.

'How can I get in there?'

'That's just it, you can't. They don't let outsiders in.'

'I'd like to at least try. Would you take me? Or let me borrow the Jeep?'

I hated to ask but there was only the one Jeep, and he had control of it. I could walk, but it'd take a whole day there and back. He knew I'd nag him till I got my way, so he dug into his pocket and threw a key on the table.

'There you go, but be back by lunchtime – I've got to get back to the hospital.'

The farther I drove, the bumpier the road. It became a narrow track, two deep furrows cut into the sandy red earth with an overgrown bank between them. I drove slowly and prayed that the flatbed truck would not suddenly appear, driving towards me. There was no space to turn; if that happened, one of us would have to reverse for miles and it would probably be me. I was the intruder here. This road led nowhere but to Jonestown. It was, in fact, their own private driveway. Jonestown was truly at the end of the world; if anything untoward was going on there, nobody would ever know. In fact, they could all kill each other, and nobody would know. They were a universe unto themselves. If it weren't for the noises at night, nobody would even think of them.

That thought was disturbing. How much truth was there to Lucy's garbled story? Her fear was real – but what was it based on? And then the talk of the CIA, and the FBI. Bribery and corruption. *Don't tell the Embassy*, she'd said, *it's full of spies*. It was worse than a bad thriller. But then the sirens and screams at night, the gunshots, the night dramas: those were solid facts. Could they really be killing each other? How terrifying to be in the midst of that! There must be some truth to her story. Most of all, who the hell was *He*? Actually, I knew the answer to that: *He* was the voice on the loudspeaker.

But who the Hell was *She*?

The road cleared and widened, ending in a loop before a high fence, and a wide gate, and over it a broad sign: WELCOME TO JONESTOWN. PEOPLE'S TEMPLE AGRICULTURAL PROJECT.

I parked the Jeep and got out, taking care not to slam the door. Nobody was in sight. I walked up to the gate and peered inside. It looked much the same as from the back, from the jungle: the same low buildings, the same sentries, yet something felt wrong. It took a minute for me to figure out what: the loudspeaker was off today. The stillness was unusual enough to be eerie.

The buildings looked flimsy, as if they could collapse at any moment, but the gate was sturdy, heavily chained, and locked with a thick padlock. I rattled at it and called. Within seconds a mangy dog ran up, barking and snarling. The nearest sentry turned, saw me, and approached.

'Shut up, Diablo!' he said to the dog, which barked all the wilder. To me, he said, 'Good morning, ma'am. Can I help you?' His voice was friendly enough.

'I'd like to come in, if you please. I'm a journalist, writing an article on your agricultural project.'

'Do you have a permit to enter?'

I shook my head. 'No, but if you let me in I can talk to your leader and get a permit.'

'No, ma'am, sorry. You need a permit first.'

'How do I get a permit?'

The question stymied him. He shrugged, as if he couldn't care less and hoped I'd go away. When I didn't, he shrugged again, and said, 'Put in a written application.'

'If you could just let me talk to someone in authority, maybe...'

Behind him a second guard approached. I could tell by his stride that this one was higher up the food chain, and even from a distance his glare could send a person slinking away like a guilty cur. But it was his size that said the most. He must have been at least seven feet tall, and built like a bulldozer.

He wore the same black uniform as the other guards, and from this distance appeared naked, as his skin was the same colour. The clothes were too small, and his muscles bulged around the tight shirtsleeves and strained against the fabric of the trousers; he looked about to pop. All the Jonestown people I'd seen till now seemed emaciated and malnourished; , not this monster.

About five yards away from the gate he stopped. He whistled once, and the dog stopped barking and ran up to him, only to cringe and cower at his giant booted feet, gazing up at its master in adoration.

The guard at the gate left me alone and walked up to this giant. They exchanged a few words; rather, the guard spoke, and the giant simply shook his head, his eyes fixed on me and his lips not moving. The gate guard returned.

'Ma'am, you're standing on private property. If that's your Jeep, I'd be grateful if you'd just turn round and return the way you came.'

His voice could not have been politer. So, I tried again: 'I just wanted to—'

'Would you just leave, ma'am. This is not a tourist resort. No sightseeing.'

I ran my hand through my hair and looked past him to the giant. He still stood there, immobile, staring at me, a glassy glare that froze me. I tried to remember the name of that human killing machine in the James Bond film *Goldfinger*, but even my thoughts were frozen.

I returned to the Jeep, drove round the loop and started back the way I'd come. I looked back. The guard had been joined by the giant, and both stood at the gate watching me drive away. The dog must have found a gap in the fence for it raced behind the Jeep, barking with bravado as if it'd personally chased me away.

My writing continued to go badly. I started an article on Jonestown, but I knew far too little. Two pages were all I could manage. It was all too vague, too thin, too lacking in substance. I had no hook – I needed a *hook*.

My days grew long and empty, but the nights were worse. The bats thought it an amusing circus trick to flit through my hut at night, in one end and out the other, sometimes bouncing against the mosquito net with a squeak of indignation.

I considered buying wire mesh to close up all the gaps, keeping out the bats and the mosquitoes and the bugs I found crawling up my net each morning, but I balked. I refused to be a softy, a squeamish city girl. Nobody up here minded the nightly invasions; neither would I. *Get over it, Zoe*, I told myself. It was all a test, a challenge. Nature was not my enemy. It was I who was out of place here, I who had to adapt, peel off the layers of alienation that separated me from this world and its formidable creatures. I had brought myself here with a goal; it was up to me to adjust. Rediscover the happy child who had once played here without a whit of fear, at one with the environment, at one with herself. This world was not hostile towards me; I was hostile towards it.

The only hostile thing here was Jonestown.

It was an abscess, plonked into the midst of a wholesome, healthy organism. I understood Aunt Edna now; it was an inner knowledge growing on me, a sensation of dread, of growing evil.

I longed to know more and yet I feared it, and it seemed a reflection of my own inner turmoil.

My greatest ally in fighting back those monsters was Aunt Edna's little radio. She must have known how much I'd need it. The radio became a crutch so vital I kept it on at all times, even while writing, for it helped fight back the inner beasts and drown the jungle noises.

I began to crave the news, pausing to listen every hour on the hour. It was my only link with the outside world. I itched to pick up a phone and chat: with Mum, my sister, with my old colleague Donna Ramdehall, with friends and colleagues from town, the very people I'd fled.

I lived in a vacuum into which the Jonestown parasite inched itself and nestled. The brooding evil gnawed at my soul, nipped at the edges of my very sanity. I longed to flee, and yet I couldn't: it held me in its claws.

I could not sleep. The full moon cast a silvery light into my hut, but the shadows seemed darker than ever before and the jungle's cacophony kept me awake: the high-pitched buzzing of a zillion insects, the crashing of branches, and even, once, the vicious snarling of a larger animal, and the desperate death-cry of its prey. And floating in over the ether a faint tendril of sound weaving in and out of the jungle noises, rising, falling, sometimes drifting off into silence only to return, potent and masterly: Jonestown's whisper.

Towards midnight I drifted off. Black spider monkeys slid edgeways through my mind, their long, lazy arms pulling me into shadowed alleyways of sleep. Then suddenly I was wide awake again, my heart pounding. Instinct told me: someone, some*thing* was in my hut.

I raised my head slightly, holding my breath, the rest of my body immobile. And in the moon's pale glow, I saw it. A black shape crouched at my feet: a small, black, creeping shape. A hand? A vampire!

I screamed, kicked and thrashed. The bat screeched in indignation, flapped its webbed wings and bounced away, out into the open. I jerked upright, threw back the mosquito net and fumbled for the matches on my bedside table. Hands trembling, I opened the matchbox. The matches fell to the floor. I leaned over and scrambled for them, found one, scratched the box. In its flare I found the candle, lit the wick.

I inspected my foot: it was covered in blood.

The vampire myths are not quite true. Real vampires do not bite your neck, nor do they suck your blood. They bite your toes and wait for the wound to bleed. And then they lick up the blood.

Thank goodness, I'd been vaccinated against rabies – Uncle Bill had insisted – but even then, this was the last straw.

The next morning, Sunday, I went out to find Aunt Edna.

She was not in the house, and I remembered that today she was planting the pineapple shoots, a weekly task. Last weekend she had shown me how to cut back the base of the pineapple heads till the tiny dots showed. I'd then stripped back the outer leaves to reveal the pineapple stump containing the shoots, and placed these in water, where they'd grow into roots.

Hers was the biggest pineapple farm in the North West, but the work was simple: preparing the stumps, planting them, harvesting them. For such an exquisite fruit, pineapples are undemanding in their needs: sandy soil, water and sun. Here, they got all three, all year round. Aunt Edna did the rest, managing nature's process.

I walked into the pineapple field, where the bushes waited

in neat rows, each row at a different stage of development. Some of the pineapples were no more than tiny buds sitting at the top of the bromeliads. The ripest ones, plump with succulence, gave off a fragrance so sublime they could be found with closed eyes. If ever there was a food divine, then surely it was these.

I did not see her at first. I found her stooped at the last row, planting the shoots.

'Aunty, is there anywhere I can get some wire mesh around here?'

'Wire mesh? What you want with wire mesh?'

I told her about the bat, about the bite, and she clicked her tongue in sympathy.

'Vinnie's shop in Port Kaituma,' she said. 'Ask Uncle Bill to get a roll for you.'

'I hate behaving like a spoilt city brat.'

'Don't apologise,' she replied. She stood up and wiped her hands on her apron. 'See, for us, bats are – well, I suppose like mice for you. You learn to sleep with your feet drawn up and away from the net. You'll get used to it, but wire mesh won't hurt.'

I said nothing. She looked at me: 'It's not just the bats, right?'

I looked up and nodded, and she must have seen the silent dread in my eyes, this thing inside that was eating me up, for she reached out and took my hand.

'It's all right,' she said. 'They're not after us. There's no danger for us, it's the people in there I worry about. It's the blight lying over the land. Bats are nothing to that. Listen, you need some distraction. Why don't we do something different today, have some friends over, Andy Roper and some others? We could—'

We both looked up. Somebody had called her name.

Stepping along one of the furrows, walking towards us, was Winston. His movements were as steady and calm as ever, and yet there was no mistaking the haste in his stride, and behind the stoic façade of his face some other emotion twitched – anxiety, suppressed alarm. He did not speak until he had reached us.

'We find a dead man in de bush. Near Jonestown. I bring he in de canoe.'

CHAPTER TWELVE

'No, you can't see the body, and that's my last word.'

I hated it when Uncle Bill spoke to me as if I were still a child of six. That chiding tone irked me more than the actual refusal. We glared at each other across the dinner table, but then I caught myself and softened my look. I could be just as stubborn as him, as nagging as a flea, but a little bowing and scraping could do no harm.

'Just a glimpse, that's all. One little glimpse. Why not?'

'Because I've had a long day and I'm dog-tired and I'm not driving you all the way to Nazareth at this time of night, and on Monday the corpse is going down to Georgetown. And tomorrow's Sunday and my day of rest.'

He looked at his watch. It was indeed late, but I was pulsing with energy and if he'd said let's go now, I'd have gone.

'I could...'

I was going to say I could drive to the hospital with him on Monday, but Aunt Edna laid a warning hand on my hand. I turned towards her. She shook her head slightly and mouthed the word 'no'. Uncle Bill took the opportunity to get up from the table, march off into their bedroom and shut the door. The lamp flame flickered with the flurry of air in the wind-still room, and shadows danced with light across the walls and along the table.

'Let it be,' said Aunt Edna. 'Why you need to see the body? It not gon' tell you any more than you know.'

I shrugged, took a deep breath, and accepted defeat. I knew she was right. What could actually *seeing* the body tell me, except perhaps put a little fizz into the sinking feeling of anticlimax, and add a little drama to a lost situation?

What had I hoped for, anyway? I knew the answer: a nice juicy murder. That would give me my story, my headline, my hook: *Death in the jungle, a killing cult.* Just like Lucy'd said.

But it wasn't that at all. Winston had told us part of the story: the Amerindians had found the body that morning, midway between Jonestown and the creek landing. To them, the cause of death was immediately clear: the young man had been bitten by a bushmaster.

The Latin name for the bushmaster snake translates as 'silent bringer of death', and nothing could be more fitting. Just hearing the name made me shudder; I'd seen the one in the Georgetown Zoo, over ten feet long, with a broad head and an upturned snout. The bushmaster is the largest venomous snake in the whole continent. It sneaks around the bush at night, and attacks with little provocation, sometimes again and again and again. The poor guy never had a chance, out there alone and probably at night. From the start I had no doubt he'd been running away; clearly, from the frying pan into the fire.

He'd been dead a couple of hours when they found him, and already the bugs and the heat had started their destructive work on the body. The two Amerindians who found the body dragged it back to the creek, loaded it into a canoe and took it to the hospital. The usual admonishment to leave a body where you found it till the police came just didn't count in the bush: 'till the police came' could be a couple of days, and by then the body would have been bare bones. In this case, securing it was exactly the right thing to do.

At the hospital Uncle Bill had confirmed the cause of death: snakebite, probably bushmaster. And that was the end of my murder story. I was hoping for a gunshot wound as well, evidence of a fight: some clue pointing towards Jonestown; I'd waited on tenterhooks for Uncle Bill to come home and relate the gory details. He came back late, and exhausted, and not at all happy with my verdict of murder.

'But what was he doing in the bush?' I persisted. 'He must have been chased out there. People just don't go for strolls in the bush like that.'

'That's all been cleared up,' Uncle Bill replied. 'I radio'd the American Embassy – a couple of times, in fact. Yesterday, Jonestown reported a missing person. Bobby Todd, twenty years old; according to them, an ex-con. Apparently, he was prone to fits of rage. He'd had a fight with someone and run away into the bush. They'd tried to find him but given up.'

'I don't believe it,' I said. 'Not a word. Remember those screams, the gunshots last night? I bet it had something to do with that. I know it.'

'You should be writing crime novels, with your imagination.'

'So, aren't the police coming up to investigate?'

He shook his head. 'No. What's there to investigate?'

'Well, you know. See where they found the body. All that crime scene investigation stuff?'

'I just told you, there's no crime. There's nothing at all sinister about it. Jonestown sent somebody over to identify the body. They've already contacted his family in America; the body's going to be shipped home some time next week.'

'I can't believe it's just going to be dismissed like that.' I snapped my fingers. 'I don't see why I can't at least see the body.'

That's when Uncle Bill cut off the conversation and marched off to bed. I said to Aunt Edna: 'I don't believe it. I mean, here's just the thing to get an investigation going. Even if there's no direct murder. Who would be mad enough to run away into the *bush*, for God's sake? If you're a stranger to these parts?'

She flinched; she didn't like me taking the Lord's name in vain. But there was no stopping me.

'I just *know* something's seriously wrong. He was running away, running *from* something, and it must have been something terrible if he ran into the bush! It's the perfect excuse to get in there and investigate. Why doesn't Uncle Bill—'

'He don't like trouble. He don't like mess. He only want peace and quiet.'

'More like, he's a coward.'

But Aunt Edna would hear no criticism of her man. She got up from the table and began to clear away the glasses – a clear sign that it was time for bed.

As I walked the short distance to my hut the bush screeched in a higher octave than ever before, a shrill dense ocean of noise I had to navigate. Or maybe it was just me; maybe I was the one who heard and saw and felt more than ever before, as if an outer skin to my senses had been ripped away and left me raw and naked and open to a trillion nuances of sound and vision. The light from my torch cut a sharp funnel of light through the blackness, and all around me, fireflies and stars and blinking eyes swirled and flickered. The hot and stagnant air quivered with swooping bats, silent yet palpable against the cacophony. I had never been so glad to reach my door and enter my flimsy little home.

I scratched a match and lit the wick. The room filled with light and I realised I'd been holding my breath. Breathing out at last, I undressed, let down the net, tucked it carefully into the mattress, and crawled into what seemed a refuge against night's phantoms. My last thought before fleeing into the very last refuge, sleep, was just one word: wire mesh.

I woke up a few hours later. The room was filled with a dull flickering glow, and I realised I'd left the lamp burning and the kerosene was running out. Sleep, and yesterday's drama, had swept my mind free of cloying indecision, lifted it into a state of alert and single-minded clarity. The man had not been murdered, true enough. Not directly. But what had Lucy whispered to me in such desperation her eyes had bulged from their sockets and her nails had dug into my flesh?

He's gonna kill us, kill us all!

I remembered the sirens, the gunshots, the screaming, muffled and faraway and yet so chilling the very memory turned my skin to gooseflesh. I shivered. What was going on in there that could induce a strong young man to flee into the bush?

He's crazy, he's a monster, and her, she's worse!

This death – and I was sure it was suspicious – was the last straw. I had to act. Three goals now stood before me, crystal-clear and unwavering.

Goals one and two meant I had to go back to Georgetown. First, I had to ring Lucy's mother myself. Lucy needed to get home, into the hands of her loved ones and a doctor. Fast. I would do as she'd asked: ring the number she'd scribbled down for me.

Secondly, I had to investigate Jonestown. I had my government contacts in town. I had Lucy's mother's number. I had the American Embassy. I would dig up all the facts relating to the community. Who were these people? Where did they come from? What were they doing here? Who was their leader, and this mysterious She? Only careful research could tell me, and research was what I did best. In all my years of travelling, this was the biggest story I'd ever come across. Some instinct told me this was just the beginning. That this would be the scoop of my lifetime. Bigger than the book I was writing. Huge.

My third goal was a logical development from the second: I had to enter Jonestown.

Satisfied, I turned down the wick to kill the last flickering flame, lay down again and slept like a baby till morning.

LUCY

I never told you about Serena.

A local midwife helped with her birth. Serena was the joy of my life. And everything was fine till Dad came from America with Moira and the rest of that Inner Circle.

Lucy stopped writing, remembering. Her hand trembled; she could not write this. Not this. It was too personal. Who would care anyway?

Mom would. Mom had to know about Serena, her granddaughter.

All had gone well the first couple of days while Dad and the others settled in. Then Moira summoned her.

'I see you have a baby, Lucy. Congratulations!'

'Thank you, ma'am.'

Somehow with Moira you just said *ma'am,* and she didn't stop you.

'I hear Ray's the father.'

'Yes, ma'am.'

'I see. But you know that Father has strictly forbidden sexual relationships between you young people. Chastity is extremely important for our work here. Father is most disappointed in you.'

Lucy said nothing, but hung her head and clutched the baby tighter.

'Of course, you will have to be punished.'

Ten days in the Box. They took Serena from me, gave her to some woman to take care of. I hear they fed her goat's milk, diluted with God knows what. Dirty river water, I bet.

After the ten days they gave Serena back. She had a burning fever and cried all the time and my own milk had dried up.

Three days later, we buried her.

CHAPTER THIRTEEN

The next day Uncle Bill drove into the hospital compound, and we got out of the Jeep. Here I'd wait until he had time to drive me to the *Witte de Roo*.

'Hope you brought a book or something,' he said, 'There's not much for you to do here all morning.'

I nodded. 'I'll be fine, thank you.'

'You can sit on the veranda, outside the staffroom.'

I followed him up the short flight of stairs to the veranda. He showed me to a wicker rocking chair in the far corner. Next to it was a group of straight-backed wooden chairs arranged around a coffee table. The chairs and the table had once been painted dark green, but the paint was chipped and flaking off, and one of the table legs had been replaced by a length of bamboo. The canes on the rocking chair were old and brittle, a couple of them broken. But it had a cushion, and it was the most comfortable place to sit.

'This is our waiting room,' Uncle Bill apologised. 'Make yourself at home. I'll give you a drop to the ferry at midday.' He entered the staffroom and returned a few seconds later with a newspaper.

Just then a vehicle drew up outside, and I looked up. It was Andy Roper, the other doctor, in a dust-caked Jeep. He was helping someone out of the passenger seat. I peered over the railing: it was an old woman. He took her by the arm and helped her hobble to the stairs, and once there, he held her firmly under the elbow and helped her up. They walked along the veranda towards me; my eyes met his, and I waved. He smiled at me, and cocked his head, and led his patient into one of the rooms.

For a while there was no activity on the veranda, and I buried myself in last week's news. In Georgetown it was the same old political squabbles. I turned to the women's page, my old domain. The new women's editor ran a right snobbish page. For today's edition she'd interviewed a newly married society lady for her predictable views on London fashion. My own articles had been snappy and fun and slightly naughty; even then, the rebel in me had shown through. I sucked my teeth and turned the page.

I looked up momentarily as the Jeep's motor spluttered and the wheels crunched into motion: Uncle Bill was driving off. I returned to my newspaper.

'Hello – Zoe?'

I looked up to see Andy Roper grinning down at me. I greeted him, smiled back.

'Been having a good time? Enjoying your stay?'

I nodded yes, though 'enjoying' wasn't the word I'd have chosen to describe the past two weeks.

Andy tried again: 'So, what brings you to Port Kaituma today? You came to visit our top hairstylist?'

It was a little joke; apart from the grocery shop down the road there was nothing in Port Kaituma.

'Actually, I'm going back to Georgetown; I came to get the steamer.'

His face fell. 'Not for good, I hope? I thought you were staying for a while?'

'Just for a day or two. I have to make a couple of phone calls.'

'A long way to go just to make some calls. What's the drama?'

I had no intention of satisfying his curiosity, and only smiled.

'When you get back,' he said, 'maybe I could show you around a bit. Not that there's much to see but I do know of a magnificent waterfall up the river. I can rent a motorboat for a day.'

I had to admit it – a picnic with Andy would not be too much of a chore. It was something to break the monotony once I returned from Georgetown. It was time to emerge from my seclusion. I knew that for him it was more, but I could handle that: it would be good to have a friend up here.

'I would love that,' I said, and I meant it. I smiled at him, which encouraged him.

'Can I bring you a cold drink? Or coffee?'

'That'd be great; a cold drink, please.'

He disappeared and returned a moment later with a frosted-over bottle of lime Juc-ee. The bottle was so cold, I flinched: 'Wow, I'm not used to cold drinks any more!'

'We've got the only fridge in the whole of the North West,' Andy said. 'The only generator. We ought to open a bar.'

His words made me think: that couldn't be quite right. Surely Jonestown had their own generator as well? It would be hard to run such a large community without electric lights and refrigerators. Then something clicked, triggered by the word 'generator'.

'Andy, what do you do with dead bodies that have to be shipped to Georgetown? Do you have a morgue?'

He chuckled. 'That's a big word for what we have, but yes, we do have our own little cold storage set-up. You want to see it?'

Immediately, I perked up. 'Yes, show me!'

The 'morgue' was in a little annex at the back of the building. As we walked along the veranda I asked casually, 'Is that man in there? The guy the bushmaster killed?'

'Oh, that Jonestown man. Yeah, he's here all right. We hardly ever get to use the freezer, most people who die up here get buried nearby in a day or two.' We entered a wooden room with the paint peeling and the shutters hanging loose on rusty hinges.

'As you can see, we can't handle too much dying!' He pointed dramatically to what looked like an oversized deep-freeze unit. As indeed it was.

'That's your morgue?'

'Yep.'

'Can I...?' The rest of the question hung in the air, but Andy knew what I meant.

'Sure.'

He lifted the lid. A cold white mist drifted out of the freezer's interior. I leaned over and peered through the swirling haze to the still, dark form it veiled. The chill that hit my face and bare arms seemed to come from inside more than out. Seeing a dead body always does that to me. He was a young man, probably still in his teens, though it was hard to tell from the cold, hard blankness of his face.

I remembered Paul. I remembered *his* cold, still body, a vacant, foreign thing. I shivered. Uncle Bill was right: I should not have come here. Andy sensed my disquiet and closed the freezer. We walked in silence back to the veranda, where I sat down, still shaken by the sight of the dead man and the memories it had evoked. Andy returned to his work, I to my newspaper. I led my mind away from thoughts of death and back to life, shallow and fleeting though it might be.

At midday, it was Andy, not Uncle Bill, who drove me to the steamer. The small talk flowed easily between us. Andy had a beautiful voice, and his lilting Guyanese accent put me at ease. The talk about fridges and generators had got me curious about him and made me warm to him.

Andy was living here without electricity and any amenities, but he didn't sound like someone who'd grown up out here. He must be from town, educated abroad. It must be tough, living out here in the wilderness. I'd had a two-week taste of it, and knew it wasn't easy if you came from the outside world.

As Aunt Edna said, when you come here you are stripped of all your props, all your conveniences, all your distractions. You're brought face to face with yourself, sometimes for the first time, and your own true face isn't always a pleasant sight. Living here took stamina, whether or not you were a native. In the case of Andy, a single man, it showed an outstanding amount of self-reliance and altruism.

Andy's natural warmth helped crumble my barriers, those inner walls that held all males of a certain age at bay. By the time we reached the dock he and I were talking like old friends. It felt good. Aunt Edna's and Uncle Bill's matchmaking attempts had failed, but I felt I'd gained a friend.

He walked me up to the *Witte de Roo*, where we said our goodbyes before I stood at the railing and watched him drive away.

A truck rumbled up through the hustle on the dock, the back of it empty but for a wooden coffin. A couple of dockworkers unloaded the coffin as if it were a crate of oranges. They manhandled it into the hold of the *Witte de Roo*. There, packed with ice, Bobby Todd's body would travel with me to Georgetown.

A promise formed silently in my mind as the coffin disappeared into the ship's belly. It was almost a prayer: *Bobby, I'll find out what really killed you. It wasn't just a bushmaster.*

PART TWO
OUR FATHER

20th October 1978

CHAPTER FOURTEEN

I paid the taxi driver, opened the gate to our house, ran up the stairs to the front door and rang the bell. Mum opened the door. Her jaw dropped with the shock of seeing me.

'Zoe, back already! What happened?'

'Hi Mum. Nothing happened. I'm going back on Thursday.'

I embraced her, but she pushed me away. 'Zoe, you stink and you look terrible! Run upstairs and take a shower, get out of those awful smelly clothes. In the meantime, I'll warm up some food for you; you must be starving.'

I obeyed. They don't make mums like Mum any more. To me, Mum means home, comfort, simple ease and well-being. Sometimes, on the road, when I was far away, in trouble or in danger, dirty and hungry and alone, I longed for just this, and I knew how to appreciate it. Everybody needs a place to return to once in a while, a place of restoration and recovery, a place to stretch out your legs and close your eyes, and someone to coddle you. Home comforts are God's gift to mankind; for me they were rare, and I knew how to treasure them. I showered for a good ten minutes, luxuriating in the water's warm caress. The shampoo smelt of heaven, and I closed my eyes and let its foam cover me, soak into me, transform into bliss; after ten days of the icy Parrot Creek waterfall, this was utter luxury.

I woke early the next morning. I had a lot to do, and only one day to do it in. First of all, the call to Lucy's mother. I smoothed out the scrap of paper and dialled the scribbled number. A child answered.

'Hello,' I said. 'Can I speak to a grown-up, please?'

'To Granma?'

'Yes.'

A few seconds later, an adult voice took over.

'Are you Lucy's mother? I'm calling from Guyana... I've got a message from her.'

The woman cried out, an animal sound somewhere between a moan, an anguished yelp, and a screech of excitement.

'Lucy! My God, where is she? Can I speak to her? Is she OK?'

'Yes, yes, she's OK, but...'

She interrupted me with a suspicious bark: reality had set in.

'Who are you, anyway?'

'I'm... a friend.'

'A *Jonestown* friend?' Her tone retreated into the far distance: cold, remote and lifeless.

'No. Listen – I'm not from Jonestown. I live nearby, though, and I saw Lucy and she passed me a note, with your number, and asked me to call. A note asking for help.'

Lucy's mother wailed in agony. 'Oh Lord, oh good Lord, I knew it, she's in trouble! Hello? Hello, miss?'

'My name's Zoe.'

'Zoe, I'm Hannah. Thank you for calling. What you know about Lucy?'

'Well, nothing, really. I live near Jonestown and nobody can get in. I met her by accident. I had a few words with her. She's terrified: she wants to leave but can't. They seem to be locked in.'

'I knew it, see, I knew—'

I suspected a long lament hung behind those words just waiting to pour forth, so I interrupted.

'Listen, Hannah, I want to help but I need to know more about this place, this Jonestown. What exactly is it? Who are these people?'

'If only I could tell you! I'm sittin' here worryin' my heart out and nobody don't know nothin'. See, it's a church, she joined this church two years ago, in California: People's Temple. They got this preacher there, and my mom was in his church, and Lucy joined too. Next thing I knew, they was talkin' about some paradise in South America; they'd be safe there, Lucy said, and I said, safe from what? And she said safe from the racist murderers and oppressors in the American government. And she could raise her little boy, her little Danny, in freedom. And I said, don't go. See, I never liked that preacher man, I don't like no man who giggles 'stead of laughin', just ain't right for a grown man – Jim Jones.'

'Yes, that's the one. I've heard him speak.'

'And next thing I knew, they was all gone: Lucy, Mom, little Danny. And I never hear a word from them again. So, tell about this place!'

I told her what I knew of Jonestown, leaving out all mention of death and killing.

'Hannah, I want to help, but I don't know what I should do. I'd like to go to the police, the American Embassy, but she was in such a panic! She told me not to go to the Embassy – she seems to be terrified of spies. Is she always this paranoid?'

'They all are! They talk such nonsense! Before she left, all she was talkin' about was the spies that were after them right here in the USA, the FBI and stuff, they was after People's Temple and that's why they had to leave the country. All nonsense, of course!'

'So, you think it's OK for me to go to the American Embassy? You think it's safe? She absolutely didn't want me to go; she said it's full of spies.'

'That girl's goin' crazy. A bright, sensible girl, did well in school and look what happened! First, she gets herself into trouble, into jail, and then she gets out and says she's gotta work for the poor and needy. Stubborn as hell, that's my Lucy.'

'OK, then I should report it to the Embassy?'

'Zoe, you know what? Why not speak to Congressman Ryan first? He's in California, he could give you a whole lot more information cos he's been studyin' the group, relatives have complained to him and he's talkin' to people at the Embassy. A real good man. I spoke to him myself, a week or two ago. He's plannin' on goin' there himself, soon.'

'Do you have his number?'

'I do. Let me find it for you...'

She left the phone, and it was a good five minutes before she returned.

'Hello? You're still there? Here's Congressman Ryan's number.'

I wrote down the number and then I took some details from her: Lucy's full name, and date of birth, and the name of her own mother and Lucy's son. I felt much better. Hannah's permission to contact the Embassy erased my last doubts. Lucy was indeed paranoid, her fears of spies ridiculous. A congressman was investigating; help was on its way. Lucy would be rescued. That part of my duty was done.

But my affair with Jonestown was far from over; talking to Hannah had only increased my curiosity. More than ever, I knew I had to get in. Not to rescue Lucy now, but to get the full story.

I dialled Congressman Ryan's office, but nobody picked up. I realised that California was in a different time zone, and most likely he wouldn't be in his office till afternoon in Guyana. My next call, I decided, would be the Embassy. However, I needed some background and I knew just the person to speak to: Donna Ramdehall.

CHAPTER FIFTEEN

Donna and I went back a long way. We had started off as eighteen-year-old trainees at the *Graphic*. We worked together till the then-editor fired me for refusing sexual favours and I ran in tears with all my clippings to the rival newspaper, the *Chronicle*. Their editor-in-chief hired me on the spot. I was out for revenge, and the only way was to excel. In no time I made a name for myself with a series of hard-hitting human-interest features – I had bylines right from the start. Guyana had started its downward slide into economic breakdown. People were suffering, and I could pick my sob stories out of the breadbasket.

But six months later, the *Chronicle* was nationalised and became a government mouthpiece. Someone high up on the food chain gave orders, and I was promoted to women's editor: more pay, more prestige, more mixing with the cream of society, yet for me a downhill move. I had to focus on safe feminine themes, fashion and society marriages and gossip. No more controversy, no more exposés.

Donna stayed on at the *Graphic* and specialised in politics. She possessed the most useful of natural gifts for her profession: she was at once the nosiest person on earth and the most discreet. Her sources talked willingly and explicitly, knowing their secrets and identity were safe. Warm and motherly by nature, she evoked the need to lay one's burden at her feet. Her exposés could be devastating, but only to the bad guys. It helped matters when she married a justice of the High Court and began to move in all the best circles. She knew everyone, or failing that, she knew their grandmother, second cousin twice removed, or – best of all – their vindictive ex-mistress.

By now, we both moved in high circles and got to interview foreign celebrities who visited Guyana: me, Mahalia Jackson and Miriam Makeba; she, Fidel Castro and Stokely Carmichael. She'd been political editor for a while, but since the birth of her children she worked freelance from home. We'd always been close friends.

I could almost hear her falling off her chair.

'Zoe, you're back! When did you come?'

'In September, actually.'

'Last month already! You bad girl! Where you been hiding?'

'Donna, I'll tell you all if you let me invite you for lunch but I'd like you to do some nosy-parker work for me first, OK?'

'Depends what it is. If I can help and the free world depends on it, sure!'

I gave her a quick account of the situation.

'I've heard about Jonestown,' she said, 'but I can find out more. Give me an hour or two.'

'Fantastic! But there's something I need to know urgently. Like, now. Who's safe at the American Embassy?'

'Give me ten minutes.'

We hung up.

Ten minutes later, she called me back.

'Talk to Rex Bennett,' she said. 'The Agricultural Attaché and Vice-Consul. He's the guy responsible for Jonestown affairs. I know him.'

Of course she knew him. She knew everyone.

'And I can trust him?'
'Absolutely. Tell him I sent you, but watch out.'
'Watch out? Why?'
'Never mind, you'll find out. See you later then.'
'Twelve thirty at the Tower?'
'That's fine. Bring your swimsuit, I need some exercise.'

I called the American Embassy and spoke to a secretary.
'Your name, please, miss?'
'Zoe Correia.'
I had decided to speak to Bennett as a private citizen, using my married name, rather than as a journalist. This was, after all, still a private matter and I wanted to keep my journalistic goals a secret for the time being. I had a feeling, even through the phoneline, that the secretary did a double-take, but a second later she put me through to Rex Bennett. Mentioning Donna, I told him I had to see him urgently.
'What's it about, specifically?'
'Not over the phone. I'll tell you in person.'
'Friday morning?'
'No. I'm going back to the North West tomorrow. It's urgent. It has to be today, preferably now.'
He hesitated; reluctance oozed through the receiver. 'OK, if you can get here in half an hour, I can give you five minutes.'
Thirty minutes later, I was knocking at his office door. It opened, and I found myself face to face with Sita Singh, older and more businesslike, but still recognisably our last head girl at Bishops High School. My nemesis in the upper sixth. I hadn't seen her for over ten years. The notepad in her hand, combined with the uniform of tight-above-the-knees-but-still-decent blue skirt and staid white blouse, told me her story. She'd done well for herself – a job at the British, American or Canadian Embassy was about the highest a girl could get in Guyana after

A-levels. If you were lucky and/or clever, but most of all pretty, as Sita was, and played your cards right, you could even end up with a foreign diplomat husband.

'Zoe!'

'Sita!'

'So, we meet again!' she said. 'Come on in, Mr Bennett is expecting you.' I could sense the curiosity in her eyes as she opened a door for me. I nodded, smiling; as we passed each other our hands touched in greeting, and then she was gone.

I walked into Rex Bennett's office. He rose from his chair behind a huge purpleheart desk. And even from the door I saw it: a slight widening of the eyes as he saw me. I did a mental somersault.

I'd met a few American ambassadors, consuls and other foreign diplomats along the way. They were all formed from the same mould: generic but bland film-star good looks; the scrubbed, elegant exteriors of men with missions to please and talents to persuade and reassure.

Rex broke the mould. He was anything but bland: dark, almost black, wavy hair, unruly as if swept back from his face by impatient fingers. Eyes of a blue so rich that even from across the room something snagged in me and I missed a breath. Nothing clean-cut about this man; his face and figure were less film-star handsome than big-game hunter, his tanned skin almost as dark as mine. He'd be right at home stalking a tiger in India, rifle in hand, eyes narrowed in concentration. His white shirt and tie clashed with his energy. The room, though spacious, was still too small to hold him. What was a man like this doing in an office, anyway? In an *American Embassy*, for God's sake, behind a *desk*? And worse – why was I even noticing? All that flashed through my mind in an instant. The reaction came just as quickly.

Wait a minute, Zoe. Focus. I despised big-game hunters even more than I disliked diplomats, and such thoughts were anyway frivolous, beside the point. I shook my head to fling away the fluff and marched forward to meet him.

He came forward and shook my hand. It felt too soft and vulnerable within his grasp, so I pulled it away, only to feel him touch my elbow lightly to escort me to my chair. The desk before me was so highly polished I could see my reflection in its rich dark-purple wood. He sat down opposite me. My glance swept over the few objects on the desk – a telephone, a lamp, a large writing mat, a spiral notebook with a pen – before reluctantly moving up to meet his rather amused gaze.

For someone with 'only five minutes' of free time he now seemed perfectly happy with the time-wasting, small-talk routine. No doubt that was his job; get the background stuff first, and as diplomatically as possible. He wrote down my contact details, and remarked on my address, tried to guess if he knew the house, who my neighbours were; and then mentioned Donna and how pleasant she was, and so on. His voice was warm and rich and had a melodic, almost mesmerising cadence to it and I caught myself listening more to the timbre than to the actual words. I sent out a swift appeal to my beloved and never-forgotten Paul, cut short the repartee, and launched into my story: 'Mr Bennett, I'm here about a young woman, Lucy, and her son, and her grandmother. I believe they're being kept at Jonestown against their will. It's a long story...'

'Go ahead. I'm listening.'

For the third time that day I gave a run down of all I knew, leaving out only the bit about the spies in the Embassy – I didn't want Lucy to sound a fool. He listened attentively, taking notes. When I stopped speaking, he spoke.

'Miss...' He hesitated, shuffled the papers on his desk to find my name, looked at me and cocked an eyebrow, now more little-boy-coy than big-game hunter. He was fishing for my first name.

'Correia. Zoe Correia.' I didn't bother to correct the 'Miss' to 'Mrs'. He launched into a formal speech. I found the words incongruous – as if he'd learned them off by heart. I took another mental step back.

'Miss Correia. We're very grateful for this report. We do carry out periodic inspections of Jonestown and I assure you we are doing our utmost to make sure that everything's fine. We have had a few negative reports and complaints from outside, but on the whole, our impression is positive. I myself was there in April; I spoke to several people, and they all seemed happy.'

'But she's not. Believe me, that girl's desperate. She's terrified. That's why I think it's serious. You've got to do something. Get her out!'

'Anybody who wants to leave can leave. They have only to report to us. The people we spoke to up there seem pretty enthusiastic about their little utopia, but we'll certainly help anyone who's there against their will. But they need to tell us themselves.'

'But what if she *can't?*'

I told him about the guards, the jungle, the impossibility of leaving. 'If you've been there you know what it's like. A prison. And the sounds, in the night – it's creepy. In fact, Mr Bennett—'

'Please call me Rex.'

I bit my lip. Now was the time to tell him about Lucy's fear of Embassy spies. But I held back. I'd already broken her trust by speaking to the Embassy. Instead, I spoke of Bobby Todd. Didn't Todd's death make him, Rex, just a little suspicious?

Rex shrugged.

'No. Why should it? As I told Dr Turner, Jonestown reported him missing *before* the body was found. He was a young man they'd saved from a life of crime. He was rebellious and given to running away. This wasn't the first time, but this time he got unlucky. You can't blame Jonestown for his death. Dr Turner said there was nothing at all suspicious about it. The jungle's a dangerous place, and anyone who tries to cross it is asking for trouble. He was bitten by a poisonous snake, and there's nothing more to it.'

'But why was he running away? What was he running from? What's going on in there? What if Lucy's right?'

Rex shrugged again, then smiled as if to reassure me that he took me seriously – that whatever he personally thought of the matter, he wanted me to feel my fears acknowledged. This, coupled with the glib we-have-everything-under-control speech, set all my red lights flashing. My five minutes were long over, and I knew exactly which way the wind was blowing. The initial timeframe was only a shield against nuisance visitors, and his eyes told me I was no pest. But that's what good-looking men do – they think they can charm the pants off every woman. Not me.

He leaned forward, locking my gaze into his.

'Zoe – may I call you that? – let me reassure you that we're looking into it. Maybe I shouldn't be telling you this – it's purely off the record, OK? A congressman, Leo Ryan from California, has the same fears you do. He's got a group of people behind him lobbying to get their folks out. Anyway, Congressman Ryan is planning a visit, some time in the next few weeks, and he's going to take home anyone who wants to leave. So, your Lucy can go along with him. I'll let him know about her.'

Now, this was different: this meant action.

'Fantastic!' I said, 'Do you know when he's coming?'

'No idea. It's early stages yet. He wants to bring a group of journalists with him as well, and—'

I pounced on the word.

'Journalists! I'm a journalist! Could I go too?'

'Well – they'll be American journalists, but I don't see why he couldn't take a Guyanese journalist as well. The government might appoint their own representative, of course.'

'They'll send someone from the *Chronicle* staff. Whatever they write has to be government-approved. It's all diluted stuff.

I'm freelance – I'll find out the truth. Please, could you try and put in a word for me? I'm dying to get in there.'

'Well, you might be able to bribe me...'

'Bribe?' I frowned.

'Just kidding. Sure, I'll ask him. But would you meet me for a drink later on? This evening?'

I was appalled. He had no shame, no sense of timing, no sense of what's appropriate. *This* was an American vice-consul? I hated it when men interrupted a serious talk to hit on you, and he'd done it all in one sentence. Did he think the discussion was over, and we could move on to the real business of flirting? How unprofessional. My disapproval must have shown, because he blushed four shades of purple and quickly backtracked.

'I'm sorry. It was a stupid joke, totally uncalled for. Of course I'll put in a word for you. I'll ask him if you can join the party. No strings attached.'

I relaxed and decided to forgive him. He was only a man. Men and their hormones! It was an old and slightly boring story. I didn't play that game, and as long as we both understood that, we'd be fine.

'Thanks. Thanks so much! Sorry to take up so much of your time.'

'It was a pleasure. Any time. And if ever you have more news, or questions, just give me a call. Here's my direct number.'

He handed me his business card. I thanked him and got up to leave. He stood up to escort me to the door. We shook hands, but when I let go he didn't. I avoided his gaze, which was trying to catch mine, and tried to pull my hand free, but he held it too firmly.

'You know, I just thought of something,' he said. 'Maybe I *can* help you further.'

I looked up at the words. He let go of my hand, for his eyes had at last caught mine.

'Yes?'

'Congressman Ryan sent us some films and tapes. Films of Jim Jones, his early years, tapes of his speeches. I could show you, if you'd care to watch.'

'Now you tell me!'

'Can't send you away empty-handed. Come back here at two thirty, and I'll show you.'

Even at the office door, he didn't let me go. Keeping up the small talk, he escorted me all the way out of the building, stood watching as I took my bicycle off its stand and unlocked it, walked beside me as I wheeled it out the gate onto the pavement. Cars whizzed past as we looked at each other, the bike a barrier between us.

An awkward silence fell over us, as if there was something still unsaid but we didn't know what. And then I smiled and nodded, wheeled the bike off the kerb, set it into motion, and sprang onto the saddle. It sailed me away from him. Five yards down the road I could no longer resist; I looked back: he was still standing there, watching, hands in his pockets, a half-smile playing on his lips.

My front wheel wobbled, and I veered off the road towards the ditch. I crushed the handbrakes. The bike screeched to a standstill, forcing me to leap from the saddle. Embarrassed, I looked back at Rex; he was laughing, clapping slowly. I blushed, made a face and laughed too. We waved at each other and then I rode away, and this time did not look back.

CHAPTER SIXTEEN

Donna was waiting for me in the foyer of the Tower Hotel, just like way-back-when. The Tower stood opposite the *Chronicle* offices on Main Street, and in the old days we used to meet there for a drink or a swim at least twice a week. She saw me first, rushed towards me and buried me in mounds of soft, scented flesh.

'Darlin', darlin', darlin'! Let me look at you!' She pushed me away, holding me at arm's length. She pinched my arm.

'You lookin' evil. But thin. Thin, thin, thin!' It came out as 'tin, tin, tin'. Donna always spoke in exaggerated Creolese, in present tense and dropping the th's. Unless, that is, she was interviewing a foreign dignitary, in which case she spoke an almost impeccable Queen's English.

'You need a bit of flesh, girl. Want some of mine?' She chuckled, pinching a chunk of her own ample arm and wobbling it. I laughed with her.

'You haven't changed at all!'

It was only partly true. Donna always dressed to kill no matter where she went, and today was no exception. She had gone all out in a soft, flowing, tunic-topped trouser suit of amber silk, high-heeled shoes, the usual lustrous assortment of rings, bracelets and earrings, and a sinuous multicoloured chiffon scarf – her extravagantly feminine style hadn't changed. Her body itself, however, certainly had, and if I hadn't noticed, she made sure I did.

'Don't lie to me. Forty pounds extra I luggin' around with me. De price of pregnancy. I'd a thought runnin' around after dem kids would take it off again but no luck. You brought your swimsuit?'

I nodded, and we walked out to the pool and the changing cabins, holding hands.

We swam for half an hour. I was content to float, enjoying the coolness of the water and the warmth of the sun, but Donna was serious about the exercise, and with great diligence swam her hundred lengths.

'How many calories you think I just burn up?' she asked as we changed back into our clothes.

I shrugged – I never thought about calories.

'Well, I just about to put dem right back on again! I'm famished! Come on, time for lunch, and I want to hear everything, you hear, *everything*.'

We found a table at the far end of the pool and sat down in the shade of a huge parasol, once gaily coloured, now faded and ripped around the fringe. The tables, too, and the chairs, had that shabby, old-colonial look: chipped paint, wobbly legs, missing slats. Like everything else in the country, the Tower was sliding into neglect. Nobody bothered to renew or refresh or replace the broken and the worn. Nobody cared.

There were few other diners: an elderly foreign couple, three white men, a mixed-sex group having some sort of a party. Donna recognised them; they waved her over and as she stood up, she asked me to order.

'What do you want?'

'Whatever – you know me. I eat—'

I chimed in and we chanted together: '...anything but rope, soap and iron!'

We laughed and she bent over to kiss me, then walked over to the other table. I groaned inwardly; knowing Donna's tendency to lose herself in gossip, this could take ages. In spite of her perky chit-chat, I'd seen a glint in her eyes that told me she had all the dirt, and I was eager to get it. However, she was back within five minutes, and a further five minutes later, lunch was served: for me, an omelette and for her, curry and roti. We ate in silence, she with all the intensity of a prisoner ending a hunger strike. I knew better than to interrupt.

'That was good!' she said at last, wiping her lips with her napkin. 'So now, let's talk. I got plenty of goodies for you.'

'Shoot!' I settled back in my chair.

'OK, let me find my notes...' She rummaged in her handbag, removed several sheets of paper – bills, old letters, leaves from a notebook – and shuffled them around on the table. Donna's disorganisation was classic, the stuff of caricature. Finally, she found what she'd been looking for and frowned, trying to decipher her own scribbles. When she spoke again her speech was formal.

'The People's Temple, that's what they call themselves. From California. They leased eight hundred acres up in the North West District, ostensibly for an agricultural project.'

'When was this?' I began to make my own notes in an exercise book I'd found at home.

'The first settlers – I suppose you'd call them pioneers – came in 1975. But last year, they began to come in planeloads. Hundreds of them. Now, the thing is, you know we have strict rules about foreigners settling in Guyana.'

'Yes. How on earth did they get permission?'

Donna rubbed a finger and thumb together. 'What you think? Baksheesh. On paper the land was leased for ninety-nine years; de facto, they bought it. Somebody's back pocket got nicely lined. I wasn't able to find out *who* yet, or how much – but I will, later. All I know is, they work those big boys in government for all they're worth. The leader is a man called Jim Jones. He don't come to town often but he knows every single minister. Best friends with our dear Comrade Burnham.'

Forbes Burnham had been the Guyanese Prime Minister for over a decade by now, held there not by popular vote but rigged elections.

'People's Temple has a house in town. The women there work our government officials big time. One of them... let me see, what's her name, Paula something...?' She shuffled among her papers, checked the name. 'Paula Adams. Paula's having an affair with our ambassador to the US. That's public gossip, and it's true, and she's not the only one to play the charm card. You know Guyanese men. Those government big boys only gotta smell a white woman, their brains turn to mush. Russian and Cuban diplomats, same thing.'

'Why Russian and Cuban diplomats?'

'Hang on, not so fast. Recently, they been having trouble with the government. Complaints been coming in from America. Some kind of custody battle; they got a little boy there whose parents in America are suing for custody. They want him back. But this Jim Jones, he claims he is the biological father, so there was this big custody case going on. Now *this* next information is hot, hot, hot, and I can even tell you my source, my own dear High Court husband, since it went on right under his nose. There was going to be a trial in Georgetown to get this child out but then the group began throwing their weight and bags of money around and all of a sudden, the case was dropped. And you want to know why?'

She waited for me to ask. Donna knew how to be dramatic. She opened her bag again, leisurely removed a packet of cigarettes and a box of matches. She passed the cigarette box to me, I refused. She took one herself and lit up.

'Why?'

Donna took a long, luscious drag on her cigarette, obviously enjoying the drama. She blew out a cloud of smoke and slapped it away from my face.

'They sent a threat that if they don't drop the case every last one of them up there, a thousand or so people, would commit mass suicide.'

'What?!'

A chill ran up my spine, like a furry animal: a spider, the brush of a bat's wing. I remembered Lucy's words: 'He'll kill us all!'

I was at the heart of the story, the heart of her terror.

'I told you it was hot!'

'But that's ridiculous, an empty threat!'

I calmed myself. Lucy had been hysterical. Hidden in the bush they might be, but you can't commit mass murder and hope to get away with it, and mass suicide was even harder to pull off. I said as much, and Donna nodded.

'And even if you could – you got a bunch of kids up there, with their mums. They not gonna kill the kids, and the mums ain't gonna leave those kids behind. It just can't happen.'

'Did anyone take them seriously?'

'That's what we don't know. Hard to believe but government caved in, dropped the case. Most likely, another case of this.' She rubbed forefinger and thumb together again. 'Somebody got his pocket lined, gave orders. That's how this place is run these days – you rub my back and I rub yours.'

She sucked her teeth.

'Was this suicide stuff in the news?'

'Of course not! All underhand, behind closed doors. Top secret. And anyway, who in Guyana cares what a bunch of crazy Americans doing in the bush?

'Anyway, after that little drama apparently things soured between the government and Jim Jones. Seems like they now thinking of moving to Cuba or Russia. So that's why those women trying to soften up the diplomats.'

'But I don't get it. Are they a church, or what? People's Temple – it sounds like a religious group.'

She sucked her teeth again. 'Baloney! That ain't no church. They call themselves socialists. A socialist experiment – that's how they try to project themselves anyway, that's how they got into the country in the first place, bad-mouthing America and the capitalist system. Sucking up to Burnham, getting all that land.'

'Who in their right mind would want to go and live in the bush?' I shook my head in bewilderment. In Guyana, we all knew what the bush was like. The only town folk who went there to live were masochists who took a perverse delight in mosquito bites, vampire bats and vipers, or freaks like me looking for a place behind God's back. People fled *from* the bush, they didn't *go* there – the idea of Americans going there to live was surreal.

I told Donna about Bobby Todd: 'And I don't care if they didn't kill him directly. There was some madness going on the night he ran away, Donna, and I think he was driven away by that. I can't believe it won't be investigated. I have a good mind to go to the police myself and—'

Donna laughed. 'The police? Look here, darlin'...' For the third time, she rubbed forefinger and thumb together. 'That's your police for you. Every one of them for sale. How much you gon' offer them to investigate? Because you gon' have to outbid whoever pay them *not* to!'

She laughed and looked at her notes again.

'Anyway, talking of escape... In May this year, one of them got away. A woman, Katy Harris. She went back to America and she too told this story, that they were planning mass suicide. The story trickled back down here, of course. Didn't make the newspapers, but people in government knew. It was dismissed as twaddle.'

'You could call it blackmail.'

'Yep. It seems that they use this threat of suicide every time they want to get their way. And they get it, too.'

'It's all beginning to make sense. That's what Lucy must be talking about, what she's scared of.'

'Seems to me that this Jim Jones fellow is the key to everything. He uses the threat of mass suicide to get his own way, to get outside forces to take him seriously, and to get his own people to obey him. Because for them, of course, it would be murder. You can't get a thousand people, women and children mostly, to commit suicide. No way, not mothers.'

'That's it, Donna. That's what she's so scared of. Lucy has a child, a little boy, and a baby – she's terrified.'

'Must be awful for her, but, you know, it's all hot air. Some people are like that. They can convince others the sky's about to fall. Get them into a panic, just to keep them in line. This Jim Jones seems to have a hold on his people.' She leafed through her notes again. 'Speaking of kids – there's Patsy Boyle. That's an easy one for you.'

'Patsy Boyle?'

'Yep. She's got three kids, and all of them call him Dad.'

'So, Jim Jones is their father?'

Donna shrugged. 'Not necessarily. Patsy calls him Dad too – all the women do.'

'Cheez! Wonder what Uncle Freud would say to that.'

'Uncle Freud would have a field day with all of those ladies. Anyway, Patsy's the one you want to speak to next.'

'And how am I supposed to do that?'

'Just go visit her. She's the one running their Georgetown branch.'

'They have a Georgetown branch?'

'Yes, of course. Didn't Rex tell you?'

'No, he didn't, as a matter of fact. And he didn't even mention her.'

'Well, next time you see him, ask him. He knows her well. How you like him, by the way? A dreamboat, right?'

'Yes, and he knows it too – the way he ogled me.'

'Really? Inter-es-ting!' She drew out the word for emphasis and raised her eyebrows meaningfully.

'What's so interesting? Those foreign skirt-chasers, they're all the same. As if we local girls just lying back, panting for them.'

Donna shook her head. 'Uh-uh. Not Rex. He's kind of – well, let's just say, lady-shy. The most hard-to-get foreigner in town. No local girlfriend, no flirting, nothing. And you know how Guyanese girls go ga-ga over white skin! Those men just got to snap their fingers and they can take their pick. But Rex Bennett? Nothing doing. You got a lot of frustrated beauty queens in town. They been saying he's... you know. The other way around.'

I sucked my teeth. 'No danger of that, the way he behaved with me.' I told Donna about the invitation to drinks, and my movie date at the Embassy. She laughed.

'He must like you a lot,' she said. 'Have fun, but like I said, watch out.'

'Don't worry,' I said, 'it's strictly business.'

CHAPTER SEVENTEEN

Punctually at two thirty, I was back in Rex Bennett's office.

I had prepared myself well, for I no longer trusted him. Donna had confirmed that Rex knew much more about People's Temple than he'd revealed, but then again, in his position he probably wasn't allowed to talk. The fact that I'd blabbered to him of these things both embarrassed and irritated me. He'd put on an act, played the part of the concerned official doing his duty, all the while hoarding secrets he knew I'd die for. Typical diplomat!

Suicide threats, child abduction, seduction; sex and money; bribery and corruption: Jonestown was an investigative journalist's dream come true. Rex knew it all, yet treated me like a child to be placated, reassuring me that Lucy would be rescued as if that was the beginning and the end of it.

On the other hand, I was grateful to be here now. Surely not every citizen off the street was invited into the Embassy's screening room. Thank goodness for male hormones – I had them to thank for the favour. I decided to play it cool and hide my irritation.

Rex must have noticed my reserve for he responded in kind:

friendly but formal. He led me to the screening room, where I took one of the plush seats at the back, just in front of the projector.

Rex had already prepared everything. He turned off the lights and the projector whirred into movement. He took a seat next to me, leaned over and whispered: 'These films were made by the People's Temple. They're propaganda films from the late sixties, made for public consumption. Take them with a pinch of salt.'

I nodded. We fell silent as the film began.

After a minute of preliminary numbers, screen snow and lightning flashes, a good-looking man in sunglasses walked on to the screen. He held his hands up high, waving to people, smiling and affable. Others joined him, a family; he embraced them all, took a small child in his arms, kissed and hugged it.

'Jim Jones!' announced a bombastic voice. 'A light shining in the darkness. Hope for those in despair. A helping hand reaching out to the lost. The Voice of Salvation.'

I watched spellbound as the film related the biography of the man at the centre of the Jonestown enigma, and as the story unfolded, I felt my mental sands shifting once again. The Jonestown loudspeakers and the night noises had chilled my heart, revolted me. Lucy's paranoia had rendered me sceptical, yet suspicious. Rex's reassurance and promise of help had calmed me. Donna's news had set off a thousand alarm bells.

The story I now heard, told in black and white with a wobbling amateur camera, turned everything I'd learned till now on its head. I had to remind myself that this was propaganda, that I must temper it with what I'd seen with my own eyes, heard with my own ears, as well as the known facts. And yet – pictures don't lie.

. . .

Jim Jones, I now learned, was the son of a Pentecostal preacher, and spent his youth in a congregation called the Gospel Tabernacles. The members of this church earned the nickname 'holy-rollers' for speaking in tongues, and Jones grew up with this rapture. He lived, moved and had his being in the Ecstasy. By the time he was sixteen, he knew his calling to do the Work of God. He was God's voice, God's instrument.

God told him that racism was wrong, and he must bring about a new order, so he obeyed. In 1947 he began to preach on street corners in mixed-race neighbourhoods – a thing unheard of in those days. *You are God's children*, he said to Blacks, and to whites he raged, on God's behalf: *How dare you treat my Black children thus?* Jim Jones breathed fire and brimstone, his words charged with such power those who heard him, Black or white, trembled for they knew that God spoke through him, a God of wrath, but a God who loved Blacks as much as he loved whites. Indianapolis had never known such a gifted preacher, and such a daring one too. But then he did the unthinkable: he invited Black people into his church. Anarchy!

The Pentecostal Church fell into chaos. The Church elders forbade him from doing so; Jones insisted. Finally, he was given the choice: keep the church white, or leave.

He left and started his own church.

From the start, People's Temple was different, a new force unheard of in America, a church bent on breaking down racial divides. '*Come unto me, you poor and needy!*' said this church, and America's outcasts flocked into its warm and loving embrace. As the years passed, the People's Temple became a home and a place of refuge for one and all. Its members felt themselves siblings of one great family.

Jim Jones reached his peak in the sixties. This was a time of revolution and renewal, a time when America's educated white middle-class youth rose up in rebellion against old values, looked at the world their fathers had given them and found it wanting and dreamed of a better nation. In People's Temple they found that utopia. They longed to change the world, to usher in a new age of peace and love, and through People's Temple they could. These young whites gave money and expertise, time and effort to The Cause. The times were changing, a new wind swept through America, and People's Temple was the first fresh breeze.

Jones's church established a soup kitchen and gave shelter to the needy. The sick came and were healed. Drug addicts came and were cleansed. Criminals came and were made whole. The hungry came and were fed. People's Temple was a place for lost sheep, a place where man could truly be free and fearless. All were equal: men and women, young and old, Black and white. Jones encouraged interracial marriages and was the living example of a rainbow family; he and his wife adopted a Black child and a Korean child. People's Temple members loved one another, and most of all, they loved their Father, the man who had wrought this miracle in a cold and hostile country.

The story unfolding onscreen was that of a hero, a man who would speak for those who had no voice and stand up for those whose legs were crippled.

Sitting there in the darkness, I finally understood.

Up there on the screen was the leader I'd dreamed of all my adult life. And had I not known what came later, I too would have rushed straight into the compassionate arms of Jim Jones.

Charisma had created the phenomenon of People's Temple, but somewhere along the line that charisma had turned to rot.

CHAPTER EIGHTEEN

Rex turned off the projector and switched on the light. I blinked and looked up at him.

'That was – enlightening,' I said, and stood up. 'Thank you so much.'

He removed the reel from the projector and placed it in its box, walked over to the window and opened the shutters. I did the same to the second window. Sunlight streamed into the room.

'You understand now why I take these scare reports with a grain of salt,' he said. I opened my mouth to speak, but he held up a hand to stop me.

'It's OK, I don't doubt you, and I don't doubt Lucy. We'll get her out of there, and anyone else who wants to leave. But, see, Zoe – for the most part they're all there voluntarily, and there's nothing we can do about it. They are here legally; they have their 99-year lease on the land. The paperwork is in order. It's all above board. They're American citizens and they have the right to live the way they want to.'

Resentment boiled up in me. Was he playing games, or did he really believe this?

'What about the gunshots?' I protested. 'What about the armed guards?'

'We have armed guards outside the Embassy,' Rex replied. He wheeled the projector into a corner and placed a cloth over it. 'Does that make us prisoners? Many middle-class Guyanese have armed guards outside their homes. Does anyone arrest them? Jonestown is isolated, and there's a lot of crime in Guyana. Foreigners especially are at risk. There are wild animals up there, tigers—'

'Not tigers,' I interrupted. 'Jaguars.'

He smiled, and nodded, and gestured towards the door. I retrieved my bag and my notebook from the chair. 'Americans like to protect themselves. They have licences for their guns, and that's all that matters to us. These are adults.'

'Not all of them.'

His hand was on the door handle, but he did not press it down. We faced each other and again, our eyes met. In his, a blank wall. The ease of our last meeting had fled, I knew not where. This was the American Vice-Consul, not the man Rex.

'OK, there are children there. With their parents. What can we do? The children are being educated. As far as I know, the schools are pretty good.'

'What about...' I leafed through my notebook. 'Patrick Hugo Stenton?'

Patrick Hugo Stenton, the child at the centre of the custody battle, the boy who Jim Jones claimed as his own son. Rex blinked. The silence before he replied was a second too long.

'Where did you hear about Hugo Stenton?'

'I have my, um, *sources*. And I wish you wouldn't treat me as a child who needs to be placated. That film was interesting, yes, but I'm not convinced. That was a decade ago, and it's obvious propaganda. A lot could have happened in that time. Jim Jones may have once been a nice man with a good heart, but he acquired a lot of power and we all know that power corrupts.

You're insulting my intelligence if you want me to believe that that's' – I turned and gestured towards the projector – 'the whole story.'

Rex looked away. He looked mortified, and suddenly I felt sorry for him. *Of course* he knew more than he was telling me, and of course he couldn't tell me everything. Here was I demanding that the American Vice-Consul tell all as a personal favour, just because he found me attractive. But I refused to back down now; I had an advantage, and I would use it.

I did not speak. I waited. I held my breath. And finally, he turned to me, our eyes met, and the blank wall crumbled.

'OK. You're right.'

I breathed out; I knew, at last, this was the real Rex speaking.

'It's not the whole story. Jim Jones is more than a gifted preacher helping the poor and needy. I don't think he even believes in God any more. The reason I wanted to calm your fears, Zoe, and keep you out of it, was personal. I like you, and I'd like to get to know you better. And I don't mind telling you a little bit more. Yes, the Embassy is watching Jonestown carefully – more carefully, and with more suspicion, than I've let you believe. The reason is twofold. There are taxation issues I won't go into. Plus, Jones now openly admits he's a communist, that Jonestown is a communist group. And you know how we Americans love communists!'

He chuckled as if to take the political edge out of his words, and then quickly continued. 'And that's all I can tell you, Zoe. That's already too much. There's more to this than meets the eye – in that you're right. But I wish you'd stay out of it.'

'But why?'

'Oh, come on. Do I have to spell it out? I told you I like you. You know they have guns. I don't want you anywhere near those guns.'

'You think it's a communist training camp? Guerrillas, Che

Guevara, that sort of thing?'

'I really can't tell you any more.'

'Classified stuff?' He was hedging again, rebuilding the wall. Yet I was satisfied. 'OK, I won't dig any further. Not with you, at any rate. I'll find another source.'

At last Rex opened the door, and we walked through into the corridor. Immediately, he changed the topic.

'So, you're a journalist,' he said as we walked downstairs, side by side. 'I meet a lot of journalists at diplomatic events. How come I never met you before?'

I raised my eyes to meet his. The sparkle of this morning was back in place. I smiled to acknowledge that, and relaxed. Not so much big-game hunter, I reasoned with myself, as maybe *conservationist*. They stalk animals too. Not with a rifle but a pair of binoculars and a long-lens camera, or at the most a stun gun. I'd met a couple of those and liked them.

'I've been away. I just returned a month ago.'

'Aaah, I see. And which paper do you work for?'

'Well – I'm published in the *Chronicle*, but I'm freelance.'

'The *Chronicle*? The government rag? I wouldn't have thought it. Why not the *Graphic*?'

'It's a long story.'

That, of course, was the perfect cue, and he grabbed it.

'Why not tell me it some time? Like this evening?'

He had me there. We both knew that he'd showed me the films as a personal favour. I'd been bribed after all, and it was payday.

We reached the bicycle stand. I took my time to open my bag and find my key. I was under no obligation, I thought, as I bent down to unlock the bicycle. I didn't have to do anything, go anywhere with him; I already had what I needed, and I knew he'd said all he could.

He hadn't really lied to me; he'd only covered up, tried to sidetrack me. He was a diplomat; that was his job. Diplomats are by nature smooth and non-confrontational. They have to be tactful and considerate. I could hardly blame him for keeping secrets that were his business to keep. His concern for me was genuine, and that made me warm to him. The suave diplomat persona was riddled with cracks, and in those cracks, I'd seen a real live person. Diplomats have a right to friends, and to human reactions.

I could very coolly look him in the eye, say thanks but no thanks, and goodbye. But I had two reasons to say yes.

The first reason was the thing I'd known since the moment I first met him. It was so simple: I *wanted* to say yes. I *wanted* to be with him on more personal ground. I *wanted* to escape the straitjacket of our formal relationship. Everything in me leaned out and away from it, wanted to break the rules of this stupid game of protocol-following we had to play. And I knew it was the same for him.

Yet I knew I couldn't – not yet, at least. It would interfere with my goal. My second reason to say yes was pure calculation: I wanted yet another favour from him, a bigger one. I turned the key in the lock and looked up. His question still hovered between us, but instead of answering, I replied with a question of my own.

'Do you know Patsy Boyle?'

He flinched. 'Well, ah, um, yes, I do, in fact.'

'I really need to speak to her. Can you get me an interview?'

'I don't know. They don't like journalists.'

'Can you at least ask? As a personal favour?'

Our eyes met, and something passed between us, a private joke, a delight in this cat-and-mouse game. We both smiled.

'I can try,' he admitted.

'Good,' I said. I wheeled my bike to the front gate. The guard opened it for me, and we walked out into the street. I stopped, turned to look at Rex. 'And yes, I'd love to go out with you.'

CHAPTER NINETEEN

Mum held a rich red dress against me, low-cut, of a soft and flowing material. It had once been my favourite dress. And Paul's favourite.

'What about this?' she said. 'You always looked ravishing in it!'

'Put it away.' I grabbed it and flung it on the bed. Already I regretted saying yes to Rex. The moment I'd left him I'd felt the guilt. What about Paul? Why had I been so eager to say yes? Where was the loyalty I'd held for so long to the only man I'd ever loved? I felt weak, unfaithful, annoyed with myself.

Worse yet, Mum and my sister Becky seemed to equate that *yes* to going out with Rex with a *yes* to marrying him. Getting back into Single Available Girl mode was all rather tedious. As I flung away the dress they exchanged glances; surreptitiously, but I saw. Mum frowned and tried again.

'Sweetheart, every one of your dresses has memories of Paul. But what are we to do? You won't buy new ones, and you won't wear the old ones. You can't go on a date wearing jeans!'

'It's not a date.'

'Of *course* it is, and you said yourself you're ready to meet new men. But if you refuse to even look nice, like a woman, like the beautiful woman you are...'

Becky held up another dress.

'This one's gorgeous! I remember when—'

I took it gently from her and replaced it in the wardrobe without a word. I walked to the tallboy and rummaged in the drawers. Behind me, Becky said, 'I'd lend you one of mine but you'd be lost in it! I had to say goodbye to nice clothes after pregnancy. Be grateful you don't have children—'

Becky was never known for her tact. 'I'll wear this,' I said, so she wouldn't have to finish. I held up a pair of trousers. Mum and Becky looked horrified.

'Darling, please!' Mum walked back to the wardrobe, removed yet another dress, a beautiful white one, one I'd never worn, the price tag still attached. Just looking at it made my heart ache.

'No. I was going to take it to Barbados. On the honeymoon.' I took it from her, hung it back in the wardrobe. But Mum was never a quitter.

'This one, then.' She held up a simple blue one, sleeveless, soft and flowing, the neckline high enough to hide my pendant. I took it from her, inspected it. I'd only worn it a few times, and never with Paul. I sighed. I'd have preferred trousers. I hadn't worn a dress for years – not since the wedding dress, itself packed away in paper, unusable, my most precious souvenir.

'OK. That'll do.' I took it from Mum, undressed and put it on. She grabbed my hand and dragged me in front of the mirror.

'See? See how wonderful you look? Oh my, I'm so excited!'

I rolled my eyes and turned away from the reflection. The woman in the mirror wasn't me at all. She was an actress, playing a part. But worse was to come. Becky, chattering all the time, pushed me from the room and into her own, next door. Becky was married now, with a growing family, but this was still 'her room', and entering it was like walking into a teenage girl's version of paradise, every inch of wall covered with the face of Paul McCartney.

Ignoring my violent protests, Becky sat me down at her vanity table and attacked my face with an impossible array of creams, lotions and powders. She did something to my hair to tame it, and finished up by engulfing me in a cloud of spray. I looked like a clown, and told her so.

'Nonsense! You look fantastic! He's going to fall in love with you the moment he sees you!'

With that threat she picked up a stick of bright red lipstick and pointed it dangerously close to my mouth. I pushed her hand away, and at that moment the doorbell rang. I rose.

'That's him. I have to go.'

'Let me just...' The lipstick briefly touched my lips before I turned away.

'Zoe! Wait!'

She caught up with me at the door and shoved a pair of pointed-toed stilettos at me. I realised I was still barefoot.

'Nope,' I said, and returned to my room. Under my bed I found a decent pair of sandals and shoved my feet into them. I was ready.

Downstairs, Mum had already let Rex in. He smiled up at me as I walked down, and came to meet me with a bunch of roses.

'Zoe, hi, you look fantastic! Nice dress!'

I smiled, thanked him, took the flowers and handed them to Mum, who took them without a glance; her eyes were glued to Rex's face, as were Becky's. Becky had followed me downstairs and now stood staring as if he were an alien; which of course he was. An American, alien to our shores. Mum spoke.

'Can I offer you a drink, Rex? Would you like to stay for a few minutes?'

Rex looked at his watch. 'No, thanks, I've booked a table at the Pegasus... we'd better go. Another time?'

He held out an arm to me to squire me towards the door, and I let myself be squired. I looked back at Mum to say goodbye, and caught the smug smile she exchanged with Becky. I'd never live this down; I should have arranged to meet him elsewhere, and never let my family know. We walked down to Rex's car.

'This is probably the corniest line a guy ever asked a girl, but how come a beautiful woman like you is still single?'

I met his eyes across the table. He had planned it well. Garlands of coloured lights cast a soft glow on the poolside terrace, while a single candle in a tinted wind-glass lit each of the tables circling the dance floor. A single rose in a slim vase scented the space between us with intoxicating fragrance, while above us coconut palms, silhouetted black against the moonlit sky, waved gently in the ocean breeze. A steel band played a gently rippling calypso, to which a few couples danced.

'Actually, I'm a widow.'

He lowered his eyes. 'I'm sorry. My condolences.'

'It's OK. It happened long ago.'

A waiter appeared and saved the moment; Rex and I studied our menus and he ordered wine. Ordering the meal took longer. The Pegasus seemed untouched by either import problems or the economic slump that condemned normal Guyanese people to the standard fare of rice, plantains and chicken curry.

'I can really recommend their Peking duck,' Rex said. 'Like to try it?'

'Whatever you say. I eat anything but rope, soap and iron!'

Rex laughed, looked up at the waiter and ordered, after which he launched straight into the usual small talk. I countered his questions with my own, and learned that he was from

Boston, thirty-nine years old, had been in Guyana only since May, and liked it here; the last, of course, a huge whopper.

Guyana was a hardship post for diplomats, and everyone knew it. Who could like this country, clothed as it now was in rags? We who had grown up in its heyday and knew the real Guyana loved our homeland with a fierce passion – but nobody else. No tourists came; they all went to the turquoise seas of the Caribbean instead, and other West Indians laughed at us and called us mudheads. Guyanese fled to the US, Canada, England in planeloads.

'Oh, come on,' I said. 'Guyana's a dump. Admit it. No foreigner in their right mind would come here voluntarily. What's there to like?' I laughed and raised my glass. 'Let's drink to that.'

He ignored the glass. Instead, his eyes caught mine and held them. 'The people,' he said. His voice was quiet and, I knew at once, sincere. 'Their warmth. Their humour. Their sheer...' he hesitated, searching for the right word. '...*lovability*. They drown you in hospitality. They want to make you feel at home. And they succeed.'

I tried to look away but couldn't. His gaze reached deep within me, and something there thawed: a ray of sunlight glanced against a block of buried ice.

'That's how I feel with you: at home.' Inexplicably, I felt my eyes about to brim; perhaps the thaw had reached them.

'Tell me more about yourself,' I said quickly.

'Me? Oh, you don't want to know me. I'm just an old vagabond at heart.'

I chuckled, relieved at the lightness to his tone. We'd sailed clean around the iceberg and into safe waters.

'You, a vagabond? No way. You're the quintessential clean-cut American. Like every diplomat I ever met.'

What was I saying? Now I was the one telling lies. Rex was

everything BUT the clean-cut American. But he *was* a diplomat, deserving of a bit of teasing.

'You mean boring? Not fair!'

'I didn't *say* boring...'

We were both smiling now, our eyes playing with each other. He mimicked me.

'I *didn't saaaay boring*... naw, not in so many words. But *clean-cut* – hey, you insult me!'

'OK, I take it back. What are you then?'

'I just told you. A vagabond.'

'Well, I still don't believe that; *I'm* the vagabond around here. What did *you* do to earn the title?'

'Drop out of college? Way before it was the thing to do. Way before men grew their hair long and smoked pot and went on protest marches. I was a hippy ten years too early.'

I spluttered over my wine.

'I'm sorry, I shouldn't laugh. Just the thought of you as a hippy...' I shook my head at the image. Rex looked even less hippy than he did diplomat.

'Well, I didn't have long hair. And I didn't float around with a broad grin giving the peace sign, sticking flowers in strangers' hair. But I dropped out of school and ran off to Burma and almost gave my folks a heart attack.'

I looked up at that.

'*Burma?* Why Burma, of all places?'

He shrugged. 'You know how it is. You read a book, something catches your attention, you can't forget it, it gets to be an obsession. You can't get it out of your mind. For me, it was that book, *A Town Like Alice*. The lush descriptions of the Burmese jungle. I just had to go, see for myself. Experience it. I lived there for two years, with a native tribe. I loved it.'

So, I'd been right. The wildlife conservationist type – possibly my favourite in all the world!

'Burma was one of the places I was dying to go to. I loved that book, too. But I couldn't get a visa.'

'Yeah, the borders are pretty tight. But it's possible. And then I went to Thailand.'

And that did it. Now it was my turn. My gaze grabbed his eyes and held them, excitement bubbling up within me.

'I spent eighteen months in Thailand!'

'Really?!'

And we were off: words tumbling into hearts, stories chasing stories. We had both discovered martial arts there, gone to the same school in Chiang Mai. He knew my master, Kuanan; we compared our knowledge, discusses techniques, promised to practice together one day. Great lumps of ice dissolved into pools of kinship, at least for me.

And then he made his first mistake of the evening.

'Zoe – look, I'm sorry, and I hope it's OK to say this, but your eyes – they're so beautiful, but there's such sadness in them. Such a deep sadness. Is that because of, you know...?'

I stiffened and immediately regretted letting down my guard. 'Please – can we change the subject?'

Rex looked abashed. 'Sorry. I put my foot in it again.'

Once again, the waiter saved the day, this time with the wine. We waited in silence while he served us.

'Cheers!' Our glasses clinked, and we each took a sip. The steel band launched into a tender rendition of 'Moon River', and several couples got up to dance. He took that as his cue.

'Shall we dance?'

I shrugged. 'All right.'

We walked to the dance floor, Rex's hand light on the small of my back. He held me loosely as we danced, keeping a respectful distance. I felt his eyes on me but averted mine, looking beyond him to the palms nodding black against the sky. I turned my head, and his eyes caught mine for a second. I felt the pressure of his hand on my back and resisted. Without a pause the music merged into 'Yesterday'. Memories flooded me – so often, Paul and I had danced to this. I couldn't bear it. I pulled away, shook my head, and led the way back to our table.

'Zoe... I wish...'

'What?'

'I wish I could put the light back into those eyes. The light that should be there.'

Inside, I curled up into a tight little ball, and he knew it, though I said not a word. That's what reminders of losing Paul did to me; they rose from the deep with a mighty punch and laid me flat. Now they'd destroyed whatever there was between me and Rex.

'Oh heck. Look, I'm sorry again. I'll try not to intrude. I promise, I promise really.'

I nodded. I hated these onslaughts of grief, but when they came like this, in great floods washing through me, I was helpless, and sorry for those caught in their wake. I didn't blame him. I hated myself for my weakness, and longed for the safety of small talk, but the waiter arrived then with our meal, and in the time he took to serve it the grief had slunk back into its cave.

Rex made a valiant effort to keep things light and slung me a whole new barrage of clichés. I guessed he was nervous and playing it now by the book: chapter one, instructions for the first date: 'Ask her about herself.'

'So, what do you do with yourself?'

'Didn't I tell you? I'm writing a book, up in the North West.'

That was a great opening hook, and as we picked up our knives and forks he grabbed it gratefully.

'A book! Amazing! What's it about?'

I told him, and that took care of the next few minutes of conversation. I told him about the Amazon, and the turtles in the shower, and Peru; arriving in Lima, bedraggled and dirty. Before long I was laughing and joking again, my stories of South America rivalling those of Thailand.

'...see, I'd just arrived from the jungle and I hadn't had a proper shower for weeks. I was just dying for a shower! I would have *killed* for one! And I was staying in this commune of hippies in Lima, and they didn't have a shower either. So, this American guy says, you know what, there's a monastery down the road and the monks go for Mass every day at nine. The gates are always open. We can go and use their showers while they're at Mass! So that's what we did: we hid outside the gates till the bells rang for Mass and when the monks disappeared, we all slipped in. God, that was the best shower of my life! After that we went there once a week for our showers and they never caught us.'

Rex laughed. 'I can imagine the shock if they *did* catch you!'

'Maybe that's the way to get into Jonestown: wait till they all go to church or whatever, and then sneak in.'

Rex frowned. 'You're obsessed with Jonestown, aren't you?'

'That's what we writers do,' I told him. 'We fall in love with our projects; we're like a dog with a bone when we get our teeth into something. I can't wait to get back to the North West, to writing.'

He paused. Ease and levity vanished from his eyes.

'When are you going back?'

'I was going to take the ferry tomorrow,' I replied, 'but I can't; I can get much more information right here in town, and I've decided to stay a week longer. I want to speak to Patsy Boyle and a few others. Jonestown won't disappear.'

He fell silent. I waited. At last he spoke.

'Zoe, I know I promised not to interfere, but I wish you wouldn't.'

'Wouldn't what?'

'Get involved. With Jonestown.'

'I already *am* involved, Rex. And if I wasn't involved we'd never have met.'

'It's just that Patsy, she's... weird. Oh, very nice, very

approachable. But they're all paranoid as hell about journalists. Some magazine back in the US published a negative exposé; apparently that's what forced them to leave America in the first place. They don't trust journalists. She won't trust you.'

I ignored his last sentence. 'Can you get me a copy of that exposé?'

'You've got a one-track mind, haven't you? You weren't even listening!'

'Can you get it for me?'

'I suppose so. I'll Xerox it for you tomorrow, if you insist.'

'I insist. So... what's so strange about Patsy?'

He sighed. 'Can't we talk about something else? Machu Picchu, or something?'

He met my glare and sighed again. 'OK, I'll take you to her, you'll see for yourself. But tonight was supposed to be about pleasure, not business.'

I laughed and shrugged. 'OK, sorry. Let's get back to pleasure.'

He laughed with me and fanned himself in jest. 'Whew! Great! No overtime!'

'So, go ahead! It's your turn!'

'OK, let me think... An extraordinary date; something breathtaking...' He paused, thinking. I sipped at my wine, watching him. I couldn't believe how well the evening had passed. Rex had gone where no other man had since Paul.

The last three years I'd lived behind a shield, an inner screen that kept the world – and in particular men, eligible men – at arm's length. Since Paul's death I felt like a character in a film or a novel, observing the world, asking my questions, playing the role of myself, Zoe Quint, footloose journalist without attachments. Yet here, now, with Rex, in this ridiculously corny atmosphere, that screen had dissolved. Was it the wine, the music, the moonlight? Or simply... Rex?

'I know!' He snapped his fingers. 'How about flying with me

up to Kaieteur, on Sunday? Some American tourists are going up and I happen to know there's a couple of seats left in the plane, and—'

I choked and spluttered, jerking my glass so that the wine splashed out and all over my dress and all over the table, flooding my plate.

'Excuse me.'

I grabbed my napkin and fled. In the bathroom I didn't even bother with the wine stain on my dress. I leaned over the washbasin and retched. Nothing came. I dry-retched again several times, then splashed my face with cold water, washing away the last remnants of Becky's make-up. I looked into my eyes in the mirror and saw a stranger, a stranger I knew well, for she was the one who had walked with me for three years, who occupied my body and my mind. She had left me for a while tonight, but now she was back, with that thin drained face, those empty eyes, portals to an inner abyss. The mask I wore for the world's sake completely stripped away. The evening was over.

After a while I returned to the table and sat down. Rex's hollow chuckle greeted me; he had replaced my glass and had my plate removed.

'You OK?'

I nodded, glancing at him momentarily. He handed me the dessert menu, but I shook my head. I did not touch the wine. My eyes must have spoken for me, for he said, 'Zoe, I'm so sorry, I put my foot in it again, but I've no idea what it was. I don't get it. It's like no matter what I say, it's wrong. So many taboo subjects. Hey, what's the matter?'

Tears welled behind my eyes, and though I knew I wouldn't cry — I never cried — I looked down so he couldn't see. I bit my lip and shook my head. I put my hand on the ring round my neck and took a deep breath. Those two actions calmed me, cleared the tears, and I looked up again.

'It's OK. It's not your fault. You couldn't know.'

'Know *what?* Zoe, I don't want to step on thin ice again but if you'd only tell me I'd know what not to mention.'

'I guess that's only fair. OK.' I paused. The steel band was playing Schubert's 'Ave Maria', and I listened a while. It soothed me and felt most fitting. Rex waited for me to speak, and at last I did. I kept all emotion out of my voice.

'My husband was killed on a flight to Kaieteur. The plane crashed into the jungle.'

'Oh my God... I'm so sorry, I really stepped in it this time.'

'You couldn't know. It was supposed to be our honeymoon. Just after our wedding. I was the only survivor. Even the baby died, the one inside me.'

As I spoke the words the moving pictures flooded my mind, a slow-motion film of the worst day of my life.

We had planned two honeymoons: a short one and a long one. The long one was to Barbados, in a week's time. The short one was to Kaieteur Falls, which neither of us had ever seen or was ever likely to see unless we did it now, together; a trip to Kaieteur was something we locals postponed into perpetuity and left to tourists. It was now or never, Paul's father had said, and he had given us the trip as a wedding present, along with the house in Bel Air Gardens.

I had a window seat but made little use of it; there was little to see. Instead, my gaze clung to Paul's; we giggled and whispered together in the manner of honeymooners, paying much attention to the round firm swell of my belly. I was five months pregnant, but this was no shotgun wedding. We'd planned it and fixed the date six months before; we were ready to start our family, not imagining that I'd conceive at the very first attempt. When it happened, we saw no reason to bring the wedding forward just for propriety's sake.

Now, we touched and kissed with little care for the outside

world, except once, when the plane slanted into the wind and I glanced outside and pointed, and Paul leaned across me to peer out. Beneath us, an endless sea of broccoli as far as the eye could see: the rainforest, vast and dense, a world unknown to both of us.

Had we been more attentive to the outside world we might have noticed an ominous black stripe creeping up the northern horizon, behind us. As it was, we soon tired of the broccoli and turned back to ourselves, and before we knew it, the storm was upon us.

The little plane fluttered and lurched, a helpless moth caught in the wind's fury. Sheets of rain tore into it, pounding it off-course. One propeller snagged and stuttered and struggled valiantly against the raw elements battering against it.

Strapped to our seats, Paul and I clung to each other. Loose items – bags, drinking bottles, several oranges – rolled and tumbled about the cabin as the plane pitched and dived, then plummeted. Other passengers screamed; in silence, Paul and I gazed wide-eyed at one another, each capturing the other's image for one last moment. Those moments are etched forever into my mind. The longing, the regret in Paul's eyes. His last words, as he clutched my hand and kissed it: 'Zoe, I love you.' What else was there to say? I told him the same. We knew it was over. Then, a fleeting moment of hope as the plane caught itself for one last time. One last plunge, and the jungle heaved up to greet us.

'Mayday! Mayday! Mayday!' the pilot screamed. And then the world outside turned from grey to green, and from green to black.

I don't know how much time passed before my eyes blinked open. Pain, so much pain I could not even localise it. It had stopped raining, but I was soaked through. I could feel that the wetness on my thighs was of a different quality, not water.

Above me in the treetops, the plane's fuselage, caught in the branches and torn open like a Christmas cracker. We had all spilled to the ground, still strapped to seats so flimsy they had been ripped from their fastenings. I managed to move my arm enough to bring my fingers to the buckle and open it. I twisted my body till I fell from the seat and into a tangle of bushes. In the distance a helicopter chugged, but otherwise all was silence.

'Paul?' It came out as a whisper, so I tried again, louder. 'Paul!' My trousers were drenched in blood: the remains of our precious baby.

I crawled along the soft moist forest floor, looking for him. The first passenger I found was dead. The second was Paul. He too was still strapped into his seat, but I unbuckled him and laid him out as flat as I could on the forest floor. Blood everywhere, so much blood I could not tell where his wounds were. But when I felt his pulse, I detected something faint, a whisper. I tore off my shirt and ripped it into strips. Whimpering his name, I searched his body for wounds and pressed the strips of cloth into them, but on and on he bled. It soaked into my clothes and into the earth and there was nothing I could do to stop it. I leaned against a tree and laid his head upon my lap and stroked his face and his wet hair, and whispered his name until the life fluttered out of him, and I did not cry because the life in me had turned to stone.

The steel band music rippled with Schubert. Rex shook his head slowly: 'Christ.'

'Since then I never stepped in a plane again.'

'But you've been travelling around the world.'

'Yes, on a shoestring! That's the name of my book. See, if you know how, you can find ships that'll take you anywhere.

Cargo ships, freighters. They usually have a few cabins for passengers. Takes longer, but it's far more interesting. Then there are trains, buses. You get to meet people, see places, experience things. All fodder for a journalist. If you've got the time it's the best way to travel. I've got the time. Loads of it. The rest of my life, in fact.'

My hand lay on the table; Rex placed his own hand lightly upon it.

'Zoe,' he said. 'I don't know what to say. *I'm sorry* sounds so – inadequate. But I – I know what you mean. Exactly what you mean. About the pain, I mean.'

I looked up at him and then I saw it – the raw wound laid bare within his eyes. And I knew, I just knew, he'd been where I'd been. The knowledge jolted me out of my own self-pity. How selfish, to wallow in my past misery and spoil the night! So, I turned my hand over to meet his and my fingers closed around his and I whispered: 'Tell me!'

It took a while for him to speak. His eyes misted over and I knew he was somewhere else, in another place, another time, with someone else.

'We'd only been married a year but I'd known her, like, forever. We actually met in Thailand – she's the reason I went back home, and back to school. Her dad was a diplomat, posted in Bangkok. It's for her I went back to college, got serious about my life and my career. Became *respectable*. So, we went back to the States, I finished school. Babes in the woods, we were. If there's such a thing as perfect happiness, perfect love, we had it. I know it sounds corny, but it's true.' I nodded, knowing of what he spoke, and still holding his eyes. Our bitter-sweet smiles mirrored each other, comforting and reassuring.

'We married straight out of college, the moment I got my first post. We had so much to look forward to. And then it happened. Out of the blue.'

He stopped speaking. I waited. His eyes had misted over again, and I did not want to intrude.

'Cancer. Who would have thought it? She was so young, so perfect, so – so healthy, till it struck. The last person you'd think of as lying sick in bed, wasting away, before my eyes. It took an eternity – and yet it happened so quickly. She had the best treatment, of course. The doctors did all they could. We were all just so... helpless. And a year later she was – gone. Poof.'

He showed me, raising his hand: closed fingers before his lips, blown apart. A life leaving the body with the last out-breath. A soul moving on, never to return. I knew it so well. No need for words.

The band played 'Strangers in the Night', softly, gently, and when Rex spoke next his words again were so familiar I could have spoken them myself.

'At first you want to die too. That's the first stage in grieving, the worst. Then it settles into a dull ache. Life goes on. Time takes the raw edge off the pain, but never heals it. People say loving again can heal it. But I never loved again.'

I looked down and slowly shook my head; not to deny what he'd said, but to hold back my tears.

'Fifteen years,' Rex said. 'Too long. Zoe, don't let that happen to you.'

I bit my lip to steady it, then looked up again and gave him a wobbly smile.

'I'll try.'

'OK, enough of the blues,' he said at last. 'Let's dance.'

CHAPTER TWENTY

Rex rang me soon after I came down for breakfast. Mum answered the phone and her eyes oozed questions as I took the receiver from her. I only smiled and shook my head, and hoped she'd let it rest.

'First the good news or the bad?' Rex said after a few warm preliminaries. His voice was businesslike, as it should be. Personal and business matters should never mix. As wonderful as our date had been, as well as we knew each other now, Jonestown had to stay in its own compartment.

'Oh heck. Go ahead, the bad.'

'I spoke to Congressman Ryan and he says no, you can't join the Jonestown group. People are already clamouring to go with him and he's turning them all away. It's nothing to do with you specifically. You'd have been proud of me; I really fought for you. Told him that as a Guyanese journalist, you'd be invaluable, but no go.'

'Didn't you tell him that I live nearby, about Lucy, the note, everything?'

'Of course. In fact, he's spoken to her mother. And he was interested in your story. He says he's willing to meet you afterwards and you can talk to one of the journalists, but you can't join the delegation. Sorry.'

'Well, I like that! He wants *them* to interview *me*?'

'That's right.'

'No way! Either I join them officially or I don't talk.'

'I thought you'd say that.'

'OK. So, what's the good news?'

'I called Patsy Boyle. She's agreed to see you...'

'That's amazing! Thanks!

'...on one condition: that I come with you.'

I frowned. 'What's that supposed to mean? Why?' The last thing I needed was a babysitter. As much as I liked Rex, as much as I was attracted to him, as much as we had in common on a personal level, he was still the American Vice-Consul. That was a big issue, one I didn't want to deal with just yet.

'I told you: she's paranoid as hell, they hate journalists, and the only reason she agreed is because you're Guyanese, and... well, I kind of made her think you'd be well disposed towards them. Kind of calmed her fears.'

'You didn't!'

'You don't mind, do you? All you have to do is be friendly and pretend to be on her side.'

'Well, I can see what got *you* into the Diplomatic Service.'

'It was the wrong thing to do?'

He said it like a little boy afraid of a rebuke, and I realised how insecure he was: even a diplomat, deep inside, is just a man, and he wanted to please, to please *me*. I'd been so quiet when he brought me home last night, hardly saying a word, unresponsive towards him, he must have thought I was withdrawing from him again. But I wasn't; I was only stunned. I had actually *talked* about the accident, for the first time ever, after three years. And I was beginning to have feelings, real feelings, for a man who wasn't Paul.

Rex had opened a tiny window into the deep dark vault of my grief. And he didn't even know it.

Later, though, in the night, the thoughts had come. Destructive thoughts.

The problem was his official role. For me, a huge turn-off. There were three kinds of people I never hobnobbed with: royalty, bankers and diplomats; and of the three diplomats were the worst: paid to lie and distort the truth. Could Rex be the exception? From the start I'd known he was different. And yet, and yet... There he was, in the American Embassy. I was torn in two, and doubtless he felt my ambivalence.

Now, I paused for a moment; a decision had to be made. Rex was encouraging me to do just the thing I abhorred in diplomats: 'be friendly and pretend to be on her side'. Didn't that prove my point about his character? What about last night? That was genuine, wasn't it? And I wanted, desperately, to meet Patsy and get the goods on Jonestown, didn't I? Why not play the diplomat game just once in my life? No harm done, and it was all for a worthy cause. Anyway, he'd helped me far beyond the call of duty, and the least I could do was respond in kind.

'No, no, that's fine. You're welcome to come along,' I said, and I knew I'd stepped over the fine line between viewing him as diplomat and as a man. Rex must have felt it, because the delight in his voice was palpable.

'Great! I made an appointment for this afternoon, five o'clock, after work. I'll pick you up.'

Sita Singh closed the office door lightly behind her. Rex had left behind a mess of papers; she straightened them, glancing at each as she riffled through them, taking mental notes. She didn't need to write anything down, she kept it all in her head. That had always been her strength.

One particular sheet of paper caught her eye. She had never

seen that name before: Lucy Sparks. She filed it away mentally for later.

That night she wrote a letter. She put it into an envelope, and scribbled a name, and an address: *Jonestown Postbag, Poste Restante, Port Kaituma, North West District.*

The People's Temple Georgetown headquarters was of the style called 'modern' in Guyana: on stilts, like most houses, but made of concrete instead of the traditional wood. It was one-storeyed, with a large balcony at the front and the ground level, known as 'the bottom-house', converted into living space. An outside staircase led up to the front door. A child of about ten opened the door to us.

'Hi,' she said, 'I'm Christina. Mom said come in, she won't be a moment.'

We entered; the child pointed to the balcony, and then ran down the front stairs.

'Mom!' she called. 'They're here!'

We walked as directed through a haphazardly furnished living area and onto the balcony, where we sat down on fraying wicker chairs, part of a group around a coffee table. Various items lay around: an untidy heap of newspapers, a child's book flung in a corner, an empty Coke bottle on its side. On the tiled floor, along the walls, and especially in the corners, several weeks' worth of dust had settled comfortably. Dustballs and sun-dried leaves rolled across the floor, pushed by the breeze. We sat alone for at least ten minutes, talking quietly. Rex told me he suspected Patsy was downstairs, in the radio room, talking to Temple members in Jonestown or in America.

At last we heard the front door open. A moment later, Patsy joined us on the balcony. We both stood up.

'Hi, Rex, and this must be Zoe. Hi...'

I half-stood and took the hand she held out. It felt like a

limp rag; I squeezed it once and let it fall, and she shoved it into the pocket of her too-tight jeans. She sat down opposite me and smiled, but it was a dull smile that did not reach her eyes. There was no mistaking the wariness, even hostility, in her stare.

'So, you're a journalist? Before we begin, could you please write down your name and address? And the name of your newspaper. Just a minute.'

She got up, went inside and returned with a notepad and a ballpoint pen, which she handed to me. I wrote down my pen name and my address in the North West and handed it back to her. She read what I'd written and looked up, frowning.

'Zoe *Quint*?'

It only took a second. Her eyes lit up: a cat that had found a secret stash of cream.

'The *Sunday Chronicle*? You're *her*? The writer of those wonderful articles? Wow!'

'"Travels on a Shoestring". Yes, that's me.'

Rex's eyes opened wide.

'That's YOU? Wow, I'm slow! You said your name was—'

'Correia? It is. But Quint is my maiden name. My professional name. I've always used it for my articles, why should I change it to my married name?'

Patsy quivered with excitement. She licked her lips and launched into a long, embarrassing gush.

'I'm one of your greatest fans, Zoe! See, it's journalists like you the world needs! You're just like us. You write about real people, real issues: the downtrodden, the oppressed. You care about them. You ask tough questions; you right wrongs. That article about the untouchable woman in India: brilliant! Wait a minute, I'll be right back.'

She stood up and hurried back inside. She returned a moment later, a folder in her hand. It was filled with newspaper clippings glued to sheets of paper; she opened it at one of the sections and handed it all to me.

'See, I even collect your stuff! It's brilliant, you should write a book!'

'I will. Glad you like it! Now, about Jonestown...'

'Zoe, you and me, the People's Temple, we're all on the same page. You're one of *us*. It's a great story for you, a scoop! Jonestown is quite simply the most progressive form of communal living on the face of the earth! You have to tell the world; we are so misunderstood.'

'Just a minute,' I said, and took my own notebook and pen out of my backpack. Patsy waited till I was ready, then launched into her spiel.

'You see, people talk about an end to racism, an end to discrimination: well, we at Jonestown actually *live* that dream. America today is a morass: a morass of greed, materialism, hatred, violence. We're different. We're a community: one for all and all for one.'

'So, you're Marxists?'

Patsy frowned and glanced at Rex. She'd wanted him here, but now he cramped her style; he represented the very evil that was America.

'A dirty word in America! That's why they persecuted us, chased us out!'

'Patsy, I've seen a lot of communes, lived in a few,' I said. 'Most of them fail. What makes Jonestown different?'

'Jonestown won't fail. Jonestown will make history. The difference is Jim Jones.'

I scribbled as she spoke. 'Ah, your leader. Tell me about him.'

'Our Father. Jim Jones is quite simply the living example of what a human being should be. Zoe, you'd like him, you'd support him.' She reached out and grasped my hand. Hers was no longer limp; it was like a claw, but hot and moist instead of dry and cracked as a claw should be. She drew it away and gushed on, gesticulating, grasping the air, hacking at it as with an axe.

'You have to show the world the *real* Jim Jones. See, when white America wouldn't let Blacks into their churches, he went out and founded his own church. He gave to the poor, he healed the sick. He helped the downtrodden, the forgotten. He's like a loving father who *cares* for his children. And that's the difference between us and every other so-called communist experiment: we have a father who *cares* about each and every one of us. That's why we love him so. Just a minute...'

She sprang up again, walked to the open balcony door and called, 'Freddy! Liane! Come here a minute!'

A minute later two children, a boy and a girl in their early teens, entered the balcony.

'These are my older kids. Kids, this is Zoe, a journalist, a good one. I want you to tell her how much you both love Dad.'

The children nodded, smiled, confirming Patsy's words. She dismissed them.

'See? Now, when children say so you know it's true. You can't fool kids. They would do anything for Father.'

I felt I had to say something, so I said the obvious: 'Beautiful children!' As indeed they were.

'They're my pride and joy.'

The interview continued with Patsy speaking as if reading from a brochure: she gave me a rundown of all the Jonestown facilities, and emphasised again and again the delirious happiness of every single member.

After an hour I closed my notepad.

'Well, Patsy,' I said, 'thanks so much for this interview. I'm really grateful. Just one thing—'

'You're going to write nice things about us, aren't you? We've had enough of journalists trying to destroy us. But you, now, you're Guyanese, and you're on our side.'

'It all sounds great but what I really want is to see for myself. Can I visit Jonestown? Look around, experience first-hand what you've talked about? Maybe stay with you for a few days?'

Patsy's face snapped shut. 'I don't have the authority to make that decision... Father doesn't like journalists.'

'But I'm different. You know that. You said so yourself! Think of what I can do for you!'

She hesitated, her eyes softening as she played with the bait I'd tossed. Finally, she grabbed it.

'OK, I'll talk to Father. I'll tell him about you. I'll tell him you can help us.'

I almost hugged her in gratitude, and my smile must have erased her last doubts.

'I have quite some influence with Father, you know. He trusts me implicitly. If I say you're clean, he'll believe me. I'm sure I can persuade him. Leave it to me!'

Her voice dripped with complicity, and she took my hand one last time. I squeezed it.

'Who knows,' I said, and threw her one last titbit, 'maybe I'll want to join the Temple!'

On the way home Rex turned to me. 'Hey, why didn't you tell me you're a famous writer with a fan club?!'

'Oh, shut up! Don't know if it's an honour to have *her* as a fan.'

'I told you she's weird.'

'She's not weird, she's dangerous.'

'Oh, come on.'

'Don't laugh. I've got a sixth sense about people, and she set all my red flags waving.'

'Maybe you went into the interview prejudiced? Because of Lucy?'

'It's not that. It's more... instinct. Her eyes – you can't look into them. There's a silver glaze in there – the glaze of a fanatic.'

'What if all they want is to live at peace with each other and with nature? Like she says?'

'Ha! Don't talk to me about returning to nature. The North West's a beautiful place, but the jungle's tough, no paradise. The only way to tame it is to concrete the whole place over. I've seen it all before, all these back-to-nature tourists. None of them can stick it out. After a while, a hunger for civilisation sets in. No way those Jonestown people are as happy as she says.'

'But you don't know. The only one you've met before now is Lucy. And you said yourself that Lucy's hysterical.'

'I believe Lucy more than Patsy. I have to get in there, find out for myself.'

'I wish you'd keep away from them.'

'I don't get you, Rex. One minute you say Jonestown is harmless, they're just a bunch of kooks but no big deal, next minute you tell me not to get involved, as if you care about me going in there.'

'Well, I do care. Maybe I'm just jealous of the attention you give them. Maybe I'd like some of that attention myself.'

Only later, remembering those words, did I realise how sleekly he'd avoided the question of why he was afraid for me, turning it into an intimate confession. At the time, though, I was touched, and looked up at him. Our eyes met, and I looked away again. I knew I had to say something; it was only fair.

'Rex – I like you. You're a good friend but I'm not ready for more yet, OK?'

'OK. But I'm a stubborn guy. I'll wait until you're ready.'

'It might be a long wait.'

'I'm patient as well as stubborn.'

The car drew up outside my house. I looked up at him, met his gaze, and knew more than I wanted to. I looked away.

'OK then. Thanks for everything.' I pressed the car door

handle, but as it clicked Rex snapped his fingers and I looked back at him.

'Hey, I almost forgot! I Xeroxed that Jonestown article for you. Here it is.'

Leaning forward, he rummaged in his briefcase, removed a large manila envelope and handed it to me.

'Oh, thanks!' I tugged, but he held on to it. I looked up.

'At the risk of you fleeing into your house screaming,' he said, 'I'm going to mention the unmentionable.'

'And that would be?' But I already knew. The word had kept me awake half the night, hammered at the back of my brain all day. I'd known for a long time that one day I'd have to face it, I just hadn't thought the day would come so soon.

'Kaieteur. You never actually said no. I went ahead and booked that flight for us. There... Go ahead, run away.'

He waited, but I did nothing but bite my lip and gaze ahead through the windscreen. We were holding up the traffic; Lamaha Street is only two lanes wide. A donkey cart creaked past on Rex's side, overtaking us. The Indian driver flicked his whip and cried 'Kurrrr-up!', but the donkey just flipped his tail and laid back his ears and quickened his gait for two reluctant steps.

In the rear-view mirror I saw the cars backed up to the corner, while ahead of us, in the opposite lane, another line of cars waited. The donkey was in no hurry. He wandered with exquisite leisure well over the middle line, and as the whip bounced against his matted grey haunches, he actually slowed down in blatant protest.

I had thought about it deep into the night. Rex's invitation had opened up a vipers' pit of fears – ugly beasts writhing in a deep, dark place. I'd tossed and turned for hours, trying to push them back into their lairs. But there was something else – another me, calm and cool, standing back and *knowing*. Knowing that there was just one way to conquer those beasts, and that was to let them out and face them – best of all with someone fearless. I'd feared the jungle, but Winston had taken me through. Now this.

This was worse – it was physical, a visceral terror coursing through my body. I watched my hands, as if from a distance. The left one gripped the door handle in a white-knuckle clench. The right one lay on my knee, trembling as if it held a jackhammer.

At last the cart moved into the lane ahead of us, and the traffic streamed past.

In the end it wasn't a conscious decision. My right hand, wobbly still but shyly bold like a child taking its first steps, reached over to cover Rex's on the gearstick. My eyes lifted, to meet his in the rear-view mirror. I heard a faraway voice, and it was my own.

'I'm not running anywhere,' I said. 'I'll do it. I'll come. I'll fly.'

CHAPTER TWENTY-ONE

The plane dipped slightly and I clenched the armrests, pressed my body back against the seat. Eyes closed, I focused on the in- and out-flow of my breath. In. Out. In. Out. Slowly. Watching my breath kept the thoughts away, the memories, the panic. Rex had mercifully left me to myself for most of the flight, but now he nudged me; I opened my eyes and saw that he was pointing out of the window: we were there.

A spectacular rainbow curved over the Falls, each colour brilliantly etched against the next and against the cobalt blue of the sky. Kaieteur itself, eight hundred feet in a single drop, fell in a sharp silver column over the canyon's edge, a glistening knife cutting through the dark green of the forest. A fine mist hung above the Falls, suffused with sunlight and sparkling with a million glorious gems. Despite myself, I gasped. Wonder seeped through me, radiant and full, dissolving all fear: an ineffable bliss, and gratitude for the gift of such splendour.

The plane lurched and fear surged up like a black hand from the depths. I gasped again, grabbed for the armrest and found Rex's hand instead. Gently he squeezed mine, as if to say all's well. My hand was a receptor, soaking up his calm; it relaxed, and the calm spread upwards, through my body, and into my mind. I breathed easily again, looked at him and smiled, then drew my hand gently from his.

Fifteen minutes later, he and I stood at Kaieteur's edge. Though it was midday a light mist surrounded us and veiled the sunlight, moistening our skin and cooling the air. But the shiver that went through me and the gooseflesh on my bare arms came not from cold but from sheer awe.

As smooth as a vast silver ribbon, the water plunged over the gorge's lip. From the plane the Falls had seemed a vision, a toy, even, unreal and far away, but here it was *we* who were the toys, minuscule against nature's majesty. The Potaro River surged forward, merciless in its might, pulled as if by a magnet into the abyss. I felt helpless, weak and small; and that was when the trembling started, merged with the giddy certainty that I, too would plunge down into the gorge.

Far below, the silver ribbon of water met the rocks with a roar so thunderous it drowned my every thought, filled my every cell until there was nothing of me left but the thunder, and the thunder morphed into another sound, a deafening crash that would not stop but echoed on and on and on inside me...

Paul's face appeared before me, a rippling, fluid portrait painted in the water, his eyes the very same as in those moments before the crash. His voice called: *come, come, come to me.*

My legs buckled, I felt myself falling... but no, falling was too passive, I was *pulled*, down, down, down into that abyss, with the water, with the roar, a helpless rag doll tossed in the careless hand of a water-giant; and I was fearless, glad even, because I knew I would fall soft, into Paul's waiting arms. I was going home...

I jolted back to reality. My eyes opened. My hand was in Rex's, his voice louder than the roar.

'Zoe! Zoe, what's the matter? Are you OK?'

I looked up at him. I spoke, and my own voice seemed a mile away.

'I'm bit... dizzy.'

He took my elbow and led me away. I leaned against him, trembling, and he laid an arm round my waist to support me. He led me to a bench and sat me down. After a while I began to breathe naturally.

'Thanks. That was... weird.'

'What happened?'

'I wanted to... jump. No. To fall. To go to... Paul.'

He didn't speak, but his arm around me tightened and his hand squeezed mine. After a long silence my words came.

'For a long time after he died, I wanted to die too. Throw myself under a car, jump from a high place. I just didn't care about life.'

My voice faltered. I thought I would cry. The tears banked up behind my eyes and I longed for them to come, to finally weep and weep and weep out the ocean of sorrow inside me. I turned towards him to bury my face in his shoulder and he was there to meet me; I heaved against him once, twice, but that was all. I pulled away and looked up at him. My eyes felt blotted dry by sandpaper. I could not cry.

'I know, Zoe, I know. I've been through it too. It takes time. With me, it was five years before I stopped wanting to die. It's normal. It's OK.'

We had to shout to make ourselves heard above the roar of the Falls, and shouting quickly dissolved the intimacy. Foolish me! A silly, sentimental little girl, weak and hysterical! I so wanted to be strong, overcome the past, wear a brave face for all the world to see.

But Rex was different. With him, I needed no mask, no

disguise. With him, for the first time in years I could be *myself*, foolish, and even weak, if need be, and what a relief that was.

On the flight back to Georgetown I felt no panic at all. Rex and I hardly spoke. At one point he reached out and took my hand, held it loosely in his. I left it there.

CHAPTER TWENTY-TWO

Over the following days Rex and I met for lunch every day, and every evening he took me out: Palm Court, the Belvedere, and once again the Pegasus. On the third night, after dinner, we went for a walk along the Sea Wall. The balmy Atlantic breeze came in soft caressing gusts that billowed his shirt and wrapped the hem of my dress against my legs, and beside us the surf lapped and sucked at the rocks. The ocean stretched away to a distant horizon, catching the full moon in its ripples. I knew what was coming a second before he stopped, pulled me to him, and kissed me.

'Zoe,' he whispered as our lips pulled apart, 'I'm falling in love with you.'

I found I could not meet his eyes. 'I need... time.'

'I know.'

We kissed again.

'I want to, but I can't.'

'I know.'

And again.

'Do you *have* to go back to the North West?'

'Yes.'

'Can't you stay – just a week longer?'
'No.'
'Can I come and visit you, up there?'
'Yes.'

But I did not forget Jonestown. I met Donna every day at the Tower, and every day she had more news for me. She had a penchant for the juicy stuff; gossip and scandal found a natural home with her, and though I took some titbits with a pinch of salt, I listened carefully.

'There's a woman called Joyce Merridale,' she said. She wrapped herself in a towel and sat down opposite me, patting her face dry with another, smaller, towel. I wasn't swimming today; I'd been out with Rex and hadn't had time to go home and get my swimsuit. 'She's having an affair with Dr Singh. She comes down from Jonestown at least once a month. Officially she's got some female condition but they've been seen together.'

I scribbled the names into my notebook. 'Dr Singh – isn't he the one with that private clinic on Brickdam?'

'That's the one. Married, of course. They meet secretly there, she's got a key. And the Minister of Home Affairs, Eric Clark – she's seeing him too. These white women only have to snap their fingers.'

'How do you find out all this stuff?'

'My spies.' She winked.

'And there's a woman called Moira – Jonestown top brass. She's a medical doctor, close as you can get to Jim Jones. His personal doctor as well as right hand, so to speak. Maybe even his lover. Cushy with both the American Embassy staff *and* the Russian Ambassador.'

'How on earth does she manage that?'

Donna shrugged. 'Who knows?'

'I'll have to ask Rex about that. He's never mentioned her.'

'If he ain't mentioned her, he got his reasons. How you

manage that, a love affair with a man who got all the secrets you want, but can't tell you? Or won't tell you?'

'It's not a love affair, Donna.'

'Ha!' She snorted.

The waiter brought our drinks, Lime Rickey for me and for her an ice cream soda.

'I thought you were on a diet?'

'I lost two pounds last week, I deserve this. And don't change the subject. How you manage it? With Rex, I mean.'

'We just don't talk about Jonestown any more.'

'So, y'all not even start up properly, and you already got a taboo between you?'

'It's not a taboo, it's just that we disagree about it. No big thing.'

'What's no big thing? You and Rex, or Jonestown?'

'Neither. I mean, disagreeing about Jonestown isn't a big thing. He prefers me not to research the story, I insist, so we leave it at that. He doesn't own me.'

'Men always think they own women. Even when they pretend not to.'

'Not this time. There's really nothing going on. Not much.'

'You mean, no hanky-panky yet?'

I laughed. 'None of your business!'

'Everything's my business. You better hurry up; a thousand Guyanese girls can't wait to get they hands on him.'

'You told me that already. I'm not in a hurry.'

'You probably right. Men always want the one girl they can't get.'

I shrugged and drained my glass. 'Men always this, men always that. What *don't* you know about men?'

She laughed. 'I know all about men, girl, an' I know what they all want. You probably right, keep him dangling.'

'It's not that, Donna.' I was tired of the banter. I needed to talk about Rex, and Donna was the perfect sounding board. It was impossible to talk to Mum, who only wanted to see a ring on my finger again, and Dad just said, 'Do what you think is best, dear.' But what was best?

'It's just that... I like him a lot. I'm attracted. I like being with him; he's comfortable, a bit like an old shoe. But...'

'Hmmm... Wonder what Rex would think, you calling him an old shoe.'

'You know what I mean. I like him all right. I have – *feelings* for him. But I don't *love* him, Donna. Maybe I can't. Something's holding me back.'

Donna sucked her teeth. 'Paul, Paul, Paul... A stuck record with you. You need to move on. Here's your chance.'

'Not true. It's not Paul. I've changed a lot, since Kaieteur.'

It was true. The trip to Kaieteur had lifted a cloud from my mind. For one, my fear of flying had vanished as if it had never been; the flight back had been as easy as crossing the road. But more important, the sting of grief had left me. Momentarily I returned to that moment at the Falls' edge, saw Paul's face, heard his voice. Felt the pull down into the gorge – and resisted. In that moment I had returned to life. I still loved Paul – always would – but I had walked free from the shadow of his death.

'So, if it's not Paul – what is it then?'

'It's what Rex *is*. What he stands for. The American Embassy. He represents the worst of everything.'

America had a bad name in Guyana – ever since they helped oust the democratically voted premier who cared and could have led us into Independence, and replaced him with a crooked puppet. The ruin we were in was the result. And they were still in charge, allowing the corruption, the rigged elections, the rape of our beautiful land by its leaders.

'Well, well, well... Just listen to Miss Pride and Prejudice herself.'

'I know, it's terrible of me.'

'You need to see past that. It wouldn't matter if you really loved him, you'd deal with it. Compromise.'

'Exactly. And I'm *not* in love. I remember what that's like: you can't think, you can't sleep, like a madness. And that's just not there. And it's not Paul holding me back any more. It's weird. All I think about the whole time is—'

'Jonestown. Lucy.'

'Right. If I loved Rex I wouldn't want to leave him, would I? Leave town? But I do. I can't wait to get back to the North West. It's like an obsession, a mystery I've got to solve, and Rex is in the way.'

Donna nodded. 'It's a question of timing. First things first. Get Lucy home, get the People's Temple evicted, wash your hands of them, and you'll be free again and ready for Rex.'

'Ha! As if it were that easy!'

Donna noisily sucked up the last of her ice cream soda. She fished for the few last lumps of ice cream stuck to the base of the glass and licked them off the straw.

'I know it's not. It's what Rex knows that he can't tell you. His secrets.'

'That, too. But somehow that doesn't bother me that much. He's just doing his job. Rex can keep his bloody secrets. I've got mine too.'

Donna's eyes narrowed. Sentences with the word 'secret' in them were her bread and butter. I could clearly see her ears pricking, her nostrils flaring.

'You've got secrets?'

'Shhh!' I put my finger on my lips, hunched my shoulders, looked warily over my shoulders, let my glance dart furtively around the terrace. Then I crooked my finger and leaned across the table. She played the game, leaned in to meet me.

'Don't tell a soul, right?'

'Cross my heart!'

'I'm going to go in and get Lucy out myself.'

. . .

The next afternoon, Rex and I met on the beach. We'd planned this for days, and I was looking forward to it: a kung fu practice. We arrived simultaneously, both dressed in the loose wraparound cotton trousers and tunic appropriate for the art. The tide was out, and we had a vast stretch of beach all to ourselves. Beneath our bare feet the sand was firm and barely moist, baked solid from the past day's sun, the Atlantic so far withdrawn it was no more than a silver line across the horizon.

After an initial warm-up we moved into a now-slow, now-fast perfectly synchronised dance, feigning attack and defence, bodies, legs and arms swirling and lunging, sometimes coming within a hair's breadth of a strike.

Our faces were glued to each other's. His eyes, wiped clean of all softness and sentimentality, held mine in an almost hostile gaze of steel, which I met with equal unswerving focus. In kung fu as in all martial arts the mind is the chief asset, and my teacher Kuanan had taught me well. Rex was undoubtedly the more experienced and more skilled, but I held my own right up to the end.

It was magnificent: our bodies surrendered to a ballet of our minds in which grace met force in perfect harmony. Our session drew to a close with one last high kick and swirl from me followed by a sudden perfect standstill, our grim faces just inches apart; and then we bowed simultaneously and it was over. Immediately the sound of clapping burst the spell that had enclosed us. We looked up, and both smiled – on the Sea Wall behind us stood a long line of spectators. They had remained politely silent during our session, but now they clapped enthusiastically and some cheered. We waved and bowed again, and hugged each other, and I felt even closer to Rex than when he'd kissed me – and forgiving. Perhaps I'd misjudged him. Perhaps my doubts were all born of my own insecurities. Perhaps they had nothing to do with him at all.

We sat on the sand and talked for a while, discussing our moves and our strikes. Rex thought I should learn other methods of self-defence and promised to teach me a three-shot combination that could bring down a man twice my strength: knee to the groin, then to the face as he doubles over, followed by an elbow strike to the back of the neck. It would only take a few hours of training, and we arranged to meet again the following day for that; which we did, and the day after, and the day after.

To my surprise these fight sessions brought me closer to Rex than any of the romantic interludes that had gone before. His attitude, considerate, warm and totally involved, made me think I'd misjudged him. Most men, when you tell them you need time, try to cut that time short with even more advances, deeming themselves irresistible enough to break you down. Not so Rex. He gave me space and he gave me time and he gave me his skills, and never again tried to kiss me.

I considered telling him of my plan to rescue Lucy, but something held me back. Not mistrust, this time, but the sure knowledge that Rex cared too much for me to maintain the distance if he knew. The poor guy would freak out. And to my surprise I found I cared too much for him to put him through that.

He would also try to change my mind, and I had no intention of letting him.

'So how do you like your job?'

He shrugged. After training we'd gone to the Pegasus for drinks and a swim, and now sat at a poolside table, sipping piña coladas.

'Not much to say about it. You know how it is.'

'No, I don't. From the start, when I saw you in that office, I felt you were out of place. Why the Diplomatic Service, for heaven's sake?'

'I liked travelling; I thought it would be a chance to see the world. My father-in-law was a diplomat – he recruited me.'

'Ah, I see. Made a respectable man out of the vagabond.'

He laughed. His hair was still wet from our swim, his skin glistening bronze. He looked like a young god.

'Something like that. But sometimes I feel like a round peg in a square hole.'

'Don't you have to – you know – do things you wouldn't do, say things you wouldn't say?'

'Isn't it like that in most jobs? That's what it is, Zoe – just a job. I wish you weren't so prejudiced. So anti-American.'

'It's just that I see the potential in you. It's wasted in that office.'

He chuckled and reached for my hand. 'I hope you mean that on a personal level, too! It gives me hope!'

'Well...'

'Well, what?'

'It's hard to separate the one from the other.'

'It's like an actor, playing a role. Just because you're playing Hitler doesn't mean you *are* Hitler.'

I pulled my hand away. 'It's a bit different in real life, I think.'

His hand chased mine, closed around it. It felt strong, reassuring.

'Zoe – I am not my job. I am not the United States of America or its policies. Can't you see me as a man, and let everything else follow? We could work it out, if you'd only give me a chance.'

I hesitated, took a deep breath, and whispered: 'I'll try.'

LUCY

Something important has happened. Everything has changed.
 Now I know Moira's secret. Now I know how to get her. I know how to set us free. I know—

Some instinct made Lucy glance up in mid-sentence and look out the window. Her heart lurched. Moira was striding across from the radio room, headed straight towards the office, speaking into the walkie-talkie as she came. Even from this distance Lucy could see the lines of her frown and even the glint in her eyes. She knew that look well.

She tore the page from the notebook and ran to the bookshelf. A moment later the office door flew open and Moira burst in.

Lucy stood with her back to the wall, hands behind her back. Moira, who had flown in the door like a tornado on the rampage, came to a stop. They faced each other across the room, neither moving.

Finally, Moira spoke.

'Come here.'

Lucy stepped forward.

'What have you got in your hands? Show me!'

Lucy held out her empty hands. Moira's tongue flicked across her bottom lip.

'So, you're not happy here?'

'I-I...'

'Running to the American Embassy? Begging for help to get out?'

Lucy's shoulders drooped. Moira's stare bored into her eyes, forcing her to look down and hang her head. The inside of her mouth felt like sandpaper, and her heart galloped at full tilt. She wanted to pee, and feared she would, right then and there.

'I want to know just how this happened. Someone must have helped you. Who?'

Silence. Her knees felt suddenly weak and wobbly; in a minute she'd fall to the ground. She wished it would happen, right now. *Pass out, Lucy. Better yet, just die, right now.* As if in response, her body refused to breathe in. The whole room swayed.

'Answer me, you Black idiot!'

Moira's furious yell tore through her fragile senses; she gasped, and stumbled, and her knees buckled. And then a cold dry hand closed round her wrist. She let herself be dragged to the door.

As they emerged into the sunlight she looked up. At the bottom of the stairs, waiting for her, stood that hulk of a guard, Bruno Grimm.

Lucy found one last ounce of strength, enough to gasp a terrified 'No!' and struggle against Moira's grip. Something whipped across her cheek, a biting sting that knocked the breath out of her. And then at last delicious oblivion. In one last sliver of her awareness she saw Bruno reaching out to catch her.

CHAPTER TWENTY-THREE

Rex saw me off at the Georgetown dock, watched me board the *Witte de Roo*, waved as she chugged away from the dock.

Waiting for me at the other end was Andy.

I'd forgotten all about Andy.

'Hi,' I said as he walked up. 'How'd you know I was on the boat?'

We meandered through the milling crowd towards the road, which doubled as a congested car park. He held open the Jeep's door.

'News travels fast up here.'

It was easy to figure out. Aunt Edna's loyalty to *Deaths and Messages* had paid off: I'd sent her a radio message last week to let her know I'd been held up in town for a week, but of course that way, the whole world knew.

'Uncle Bill asked you to pick me up?'

'Nope. I offered.'

'Well... thanks. That's nice.'

The Jeep inched its way forward. This part of the North West District is a vast, sparsely populated area. On most days you'll see no more than four or five vehicles. On ferry days –

twice-weekly – though, every vehicle in the vicinity descends on Port Kaituma, and every one of them now criss-crossed our path. These were no sleek motorcars, of course: they were pickups, trucks, vans, Jeeps, ancient or covered in dust, or both. I scanned them all for the Jonestown flatbed truck, but in vain.

At the end of the village Andy turned off down a small track leading off the main road and pulled up outside a ramshackle building, a shop with living quarters above it. I read the faded sign above the entrance door: PEREIRAS HARDWARE AND SUPPLY'S. The writer in me longed to edit the sign.

'Your uncle asked me to bring you here to buy some chicken wire,' Andy explained. A mangy dog barked furiously as we left the Jeep, announcing our arrival more thoroughly than a bell, yet keeping its distance, and in fact backing off as we crossed the bridge into the shop. Inside, it was dark and dank, but as my eyes adjusted I saw shelves filled with all manner of metal gadgets, while the floor itself held a wide assortment of larger items – wheelbarrows, metal pails, spades and rakes, and several rolls of wire mesh, including the chicken wire I wanted. There was nobody to be seen.

'Vinnie must be down with the boats,' Andy said, and led the way out the back door. We walked along a wooden causeway and down a rickety stairway leading to a separate building on the riverbank.

We entered, and it turned out to be a large boathouse. Two rowing boats, two motorboats, all of them faded and ancient, bobbed on the water, while several canoes were stacked against a wall. A smart white launch was moored at one end; it looked new and almost luxurious compared to the other vessels. A grizzled Portuguese man came forward to meet us. He wore a ripped and grimy singlet tucked into an even grimier and more ripped pair of khaki trousers, and a tattered pair of tennis shoes with the caps cut out to reveal long, bony and very grubby toes. The man's long, hollow-cheeked face was pockmarked and coarse with several days' stubble, and when he spoke, he revealed several gaps in his teeth.

'Eh-eh, long time no see, Doctor, how yuh doin'?' He turned to me. 'And who's dis charmin' young lady yuh bring fuh me?'

Andy introduced us; we shook hands. I didn't much appreciate the man's – Vinnie Pereira's – eyes on me, but he shifted them away as Andy spoke.

'So, Vinnie, how's business?'

'Bad, man, bad. Nobody not comin' up here.'

Andy turned to me to explain: 'Vinnie also runs a small guest house and rents out these boats. Trouble is, we don't get much visitors up here. I see you got a new boat, though.' He pointed to the launch.

'That? Yeh, she new. Ah thinkin' of doin' nature tours into the interior, me brother in Georgetown tryin' to get business goin' down there, send me up some people. So, tell me, dis yuh new girlfriend?'

He leered back to me; I had the feeling that if Andy said no, Vinnie's paws would be all over me. I shuddered, and nudged Andy to put an end to the small talk. He obliged.

'We came to get some chicken wire, against the bats.'

The talk turned to bats as we walked back up to the shop, Vinnie leading the way. I bought a roll of wire, and Andy and I returned to the Jeep.

'What a creep,' I said to Andy as he drove off.

'Vinnie? Yeah, he has a bit of a reputation as a ladies' man up here. Trouble is, the Amerindian ladies don't like him, and all the girls he brings up from town run away again.'

'Not hard to understand why.'

'But that launch looked nice; I was thinking of renting it myself. It's a lot more comfortable than the hospital motorboat – which I shouldn't take anyway, in case it's needed. Think I'll go back and have a talk with Vinnie later... what about this Saturday?'

'*What* about this Saturday?'

'Don't tell me you forgot – our trip to the waterfall? I've been looking forward to it all week.'

Ouch. I had completely forgotten that promise. But Andy was still speaking and didn't notice my discomfort.

'Saturday's my day off. Can you make it?'

I hesitated. I had avoided men for so long that the ethics of the situation were unclear to me. I ought to tell Andy about Rex right now. And write to Rex about Andy.

But then again, why? There was nothing between us. I liked Andy; a lot. But as a friend. I knew that Andy's interest might not be entirely platonic; that Uncle and Aunt were encouraging a romantic attachment that would never be. But I could handle that. I needed a friend up here. Moreover, I'd promised him this trip before I'd met Rex. And I had certainly not committed to Rex. But then again... it just didn't feel right, to go out with Andy. Not after that trip to Kaieteur. Not after growing so close to Rex.

'I'm sorry,' I said. 'I need more time.'

'That's fine,' he said, but I could hear the disappointment in his voice.

'It's just...'

'You don't have to explain anything, Zoe. I understand.'

I reached for his hand, and squeezed it in gratitude.

The conversation shifted; I decided to talk to Andy about my interest in Jonestown.

'So, you're really going in there?'

'Or die trying. I want to write an article about it and I've got someone who's helping.' I told him about Patsy Boyle.

'It'll make a good story – if you can get information,' Andy said when I'd finished speaking. 'They're a strange bunch. You get the impression they're – well, not speaking their minds. As if they're hiding things.'

Finally, we were free of the crowds, and picked up speed.

Port Kaituma is so small that five minutes later we were on the open track. Andy drove easily, half-turned towards me, one hand on the wheel and the other resting on the gearstick.

'You've been that close to them?'

'Sure. About six months ago they sent a radio through to us – a complicated birth. I went over and performed a Caesarean. Twin girls. A bit premature, but they survived.'

'Don't they have a doctor in there?'

'Normally, yes. She happened to be in town at the time.'

'What was your impression?'

'With a few exceptions, they're malnourished. Dark circles under their eyes, bad skin. They call themselves an agricultural project but it doesn't look like a roaring success. It can't be easy, producing enough fruit and vegetables for a community that size. I think their staple is rice. Breakfast, lunch and dinner, rice.'

'But did you meet anyone? Talk to anyone?'

'I worked with a Black girl; said she had some medical training. She acted as my assistant during the operation. An intelligent girl, too good for a place like that. I even remember her name: Alexis. I remember she kept looking at me in this strange way. As if she wanted to tell me something but couldn't.'

Alexis? I made a note of the name. Perhaps she was another Lucy, with stories to tell of inside Jonestown. I'd try to find her once I entered.

'Did you meet Jim Jones? Or anyone high up?'

'No. His right-hand is a woman called Moira, who's also his personal doctor. Alexis kept mentioning her: Moira said this and Moira said that.'

'I've heard of this Moira. She seems to be quite active in courting foreign diplomats. Can't wait to meet her. Hopefully, Patsy can get me in.'

Andy did not reply. We had reached the jungle now, and the road narrowed. The trees on either side had been felled to make room, and half-high strips of shrubbery in a lighter green lined the road. I felt his eyes on me and turned to meet them.

'Zoe, just be careful, OK? I don't like that place. It gives me the creeps. You ever hear that voice at night?'

'Yep. And the sirens, and the gunshots. I'm surprised the police haven't raided them yet.'

'What police? You're in the North West. No crime, no police.'

Our talk turned casual after that, and by the time we reached Parrot Creek Andy was – well, I'd called Rex an old shoe, and it was a compliment, but Andy was an old glove, an even bigger compliment. Being Guyanese himself, his background was familiar, and we had no need to verbally fill in the details of our lives. We spoke easily about the schools we'd gone to, the people we knew, the places we'd been.

And, I realised, that was how I felt about him: he was like a brother. I looked forward to spending more time with him, but I knew there was no danger of romance; it would feel like incest. I hoped he'd feel the same.

CHAPTER TWENTY-FOUR

I found Aunt Edna squatting at the woodpile under the house, axe in hand, hacking at a chunk of wood till all that was left of it was a heap of evenly sized slivers. She pushed those off the chopping block and reached for the next chunk.

'Good morning,' she said in that moment of quiet, and only then looked up at me and smiled. 'How was the trip?'

I squatted down beside her and picked up the second axe.

'Morning. Couldn't have been better,' I said. I hadn't seen her last night when I returned home; she'd been out attending a birth and had come home long after I'd fallen asleep. As we chopped wood, I gave her a brief rundown of the events in Georgetown, told her about Rex and Patsy and the help they had given me, about my phone call to Lucy's mother and Congressman Ryan's anticipated visit.

The rhythmic splitting of wood soothed my jagged spirits and brought me right back into the farm routine. My efforts with the axe were slow and clumsy compared to hers, yet had improved a lot over the last few weeks. Aunt Edna had first taught me to split wood when I was only six years old, and that latent skill was returning.

'So, what now?' she asked between the slashes. 'You got enough for your article?'

'No,' I said. I gashed open a new piece of wood. It fell into two neat halves, my best work yet.

'No what?'

'No, I haven't got enough. I need to talk to Lucy again, properly. I need to get into Jonestown. I've won Patsy's trust, and she'll help get me in.' I was hedging. That wasn't the whole truth.

'But you gon' be careful, right? Don't take no risks.'

It was no use. I had to tell her.

'Aunt Edna, that's not all. See, once I get in there I want to escape with Lucy, through the bush. And I need your help. I want Winston to teach me the way out. The back way.'

Aunt Edna's axe was on its swift path down as I spoke, but she started and the blade missed the wood and buried itself in the block. It was the first time I'd ever seen her miss.

'No!'

I laid down my own axe and put a hand on her wrist. We looked at each other over the block. Fear flickered in her eyes.

'I'll be all right. Don't worry.'

She pulled her hand from under mine. 'Don't *worry*? Zoe, you crazy, or what?'

She jerked the axe's handle and freed it from the wood, hacked it into two.

'I have to do it. I know I can. I'll be fine.'

'No! That's not what I asked you to do! I wanted you to write an article; to expose what's going on in there, get it closed down!'

'But Aunty, I can't do one without the other. You know Guyanese bureaucracy. If I write that big exposé, what's going to happen? Nothing. A flurry of agitation and then it'll all settle down again. They bribed their way in and they'll bribe their way forward; if they want to stay, they'll figure out how to. Lucy wants to get out now, and I'm going to get her out.'

'But you said this congressman is coming to get them out!'

'Congressman Ryan? You know these official visits – it might be months before he comes. And anyway... look, if the American Vice-Consul can't get people out, why should some congressman be able to? I don't trust the official channels, never did, never will.'

'I thought you trusted this vice-consul of yours.'

I shrugged.

'He's a diplomat. He's paid to smooth over differences. He avoids conflict. He believes everything's fine in there, and all he does is try to placate me. He wants to protect me.'

I inspected the axe in my hand, running my finger gently along the blade. 'Rex's nice, but he doesn't really believe my story about Lucy. Thinks she's hysterical, paranoid, which she is. Thing is, he didn't see her *face*. I did. Aunty, I don't care how true her story is. I see her face all the time. That terror in her eyes. She even comes in my sleep now, begging me to get her out. I've got to do it. It's almost, well, personal.'

'You're like obsessed with this Lucy. Like if she's family.'

I nodded. 'It's weird. As if she's *me*. Those eyes of hers – I can't explain it. I just know what I have to do.'

'I wish I'd never said a word. Your mother would kill me.'

'Ah, but she won't know, will she? Not unless you tell her. Or not until it's all over.'

'It's not a good place, Zoe. It's one thing to go in there to research it, to write an article, but any kind of rescue attempt – it's madness. You saw those guards. They got guns!'

'Don't you worry, I'll be fine! I've done far more dangerous things than this!'

'Like what?'

'Like, hitchhiking alone through Colombia? I nearly got

raped six times!' I reached into the woodpile to remove another chunk of wood. I tossed it into the air and caught it jauntily, adding for emphasis, 'If I can survive Colombia, I can survive Jim Jones!'

'Watch out!'

Aunt Edna's shriek drowned my last words. A scorpion rushed out from the woodpile, straight towards me, tail raised for the attack. I had no time to think. My axe slashed down upon it. Aunt Edna and I stared at two severed pieces of scorpion, still writhing in its death throes.

Aunt Edna shook her head. 'A bad omen. When you talk cocky like that, God does teach you a lesson.'

'I'd say it's a good omen. I killed the bastard, didn't I?'

I scooped up the pieces of scorpion with my axe blade and flicked them away.

That night I tucked the mosquito net carefully into the mattress, leaving the smallest entry gap. The chicken wire was firmly in place, nailed into the window frames; no more bats would visit me at night. I put on my nightshirt, washed my face in the basin, cleaned my teeth, plaited my hair for the night and stepped across to the shelf I kept as a shrine. The centrepiece of that shrine was a photo – our wedding photo.

Every night for the last three years the last thing I had done each night was to pick up this photo and speak to Paul, kiss him goodnight. My little goodnight ritual. I had taken it with me to Georgetown, but since the trip to Kaieteur the ritual had lapsed and then disappeared altogether. But now I needed an official closing ritual.

Tonight, I held the photo a little longer than usual. I kissed and stroked it one last time and laid it down. I reached behind my neck to unclasp the chain. I let the wedding ring fall into my palm, touched it one last time, then closed my fingers over it, and whispered one last time to Paul: *Forgive me.* I wrapped the ring and the photo in a third souvenir – a handkerchief embroidered with his initials – slid open the drawer in the table and slipped the slim little package into it, then closed the drawer.

CHAPTER TWENTY-FIVE

My mind was made up, and Aunt Edna knew that argument was futile. And so she gave in to the inevitable, and I told her of the next phase of my plan. I had to learn how to find my way through the jungle, on my own. And I needed a teacher.

'What about those guards?' Aunt Edna asked in a last appeal to my sanity, but I only shrugged.

'I'll cross that bridge when I get to it.' Once inside Jonestown I would use my wits to figure out a way past the guards; any plan I made now could only be speculation, and futile. Lucy would help me.

As both the local teacher and the district midwife Aunt Edna commanded respect, and though Winston was sceptical, she convinced him and he appointed me my personal trainer, a young man named Errol. Frankly, I was disappointed; I'd hoped for Winston himself. But obviously he had better things to do than teach me my jungle abc's. I could have Errol for two weeks, Winston told me. Not one day longer.

. . .

The bush was a city, the creeks its roads, the canoe my vehicle. I was a stranger to that city, and a tangled mess it was, but with Errol as my guide I learned to drive and to navigate and find my way. Up and down we travelled through the gridwork of creeks until I knew its pattern by heart and could travel it on my own, until the miles of tangled mangroves lining the water-road became almost as familiar to me as my home town, and a fork in the creek no more a mystery than the Lamaha-and-Camp-Street junction.

Familiarity drives out fear. Now I was ready for the real challenge: the bush. I took a deep breath, and plunged right in behind Errol. I followed him a while. Then:

'Stop here. Close your eyes. *Listen.*'

I obeyed. At first, I heard nothing out of the ordinary: a shrill sound-curtain, the same as everywhere. Yet it was not the same. Unable to see, I began to truly listen, and as I listened, the dense fog of cacophony opened and split into isolated sounds: a thin high whistle here, a staccato peeping there, a rich full warble somersaulting through the backdrop, a siren fluting in the foreground.

I jumped; Errol had touched my face, but only to tie a blindfold over my eyes. As he led me forward through the bush a veritable pathway of sound opened up to me, as clear and obvious as a visual track, and I learned to follow and to heed and to listen.

Next, I learned the pathways of smell, for every tree and every bush has its own distinctive scent, and the earth and the insects and the sprayings and droppings of beasts leave trails of odour, hidden from us only by ignorance. Errol taught me to find those olfactory tracks.

Next, I learned to switch off both sound and smell and actually *feel* my way forward, not by touch but by silence; I learned to turn away from thought itself and pitch my being towards that silence which, once trusted, led me on into the secret world of the rainforest. I began to understand, all senses merging; to hear, smell, feel and think like an Amerindian.

And only once those more subtle senses opened did Errol allow me to use my primary sense, that of sight. He divided the path between the creek and Jonestown into short sections, and made me memorise each section, walk up and down it until I knew each tree, each shrub, each overhanging branch by heart.

Day after day we walked the distance, up and down, bit by bit, until I could do it not only blindfolded but on my own; then, and only then, I walked the distance and painted white arrows on tree trunks, pointing the way. On the last day of my last lesson I brought an extra canoe and hid it in the mangroves. I was ready for Jonestown.

But, it seemed, Jonestown wasn't ready for me. I had not heard a word from Jim Jones. The only person in Georgetown I heard from was Rex.

10th November

My dear Zoe,

Your letter came yesterday; what a joy! I'm glad to hear you've settled well, and don't miss Georgetown. I had hoped, however, that you do miss me because I miss you so very much. I think about you night and day.

It seems to me I only began to get to know you when you ran off again. But on the other hand, I feel as if I've known you all my life, as if I've been waiting for you all my life and everything I've done till now was only a detour, and every event that has brought us together had only that as its aim – yes, that even Jonestown was simply a ploy by destiny to bring us together. Me from Boston, you from Georgetown – it seems impossible that we should ever meet, but it happened and it had to happen, and I hope that you feel even a small part of that sense of destiny. Or will one day.

I know you need time. I'm willing to wait.

As for your question: yes, I spoke to Patsy again. She says she's discussed you with 'Father' and has given you an enthusiastic endorsement. But the answer is still no. Jim Jones doesn't want you in there. Patsy can do no more than ask, she says. It's up to him. She promised to ask again after Congressman Ryan's visit, but I wouldn't depend on it. If he says no now, it'll be no then, too.

Zoe, I know your hopes were high and I'm sorry to disappoint you. As I told you, he's incredibly paranoid about journalists and this comes as no surprise to me.

You know my feelings on this. I wish you'd leave well enough alone. I wish you'd stay out of it. But at the same time that's what I love about you: your stubbornness and determination to see things through to the end, your compassion for that girl, your courage. I know how much you want to see Jonestown. And maybe I can help.

What if I made you an offer? Let all this business with Ryan pass by. Things are very volatile at the moment. With the congressman's impending visit, they're all on edge and it's just not the best time to go. Let things cool down. Let him get your Lucy out, and things settle back to their old rhythm. I promise to work on Ryan to the best of my ability to get her out.

But if he doesn't – I'll go myself, personally, and escort her out, and I'll take you with me. How's that? I realise it's a compromise; I know you're in a hurry to get in, I know you want to help, I know you want to research for your article. But what's the hurry? Jonestown won't disappear – not for a while. It's only a matter of weeks. We expect Ryan later this month.

As for me, life goes on here. You know Georgetown. Not much happening. The usual round of parties and receptions – you Guyanese love your fêtes, don't you?! Every weekend something else but always the same, same rigmarole, same people, and I'm heartily sick of it. I wish you were here.

In that spirit, my dear,

Yours very warmly,

Rex

I smiled to myself, folded the letter and put it back into its envelope. It was Rex's third letter since I'd left Georgetown, and the third time I'd read it. I had brought it down to the creek to read again, and to think, to clear my mind, to make a decision. I sat in my swimsuit at the edge of the jetty, my legs over the edge, my feet just skimming the water. I'd had my first swim, a delicious cooling-off in the midday heat, and now the sun's rays caught each little drop of water on my skin and made of each a jewel glistening in rainbow colours and dissolving into nothing. By the time I finished reading I was all dry. I put the letter aside, pulled up my knees, hugged them, and thought of Rex.

Each new letter seemed to open the door to him just a little wider and close the door on Paul a little more. More and more, a little more each day, my thoughts returned to Rex.

Could I ever love him? Did I even want to love him? Should I encourage him by writing letters, responding to his? Should I just tell him there was no chance, and break it all off now, before he hoped too much? Was I ready for all he hinted at?

Rex had done so much for me. Taking me to Kaieteur was exactly what I'd needed, exactly when I needed it. For three years I'd nursed a wound that would not heal. For three years I'd been haunted by an unlikely, incompatible pair of emotions: fear of death – concretised in my fear of flying – and yet longing for death as the portal back to Paul, climaxing at Kaieteur's edge.

Rex had helped me kill two birds with one stone: face the fear and resist the longing. Rex's hand had held me through both. And then there was our shared experience of losing a beloved spouse. Rex had helped heal me. Was this a sign, a portent, that he belonged in my life?

And then there was Paul himself. The little ceremony of putting away the ring and his photo had brought new closure; Paul now belonged firmly in the past. And yet I knew he was still there, watching, knowing, a guardian angel, seeing all and guiding. Was it his, that little voice that said of Rex: *not this, not this, not yet?* Or was it mine?

For why this wall between us? Why the reluctance to see him again soon? Why the basic – I had to say it – *mistrust?* In my heart I knew.

Donna was right. Jonestown had not just brought us together, as he had mentioned in his letter; Jonestown also kept us apart. I knew that he was more involved than he liked to say. I knew that he spoke with Congressman Ryan, and Patsy, and the Concerned Relatives. Perhaps he even spoke with Lucy's mother. The American Embassy was at the very heart of the Jonestown controversy, and he was at the heart of the American Embassy, the liaison officer between Jim Jones and everyone else, and he knew the things I needed to know and would not, could not, tell me. As for this offer to take me into Jonestown himself – was that just his guilt speaking? Or was he trying to pacify me, distract me, keep me from digging too deep? *What did Rex know?*

His secrets were a wedge between us and forced me to keep my own secrets. Rex did not know what I planned. I had not told him of my training with Errol. I did not share with him the sensory adventure that was my daily trek to Jonestown. If he could keep his secrets, so could I.

Time, I said to myself. *I need time.* I stood up and dived into the creek.

. . .

Later in the languid afternoon heat I lay on my bed, rehashing the same old problems. I was bored, restless. The inactivity was getting under my skin. What was the point of all my preparation if I couldn't get into Jonestown?

The furious barking of the dogs shattered my thoughts, and a moment later Aunt Edna called my name. Thankful for the break, I stood up.

I stepped out into the midday sunshine. Two men, both dressed in black, stood in the yard, both in exactly the same position: legs slightly apart and hands clasped behind their backs. Even without an introduction, I placed them immediately. The now-familiar flatbed truck outside the open gate gave them away, but even without that clue I could tell from their faces where they were from. Their expressions were flat, almost zombie-like. No sign that any humans lived behind those faces. Their indifference was in sharp contrast to the anxiety written on Aunt Edna's face.

'Zoe, these two men asked for you.'

I turned to them, hardly daring to hope. 'Hello. What can I do for you?'

'Are you Zoe...' the speaker frowned and brought forward one of his hands. It held an envelope, with handwriting on the front. He read the words. '...Zoe Quint?'

'That's me.'

'I have a message from the Reverend Jim Jones for you.'

I was speechless for a moment; but only a moment.

'Yes? What does he want?' I was breathless, a bit too eager, perhaps. The man handed me the envelope.

'This is for you. An immediate answer is required.'

'Oh. OK.' I took the envelope, opened it, removed a single sheet of paper, and read the two typewritten sentences. The note was unsigned. I looked at Aunt Edna. Her frown had deepened, and her lips formed a silent 'no' even before I spoke.

'He says I can come to Jonestown – for a day and a night! This Friday!'

She said it aloud, then. 'No! Oh, Zoe, no! Don't go!'

I looked at the men, who stood like statues, with no seeming interest in the outcome of their mission. Their faces were inscrutable; dead.

'Tell him, tell the Reverend Jones, that I thank him for this invitation, and of course I'll come.'

PART THREE
INTO THE LION'S DEN

17th November 1978

CHAPTER TWENTY-SIX

The Jeep came to a stop in a cloud of dust before the Jonestown gate. Uncle Bill switched off the ignition and turned to me.

'You're sure about this?'

'Absolutely.'

He shook his head in discomfort, then shrugged and leaned towards me, reaching out to draw me into his clasp. We hugged.

'Be careful. Keep your eyes open.'

'I'll be fine, Unk.' I felt his hold slacken and pulled away. Our eyes met, and I kissed him on his forehead. 'See you in a day or two.'

'I can come and pick you up, you know.'

I opened the door. 'No, that's fine. I'll get back somehow. If need be, I'll walk.'

I was thinking more in terms of the canoe hidden among the mangroves, but that was still my secret. I reached behind me for my rucksack on the back seat, and climbed down from the Jeep.

'Bye then.'

I felt his eyes on my back as I walked to the gate. The guard stood ready to meet me, his hand gripping the two halves of the gate together as if to reinforce the chain wrapped several times around it. I looked him in the eye, took the letter out of my bag and passed it through the bars to him. He let go of the gate and took it, unfolded and read it, slowly. He looked me up and down as if to verify my identity, then fished in his pocket for a bunch of keys. He took his time looking for the right key – he seemed rather slow-witted, for the keys were all very different in size and shape and many of them obviously wouldn't fit the padlock. While he did this, I turned to Uncle Bill and gave him a thumbs-up; he waved back and the motor coughed and spluttered as he switched on the ignition. The tyres crunched on sand as the Jeep moved off.

The guard clicked open the padlock, loosened the chain and tugged at it; its heavy links clunked across the crossbar of the gate as it rattled forward into his hands. I looked back at the Jeep, bumping away back home, and felt a lump rise in my throat, a rush of desolation, regret even, at the final breaking-off from all that was safe and familiar. Perhaps it was a fleeting premonition, a knowledge that I'd passed the point of no return.

Into the lion's den, I thought, and swung round to march into the compound.

The chain's jangle had alerted the dog, and it pounded up to the gate barking furiously. I stood still.

A piercing whistle split the air; I looked up and saw, standing near the first building, the giant guard. The dog immediately turned and raced back to its master, a whimpering half-moon, tail between its legs, and circled to the ground in shame, and I knew at once that its training had been a violent one. The giant stood his ground as I walked past. The dog's eyes twisted to look up at me, contritely white. I resisted the urge to bend down and pat its head and walked forward towards the first building.

As we walked under a loudspeaker attached to a tall pole, the droning voice I'd been hearing even from the gate grew louder, and I could hear the words. It was a voice I'd recognised, the same voice I'd heard while watching from the protection of the rainforest. Again, it seemed to be reciting news stories.

> *The military government in Iran has stepped up its campaign to settle public oppositi—opposition against the Shah imposed upon them in a dreadful murder of their president by the CIA. One move is they are arresting of many public officials and numerous prominent rich Iranians. Among the latest to find himself behind bars is the former prime minister. In addition, the reigning officials have also arrested the United Press International...*

It was a one-storey wooden block, much longer than it was wide, built on short pillars with a flight of stairs leading up to a landing and a door. A small sign on the door proclaimed that this was ADMINISTRATION. I walked up the stairs and knocked on the door. It opened.

The woman who had opened the door for me first frowned, but then understanding flashed through her eyes and she smiled, showing a row of uneven, yellowed teeth.

'You must be Zoe!' she said and held out a hand. I took it; it was warm and moist and lay limp in my own like a dying bird, but only for a moment, for then her fingers clawed around mine and she drew me into the room.

'Come in, and welcome! We've heard so much about you and we're looking forward to meeting you. I'm Miranda!'

Miranda was of medium height and build, dark, probably mixed race, with black hair drawn away from her face and bound together into a ponytail of languid curls. Her eyes were dull brown, and darted all over the place, resting everywhere except in my gaze, and her movements were quick and somehow self-conscious, as if finding herself alone with me in a room was somehow too much for her to deal with.

She trotted to a desk at which it seemed she'd been working, snatched a half-typed piece of paper from the carriage of an old typewriter and walked over to a filing cabinet against the far wall, next to a closed door. She jammed her hand into her pocket, produced a key, and fumbled with it to open the cabinet's top drawer. It was stuck, so she rattled and pulled it so that it shot out, throwing her off balance. She turned to grin at me, threw the page into the drawer and locked it, then stepped over to the desk and pulled out the chair – a simple wooden chair, not a swivel one – so awkwardly it fell from her grip and clattered to the floor. We both bent to pick it up, knocking our heads together, at which Miranda giggled like a child. She stood up, rubbing her forehead, gestured to me to take a seat, gasped something about going to get Moira, and fled. I was alone, still standing in the middle of the room, my backpack slung over one shoulder.

I glanced around. The sparsely furnished room was square, and small, but a door in the middle of one wall, directly opposite to the front door, seemed to lead into another room. I tried it, but it was locked. A frayed and faded woven rug – a handwoven Amerindian one, I recognised – graced the centre of the polished wooden floor. Above it an overhead fan rotated slowly, making little difference to the hot thick air, stagnant in spite of an open sash window adjacent to the desk. Another window, this one closed, completed the symmetry in the opposite wall: two doors, two windows, rug above, fan below, a central empty space and clutter around the edges.

The furnishings, too, followed a pattern, for matching wooden bookshelves – most of them empty – filled the spaces between doors and windows, the only break in the pattern the filing cabinet and the desk shoved together into one corner. On the desk stood nothing but the typewriter and a glass jar with three pencils and one ballpoint pen sticking out of it. A small plastic bowl held other writing paraphernalia: two dirty erasers, a sharpener, several paper clips and, incongruously, three blue buttons. A fat spiral notebook occupied the far corner. The desk itself was of clunky wood, simply a rectangular slat nailed to four legs.

On the wall above me – painted the same creamy yellow as the outside walls – hung an oversized photograph of a man, whom I recognised from the films I'd seen as Jim Jones. Half-turned towards the camera, he smiled a sickly smile and watched me from behind black sunglasses as I reached out for the spiral notebook and opened it. It was half-filled with writing, and I leafed through it, hoping to find something of interest, but it seemed to be nothing but a sort of housekeeping diary, each page with a date above it: lists of foods, amounts used, menus, names of people with jobs next to them, such as cooking, laundry, washing up. Disappointed, I flipped to the back of the book, but that was empty; however, a wisp of paper caught within the spiral showed that someone had torn out a page, and I could see the impression of handwriting on the clean back page. Somebody had been writing in the back of the book and had torn out the last page, leaving a slight imprint.

Voices. I slammed the notebook shut and replaced it and looked through the open window. Two women were approaching, Miranda and another, taller and blonde.

She looked strangely familiar. In spite of her old and faded clothes – a cotton shirtwaist dress, so washed out its colour was indistinguishable, hanging on her in a straight up-and-down line, for she had neither waist nor bottom – she wore a look of regal elegance. She had that leathery skin white people get after too much tropical sun, and that tough look extended to her hair, cut in a pageboy as if cast in iron. Her every feature seemed hard and dry, including the tongue-tip that moistened her lower lip in a quick flick. I stood up before they entered the room and walked over to greet them.

'Moira, this is Zoe,' said Miranda in a whiney voice, and it was then I realised where I'd seen her before. The white woman from the *Witte de Roo*. The hand she stuck out to shake mine was a sharp cleft held close to her waist, like a butcher's knife protruding from her belly.

I reached forward for it; it was dry and hard, the opposite of Miranda's, and unyielding in my clasp. Her eyes were blue and cold, giving the lie to her words.

'Welcome to Jonestown, Zoe! We've heard all about you, and we're so pleased that you came.'

Her voice was as chilly as her entire appearance, somehow out of place in the gathering morning heat. She drew back her lips in a stiff smile, revealing one crooked tooth, slightly overlapping its neighbour.

'Thank you for the invitation; I'm pleased to be here.'

'Miranda will show you to your room and give you a guided tour of Jonestown.'

She said the last word with as much pride as had it been Buckingham Palace, and I bowed my head slightly to acknowledge the privilege granted. That was my role: the admiring journalist. From Patsy's scripted talk and the propaganda film I knew they viewed their home as one of the twentieth century's most advanced experiments in communal living, and I – Zoe Correia, or, rather, Zoe Quint – had been chosen to reveal this to the world. I was not about to burst her bubble till I was ready for it.

'I have the schedule!' said Miranda proudly, waving a piece of paper at me. 'Come with me!'

She led the way down the stairs. I followed, while Moira, bringing up the rear, stopped to lock the door. We waited as Moira took a walkie-talkie, a battered old thing held together with a strip of grubby plaster, from a deep pocket and spoke into it, half-turned away from us. She passed us and led the way onto a raised wooden walkway that led straight into the centre of the settlement, criss-crossing with other walkways. In the rainy season, I guessed, Jonestown would be an unbroken lake and, as the water sank into the earth, a sea of mud. These 'roads' made good sense, as did the style of the houses, built on short pillars to keep them above ground. Respect for water is the first rule for living in Guyana, this land of many waters.

The disembodied voice had moved on to a different topic, another news story:

> *The Venezuelan operation of that general is a perfect front. He is a candidate for the next presidency. There's hope that he will be defeated. If not, we have a perfect ground then to say we are going to the Soviet Union and the Soviet Union has said they'll take us. They'll cause us no conflict with Guyana because Guyana will have nothing to say about this land. We will just get out because we didn't make any agreement with them — with Venezuela — and the Soviets have promised us protection against any kind of an invasion or any attempts on the part of reactionaries that would take over Guyana. But it's more serious than some people want to see. We have several enemies.*

I gazed around me. I could see people in the distance. I tried to make out if any of them was Lucy, squinting against the sun in my eyes. Two people came out of a building on our left, and I looked for her that way. When Moira stopped and turned at one of the crossroads, I bumped into her.

'Goodbye, Zoe, and I'll see you again later. Enjoy Jonestown.' She nodded, then turned and walked away. I stood watching her.

'Come on, Zoe!'

I hurried to catch up with Miranda.

CHAPTER TWENTY-SEVEN

In Jonestown's centre the causeways were wider, allowing people to walk side by side, or to pass each other, and I noticed the quick and furtive glances of the few we passed – glances never meeting mine, heads bowed at our approach, muttered greetings in reply to my own. Miranda led me right through the middle of the community, past what looked like a large round pavilion, and on to the furthest outskirt buildings on the other side of town.

I followed her over to a group of low wooden cottages, just small cabins, really, on short stilts.

'This is your room,' she said as she led the way up the short staircase leading to the front door of one. There, she fumbled again with her jangling keyring, found the right key, shoved it into the lock, and turned. She pushed at the door, but it was jammed in its frame. She pushed again, this time with her body weight, and the door yielded so that she flew into the room and almost tumbled to the floor.

'Watch out!' I reached out to steady her.

'Thanks! Whew! The wood here swells because of the moisture and then the doors stick.'

'I know; I'm from here.' I paused, then said, 'How long have you been here, Miranda?'

'Oh, I've been here right from the beginning! I'm an old hand at the jungle!'

'And you're happy?'

She laughed, her glance darting to one side. 'I have to admit it took some getting used to at first, the climate, the mosquitoes, and so on. But now I love it!'

A silver glaze drew across her eyes, just like Patsy's; it was as if the fervour shining there was merely glitter sprayed upon a blank screen.

Like the office, the room was sparsely furnished, with everything jammed against the walls: a bed, a table with chair, a basic cupboard without doors. I tossed my bag down on to the bed.

'Are you here with your whole family? Excuse my curiosity, but that's what I'm here for – to talk to you all. Might as well begin with you!' I chuckled to put her at her ease, and it seemed to work, for she replied: 'My daughter Dana is here with me, she's fourteen. She loves it here too, but she's a bit afraid of the tigers. When they roar at night.'

I couldn't let that stand. 'They aren't tigers. We don't have tigers in Guyana, or in South America. They're jaguars.'

'Oh, really? We call them tigers here. It's all the same, isn't it, the roaring? Come on, let's move on, I'll show you around.'

We returned to the walkway outside, and Miranda led me away from the living quarters, accompanied as always by the news:

The League of Red Cross Societies at Geneva, Switzerland, has appealed desperately for nearly one million dollars to help save two million people, who they say are facing starvation in Nwala region near Ethiopia, due to the awful drought created by what many reports have said was CIA efforts – CIA efforts at cloud-seeding.

She headed towards a low, white-painted wooden building, from which I could hear the high-pitched chant of children's voices. The typical sounds of a school. Miranda walked up a short flight of stairs to a narrow veranda, rapped sharply at a door, and entered without waiting for an invitation. As I followed her into the schoolroom some thirty children, aged between six and eight, shot up to standing. The teacher smiled. It seemed she had been expecting us – or rather me, the visitor – for she turned to her class, said one word – 'Children!' – and immediately the response came, almost shouted in enthusiasm, an obviously practised chant:

'Good-Morn-ing-Miss-Quint!'

At the teacher's gesture the children sat down again, on low, backless benches before very basic communal desks. They sat five or six to a desk, scuffling, giggling, pushing their little bottoms together to fit in, and looked up at me with the bright-eyed innocence and curiosity of yet-unspoiled childhood, as if waiting for a story. I felt the old familiar wrench, and stepped back involuntarily, lowering my head in acknowledgement of the greeting but giving them no more than a tepid smile in return.

The teacher pointed to the chalk words on the blackboard, and I recognised the Cyrillic lettering as Russian. As her rod moved along the indicated sentence the children resumed their chanting, unhesitating, as if they had already learned the words by heart and were simply matching them to the lettering. I wondered what they were saying but decided not to ask. Above the blackboard the portrait of Jim Jones looked down at them. We watched for a minute, and then Miranda excused us in gestures, and we left.

I stepped forward to walk next to her. 'How many children do you have here?' I asked.

She beamed at me. 'Over two hundred! Those you saw were the first-graders – we also have a pre-school, and a high school. Really, it's a paradise for children, growing up so close to nature!'

I couldn't resist it. 'In spite of the tigers?'

My little barb went unnoticed.

'Believe me, no tiger has ever attacked one of us! Never! Not once! The Lord protects us.'

'Actually,' I said, 'jaguars hardly ever kill humans, unless provoked. They prefer small animals.'

But Miranda wasn't listening; she was busy recounting the glories of Jonestown.

'Our children know how it is to grow up without fear, without greed, how to share and live as one big happy family. Where else in the world can they live with such freedom, such... such...' She searched for the right word, all the time directing me towards another building, designed to the same model as the school but a few rooms longer. Not finding the word she was looking for, she left the sentence unfinished and darted off on a related tangent.

'All these rumours about people being kept here against their will – garbage! You see, any group that refuses to adapt to the norm will have enemies, and ours are legion.'

'But why, Miranda? Why's that? Why do you think you have enemies?'

The answer came as if shot from a pistol.

'Jealousy. People don't like to see others finding happiness. They wouldn't leave us alone in America, that's why we came here, to start our own society. This place is a model of what society should be. One day we'll be famous for what we have done here, here in the remote jungle. Who ever heard of Guyana! But Father will put Guyana on the world map, mark my words. And you, Zoe, you, you have been chosen by Father to be our messenger. You see, American journalists are prejudiced. They already have a fixed opinion about us, a negative one. You, now, you're different. Patsy sent us copies of your articles and many of us read them, and we know you are the right one to tell our story. You are just like us; you share our ethics, our philosophy. You are on the side of the underdog; that much shines out of your articles. Father said. Here's our hospital.'

Again, she led the way up the stairs. This time, though, she did not open any of the doors; instead, we walked along the veranda, and I was permitted to peer into the open windows. The first room, Miranda explained, was the staffroom; a central table, a few chairs, shelves and cabinets along the walls. As we passed the open door a nurse inside saw us, signalled to us to wait, and came out to join us, closing the door behind her. She pulled down her surgical mask and looked expectantly at Miranda.

'Zoe, this is Fiona, Fiona—'

'Zoe! Yes, I know! So glad you could come, Zoe, pleased to meet you!'

I smiled, and shook the proffered hand, but then she turned to Miranda, frowned, glanced at me and said, 'Miranda, I need to have a word...'

I took the hint. 'Don't mind me, I'll show myself around!'

Which was, of course, exaggerating. There was nothing to see except more wards and a few smaller rooms. I glimpsed two or three female patients in the first ward, a few men in the second, children in a third. One double room appeared empty, as did the next. I had almost reached the end of the veranda: only two more doors to go, and only one window. The next was a single room, and looking through the window I saw a young woman sleeping on her side, her face turned towards me, a woman whose big hair, twice as big as her face – probably, in healthier times, a voluminous Afro – had obviously not been tended in days, if not weeks, and had suffered badly from being slept upon, for the portion visible was matted and coarse, like a thick pad of black sheep's wool. Behind her was a second bed, also occupied. Whoever was sleeping there had her back to me.

I moved on; the next door, it seemed, led into a smaller room, one without a window; or the window was at the back, on the other side. I might have walked on, around the building and out of sight, had Miranda not called me to attention and hurried towards me.

I walked back to meet her, stopping again to have a closer look at the woman sleeping with her back to me. Was she Lucy? I desperately wanted to know. But by this time Miranda had reached me, and she grasped my hand and pulled me away from the window.

Out on the wooden walkway, I turned to Miranda: 'Do people get ill here often? Do you have doctors?'

She answered the last question first.

'Of course! We have in fact two doctors, Dr Gilbert and Dr Sutton, Frank and Gary, both excellent practitioners. Moira is also a doctor, an anaesthetist. And nurses; you saw Fiona, we have a few others, and many health workers who also help out. Believe me, all our patients are in the best of hands.'

'Do people get sick often?'

'Well, obviously sometimes.'

'What kind of illnesses do they get?'

No hesitation this time. 'Diarrhoea! Oh my Lord, diarrhoea! I bet all of us have had it at one time, in the tropics you have to be so very careful, you know, and drinking that river water, you never know what's in it. Once we had a hepatitis outbreak – oh my!'

She launched into a blow-by-blow description of her own hepatitis bout, but after a few sentences I managed to interrupt.

'That girl – woman – for instance, in the last room, the one with the big Afro – what's she suffering from? Is she contagious?'

'Alexis? Oh, Alexis, yes, she has some kind of a liver thing, some long name, she's responding well to treatment though. Look, here's our pavilion.'

We had arrived at the geographical heart of Jonestown, a huge round building of a primitive wooden construction, yet sturdy-looking and impressive through its sheer bulk. All paths led here. Miranda as always in the lead, we walked up the short flight of stairs and entered the main hall.

Meanwhile:

...all strikes have been made illegal, and in case of trouble, all police leaves are cancelled. Ghana, spelled G-H-A-N-A, is the place that W.E.B. DuBois, the great scholar, of which Lenin quoted much in his writing about capital, went to make his home at ninety-one years of age, and spent the last four years of his life, Ghana, the head of state has declared a state of emergency in an attempt to combat the wave of ...

Sometimes he stumbled over words, sometimes I couldn't understand. But always he droned on. It was clearly a pre-recorded tape of him regurgitating an unedited list of news stories, one after the other, without pause. Loud enough to drive a sane person crazy; too loud to ignore. Did people really listen to that voice, or did they over time become immune?

The pavilion appeared even larger from the inside. The interior space was filled with long benches, similar to those in the schoolroom but adult-size, the front of the room indicated by a dais on which stood four or five chairs. One chair obviously, going by its sheer size and weightiness, belonged to Jim Jones. The pavilion itself had a conical banana-leaf-thatched roof, supported by several tall poles evenly placed around the interior.

My eyes were so drawn to the front of the room that I didn't notice a group of benches arranged in a circle near the entrance, on which sat several people. As I walked forward they all clapped, and that's when I turned and saw them: the welcoming committee. I quickly scanned the group to see if Lucy was among them. She wasn't.

As I approached about twenty faces smiled at me, while forty hands continued to clap, this time in a slow, marching rhythm.

'Welcome, Zoe!' cried one woman, and her cry was echoed by several other voices. The faces beamed at me, and all eyes followed me as I walked into their midst and sat down on the only empty bench, smiling my acknowledgement. I felt as if I was walking into a revival meeting. Miranda followed me into the circle but did not yet sit down. By now she had lost all awkwardness, and when she spoke it was with confidence and authority. Miranda, in fact, came to life. Her voice rang out.

'Well, everyone, I'm so happy you could all come, and so happy to introduce Zoe Quint to you all. We all know of Zoe's writing, of course. She's come to Jonestown to make sure we are all happy and free here.'

They all laughed heartily at these words, as if to ridicule the very idea of doubt. The woman nearest to me turned and extended a hand for me to shake; I shook it. Her grip, unlike Miranda's and Moira's before her, was at once firm and heartfelt. She was a middle-aged, buxom Black woman; her eyes were warm and kind, and I imagined her as a Church Mother, organising cake sales for a new church bell and charity drives for the poor in Africa.

'Welcome to you, Zoe, I hope you enjoy your stay in Jonestown! My name is Gladys!'

Other scattered voices echoed her words:

'Welcome, Zoe, welcome! Welcome to Jonestown!'

Miranda beamed at them. 'That's the spirit, comrades! Now, Zoe has a few questions for you!'

'Fire away!' said a man sitting opposite me. He wore a yellow shirt, faded now and limply hanging on wide shoulders. Large gnarled hands clutched a straw hat in his lap.

I reached into my backpack, removed and opened my notebook, leafed forward to the page where I'd written down my questions. I looked up, smiled, and spoke.

'First, I'd like to thank you for the warm welcome. I hope you don't mind my poking my nose into your affairs, but I'm a journalist, and that's just what we do!'

On cue, everyone laughed.

'Poke away!' cried Yellow Shirt. I smiled at him and continued.

'I'd just like to hear a few of your stories; your names, why you came here, what you expected, if you have found what you were looking for?'

Miranda looked pleased. 'That's a good idea... why don't you begin, Gladys? We can then move clockwise round the room.'

'Sure! Me, I'm a kindergarten teacher, and I met Father through my mom, who used to go to his church in San Francisco. Me and my husband Joe came to see him. Right away I knew People's Temple was my home! See, they really cared about Black people like us, they really looked after us folks. Father cares.'

That seemed another cue, for immediately heads nodded and voices, scattered around the circle, chimed in.

'Yeah, yeah, right, Father cares.'

Gladys paused, as if thinking what next to say. 'So,' I prompted, 'when he moved you all to Guyana, you came willingly?'

Gladys needed no more prompting. 'But of course! What do you think?! I'd have gone with Father to the moon! Father told us, we Black folk ain't never gonna feel at home in white America, he's gonna find a home for us, far away from it all. And that's just what he did, and here we are!'

'And your husband? Joe? Is he here too?'

'Him? Ha! Nope, he stayed back. Couldn't see paradise if it was in his backyard!'

Everyone laughed, as if this was a running joke. Yellow Shirt raised his hand, like a kid in school, then spoke anyway.

'See, before we had Father, all we Black folk had was troubles – white people don't want us, ain't never gonna. Father said, that ain't no way to live, in a country where nobody don't want you. So we come here. I bring my wife and kids, and since then we happy like Adam and Eve in Eden. Father cares!'

Again, everyone laughed. I was growing tired of the canned outbursts.

'And the children? They don't miss home?'

'This is home now! This is one big happy family! All we want is to be left alone, and no people botherin' us! We doin' fine! The kids happy as larks! Only thing they scared of is them tigers in the night!'

Again, the laughs, this time interspersed with murmurs.

'And your relatives, back in America? Don't they miss you? I've heard some of them are concerned?'

The only other man in the group, two places away from Gladys at my left, spoke up. I had to lean forward to see him, and our eyes locked. He was much younger than Yellow Shirt, barely out of his teens. In his gaze lurked coiled energy, anger, even, just waiting to leap forth. He seemed vaguely familiar, and when he spoke I remembered his voice, and where I'd seen him. The slight lisp was unmistakable. He was the guard who'd blocked my entry on my first failed visit to Jonestown.

'Those relatives that complainin', why they don't come and see for theyselves, like you? How they could complain about something they don't know, ain't got the experience of? If they was to come here, they'd see we're happy, like you seein' right now!'

'So, relatives are allowed to visit?'

Several voices piped up. 'Yeah, sure!' But before any single person could speak for them all, Miranda explained: 'Of course! Just a few months back we had the Armstrongs here, Mike and Edith Armstrong, the parents of Jennifer and Bev. They were most impressed with what we have here! That's what they told us! They spoke to Jennifer and Bev. They came and had a look and went away satisfied. Isn't that true, folks?'

Nodding heads, murmurs of assent. 'Right, right. Yeah, that's true.'

I was getting tired of this; it was as if the whole thing had been rehearsed many times in advance, and they all had it down pat. I asked questions for half an hour, and each one was answered in a similar manner: everything was fine and dandy and they were all deliriously happy, all they wanted was to be left alone and Jonestown was the best thing that had ever happened to them.

Finally, Miranda looked at her watch. 'Well, everyone, I thank you for coming here and giving of your time so that Zoe could ask her questions. It's now time for lunch, so why don't we go over to the dining hall? Or do you have any more questions, Zoe?'

I was glad to say it: 'No, thanks, I'm fine. Thanks, everyone!'

Scattered voices replied. 'Thanks, Zoe! Enjoy your stay! Welcome to Jonestown!'

With an enthusiastic outburst of clapping, and even a few cheers, people rose to their feet. Miranda walked over to speak to the young guard, and as she walked past, Gladys turned to me again and shook my hand, and this time there was something more in her fingers, a hesitant pressure; her eyes changed their expression. The forced heartiness shifted aside and the undefined shadow of fear crept through her gaze. Spontaneously, I recollected Lucy's eyes. That same fear.

Taking their cue from Gladys, the happy Jonestown crowd lined up behind her and one by one, they came forward to shake my hand and thank me individually; and one by one, I looked into their eyes and saw the happy masks crumble. And as the masks fell I saw what lay behind: caverns of terror, black holes of despair, chasms of dread. And unlike the merriment that had underscored our meeting, it was all too real. No word was exchanged, but in the tremors of their hands I felt silent messages passed along, and their lips quivered with unspoken truths.

Miranda finished talking to the guard. She came up to supervise the goodbyes, and immediately the masks returned, but now I was alert for nuances I had missed before, and saw the fleeting sideways glances at Miranda standing at my side, flighty approval-seeking glances, frayed at the edges with fear. And it was these eyes, more than the entire meeting that had preceded them, that told me all I wanted to know.

As Miranda and I walked over to the dining hall self-satisfaction oozed from her being. In her eyes, the meeting had been a huge success. Hungry for confirmation, she looked at me, smugly smiling.

'I hope that talk assuaged some of your doubts!'

I had to play my cards right. My entire visit here had been carefully choreographed. I needed to break the schedule.

'Yes, yes, certainly... but I was wondering if I could speak to a few people individually? Alone?'

The smugness crashed from her. Insecurity, dispelled by all the cheerleading her charges had dutifully displayed, returned with all its shifty-eyed shadows.

'Who? Why? Do you have anyone special in mind?'

Right there and then I decided to go for the jugular. One man held the key to this whole charade.

'Well... I'd love to speak to Jim Jones himself!'

'Reverend Jones!' She unfolded the paper in her hands, scanned the list of approved activities. 'I'm sorry, a visit with Father has not been scheduled. He's very busy, you see, and not well.'

'I'd like you to change the schedule.'

She actually trembled. Her fingers fiddled with the paper, folding and unfolding it, reading it again as if to find some hidden instruction written between the lines. I waited. Finally, she replied.

'I'll ask Moira.' She walked away. I was left with that ghostly, maddening voice:

> *In Angola, at least twenty-four people have been killed in an explosion in the country's secondlargest city. Angola is a Marxist–Leninist nation led by Prime Minister Agostinho Neto, who was enabled to win the victory for the people by direct aid and substance from Moscow and Cuba. The explosion occurred in a marketplace, and many more people...*

CHAPTER TWENTY-EIGHT

A slow-moving queue snaked out of the dining hall. As Miranda led me straight to the front I felt hundreds of eyes fixed on me, faces turning at my coming, voices dying down as if I were royalty on an inspection tour. I looked at them as I walked past, smiled greetings, and occasionally my gaze caught, momentarily, a glance, a hungry clawing at me, before it was deflected by Miranda's own stern stare, and the person in question looked away in guilt.

Guilt – that was it. The awareness of betrayal, of abandoning the dream, even if only in thought, guilt born of truth revealed towards a stranger as my passing stripped one façade after another away and laid bare hearts. That was the shadow flitting through those pleading eyes, in the nanosecond before the welcoming mask changed to the hungry grasping for attention, the silent cry: *hear me! look at me! help me!* Here was Lucy, multiplied by hundreds, but nowhere the original. I knew then that with Miranda at my side I could not, would not find her.

Miranda gave me a quick tour of the kitchen before leading me to a small table separate from the other, longer ones. We sat down, and a moment later a young woman entered bearing covered dishes. Jovial and warm, she chatted easily with us as she uncovered the dishes to reveal a veritable feast: rice, vegetables and chicken, simple but beautifully presented and appetising. I looked up at the woman to smile my thanks, and in her, too, I saw the tail end of that guilt as it fluttered over her face. Her cheeriness was so thin I could scrape it off her soul with no more than my gaze. I lowered my eyes and picked up my knife and fork.

'This is delicious!' I said after a few mouthfuls.

'Specially cooked by Linda, our best cook.' I had met Linda in our visit to the kitchen, a woman in perhaps her late forties, heavily built and, compared to all the others, well padded. I supposed being a cook carried definite privileges. Miranda continued: 'She was a professional chef in a big restaurant in LA before she came here. Earning a lot of money!'

'Really?! And she sacrificed that to come here?'

Miranda frowned. 'She didn't *sacrifice* anything. You've got to get that sort of thinking out of your head. *Not* being here is a sacrifice! The freedom and love and the community of family that we get here, you can't find that anyplace in America.'

'I see.'

I could feel a lecture hovering in the background, but luckily, we were joined at that moment by Moira and three other people, introduced to me as Jennifer, Bev and Brian. The four of them sat down and the conversation turned away from Jonestown to me. Apparently, I was a minor celebrity among the Jonestown staff, recommended by Patsy, who had underpinned her enthusiasm by sending up copies of everything I'd ever had published in the *Chronicle*.

Those articles, more than anything else, had broken down the resistance towards allowing me – a journalist – in. I'd been vetted and approved from above. Jim Jones himself had read my articles.

But I persisted in my questioning: 'Where do you get your food from? Do you grow it all yourselves?'

'Yes, most of it, the vegetables at least. Have you seen the gardens yet?'

'No, I'm taking her there this afternoon,' Miranda replied for me.

'Our aim is to be self-sufficient – that's why we call ourselves an agricultural project. We haven't been able to do so entirely – rice was a failure, so we do buy that. As you can imagine, we need to replenish our supplies quite often. We're almost a thousand; we eat through mountains of it in a week!'

Aha. That was my opening.

'So where do you buy your rice from? Do you get it sent up from Georgetown?'

'Yes. We have an agent in Nazareth, a shopkeeper who orders it for us, and we go and collect it every week. That's Lucy's job.'

'That sounds interesting,' I said. It was a weak statement, and sounded ridiculous the moment I'd said it, but it was all I could think of in the moment. I seized the opportunity. 'I really want to speak to some of your people with... with specific jobs,' I continued, 'maybe I could start with this Lucy?'

'That's a good idea,' Moira said smartly, 'but unfortunately Lucy is ill this week. You can speak to her replacement, Dorothy, if you like.'

I had no intention of speaking to Dorothy.

'Oh. I'm sorry to hear that. Is she—' I meant Lucy, of course, but realised it was better to go along with her. 'Dorothy. Yes, I'd love to speak to Dorothy.'

'After lunch,' Miranda said firmly. I could see her mentally consulting her schedule in order to fit in this unscheduled talk with Dorothy. I sighed and resigned myself to her continued tyranny.

. . .

After lunch everyone streamed from the dining hall and dispersed, apparently returning to their various workplaces. Miranda, as I'd known she would, took her schedule from her pocket and examined it. It was about one o'clock, and the overhead sun scorched the very air. I was exhausted and decided to say so.

'Miranda, thanks for showing me around, but I'm quite exhausted now, I'd really like to have a rest.' I stifled a yawn, covering my mouth with my hand, to emphasise my longing for a siesta.

Miranda smirked. 'I'd forgotten you people on the outside don't know the meaning of hard work. That's fine with me, but I'll have to strike a few things from my list; it's your loss. I'll escort you back to your room. I'll show you the rest of Jonestown later.'

'It's fine, I can find my way back, I don't want you to—'

'Oh, it's no trouble at all. No trouble.'

In silence we walked towards the living quarters, at the other end of the compound. Once again, I was aware of furtive attention as I walked past people, surreptitious glances, heads dropping in guilt or fear. I wondered what it was about Miranda that evoked such fear; Moira, I could understand, but Miranda? To me she was a limp noodle, faltering and almost obsequious. I decided that she was one of those people who only felt safe within a fixed hierarchy, and adjust their social attitude accordingly. To those below, the disciplinarian; to those above – and as a visitor with the power of the pen I was evidently positioned above – a fawning sycophant. I longed to walk through Jonestown on my own, to confront and talk with whomever I chose. I needed to throw her off.

'Here you are!'

I probably would not have found the cabin again on my own; it was identical to several others in its group. Next to it was a group of bigger buildings, and as they had but one door I figured they were dormitories.

'Well – I'll be off then. Have a good rest.' She turned and walked away. I breathed out.

Alone at last.

My room felt like a haven. I entered, grateful for its shade – though even inside it was not at all cool, due to the corrugated iron roof – and flung myself on the bed for a moment of collecting my forces. Miranda's company had drained me. I lay on my back and closed my eyes.

Sleep threatened to overcome me. There's a good reason for siesta: the combination of digesting food and the midday sun can be debilitating, and here in Jonestown, surrounded as it was by jungle, I felt trapped inside a pressure cooker. The humidity pressed in on me, soporific and debilitating. A melange of sound drifted in from outside: a kiskadee's cry, a parrot's squawk, voices. Children's laughter. A hammer, a saw. Vaguely, I registered what I'd missed all morning – the omnipresent voice of Jim Jones over the loudspeaker. Today it was switched off, apart from sporadic news announcements, no doubt in my honour, and the gaping silence it left now screamed at me. But I fought the stupor and won – I had no time for the creature comfort of sleep. I sat up.

Sitting on the side of my bed, I picked up the backpack I'd left here, reached into it and removed its contents. I'd brought one change of clothes and underwear, toothbrush and soap, a torch, a notebook, a pen. I placed the torch under my pillow and the clothes back in the bag, and picked up the notebook and pencil. I opened the notebook and sketched a diagram.

My memory swung into action. I had no problem recollecting the buildings I'd seen, and with a few quick strokes, I sketched a rough layout of Jonestown. I glanced up at the window, mulling over various rescue variations. Within its frame I saw treetops, clumps of dark green against the vivid blue of the midday sun. It was my luck that the living quarters were where they were, at the far end of Jonestown from the gate, right at the jungle's edge. Across from me, less than a hundred yards away and with no buildings between me and them, stood the two coconut trees from where, time and time again, I had watched Jonestown from the jungle. I was within reach of an escape route. Now all I had to do was grab Lucy and — I remembered something: Lucy had children. A little boy, and the baby Aunt Edna had delivered.

She wouldn't, couldn't leave the kids behind, and that complicated matters no end. Where would they be? Did children sleep with their mothers? In fact, come to think of it... the question that had nudged and poked at the back of my mind all morning now pounced lifesize into the foreground: where the hell was Lucy anyway?

CHAPTER TWENTY-NINE

I closed the notebook, placed it under my pillow, stood up and walked to the window. Outside, all was quiet. In the distance, to the oblique right, people worked the fields in the hot sun. A guard strolled by, between these last houses and the jungle.

I returned to the bed and lay down, still thinking. I yawned, once, twice; sleep's temptation welled up in me, a heavy blanket pulled across my spirit, dull and fuzzy. I shook it off and sat up. I couldn't let this happen. My time here was limited, and I had not yet had even a glimpse of Lucy. Neither did I have a clear escape plan. I could not waste time with sleep; soon Miranda would be back, leading me around like a child on her first day at school.

I walked to the door and down the stairs.

I walked confidently, as if on an official mission. Two women crossed the walkway ahead of me. I waved at them and smiled, and they smiled and waved back, a nebulous hunger in their gaze. One of the women, in fact, stopped momentarily. I thought she'd turn in her tracks and walk towards me, but her companion yanked her back. I stopped to watch them walk away. The woman who'd stopped looked back at me, pleading. I thought of stopping her, asking her all the questions I could not ask Miranda, hear her story, but decided against it. Not now. I walked on.

> *Starting tomorrow, we hope to be able to get Radio Moscow again. Unfortunately, we've had the power cut off in the middle of the day, and... it has enabled us to be able to make contact with the Soviet Union that gives another side of the story. Thank you for your commitment to socialism.*

The only clue I had as to Lucy's whereabouts was Moira's words at lunchtime: unfortunately, Lucy is ill. If she were ill then she'd likely be in the hospital, so there I headed.

As I approached the hospital I became stealthy. The last person I wanted to meet right now was Miranda, or another member of the top-tier staff. In spite of Miranda's assurances of absolute equality in Jonestown the hierarchy was already quite obvious: there were workers and administrators, a clear division of labour between blue- and white-collar, leaders and followers, organised similarly to a beehive: A king, a few queens, and hundreds of worker bees. The worker bees, I figured, were the ones I needed to know; a private meeting with one was desirable. The queens, I must avoid. But the king: him I longed to meet.

The giant guard walked past me on a parallel walkway and stared. He carried a rifle slung casually across his shoulder. The dog trotted at his feet. At him, too, I smiled and waved, and held my breath. He bowed his head slightly in acknowledgement and made no attempt to stop me. I breathed out.

I had decided to bluff my way through. Most likely, the nurses were followers, not leaders, and would not know of the instructions that as far as I could tell accompanied my visit: that I was not to do my own investigating. I banked on my reputation as a 'good' journalist, the exception to the profession, the one whom their leader had permitted to enter. I had simply come for interviews, I would say. I walked up the steps to the hospital.

I rapped softly at the door to the staffroom, and when no one replied, I turned the knob and opened it. It was empty. I closed it again and walked down the veranda. I could see through the window to the women's ward. There was no nurse in it; even better. I opened the door and walked in.

There were about ten beds, five down each side; seven of them were occupied. As I walked down the middle aisle some heads raised and then fell again, but none belonged to Lucy. One of the patients called feebly to me: 'Hello... hello, miss!' It was a cry not of greeting but an appeal to come to her, but she was not Lucy, and callously, I waved and walked on.

I did not enter the children's ward or the men's; I saw no need. The next rooms, I remembered, were smaller, with fewer beds. Instead of a window at their opposite ends there were doors, perhaps leading into other rooms. Probably, I reasoned, this was a wraparound veranda and more wards or rooms could be accessed if I walked all the way round the building. I passed two empty rooms, their beds – no more than cots, really – devoid of sheets, the mattresses lumpy and, I could tell even from the window, stained. The next room was the one with the Afro-haired woman, I remembered, and a second patient whose face I had not seen. Was that Lucy?

I walked to the next window, looked in – and gasped aloud. Involuntarily, I took a step back: Moira was in there.

The Afro-haired woman was sitting on the edge of her bed, her back to me. She sat slumped, and wore only some sort of tattered nightgown. Moira sat on the bed facing her and seemed to be holding something to her lips – a spoon, perhaps, or a cup, but I could see little due to the huge matted bundle of the Afro-woman's hair. Either her instinct announced my presence, or she had heard my gasp: she raised her head and looked straight at me.

What was it in that woman's stare that could so freeze my blood? My breath stopped, my heart missed a beat, and I almost peed in my pants. I wanted to turn and flee, but I couldn't: Moira's stare rooted me to the spot. I could not move.

And yet – even in this state of utter incapacity, I noted something. My senses, naturally sharp, had grown even finer over the last few hours, picking up silent signals and messages, shadows fluttering through desperate eyes, emotions that quivered in the space between two breaths. And one of those emotions flickered in Moira's eyes right now, just for a fraction of a nanosecond, the emotion I least expected to see there. Guilt.

And then it was gone, and she was smiling. She withdrew her hand from the woman's face, placed a glass on the bedside table between the two cots, and called to me:

'Well, hello, Zoe, I wasn't expecting you here! Do come in!'

My heart, having stopped for a moment, now began to hammer so loudly I thought Moira would hear it and wonder why. Why, indeed? I had nothing to fear. I was doing nothing wrong. I was a respected guest in Jonestown, why should I feel guilty? But I did, and that, perhaps, was the cause of my present fear – had Moira seen the guilt in my own eyes?

No time now for speculation, however. She had called me and go I must. I walked on and entered the ward, a smile pasted across my face. I walked to the narrow aisle between the two beds.

'Doing a little research, are you?' Again, my heart skipped a beat. Was she being sarcastic?

'I-I couldn't sleep,' I said, 'so I decided to look around on my own. Just to make my own impressions, you know, get a feel for the place.'

Moira laughed. 'Yes, I know. It's hard to pick up the spirit of a place when someone is jabbering non-stop in your ear. Miranda's quite a chatterbox, as I expect you've discovered.

I'm glad you took the initiative. I'd like you to meet Alexis. Alexis!'

She placed her hand on the other woman's shoulder, her fingers digging in as she shook. No reaction.

'Alexis! Look!' Moira's voice was loud and sharp. She pointed to me, and this time Alexis turned slowly to face me. Her gaze rose to meet mine.

What eyes! And what a face! I could tell at a glance that Alexis, when healthy and washed and – well, *alive* – would be stunning. Objectively, her features were the very epitome of classic beauty. Huge eyes as black as coals, skin the colour of dark honey and smooth as silk, wide, full and perfectly formed lips, high cheekbones, and everything in faultless proportion.

But dead. Nobody lived behind that gorgeous face. The eyes now looking up at me were vacant, soulless. The mouth drooped at the corners, as did her entire body, and the skin was covered in a greasy film. A miasma of neglect and a faint smell of urine mixed with medication and old sweat hung in the air and made me want to step back to the door and the fresh air.

'Alexis is very ill,' Moira explained. She stood up and firmly pushed Alexis backwards until she was supine. Alexis let it happen, showing neither resistance nor compliance. A rag doll, flat out on her back, staring at the ceiling with dead eyes.

'She's in the midst of a very bad bout of hepatitis, it's been going around for the last few weeks. I tell people not to share spoons or cups but they don't listen, and so we've had to fight it in one person after the other. Once we had ten people down with it at one time; we had to clear one of the dormitories to fit them all in! The nurse is having her lunch break, she'll be back soon, so I just came to make sure Alexis was fine and give her some water. Water is of the essence with hepatitis; that liver needs to be flushed out. Come, shall I show you some of our other patients?'

She covered Alexis with a sheet and walked to me.

'Um... yes, please,' I managed to say. During her speech I had had time to organise my thoughts and to rediscover my own voice. I pointed to the other bed, where another woman lay with her back to us.

'Who's that?'

Moira half-turned. 'That? Oh, she's asleep, and I don't want to wake her. Come with me, I'd like you to meet some of the children.'

So saying, she clutched my elbow and led me firmly out of the ward and on to the veranda. What was it about Moira that reduced a person's will to nothing? That took for granted, and immediately received, complete obedience? I couldn't believe it but it was happening to me, too. I wanted to pull myself away, march round to the back of the ward, pull back the sheet to see the other patient's face, but I was helpless against Moira's command.

One thing was clear to me right now: Alexis did not have hepatitis. I had had it in Ecuador, along with six members of the commune I'd been living in at the time. In 'the midst' of hepatitis the eyes are marigold yellow. The whites of Alexis's eyes were bloodshot, yes; but they were just that: white.

CHAPTER THIRTY

'So, you want to have a look around on your own,' Moira said as we walked away from the hospital. 'Wasn't Miranda doing a good job?'

Sarcasm dripped from her words, innocent as they were in themselves. I had to be careful with this woman. She saw and heard everything.

'Miranda's a good guide,' I said, and decided to plunge right in. 'But you know, there's one thing I really want to do, and she doesn't think she can help me.'

'Really? And what would that be?'

'I would like an interview with Jim Jones,' I said. 'Miranda seems to think that's not very likely. She promised to ask you but didn't give me much hope.'

'So, you're asking me yourself.' Moira laughed. 'Clever girl! Miranda is often a little overcautious, lacking confidence, when it comes to approaching her superiors. It's an unfortunate trait because of course there are no superiors here. We are all one big happy family. There's nothing at all forbidding about Father; he loves to see his children at all times, and he regards everyone as his children, even strangers, like yourself. Father says there *are* no strangers, and you least of all are a stranger to us. He read the articles about you and he asked me personally to extend his warmest welcome to you. The thing is, he's been rather ill lately, and not seeing people. All the same, I think, maybe I can arrange something, just five minutes or so.'

'Could you really?' My eagerness spilled into my voice. I'd started to believe that an audience with Jim Jones was as exceptional as one with the Queen of England or the Pope.

'Yes. It can be done. I'll put in a word for you myself. So...' she looked at her watch. 'Is there anyplace else you'd like to see? I can't show you around myself, I'm busy, but...'

'That's fine, thanks!' I said hastily. 'Miranda's coming to get me at two thirty, and she'll show me around some more. Right now, I've a bit of a headache. I think I'll go to my room for a rest.'

'Yes – the midday sun is so draining, isn't it? Though I'd have thought, as a Guyanese native, you'd be used to it.'

Again, that tinge of sarcasm. I had the feeling Moira saw right through me and just played along for the fun of it, like a cat with a mouse. Then again, maybe it was simply her art, and even calculated; maybe that was the impression she *wanted* to give, the source of her power. For a power she did have, and if even I, a veritable stranger, found her hard to resist, how much more would those committed to live here, under her rule? For it was quite plain to me that Moira ruled here. Jim Jones might be the head of this set-up, but Moira set the daily rules and upheld them. Most likely, Jones himself sat on a throne high above this daily grind, and it was Moira who actually ran the show. But I could only tell once I'd met him.

Whatever. I ignored her last comment and said goodbye at the next crossroads. Moira promised to send me a message as soon as she had the OK for an interview, and we parted.

Supporters of Indira G – Gandhi have been hailing her parliamentary victory as an important step to her eventual return to national power. She... she... parliamentary victory by a decisive majority in spite of framed criminal sentences hanging over her. In the face of concerted effort by the ruling party to see that she did not get back in Parliament again, and in fact, be placed in jail...

I returned to my cabin. That irritating voice boomed into the room, so I closed the window. In the relative quiet of my sanctuary, I peeled off my shoes, wriggled out of my jeans and flung myself on my bed, both relieved and frustrated. Relieved, because I was closer to a talk with Jones, one of my high priorities, but frustrated as I may have found Lucy, but it had been in vain. That girl in Alexis's room, I was 99 per cent sure it was Lucy. But if it was, and she was ill, how could I possibly rescue her? What to do next?

I lay back on the lumpy mattress. What incredibly bad timing, to miraculously gain entry into Jonestown only to find Lucy so ill, she could do no more than sleep. I had a window of only one day to find her, talk with her, discuss escape plans. Less than a day, in fact; for the best time for flight would be tonight, protected by darkness. That meant I had only hours. I *had* to find her. And if the sick woman was indeed her, I had to so ingratiate myself with Jim Jones that he would invite me back or allow me to stay longer. No, not stay longer. If that was Lucy in the hospital and she was as ill as she looked, I'd have to return when she was back on her feet. All of this had to be resolved. I had to get back to the hospital as soon as possible. Should I go right now? After all, Moira was gone. The coast was clear. I could sneak out once again... But I was so tired. It was so humid, so hot... I closed my eyes.

. . .

'Zoe! Zoe, wake up!'

The loud knocking, the calling of my name, penetrated my dream and jolted me awake. Immediately alert, I rolled off the bed and staggered to the door.

'Yes, yes, I'm here,' I groaned, and opened it. Outside stood Miranda.

'Zoe! Father has agreed to see you! You have to come right away!'

'Right now?'

She tugged at my arm. 'Yes, right now! Come along! We can't keep Father waiting.'

I shook myself loose. 'Wait a minute. Can't you see how I'm dressed?' I wore no more than a crumpled T-shirt and my underpants. My hair felt like a sensa-fowl, whose feathers grow backwards, and a film of dried sweat clung to my skin. I longed for a shower.

'Can't I have a quick shower? I won't be more than five minutes.'

'Are you crazy? Showers are rationed here, and no, you can't have one. Put on some pants – quick!'

'Please excuse me one minute.'

I gently closed the door, and she stepped back to allow it. 'Hurry up!' she cried as the latch clicked. 'Father doesn't like to be kept waiting.'

Alone again, I stripped off my T-shirt. I needed water, but all I had was the precious bottle of drinking water. I'd have to use that. I dampened a corner of the T-shirt I'd just removed and wiped my face and under my arms with it. I put on a clean shirt and the same jeans I'd worn that morning, dragged a comb through my hair, put on my shoes, opened the door and stepped out into the sunshine.

'OK, I'm ready. Let's go.'

. . .

Miranda chattered all the way over to Father's house, giving me instructions on how to behave, admonishing me for going off on my own and bothering Moira, and complaining that her entire schedule would now have to be changed. I said nothing; I was preparing myself for the coming interview and considering my questions.

Even from the outside, Jones's house was obviously of a different calibre to everyone else's. Though of the same style – wooden-planked, yellow and resting on short stilts – it was bigger, grander, and stood in the rudiments of a garden. A guard stood at the bottom of the flight of stairs leading up to the bright blue door. Miranda ignored him and led me up. She lifted the brass knocker and rapped three times. The door opened.

Moira stood at the entrance to a wide hall. She smiled – almost fondly, I thought – at me. She gave me her thin crooked-toothed smile, and said, 'See? Nothing is impossible in Jonestown!'

'Thank you so much for arranging this!' I had some major sucking up to do if I were to earn a repeat invitation, so I smiled back at Moira and followed her to a door at the back of the hall. She knocked, and entered without waiting for a reply. This was a woman who feared no one, not even her leader. She stood back and allowed Miranda and me to enter. The crawling of my skin told me that she'd slipped in right behind us.

I recognised him at once. Jim Jones sat behind a huge desk, in front of which two chairs waited for their occupants. The room was simply and oddly furnished. A wooden bench with a flat cushion against the adjacent wall offered more seating, while a cot with a white sheet was pushed into the farthest corner, opposite the desk. A locally woven rug similar to the one in the office, but in better condition, lay in the very middle of the floor, beneath a slowly rotating ceiling fan. In one corner sat a man in a white coat.

Miranda walked up to the desk and gestured at me. 'Dad, this is Zoe.'

I followed her to the desk and held out my hand over it. 'I'm very pleased to meet you, sir, thank you for giving me some of your time.'

Jim Jones ignored the hand. He looked me up and down intently for a full minute. I had the feeling he was stripping me naked. I looked back at him, trying not to stare, feeling intensely vulnerable and lost for words. What to say to a man who let himself be labelled Dad, and thought of me as his child? A man who looked like this?

Compared to the younger portrait of himself hanging immediately behind and above him, the man before me was a wreck. His dark-ringed eyes glared at me from deep hollows in a puffy face; I would have judged him in his fifties, though I knew he was mid-forties. His dark hair clung lank and greasy to his scalp, one lock falling almost boyishly over a furrowed forehead. He had thick dark Elvis sideburns and loose rubbery lips. His facial skin, too, was loose, pasty and pale as if he never saw the sun, with the beginnings of jowls along the jaw. He looked old, exhausted and very, very ill; and yet a coiled tenseness radiated from him, like a wounded wildcat ready to pounce. He coughed, cleared his throat, and finally, he spoke:

'You're very pretty.'

'Thank you, Mr Jones.'

'Reverend. To you, I am the Reverend Jones. Please address me as such.'

'I'm sorry. Reverend Jones.'

'So, you live near Jonestown?'

The voice was hoarse, low, yet somehow authoritative. It was a statement, not a question. He'd done his homework.

'That's right.'

'Patsy spoke well of you, that's the only reason I let you in. I trust Patsy implicitly. And Moira. Those are the only two.

Everybody else I mistrust, yes, even you, Miranda. For all I know, you're a CIA spy.' He glared at me with yellowy eyes.

'No, of course not! I'm just a journalist! I'm Guyanese, I have relatives here.'

His features relaxed. He leaned forward, and a tone of slimy confidentiality infused his voice.

'Then you are our friend. The Guyanese people are our friends, great people, very hospitable. The Guyana government leased this land to us, forty thousand acres of paradise, for ninety-nine years. You know what that means to us? We're a beleaguered people, chased all over the world, like the Jews. Just like the Jews, searching for a promised land all over the world. All we want is the peace to live our own lives, to live side by side, Black and white in perfect harmony, perfect equality, rich and poor. Ask Miranda.'

'That's right, Dad!' piped Miranda.

'And like the Jews, we found our promised land. But that wasn't enough for them. They followed us here. See that jungle out there? It's full of tigers and snakes, swarming with tigers and snakes. Boa constrictors, anacondas, black widow spiders. You can hear the tigers roaring at night. But you know what it's also swarming with? CIA spies! They put two hundred Green Berets in the jungle to watch us, and the British too, three hundred Black Guards are out there in the jungle right now watching us, waiting to pounce. Armed soldiers. You go back and report that, write a story about us, let the world know how we have been hunted down to this, our last refuge. Tell the world. Sell your story to *The New York Times*. But they won't believe you, but Miranda here, she can confirm it. Right, Miranda?'

Miranda simpered before she confirmed: 'Right, Dad. It's true!'

'I gave a home to these people when nobody wanted them. I was a father to them. Black or white, I'm their father. I adopted eight children, Black and white. No racial barriers here, paradise. But instead of letting us live our life in peace they hunt us down. Cornered animals, that's what we are! Where are we to go? What are we to do?'

In the following pause I managed to put my first question:

'Is everyone here of their own free will? And they can leave whenever they want?'

'Who would want to leave? Tell me, if you found paradise, a place where you had everything you want, food, clothing, family, everything, would you want to leave? No! That's the position of the people here. All we want is to live our lives in freedom and happiness. But people out there, people in America, they want to destroy us. They wouldn't let us live in America so we came here and now they won't let us live here. People came to inspect us. They sent a spy. He'd heard all those lies, thought that he'd find barbed wire, and sentries and three hundred armed men. He thought they was coming in here, gonna fight – have to fight a war. Afterwards though, he said, when I came in here, all I found was children, happy children, and plenty of happy seniors, as far as the faces he could see. Right, Miranda?'

'That's right, Dad. We're all happy here and all we want is to—'

Jones stabbed a forefinger in my direction. 'But why did you ask that question? That question was aggressive; it's what all the Americans ask. So who sent you really, the CIA?'

'No, of course not. I told you – I'm a journalist! A Guyanese!'

I had to disarm him, make him believe I was neutral, a potential friend. That was the only way I'd be able to pull my plan through. I had to break down his paranoia.

'The Guyanese are our friends. I'm a personal friend of your prime minister. What newspaper you work for, the *San*

Francisco Informer? They wrote an article about us. Complete garbage. I wouldn't like to hear you work for that newspaper.'

His words ended in a violent barrage of coughs. The white-coated man in the corner leaned forward and handed him a glass of water. He took three sips, then placed it on the desk.

'...cos, if you were with them, that would make you an enemy. I want you as a friend. Patsy said you're on our side, you think the way we do. That's good.'

Another fit of coughing. He drank another sip, and the coughing stopped.

'Now listen... Zoe? Zoe is your name?'

I nodded.

'Zoe, I want you to go out there and tell the truth about us. Tell the world that we have found peace and leave us alone! Leave us alone, damn it!'

He yelled the last words, and hammered on the desk the better to drive them home.

'Leave us fucking alone, for God's sake! If I find out you're CIA I ain't gonna like that at all! You gonna be punished! But if you're our friend, you gonna do the right thing and tell the world about us! We're good people! Out there, you have Satan out to get us! So what newspaper you're with? *The New York Times*?'

He glowered at me from across the desk. I recoiled, but kept my voice steady as I replied: 'I'm freelance. I work for myself, but the *Chronicle* publishes my articles.'

'Well, then, maybe you're a spy. Aren't you? Admit it?'

'No, of course not! I'm a journalist. I told you.'

'You're CIA, aren't you? I've got a nose for that sort of thing.'

He bellowed at me again, his voice a rasping whip that descended into another bout of coughs. The doctor – if that was what the white-coated man was – stood up and patted him on the back. He hawked violently and spat into an offered spittoon.

Again, the coughing stopped. The doctor leaned forward and whispered to him, he nodded, the doctor returned to his seat.

'You'd better admit it, if it's true! Admit it now!'

'No, I'm not! I swear it!'

'Let's say I gave you the benefit of the doubt. What'll you write about us? That you found a peaceful community that wants nothing more than to be left alone?'

'Yes, exactly. Everyone seems so happy. You've done a good job. My article will be fair.'

'Really? Is that what you really think?'

'Yes, truly. You've done a good job here. They all adore you! in fact, I'd like to—' But I didn't get to finish.

'Are you friend or foe?' He yelled the words, silencing me. He scraped back his chair, stood up and paced the room. Sweat beaded his face and poured from his temples. Dark wet patches spread from under the sleeves of his light blue shirt. He turned his back and that, too, was patched with sweat. Miranda walked up to him and handed him a handkerchief. He blotted his face with it.

'Friend or foe? That's what I need to know. Ha, that rhymes, even! You can't tell the difference these days, spies everywhere, the American Embassy in Georgetown is full of spies, sent here to watch us. They was coming in here to kill people. Dead or alive. You know, there— – there's the conspirator, the head detective that did all their hiring. He was the chief he – he was the head of the unit that was laying out there in the wo— in the woods, bothering us for those seven days, when we had our White Night... Full of CIA, FBI. Ask Patsy. Patsy Boyle. You met Patsy, right?'

'Right.'

'Patsy says I can trust you but I don't trust anybody. I need to know your connections. You working for them Concerned Relatives, that group out there, that group with Congressman Ryan?'

'No, I—'

'Congressman Ryan's coming out here any day now. Says he wants to make sure everyone's safe and happy, what garbage! It's out there in America people aren't safe and happy, you ask the Black people of America if they're safe and happy, listen to what they say, just listen.'

Jones launched into a long rant along this vein, a diatribe against Congressman Ryan, the American President, America in general, the CIA the FBI, the IRA. The American Consulate; even Rex Bennett's name came up. As he spoke, he coughed; sometimes he coughed so much he could not speak, but just bent double and held on to the desk. He hawked and spat again and again. The doctor came to assist him, but Jones pushed him away, and continued.

'Here, we found a refuge, a safe place, a paradise, and what happens? CIA comes after us and Congressman Ryan with his Concerned Relatives. Let him come. Let him come, I say, and see what happens. See what he's going to find, a people they chased all over the world like animals. We found paradise, but even paradise ain't safe, turned to hell. Got us cornered. Russia and Cuba would be glad to take us. I'm gonna take all my people over there, somewhere safe, my little children. They're all mine. I'm their dad, they look up to me, follow me. I will lead them out of this hellhole, because they got us cornered, in a corner with – with nowhere to go. But we will win! We will win in the end!'

Another violent fit of coughing interrupted this speech. The doctor came over, shook two pills from a small bottle, handed them to him with the glass. Jones swallowed them, and continued his rant:

'We gonna show the world! They gonna see how we been hunted down, destroyed, when all we wanted was to live our lives in peace! In the end we – we gonna be victorious and the world gonna know about Jonestown, People's Temple gonna win in the end! If they chase us out of Jonestown, we gonna go somewhere – somewhere nobody can follow. Right, Miranda?' The speech ended in a manic cackle, turning into another coughing fit. He grasped the desk with one hand, pointed to Miranda with the other.

'That's right, Dad. We're gonna win in the end.'

Without warning, he turned to me and pointed his finger straight at me. 'Get her out of here.'

He turned his back. The silence echoed with his voice. Miranda grabbed my elbow and ushered me out of the room.

CHAPTER THIRTY-ONE

Miranda laid her arm round me as we left and gave me an amicable squeeze, as if we were old buddies. Involuntarily, I trembled, and she must have felt my revulsion, for she dropped the arm immediately. She said, 'Father was very gracious to grant you an interview. I hope you will write a favourable report on us.'

'He seems terrified.'

'Who wouldn't be? What he says is true, they are all after us for some reason.'

'What with the tigers and the CIA, you really have it tough.'

She didn't notice my sarcasm, a trait I'd seen again and again in most of those I'd spoken to.

'Yes, I'm glad you realise our plight. You must write about it in your article.'

'So, you're stuck between the devil and the deep blue sea!'

'That's it exactly. We fled America so we could have our own place, to live in harmony with each other; America is a racist capitalist country and we thought we'd find peace here. Instead, they bother us all the time. And Father is not a healthy man, as you can see. Anyway, this is our vegetable garden...'

The afternoon tour had begun.

There was no sign of Lucy all afternoon, or at supper. Miranda, as if to compensate for my little solo adventure after lunch, clung to me, a shadow with a schedule, forever peering over my shoulder when I spoke to anyone. I retired early, deeply disappointed and frustrated. The whole day, except for the interview with Jones, had been a waste; the whole precious visit squandered in useless sightseeing. Now all that was left was the night, but there was no question of getting her out tonight.

If she was the woman in the sickroom – which was the first thing I wanted to find out – then my plan was useless, and I'd have to go home empty-handed. For now. And I'd have to return. Moira, I felt, would be the one to approach tomorrow. Moira was distant and cold, but she was sane – unlike Jones – and helpful, and seemed to trust and like me. She'd let me come back, I was sure, just as I was sure that it had been she who had persuaded Jones to let me come in the first place. That was it: Patsy had recommended me to Moira, and Moira had worked on Jones to let me come. In the end, I'd get my Jonestown story. But without rescuing Lucy, it would hardly be the scoop I'd hoped for. My plan had failed.

I lay on my bed in the darkness, waiting. I'd set my alarm clock for midnight, but there was no way I could sleep; every fibre of my body, every grey cell of my brain was on edge, waiting. Outside, the familiar night noises floated in from the jungle, a shrill cacophony of piping, tweeting sound rising and falling in ensemble as if conducted by the high priest of insects, now frantic, a wave about to break, now tranquil, as if melting down to silence but never arriving, rising instead into yet another crescendo, swelling into a climax that never came. A bat flew in, and out again, and mosquitoes buzzed hungrily around my net. If I closed my eyes I could very well be back at Parrot Creek; all that was missing was the distant hum of Jim Jones on the loudspeaker. And here I was, in Jonestown.

Soft moonlight fell through the window, painting a pattern of light and dark across the wall and the floor, veiled by the mosquito net. I felt under my pillow for my torch, switched it on, looked at the clock: only eight o'clock. Too early by far. I could not dare to venture out before midnight, an eternity away. I reached under the net for my notebook and pen and began to scribble some notes in the circle of torchlight, but not for long. To save the battery I switched the torch off again, lay back with my hands behind my head, waiting in the darkness for time to pass. Breathing deeply. Gathering courage. Every now and then I checked the clock. At last I drifted off, only to be awoken by the now-familiar scream of a jaguar. It felt near, nearer than it had at Parrot Creek, and I could understand the fear of 'tigers' that seemed to haunt the Jonestown inmates.

At last, midnight. I ducked beneath the mosquito net, pulled on clothes and shoes, and looked out of the window. All was still. Jonestown slept. A blanket of peace rested on all the turmoil and kept it contained, the moonlight a benevolent hand laid upon an open wound. I stepped across to the far window, and there the jungle waited, a black wall against the night sky. I shivered. I realised that I did not know the jungle by night. And night in the jungle is a different beast to day. No way was I prepared to meet it. All my plans had been for a daytime escape. But...

Between my cabin and that black wall lay an open stretch of wasteland. Even as I gazed out, a guard strolled past, a black moving shadow in the silver light. I clearly saw his rifle, a finger pointing upwards behind his head. This, I realised, would be my first hurdle – how ever to traverse this land unseen, in broad daylight? Crossing that stretch would require the protection of night, and even then, evading the guards would need great care.

So there it was: to get to the jungle we needed night, but for navigating the jungle we needed day. The plan seemed clear: we would have to leave Jonestown as close to dawn as possible, hide in the shrubbery at the jungle's edge for a few hours, then at first light make our way to the creek. Me, Lucy, Lucy's two kids. Just the four of us.

But first I had to find Lucy. I took a deep breath and walked over to the door.

The night was fresh, and my bare skin rose in gooseflesh. I held the torch in one hand, but left it switched off – I could see well in the moonlight, for the buildings rose around me as big black hulks, the walkways clearly defined at my feet. I'd brought my backpack, just in case, lightly packed with just the bare necessities: notebook, matches and water bottle, still half full.

I found my way easily to the hospital, seeing not a single person on my way. The guards, it seemed, patrolled just the outer limits of the settlement, and for that small mercy I was grateful. I slunk up the stairs to the hospital, and along the corridor to Alexis's door. I tried it: it opened. I slipped inside the room, closed it again, and stood still to settle myself. My heart was beating madly, but the sound of rhythmic breathing seeped into me and calmed me down.

Only then did I switch on the torch. I let its beam wander around the room till it found the far bed. The spotlight fell on the bulk of the sleeping woman beneath the white sheet, only the black mat of her hair visible. I tiptoed round the corner of the bed and shone the light full on to her face.

I was so certain this was Lucy that I jumped and almost gasped aloud to see the face of a stranger, a face I'd never seen before.

My escape plan, tentative though it was, crumbled into

nothing. I'd been clinging to it, hoping against hope that somehow, Lucy would be well enough to leave. That I would wake her, whisper to her, and that she would come. That the two of us would sneak off, somehow find her children, wait for the guard to turn his back, make a dash for it to the jungle. Once inside, we would settle down for the long wait till dawn, and then make our way to the creek, the way I knew so well. It had been a vague plan, built on nothing more than optimism and hope, but even as it dissolved, I realised how very strong that hope had been, how much I'd clung to it, and how very unrealistic it had been. Ludicrous, even, entirely dependent on chance and luck and a false notion of my own heroism. My escape plan, crumbled to nothing. A pipe dream.

As I regarded the sleeping face of the second patient, I at last had to admit: my mission to Jonestown was an abject failure. It was over. I sighed. Time to go back to bed, get some sleep before the morning light. I'd make the best of my defeat, gather more material for an article, write an exposé. Perhaps Congressman Ryan could help Lucy.

I walked softly back to the door, the beam from my torch a moving circle before me. As I approached Alexis's bed, my heart lurched. I stopped.

There, slightly protruding from under the bed, was a foot. A bare foot. A bare brown female foot.

CHAPTER THIRTY-TWO

A chill slithered down my spine. Sheer terror snatched my heart in a grip so cold it missed a beat, or several. I could not think for fear; not breathe. The foot twitched.

Thinking set in and I realised: *whoever is down there doesn't know it's me. She's hiding from authority.* I stepped between the two beds, knelt down, and swept beneath Alexis's bed with my torch's beam.

'Who's there?' I whispered. 'Come on out. I won't hurt you.'

The circle of light moved up and along a body crouched beneath the bed, until it reached the face. For the second time my heart skipped a beat.

'Lucy!' I gasped.

For it was her. Here, spotlighted by my torch, was the very face I'd been searching for all day, wide-eyed with terror like on the day I'd first seen it.

'Who... who is it?' she squeaked.

I realised that I was in darkness, and shone the light on my own face.

'I'm Zoe! The woman from the shop!'

'You! What – what are you doing here?' Lucy scrambled from beneath the bed. We were both whispering.

'Looking for you! Where've you been all day? What are you doing down there?'

I helped to pull her out, giggling in sheer relief, and when she was free I hugged her. She fell into my arms as limp as a kitten, and a sob shook her body from top to toe.

'I – I heard you coming, and I hid – I thought it was Moira, or someone.' She turned to reach beneath the bed and brought out a single flip-flop. She slipped it on to her one bare foot.

'But where've you been all day? And why're you here now, of all places?'

'I've been in the Box. They let me out today, this afternoon, so I came to see Alexis.'

We were both still crouched on the floor; instinctively we knew it was safer down here, between the two beds, than standing up. I switched off the torch to save the battery.

'What's the Box?'

'A hole in the ground. They put you in there for punishment. Ten days. Ten days is the sentence for trying to escape, and – and... Zoe, you went to the American Embassy, didn't you? With my story!'

'Why... yes, I did. Your mother told me to.'

'But I warned you. I told you not to go there, not to trust them, I told you they have spies. See what happened. They put me in the Box for that!'

'But...' I could not continue. A lump rose in my throat. *Rex.* I hadn't thought of Rex all day, not once. Now I did. His face rose up in my mind's eye, and it came not accompanied by the familiar warmth and affection and trust but with revulsion. That very trust, so fragile, that tender plant that we both had tended and nourished and coaxed out into the light: crushed underfoot. Rex. He who claimed to love me, he who claimed to care, who claimed to be helping – he had betrayed me. Rex, a traitor! I could hardly believe it, I did not want to believe it, but it was so; the evidence crouched before me.

'Ten days for treason, and all privileges revoked. The little bit of freedom I had, gone. Who's she replaced me with? Miranda?'

I swallowed the lump of shock. 'Yes... I guess so. Miranda showed me around yesterday.'

'That bitch! See, if you hadn't told, it would've been me showing you around.'

My head swirled. I still could not comprehend the depth of Rex's betrayal. I did not want to think of it, or about the consequences. Or about the Box.

'I'm sorry. I'm so sorry, Lucy.'

'Never mind, that's over now. Now I'm here and you too and—'

Suddenly I came to my senses. What was I doing, wasting time with thoughts of Rex?

'Lucy, I came to find you to take you out of here! We can go – now! Listen – I know the way out, through the jungle. I can take you. All we have to do is—'

'I'm not goin' nowhere without my Danny.'

Danny. I kept forgetting Danny, Lucy's son, and the other child, the baby. Some reflex in my mind kept it constantly swept clear of children, making me keep leaving her kids out of my plans. They were indeed a problem.

'Can't you get him? Where does he sleep? And isn't there another child? A baby?'

A sob escaped her lips. 'I had a baby. Serena. They killed Serena.'

I took a moment to digest those words. Her hand reached for mine. I grasped it, and squeezed, but still – we had to plan.

'Danny, then. Can you get him? Now?'

'I could if I was very careful. It's possible he's in one of the dorms. But I won't go without Granma either.'

'But, Lucy...'

I couldn't believe what I'd just heard. Not just Lucy and a child, but a grandmother as well.

'And I won't go without Alexis.'

'Alexis! But—'

'Yep. I'm not goin' nowhere without her. It's me that got her into this fix in the first place and me that's gonna save her.'

'But she's ill – sick. She can't even sit up properly. How do you expect to...'

Lucy chuckled. I felt her hand reach for mine in the darkness.

'Give me that flashlight.'

I let go of the torch and let her take it from me. She switched it on and turned its beam on Alexis.

That was the third shock of the night – or the fourth; I'd lost count. Instead of the zombie face of yesterday, fast asleep as I'd expected, I saw a normal, very pretty, smiling face, eyes wide open and looking at me; and the smile was not just on the lips but in those dark eyes. The woman who lived behind that face was very much alive.

'Hi,' she said, and raised her upper body up on to an elbow. Her hand reached out to me. 'Pleased to meet you. I'm Alexis.'

I took the hand, too amazed to do or say anything else. She took it firmly and shook it, then turned her body to sit up in bed.

'What on earth...?'

'Alexis's not sick. She's been kept under sedation. For weeks, now.'

'Really? But why?'

She looked away. 'I'll tell you one day. I— I was being troublesome.' She and Lucy exchanged a knowing look. She continued: 'But unknown to them, I've developed a tolerance. It doesn't work the way it used to. After a few hours it wears off. But I'm a pretty good actress. I've got them fooled.'

'You mean, when I saw you last time...?'

She frowned. 'When did you see me? I don't remember. I've never seen you in my life before.'

Then I remembered – Moira had just given her a glass of water. It must have been spiked.

'I saw you all right,' I said. 'I don't think you were acting. Nobody can act that well.'

'Just try me.' Alexis lolled her head, rolled back her eyes, and indeed, she looked just the way she'd done when I'd seen her. Still, there's no way anyone can consciously be dead inside, and that's what she had been. Knocked out.

'Nope,' I said. 'You were really, really gone.'

Alexis shrugged. 'Oh well. I'm pretty good, though, and mostly I just have to sleep. That's easy.'

I could sense Lucy's impatience.

'Anyway, the two of us – we've been figuring out a way to leave this damned place. Take our folk and go. One thing the Box has taught me is that I ain't stayin' here one day longer than I have to. I'd rather be dead, shot by CIA or eaten by tigers, than let them win. Same for my Danny, and Granma.'

'We were planning that before Lucy went in the Box. At night, I've been doing exercises – getting back the use of my limbs, getting strong again.'

'And Alexis's real strong!' I could hear the pride in Lucy's voice. 'She was in the 1968 Olympic team, the women's one thousand metres! The name Alexis Harding mean anything to you?'

The name rang no bell; I didn't follow the Olympics. She could have been a gold medallist and I wouldn't have known.

'Just an also-ran,' added Alexis, 'but being there is everything.'

'Don't believe her. She's great. And together, we're gonna get us out of this damned hellhole. Away from those damned devils.'

Lucy's voice in the darkness sounded curiously disembodied. It was little louder than a whisper, but so filled with passion and determination I knew that this was a different Lucy to the one I had met a few weeks ago. This Lucy had fought fear and conquered it. She was ready for anything, and I was glad.

'Then I came at the right time,' I replied. 'Like I said – I know the way out. I've got a boat waiting for us.'

'For us all?' She counted on her fingers. 'You, me, Danny, Granma, Alexis...'

'Well – no. It's just a two-man dugout. But the main thing is to get you all out of here, and then we'll walk through the jungle to a creek. I know the way. I'll lead you.'

'No way I'm goin' through that jungle. It's crawlin' with tigers, and if it's not tigers, it's the CIA. If I escape this place, it's not to get killed.'

'Don't be silly, Lucy. It's not crawling with anything. Insects, maybe. How were you planning to escape, if not through the jungle?'

Lucy chuckled. 'Through the main gate. Whack the guards on the head. Whichever way you go, you gotta escape those fuckin' guards, at some point you gotta whack them on the head.'

'We were working something out,' Alexis said. She must have noticed how childish Lucy sounded. 'We were hatching this big plan to spike the guards' food one night. It sounds complicated but it can be done. But there's a problem. See, every night at eight Moira comes to give me my sedative and knock me out. But if I want to escape, I can't be knocked out. I have to be wide awake the night we escape. And we know what to do about that, but we can't.'

'Why not? What's the plan?'

Lucy spoke. 'There's a room. A few doors down. That's where they keep all the drugs. There's a padlock on the door and Moira's got the key but that's no problem – I can pick a lock. All I need is a pin or something. You got anything like that?'

I kept a couple of emergency safety pins stuck in my backpack. I told her so.

'Excellent. Finding a pin in this place is like finding gold. Anyway, that's problem number one solved. Problem number two is worse. See, the drug's locked up in that room. All we have to do is replace it with clear water. The trouble is, the water in here ain't clear. I don't know if you've seen it. It's river water, brownish, then they put this stuff in it, water purifier, that colours it. No way can we use that water. She'd know at once we'd messed with it.'

Instead of answering I took the torch from her, switched it on, held up my water bottle with my other hand, shone the light on it and shook it. Water sloshed around audibly inside it.

'Water,' I said with some satisfaction. 'Good, clear rainwater.'

'Oh my God! Prayer does work.' Lucy flung herself at me and hugged me into kingdom come.

'Do it now,' Alexis said into the darkness. 'Right now. I can't stand another day of zombiehood.'

'Let me do it.' Lucy took the pin from my fingers.

We slunk away, into the shadows of the veranda, until we came to a locked door. I shone the torch's beam on the padlock, and she held it steady and stuck the pin into the hole. 'I've done this a hundred times,' she whispered as she fiddled the pin around inside the lock. 'My brother Bobby showed me, when I was a kid. Before he went to jail. In my other life.'

I heard a noise, looked over my shoulder. My heart was racing and I could hardly breathe. It was nothing, an animal, maybe a rat. I breathed again. Lucy frowned in concentration as she worked, carefully moving the pin around.

'Got it!' she cried.

The padlock snapped open. Lucy slipped it off the latch

and opened the door. I glanced behind me one last time, and we entered, the torch leading the way into the black cave of what appeared to be an oversized storage cabinet. I let the beam wander over a whole wall of shelves, filled with medicine bottles of all shapes and sizes.

'You know who that stuff belongs to?' Lucy said as she walked to the far end of the wall. 'Us. The people. The first thing they do when we come here is take our medicines off us. They took all of Granma's painkillers. See – gimme that.'

She took the torch from me and beamed it onto a shelf of small dark bottles and cardboard boxes. I glanced at the labels: aspirin, Excedrin, Motrin.

'All these are painkillers. Stolen from us! Look: this is Granma's!' she said, holding up one small box of Excedrin. 'See: it's even got her name on it. It's a prescription drug. That devil!' She plopped the box into my backpack and handed it back to me.

'Might as well help myself since we're here. Can I just...'

She snatched one whole bottle from the shelf, and then another and passed them to me. And several more. 'Put these in your backpack. I'm goin' for broke.'

'Careful,' I warned. I glanced at the door, half-expecting to see Moira standing there with those flint-like eyes. Lucy, flushed with the exuberance of her newfound freedom and the tangible hope of escape, was growing reckless. The terrified bundle of nerves I'd spoken to behind the shop had vanished completely. Being in the Box must have given her just the anger and passion she needed to give birth to this new version of herself.

When she'd finished pilfering the pills she took back the torch and searched farther down the shelves. The bottles she was looking for were on the very last shelf, standing in a tidy row. Several small bottles of amber glass, just about three inches high. Almost all of them were closed with a cap, but one was three-quarters full and closed by a dropper pipette. That's the one she took. With one neat twist she lifted off the pipette cap, then walked to the door, stepped out into the veranda. She returned.

'There you go... I just knocked out a couple of ants. Be careful. Don't spill anything, and don't fill it to the brim. About three-quarters full.'

I unscrewed the cap of my water bottle and held the neck just above the bottle's opening. Carefully, I poured a little clear water into it till it was three-quarters full. Lucy took the bottle from me, replaced the cap, and put it back at the end of the row. I replaced the cap on my water bottle. We were ready.

Just before we left, Lucy shone her torch on a large metal cupboard in the corner. It had double doors and looked like a safe. Lucy tried the handle: it was well and truly locked.

'You'd never guess what's in there,' she said to me. 'You want to write a story about Jonestown? Well, the biggest story of all is behind those doors. I know secrets, Zoe, secrets nobody else knows. A big, big story I'll tell you soon as we're outta here. Not now. First, you gotta get us out.'

'There's just one little problem,' I told the other two when we were safely back at Alexis's bedside. 'I'm supposed to be leaving tomorrow. The escape has to be tonight.'

'Tomorrow? Already?' Lucy's voice rose in alarm. 'And now you tell us? We can't possibly leave tonight. I've got to arrange things, tell Granma, find out where Danny is, get him back. Tomorrow night's the earliest we can go.'

'It's all right,' I reassured her, 'I plan to stay longer. I'm going to ask Moira if I can stay a week, to live just like a normal Jonestownian. Moira likes me, I'm sure she'll agree.'

'Moira *likes you*? Who the hell are you kiddin'? Moira doesn't like anybody except herself. And Bruno Grimm.'

'Who's that?'

'You must have seen him around. One of the guards. A huge giant, muscle man.'

I knew at once which guard she meant. I'd seen him at the gate, the first time I'd come to Jonestown. I nodded.

'She and Bruno, they're thick as thieves. She hates everyone else. She doesn't even like Father. She's a devil!'

'Well, she was nice to me!'

'If she was nice to you it's because she wants something from you. She's nice to a whole lot of important men in Georgetown just so they'll give her what she wants.'

'Well, then, she's nice to me so I'll write something nice about Jonestown.'

I told Lucy about meeting Patsy, my articles, and the positive story on Jonestown Moira thought I was writing.

'See, she thinks I'm kindly disposed towards Jonestown. I think she'll let me stay. I'm going to ask tomorrow. Feign enthusiasm, and say I want to be a part of it.'

'She'll never let you. She'll be too afraid of people talking, telling you the truth. The thing is: we all want out, but we can't say it aloud. And she knows it. She doesn't trust anyone. She's a snake. And you can't trust her. Beware of every word Moira says. I wouldn't trust her as far as I could throw her.'

'Well, I guess we're even then,' I said. 'Because she shouldn't trust me. But she does.'

CHAPTER THIRTY-THREE

After breakfast next morning, I turned to Miranda.

'Before we continue the tour,' I said, 'I'd like to speak to Moira. There's something I want to ask her.'

Miranda frowned in consternation. 'What do you want to ask her? You can tell me, you know. I'm Moira's right hand. Anything you tell her, she'll tell me anyway.'

She sounded suspicious, as if she thought I was going to complain about her. I decided to calm her fears by confiding in her. Maybe she could put in a good word for me.

'It's just that I'm really impressed with Jonestown,' I lied, 'But one day is just too short. I'm here as a tourist; I want to really experience your everyday life, live the way you do for a few days. I did that with a self-help project in India; I'm sure Moira read it. I spent a week there and it was brilliant. I could do the same for you. I find it such a shame that people put you down without knowing you at all. I don't want to be a tourist. Then I'll write about you. Something positive, to counteract the bad press you've been getting.'

I considered asking if I could actually join Jonestown, but

that might be taking it too far. 'So, I was going to ask Moira for permission to stay on.'

Miranda beamed. 'I'd so glad you like it here! I'm sure Moira will say yes. We really need some good publicity. They're making things really tough for us, you know.'

She lowered her voice, looked around to make sure no one was eavesdropping.

'There's this congressman, a Mr Ryan. He's evil. He's working up a frenzy in America about us. Listening to people who've never been here, complaints. You heard what Dad said yesterday. This Ryan, he's planning on bringing a whole bunch of journalists down to investigate. I mean, can't you see what's wrong with that? Those people are already prejudiced against us. They come here looking for trouble. That's the kind of problem we have to deal with, you see. Come, I'll take you to Moira straight away. It'll make a mess of my schedule but who knows, perhaps we won't need my schedule after all.'

She giggled and waved the schedule at me, then took hold of my elbow and steered me in the direction of Jones's house. I wriggled out of her grip by bending over to tie a shoelace that didn't need tying. The woman's very touch made my skin crawl.

We found Moira in the radio room. This little room buzzed with activity, with several of the top-tier people – I had learned to identify these by now; a subtle aura of superiority clung to them, and most of them were white – hovering outside, deep in discussion, and a couple more inside.

Miranda frowned. 'Something's going on here,' she said. 'Wait a minute.'

She put a hand on my arm to stop me progressing, and hurried into the room. A moment later, she emerged again with Moira. Both looked flustered. They walked up to me, whispering in agitation together.

'What's going on?' I asked, for it was obvious something big was happening. The very air buzzed with excitement.

Before Moira could speak, Miranda blurted out: 'Congressman Ryan's coming – today!'

'Today!'

Moira tossed Miranda an annoyed glance and turned to me. 'Yes, today. Do you see what's wrong with this? Isn't it normal that some period of notice is given before an official visit, at least one day? Do you see how aggressive, how hostile this move is? The intention of it is to bring Jonestown down. This is an invasion, no less. Do you see now? Do you believe now?'

'I thought he wasn't due for, I don't know, a few weeks?'

'That's what we thought. Lies, lies, I tell you. They've been planning this secretly, to take us unawares. It's pure hostility—'

Miranda interrupted. 'When's he arriving? How much time do we have?'

'Right now, he's on his way to Ogle Airport,' said Moira. 'He'll be here within the hour. Zoe, are you really on our side?'

The question took me unawares. Fear spilled out of Moira's eyes; the news of Ryan's arrival had obviously come as a bombshell, blowing her characteristic cool to shreds. Up to now it had been impossible to read Moira; now, suspicion and doubt fluttered through the fear, her normally impenetrable armour cracked by emotion. She reached out and took my hand; hers was dry and cold, a claw. I stuttered a reply:

'Why, ah, yes, of course! I-I-'

'We need you. Now. I know you were going home today but with Ryan coming we need all the support we can get. We need you as a witness, a friendly outside witness. I want you to stay a day longer. Just a day.'

Her bony fingers closed around mine, and suddenly I, too, knew fear. The hand gripping mine *told* me I had to stay; I was not being given a choice. It was a visceral fear, instinctive, the kind of fear I'd seen in Aunt Edna's eyes, a fear born of an innate knowledge of – of evil, stark naked evil, hovering on the perimeter of reason.

'Well, actually, I...'

I wanted to go. Right now. That instinct, that primal fear, rose up in me and swept away all the carefully laid plans, all reason, the knowledge that Ryan's arrival was a good thing. Red flags waving, warning lights flashing, an inner siren threatening danger. My skin crawled. I knew at once something was wrong, something had changed. Everything in me screamed for flight, while there was still time. Lucy, Alexis, escape plans – nothing counted. My bravery, shot through. I had to go – now. Save myself. I was no hero! I tried to pull my hand from hers, but she would not let me; her hand crushed mine in a talon grip. Our eyes met, and what I saw there now was more than fear. It was panic: raw panic.

'Come with me to Father,' she said. 'Miranda, you too.'

She didn't give me the choice; still clutching my hand, she strode away, pulling me along behind her. Miranda trotted along in our wake.

As we approached Jones's house I reasoned with myself, pushed my own mounting panic away. Congressman Ryan's coming was *good* news, I told myself. Better than any stupid escape plan. The best news ever. Even Lucy's mother had mentioned Congressman Ryan to me, infusing his visit with hope. He seemed to be the key to all our aims, the one man who could bring down the community. Ryan meant freedom for Lucy and Danny and Lucy's grandma and Alexis; I was sure of it.

I only had to look at Moira to know that Ryan, above all, was her bogeyman. Why was he arriving so suddenly? The way Rex had spoken of this visit, I'd thought it weeks, even months away; but then, he might have deliberately misled me. After all, Rex had betrayed me; he'd told Moira about Lucy's cry for help when I'd told him not to. Nothing he'd said counted any more. His assurances were built on sand. Momentarily, I felt a constraint around my heart, pain and sadness and regret, but I could not dwell there.

Moira seemed to have forgotten me in her haste to get to Jones; I felt her fingers release their grasp, and by the time we arrived at the house my hand was free again; but now I followed her willingly. I wanted to be in on this.

As I hurried along behind her I felt myself go limp with relief. Hope rose up within me, and I came face to face with the terror I'd hidden from myself. What empty bravado I'd shown to Lucy and Alexis, what a mask! I'd played for them the part of the heroine, but deep inside I quivered with dread, and that dread now showed its ugly face.

The jungle. Yes, I had learned to know it and to navigate it, to beat away my fear. But deep inside me the terror still lurked. Here it was, now, freed from the need to show a brave face, naked and in the open. Yes, I would have conquered fear, if I'd had to, done what had to be done. But it was no longer necessary. Congressman Ryan was on his way.

We were safe. We'd be rescued. No need for escape now. Perhaps by the end of the day we'd all be out of here, safe and sound; Lucy could tell me all of those secrets she'd promised, and all I had to do was write my article. No escape, no flight through the jungle. Everything was fine, and it was all so easy! I could hardly wait to see the smile on Lucy's face. But I had to find her, to inform her, and Alexis, let them know of the change of plan.

We arrived at Jones's house. At the bottom of the stairs Moira turned to Miranda and me and snapped: 'Wait here while I talk to Father.' She hurried up the stairs, rapped once. The door opened to let her in and she disappeared.

'You see? You see? This is how they treat us. This is how those fascist pigs try to...' Miranda screeched into my ear and treated me to a whole new tirade on the evils of capitalism and

America's fascist government. From her flapping lips I learned that the entire aim and focus of American policy at this very moment was the destruction of People's Temple; that all of America was watching Jonestown with bated breath, that President Carter himself had nothing better to do than obsess about one thousand people in the depths of the Guyanese jungle.

'They want us all dead!' Miranda ranted on. 'All of America wants us dead because they know that we are people of light, that our way could destroy the entire capitalist system, we are a threat to them and their tyrannical racist system!'

I listened with only one ear, for I had to figure out my next moves. I had to find Lucy, first of all. I had to make sure she was prepared. She needed to see Ryan as soon as possible. I hadn't seen her at breakfast; where was she? I had to see Alexis, too. I had to—

Pandemonium crashed into my thoughts, and it came from the open windows of Jones's house: crashing, thrashing noises, like an enraged beast fighting its way out of a pen, accompanied by frenzied yelling, and at one point a long, drawn-out howl like a wounded animal.

'Father,' Miranda explained. 'Moira must have just told him. He gets very upset when he hears bad news. Poor Father.'

After a few minutes of this the tumult died down. The door opened and Moira appeared at the top of the steps, red in the face, hair and clothes dishevelled as if she'd been bodily fighting the beast.

'Miranda!' she called, and crooked her finger. Miranda ran up the stairs. Moira leaned into her, hands cupped open before her as if holding the weight of the world as she spoke.

A frenzied scream from inside the house interrupted their palaver: '*Moira!*'

'Coming!' Moira grabbed Miranda's hand and bolted back inside, pulling the other woman in with her. The door slammed shut behind them. They seemed to have forgotten me entirely; I was all alone, abandoned by the powers that be as they grappled with their new emergency.

CHAPTER THIRTY-FOUR

I hurried off, heading for the hospital. I had no idea where Lucy might be, but I did know where Alexis was, and this seemed the logical place to start my search. It took five minutes to walk across the compound. Around me, Jonestown went about its daily routine. Most people were at work by now, and the few on the walkways were calm, unruffled. The news of Ryan's arrival had not yet spread.

The overhead static, when it came, sounded like the crackle of cellophane paper at Christmas, only louder. I jumped, but before I had time to think, a disembodied voice boomed out:

Children, beloved children.

I stopped in my tracks. It sounded like the voice of God, booming down from the sky. I knew that voice. I had heard it just a minute ago, screaming and screeching. Now it was calm and collected: Father had taken his meds.

Beloved children, attention, attention! Every member of the community must come to the pavilion immediately. People's helpers must go around, escort them into the pavilion. We may have the invasion, not with guns, but with hostile racists – one hostile, racist congressmen that voted for Pinochet, who cruelly killed the President of Chile, Salvador Allende, and represents all anti-Black feeling. A few have gathered to make a little scene for him, I guess for his next election. Now whether they'll get to Georgetown, I do not know, but we are to see that we sign that he – that you do not want to see any relative accompanied by – with any congressman. You do not want to see any relative that you have not requested to see, and you will determine the time and the place that you see your relative. Thank you very much.

The words were no sooner spoken than the place erupted. People streamed out of the buildings, while those already outside turned in their tracks and rushed towards the pavilion. Some dashed into buildings and ran out carrying squalling children. All around me, sheer pandemonium. I watched in disbelief.

Meanwhile, the rallying call of God boomed down from above:

Everyone to the pavilion. Right now. Leave whatever you are doing. Everyone is to come immediately. This is an emergency. Everyone to the pavilion, please. This is your father.

I too turned in my tracks and followed the crowd. This I could not miss.

Long, straggling lines of jostling people had built up outside the pavilion, like lines of ants at the entrance to a nest with all the ants scrambling to get through the single entrance at once. Two armed guards stood overseeing the process. Miranda hurried back from wherever she'd been, escorting a crowd of latecomers.

I joined one of the queues and inched forward with the others. My eyes, meanwhile, scanned the crowds for Lucy; I had to speak to her. She was nowhere to be seen. The loudspeakers by now were silent, the uproar replaced by an eerie calm as people fell into their lines and shuffled forward. I could hear whispered conversations around me:

'You know what's going on?'

'No idea.'

At last I reached the door, the last in my own queue. The one guard whose name I knew, the giant guard named Bruno Grimm, stood there surrounded by his three dogs. The dogs snarled as I came close; could they sense that I was an outsider? Bruno raised a hand as I tried to enter.

'Not you. Only members of the community. You go back to your room.'

I shrugged, and walked away, but not to my room. I hid behind a nearby building, and once everyone had entered and the doors closed, I stealthily looked out. The lines had disappeared; everyone was in the pavilion. One guard still patrolled, but his back was turned to me. I darted forward, around to the back of the pavilion, and there I crouched beneath an open window. I could not see, but I could definitely hear.

After a few moments shuffling noises from inside and a low collective moan told me that Jones had entered the building. He'd be on the dais at the front of the room, flanked by Moira and others of importance. His voice, when it finally came – over an internal loudspeaker, this time – was composed:

'Children, children. The time has come, the invasion is imminent.'

Another low moan, this time much louder.

'Don't be afraid, my children. This is the time for you to show the strength of People's Temple, to show your loyalty. The invasion this time is not with guns. It is with hostile racists, one hostile racist congressman. Congressman Ryan.'

Again, the moan.

'This name has haunted us for the past few weeks and now the reality of his coming is upon us. Remember who this man is. He is a racist CIA investigator. A host of people will accompany him. Several journalists.'

A few individual angry shouts rose up. After a while, Jones spoke again:

'Remember this: you do not speak to any journalists if they ask you aggressive questions. You will say that Jonestown is a happy place, a paradise. That is all you will say. Any personal questions, you answer with "no comment". Is that understood?'

Shouts of 'Yes, Dad!' and 'Of course, Dad!' rose from the crowd.

'Furthermore, Congressman Ryan is bringing some of your relatives. Your relatives will want to speak to you, so listen carefully: you do not want to see *any* relative accompanied by *any* congressman. You do not want to see any relative that you have not requested to see, and you will determine the time and the place that you see your relative. Thank you very much. What's that, Moira?'

A minute or two of silence followed. I risked a peep, raising my head above the lower ledge of the window. I could see him clearly above the heads of the crowd. Moira leaned in towards him, whispering.

Jones turned back to the mike he held in his hand. I crouched down again.

'Apparently there are names of other enemies seeking to join this antagonistic group of invaders. I have requested Moira to collect these names as fast as we can, so that they can be blocked from entering the community. They will be blocked from any kind of entry, illegal entry. We will protect you, my children. You are safe. We'll have to be very alert at night. Security, do you hear this?'

Scattered cries of 'Yes!' and 'Yes, Dad!'

'Your relatives are your enemies. They are still enemies if they've spoken against People's Temple and Jonestown. You know from your mail whether they have spoken against you. We must move quickly, because the hour can approach tomorrow or the next day. This tactical manoeuvre of the fascists can take place any time now and so we will be prepared.'

The crowd stirred audibly, shifting in their seats, murmuring among themselves. One man shouted: 'Who's coming, Dad?'

'Who? We do not know more than I've just said. You can help us fill the list. The President of this country, Mr Burnham, is my personal friend. The Foreign Minister wants to know the names of all people hostile to People's Temple. All those hostile to Jim Jones and the truth that I stand for. Beware of traitors. They are everywhere and will be dealt with appropriately. We will not tolerate traitors in this community. As soon as you become aware of a traitor I expect you to report him or her to one of the leaders immediately. I will not tolerate any single one of you talking bad about Jonestown to any of these hostile invaders. Traitors will be punished severely. Do you hear me?'

At that moment I felt a poke in the middle of my back. I swung round to find the barrel of a rifle pointing straight at me. At the other end of the rifle stood Bruno. At his feet the three dogs snarled and grovelled.

'Get up.'

'I was just—'

'Get up, I said.'

I shrugged and scrambled to my feet.

'Get away from that window. Hands up.'

I did as I was told.

'OK. Now get lost, get away from there. I don't want to see you around here again.'

I walked away with as much nonchalance as I could muster. Would he report me to Moira? I thought not. What had I done wrong, after all? As far as she knew I was friendly to Jonestown. I was just doing what journalists do, gathering information. Investigating. However, those words of Jones, *traitors will be punished severely*, echoed in my mind; I remembered that Lucy had said the same thing. The punishment for betrayal, she'd said, was ten days in the Box. Did that apply to me, an outsider? If I got Jones in a bad mood, then, I thought, nothing was impossible. I resolved to be more careful.

But then again, I thought, maybe by tomorrow Jonestown would be no more. The impact of Ryan's coming was more than I'd expected – but could one congressman, with one visit, work such a miracle? Maybe I could help.

I brought to mind the faces of those I'd spoken to in the pavilion. The pleading eyes, once they thought they were alone with me, unobserved. The surreptitious glances, the silent cries for help. *We all want out*, Lucy had said, *but we can't say it aloud*. But there's strength in numbers. What if, once Ryan was inside the compound, everybody, in one strong block, spoke up? What could Jim Jones and Moira and their cronies do? All they needed was encouragement. What Jonestown needed was a revolt. Maybe *that* was my true mission here: to stir up that revolt. My heart beat faster.

Once more I headed for the hospital, and this time I arrived there without interruption. I peeked into the wards as I walked by: some of the beds were still occupied, but fewer, it seemed, than the day before. No doubt all those who could walk had gone to the meeting. I reached Alexis's room and entered. Her back was turned towards the door, so I walked round the bed and stepped into the aisle between it and the next one. I regarded her face; it was serene, eyes closed. Had last night's trick not worked?

'Alexis!' I whispered. 'Are you awake?'

Her eyes fluttered open. 'Oh, hi!' She smiled and raised

herself up on one elbow. She reached for my hand, and I gave it to her.

'So it worked!' I said.

'Even better than we'd planned!'

'What d'you mean?'

'Look behind you.'

I did so. The woman in the next bed, the woman I'd first thought was Lucy, was staring at me and smiling. She too raised herself up.

'Hi,' she whispered, 'I'm Louisa!'

'I told Louisa about our plan,' Alexis said, 'and she's joining us. If you don't mind, that is.'

'Oh, but...'

Of course, Alexis would not yet know about Congressman Ryan. In a few sentences I related the latest developments.

'So, you see, there's no need to escape at all. Ryan'll take you out. Anyone who wants to leave. I know that from reliable sources. That's what he's coming here for – to take home anyone who wants to leave. That means you, and Lucy and her son, and her grandma, and you too, Alexis. And Louisa. It's all over – he's on his way now! Maybe you'll all be in Georgetown tonight!'

Even before I'd finished speaking Alexis's face had fallen into a slump. I looked at Louisa, and it was the same. My words had brought them no joy.

'So you're backing out? You won't help us?'

'I don't *need* to, Alexis. Don't look so anxious. It's all OK; this is great news, fantastic! All we have to do is spread the word. You all tell Ryan you want to leave, and he'll take you. Just walk out. What can Jones and Moira do?'

'You don't know Jonestown, Zoe. It just won't happen.'

'It will! I'm sure it will!'

'Trust me, it won't. You know how many times we've thought we could walk out, just like that? Whenever people from the Embassy come up, we get all excited. The first couple of times I was sure I'd be able to leave. I tried to speak to that guy – what's his name?'

'Rex Bennett?' My heart constricted at the name, and a wellspring of feeling rose up in me. I pushed it down again.

'Yeah, Bennett. That's the guy. Nice guy, but he believes the lies. You don't know how well People's Temple people can act, Zoe. All those cries of *Yes, Father*, all that cheerleading – it's all an act, but they do it well and they'll do it for Ryan.'

'But I don't understand – why? If they want to leave, why can't they?'

'Ah, Zoe. How can I tell you? The dynamics of this place – nobody outside can understand. To you it seems so easy. You don't know just how much he owns these people – yes, owns them, body, mind and soul. They're completely brainwashed. He got them when they were most vulnerable, when they were down and out, poor and alone and in trouble. He was kind to them when they needed kindness. He took their trust, and then robbed them of everything else so that all that's left for them is that trust. They don't dare betray that trust. They're good people, but they're so good, they'd rather die than betray the man who saved them.'

'But saved them – from what?'

'From the misery of their lives. From the struggle, the daily fight for survival in America. He took all that from them. They won't betray him. And from his point of view, it's all about power. That's all he wants. Power. Control. He hungers for it, he thrives on it. He'll do anything to keep it. Even the ultimate. He really will. You just don't understand – you can't.'

'The ultimate? You mean...?'

Alexis nodded. 'Sure. He'll kill to retain power. What d'you think White Night is all about?'

White Night. There was that phrase again. I said nothing.

'White Night. You heard about White Night?'

'Isn't that some kind of – suicide ritual?'

She nodded. 'He makes us drink poison. Pretend poison, of course, but we don't know it's pretend – we think it's real.'

'And that's some kind of – loyalty test?'

She nodded again. Her eyes now were grave and immensely sad. 'Yep. The ultimate loyalty test. The ultimate control: *are you prepared to die for me, of your own free will? Do I have the power over a thousand lives?*'

'But that's just play-acting, Alexis. In real life it wouldn't happen.'

'For us it is real life, and it does happen. I've seen it happen, Zoe. Christ – I've done it. I drank it. I thought it was poison, and I drank it! I thought it would kill me, and I drank it!'

Tears welled in her eyes. I looked at Louisa, and she too was crying, silently. She dabbed at her eyes with the sheet. Alexis did the same with the sleeve of her nightdress.

'The man's a psychopath,' I said.

Alexis shook her head.

'No, a sociopath,' she said. 'There's a slight difference. A psychopath is more or less born that way; the kink in his mind comes from *inside*. A sociopath develops. Circumstances mould him to what he is. Jim Jones wasn't always a nutcase. I knew him way back when. Since I was a kid, in fact. I mean, do you know this man's story? He was one of the first leaders to speak out against racism, and not just that, to do something about it. The first white preacher to allow Blacks into his church. He was on our side. A good man, with good ideas.'

'But what went wrong?'

'Too much power. All that adulation, focused on himself. I'm not really religious but even I would say he used to be a man of God. As if he was an instrument of good, of God. Doing God's work on earth, a servant of God. The trouble started when he started to *be* God in his own mind. God in person. Guess he just couldn't stand being the servant and rose up to be the master. What you get is a God-sized ego. Megalomania. That spells trouble.'

'But don't people notice? Why don't they just rebel? I mean, he's outnumbered by about nine hundred to one!'

Alexis shrugged. 'You got to be inside to understand. You first saw him when he was already far gone. These people have known him, like, from way back when. It's like he's got them in his fangs. He caught them through love and made them dependent on him. It's hard to break that kind of dependency. Even abused and neglected children grow up to love their parents. Don't condemn us, Zoe. It's more complex than you think, and unless you were in our shoes, you can't understand. Look, I'm pretty sensible, aren't I? And yet it took years for even me to see through him. I saw the weird things he was saying and doing but I excused him, again and again. And let myself be manipulated. See, I believed in the dream. I wanted a socialist paradise too, and that's what he promised. I wanted to make it come true, so I closed my eyes to what was really happening. I took on all the hardship, all the weirdness, just as things I had to live with.

'Discipline – you need that. Too much laxness and people get wishy-washy, no backbone. So, in a way I *liked* the tough regime, the starvation rations, the hard work. I felt it made us strong. Then one day he stepped over the line and the bubble burst. About six weeks ago. It took me a few years, but six weeks ago I woke up.'

She fell silent. I waited for her to continue, but she didn't. Her eyes gazed into the far-off distance, telling me nothing. I couldn't bear it.

'What happened?' I prompted.

Alexis slowly turned to look at Louisa. She reached out a hand to her, and Louisa took it. The two women looked long and deep into each other's eyes. Louisa gave way first. Her bottom lip trembled; she closed her eyes, then withdrew her hand, flung herself belly-down onto the bed and dug her face into the pillow. Her body heaved and shook with uncontrolled sobbing. Alexis's dry-eyed gaze fixed once more on the darkness behind me. When she spoke at last her voice too was dry, devoid of any emotion.

'White Night is a test. It's the ultimate loyalty test, the ultimate proof of his power. And it's a manhood ritual. A demonstration of control, of power. And because it's a manhood ritual, of course, he has to have a woman.'

She was silent. I let her words sink in, ruminated over what they could mean.

'You're saying...?'

She nodded and looked straight at me. 'He chooses a woman, a beautiful one, one he's never had before. Preferably young, a virgin. Why d'you think he insists on celibacy? Why d'you think he tells us all men are homosexuals, that he's the only real man, blah blah blah, and that all women secretly crave just him? It's supposed to be the ultimate privilege. So, he picks one of us for the last grand stand – what an honour! She has to spend her last hour pleasing him. He's had girls as young as fourteen. Six weeks ago, it was me; I was the oldest virgin in the community. More recently, Louisa. Most women give in to him without protest. They either believe him or are too scared to defy him. Louisa and I defied him. We fought. He won anyway. See what we got for our efforts.'

A single tear swelled in the corner of her left eye. She did not bother to wipe it away, but let it grow until it plopped away and ran down her cheek. Then without warning, sadness exploded into rage. It flashed in her eyes, rabid and raw. She almost spat the next words.

'I was dumb. I fought wrong. That was my chance! I should've fucked the rotting brains out of him and just when he'd got his head back in ecstasy, I should've grabbed his neck and...'

She demonstrated, hands like talons snatching at an imaginary neck, squeezing it tight, her face a mask of loathing.

'Instead – he raped me.'

She looked up, her eyes full of unmasked pain. 'That's when I flipped out. I began having attacks, screaming attacks, panic attacks, seizures. That's when she – Moira – began to drug me. A tranquilizer, called alprazolam. It worked. Kind of turned me into a zombie. Since then, she kept me here. Drugged. Just like she wants to drug us all. Kill us all.'

Then she relaxed, dropped her hands in resignation, closed her eyes for just a moment only to open them again immediately and fix them on me, and now there was no more anguish, no more rage, only pleading. She reached out for my hand and squeezed it with such urgency it hurt.

'Stop this madness, Zoe. You've got to! Put an end to it! You cannot imagine it. I've seen mothers put a cup they thought was poison to their children's lips and make them drink. I've seen them take that cup themselves. I've seen them all do it, all nine hundred-odd. If you don't stop it now, it will happen – for real!'

'But – how can I stop it?'

'Talk to this congressman, this Ryan. Tell him everything. Tell him not to leave before he's closed down Jonestown completely and evacuated every single one of us and Jim Jones is locked up for the madman he is, and Moira too. Tell him it's an emergency. Tell him our lives are at stake, all of our lives. It's up to you, Zoe; it's up to you to save us.'

As if the effort had cost her the last shreds of her energy she let go of my hand and fell back on the bed, her eyes closed. Her lips moved as if she were praying. Perhaps she was. The sound of distant chattering drifted in through the open window; the meeting was over. I stood up and walked to the door, all my optimism swept away by those last words: *It's up to you to save us.* The responsibility was too heavy to bear.

CHAPTER THIRTY-FIVE

I felt like an animal set free from a cage and not knowing what to do with its freedom. Yesterday I had been the focus of all the attention, the guest of honour; with all eyes on me I'd been as much a Jonestown captive as anyone, with Miranda my constant shadow.

Ryan's imminent arrival changed all that. I walked across Jonestown on my own and nobody looked at me, nobody cared. The very air buzzed with tension. People scurried here and there like ants in distress. Anxiety was etched into the passing faces, and even panic. What were they so afraid of? It didn't make sense. If they were here against their will, as Lucy and Alexis both insisted, surely they'd be happy, relieved? Surely they'd regard Ryan as their saviour?

A woman crossed my path. I recognised her from the group meeting. I raked my memory for her name: Gladys. That was it. I called after her:

'Hello, Gladys? Just one moment, please.'

She stopped and stared at me, frowning a moment at the interruption, then nodding reluctantly.

'Yes?'

'What's going on? Why is everyone so excited?'
'Haven't you heard? Congressman Ryan is coming!'
'Yes, but...'
'Those fascist pigs – why can't they leave us alone? We're not hurting anyone. Why do they want to destroy Jonestown?'
'Why do you think he wants to destroy Jonestown?'
'See, capitalist America don't like to see its own citizens living in peace and harmony. They want to bring us back and arrest us. Put us all in prison.'
'But that's ridiculous! Of course they won't put you in prison!'
'Whose side you on anyway? Are you one of them? Huh? Listen, if you ain't heard those guns in the jungle out there, you don't know one thing. They got us circled, they been watching us for months now.'
'Who's been watching you?'
'The CIA. The American government. The enemy. Listen, lady, I'm sorry, I forgot your name, I can't talk any more, I gotta go now. See you.'
'Wait a minute, Gladys, just one more question: do you know where...'

But she was gone, leaving me to stare after her. I shrugged and continued on my way. I had to find Lucy. I had no idea where she lived, and only a vague idea where she worked – on the fields, now. Obviously, that was some kind of a demotion, a punishment. Had the field workers returned to their field, wherever that was? It seemed possible; surely Jonestown would want to appear normal.

I stopped another woman. 'Excuse me, do you know Lucy?'
'Lucy who? We got several Lucys here.'
'Sparks. Lucy Sparks. She used to buy rice.'
'Lucy Sparks? She'll be out in the field, I guess.'
'Where's the field?'
The woman gestured vaguely into the distance. 'Over there.

'Scuse me, I gotta be going.' And she too rushed off, leaving me alone to decide – should I run off to find Lucy in the field, or stay to meet Ryan?

The wail of a siren made the decision for me: Ryan had arrived.

Several people walked towards the gate. I joined them. As we trooped along the walkway I reached forward and touched the arm of the woman in front of me.

'Excuse me – may I have a word with you?' I asked. She turned and looked at me. No recognition flickered in her eyes, so I said, 'Zoe Quint – I'm a visiting journalist. My visit has been approved. I'm wondering if we could talk for a few minutes.'

Her lips pursed into a silent no, and she shook her head and hurried forward. I quickened my step to walk beside her.

'I just want to know – if you had the chance to leave Jonestown, today, with Congressman Ryan, would you go?'

Her chin stiffened, and she walked on without speaking or even turning to me. I tried again: 'Congressman Ryan says he'll take anyone out of here who wants to go. Would you consider going?'

She stopped then, and turned to face me, and in her eyes raw zeal flared, fierce and unmitigated, like the blue glare of a fluorescent lamp. Her lips parted and she muttered something I could not hear.

'I beg your pardon?'

She frowned, raised her forefinger, pointed it first up to the sky then down to me, a parent reprimanding a child.

'Thou shall not tempt the Lord thy God!' She turned and hurried forward to rejoin her group. I followed at a distance.

Several such groups of people had gathered at the gates, just as they swung open and a line of Jeeps drove in. I stood apart, watching, and realised that I had entered a theatre of the bizarre.

The Jeeps stopped and passengers spilled out, men whose pale faces and smart clothes, wide-brimmed hats and dark shades identified them as newly arrived from colder climes. One man left them and walked forward, his right hand raised as if to say, 'I'm me.' It was obviously Congressman Leo Ryan.

A cheer rose up from the waiting crowds. People were walking towards us from all corners. People waved, some flapped handkerchiefs, several clapped, including the woman I had just spoken to. I looked at the faces, and all were smiling, every trace of fear and anxiety wiped away. If I hadn't seen the transformation with my own eyes I would never have believed that this joy and exuberance was anything but genuine.

Moira stepped forward from a shiny-eyed group of Jonestown leaders, beaming with such joy I thought she'd clasp Ryan in her arms. Instead, she wrapped his outstretched hand in both her own. Her voice rang with enthusiasm.

'Welcome to Jonestown, Congressman Ryan! We're delighted to have you. These are my colleagues, Joanna, Miranda, Rhonda, Stewart, Brian...'

Ryan's face had transformed before my very eyes. As he'd left the Jeep, it was stern and brooding; when he heard the cheers, and his own name called, he broke into a wide smile, and waved back. Now he walked forward to greet Moira, hand held out to take hers. Joanna, Miranda, Rhonda, Stewart, Brian and the rest of the pack, all wearing broad smiles, stepped forward after Moira. Ryan shook hands with them all, and a moment later he melted into a human cushion of welcome and warmth. The rest of his party approached, likewise to be folded into the collective embrace.

Moira glanced away, towards us onlookers. Her pasted-on smile morphed into a scowl. She flicked her hand in dismissal and mouthed: *Go!* Immediately, people turned to leave. I alone remained standing, watching.

The introductions over, Moira spoke again: 'Come this way, Congressman Ryan. I'm going to show you around myself.' She gestured him forward. His group followed. The lieutenants dispersed. Now it was my turn. I stepped up and introduced myself.

Moira shot me a look of utter disapproval; this was not part of her schedule. I was not part of her plan. She had most likely forgotten my existence in the excitement of preparing for Ryan, and now there was little she could do. She turned to Ryan.

'Congressman Ryan, Zoe's a Guyanese journalist, spending some time with us.'

The congressman and I shook hands.

'Very pleased to meet you,' I said, and added quickly, 'Do you mind if I join your group?'

'Not at all,' he replied, and I ignored Moira's frown of displeasure and fell into place behind him.

The tour of Jonestown was identical to my own yesterday. We walked from building to building, escorted by Moira and a few other women, greeted everywhere by an enthusiasm and delight that would have melted a stone's heart. I understood, now, Rex Bennett's scepticism in the face of my fears. If this was the reception he'd been subjected to... well, no wonder.

Rex. At the thought of him, again my heart constricted. He'd betrayed me. I could hardly grasp it.

No, I corrected myself. He hadn't betrayed me, exactly. I'd never have been allowed into Jonestown, had he done so. He'd betrayed *Lucy*, and somehow kept my name out of it. But that was bad enough. It demonstrated utter disregard for me; but then again, hadn't I felt it, right from the beginning? Hadn't I told Donna I didn't quite trust Rex? I had known – and I was right – that Rex kept secrets from me, and I'd paid him back in kind: I had kept my own secrets. Now I knew that I'd been right to do so.

I snapped out of my ruminations – I'd heard the propaganda too recently to be paying much attention to the tour – when Miranda came rushing up, grabbed hold of Moira's elbow and drew her aside. This was the chance I'd been waiting for.

With two swift steps I was at Ryan's side.

'Mr Ryan, I don't know if...' I began, then started again. 'I'm a friend of Rex Bennett's? Did he ever mention me?'

Knowing what I now did of Rex I could well imagine that he'd lied to me. Had he ever mentioned me to Ryan?

'Ah, yes, I remember... the journalist. He said you might have some inside information.'

'That's right. And it's urgent. It's not what it appears to be here. Jones is dangerous. Really dangerous. You've got to stop it. Break up the whole community. Get them out – all of them. Now.'

'There's not much I can do. Everyone I've spoken to up to now insists they're happy here... that they're here voluntarily. I can't force them to leave.'

'Don't believe it. He's got half of them brainwashed, and the other half too scared to peep. I've spoken to people, heard the true story. Listen...'

I gave a brief and hurried account of what I'd learned from Lucy. I told him about White Night, how Alexis feared that it would happen again, but for real, and how Jones had raped her. As I spoke, I kept glancing up to make sure we were still alone, and we were: Miranda's issue, it seemed, was complex. She was still speaking with some animation to Moira.

When I'd finished speaking Ryan said, 'Zoe, you've told me nothing new. I've heard of these threats of suicide and these White Night rituals, and I do take them seriously – but what can I do? My hands are tied as long as they all declare themselves to be here voluntarily. Nevertheless, nobody is to be kept here against their will. Go and tell your Lucy: if she wants to, she can leave, but it has to be *today*, with me. I leave here at 5 p.m. Tell her to be at the gate at that time. And anyone else who wants to leave.'

'I'll find her. And I bet I can find hundreds more who want to leave.'

'I can't take hundreds with me now. I'll take a few, and if there are more, I'll arrange for planes to come and collect them tomorrow. Can you get the word out?'

'Wonderful! I'll do that.'

I ran off, my heart pounding in excitement. A plan began to take form in my mind, and the first step was to find Lucy. I stopped a passer-by and asked directions to the field. She pointed the way beyond the vegetable gardens. I set off.

Soon I'd left Jonestown behind me and found myself alone on a rough path that led through a stretch of wasteland, dotted with tree stumps and covered with a tangled mass of razor grass. At my feet I could see that the rich brown earth was tipped with black, like a light sprinkling of spray paint. The forest here had been cleared, then burned, I realised, to make way for farmland.

I marched for almost half an hour in the broiling sun; on either side, beyond the wasteland, the thick green walls of the forest rose hundreds of feet high. Jonestown might be expansive, but it was nonetheless a prison, and those trees were the walls.

Finally, I came upon the field. Here, the wasteland was being prepared for agriculture, ploughed by human hands. About fifty young people, bandanas tied tight round their heads, toiled with pitchforks, hoes, spades and rakes: they were digging into the earth, turning it over, raking it smooth. Again, I was reminded of slavery – except that a few of these 'slaves' were white, this overseer was Black, and he carried not a whip but a rifle slung across his shoulder.

When he saw me, he stopped his strolling and walked up.

'What d'you want here?'

'I've come to talk to Lucy. Is she here? I've got a message for her.'

'A message from whom?'

'From Moira,' I lied.

'Lucy!' the guard yelled at the top of his voice. The ranks of labourers rippled, and from their midst a young woman emerged and walked towards us, a cutlass in her hand. Yes – it was Lucy.

Her eyes bulged in fear when she recognised me, but she managed to hide her shock. Ignoring me completely, she looked up at the guard.

'What is it?'

'This woman got a message from Moira.'

Lucy turned to me, warning in her eyes. To the guard, I said, 'It's private.'

He turned and walked away a few steps. I took Lucy's arm and led her away.

'You shouldn't have come here! You'll get me into trouble! I'm not supposed to know you!' she whispered fiercely, even before I could speak.

'Shut up and listen! Ryan's getting you out, you and everyone who wants to leave. You've got to be at the entrance gate at five.'

Her voice rose in an irritable squeal. 'How you expect me to do that?! They gon' kill me first! How I gotta get my boy and my granma, and I'm not leavin' without them!'

'Just don't worry about it. I'll help. They can't do much while Ryan's here; they're all on their best behaviour. We've got to brazen it out.'

'What you mean, brazen it out?'

'It means just that. Just do it. At four thirty you get back to Jonestown, get your people together, and get to the gate.'

'He ain't gonna let me go nowhere.' She jabbed her thumb towards the guard, who stood several feet away, watching us.

'Tell him Moira sent for you.'

'He ain't gonna believe me.'

'I'll tell him for you, right now. Don't worry, just come. What's he going to do, shoot you from behind? Just tell him you have to go, and go. We have to bluff this through.'

Before she could offer more objections I left her standing there and walked up to the guard.

'Moira wants Lucy to return to the pavilion later today. She's to be there at four thirty,' I told him with as much authority as I could muster. 'On the dot,' I added. That sounded like something Moira would say.

'How I gon' know when it's time to leave?'

I felt like slapping Lucy; her whining voice was enough to give the game away.

'Here, take my watch,' I said. I unstrapped it and laid it round her wrist. Her forearm in my hands was skin-and-bones thin, like a child's, and marred with mosquito bites, fresh ones and the scars of old, scratched ones.

'Leave here at four,' I repeated as I buckled the watch. To the guard, I said, 'It's very important. Make sure she's on time.'

'How come Moira sent *you*?' he asked, quite logically.

Why me, indeed.

'Ask her yourself when you see her. I don't know.'

With that, I turned my back and began the long march back.

The first thing I saw as I re-entered Jonestown was the open-walled hut where they did the laundry. Several older women worked there. I walked over to them.

'Hello,' I said as they looked up, 'Just in case any of you want to leave, you can. Congressman Ryan says he'll take anyone out who wants to go, and if you all want to go, he'll send more planes up for you tomorrow. Just be at the gate at five.'

The women stared at me, speechless. Suspicion drew across their eyes, mingled with hope, and doubt. They exchanged surreptitious glances, and I could almost hear their thoughts: *this is a set-up. A trick.* I couldn't be trusted; I'd write them up. I was a spy, out to catch the traitors.

Nobody said a word. They stood before me transfixed, twists of laundry in their hands, staring as if I were an apparition, so I chuckled and said, 'It's true. Trust me, don't be afraid. The more of you that turn up, the better it'll be for you all. If you want to leave, just be there on time. Let Ryan see you. Let him know. There's power in numbers.'

They still did not react, so I turned and walked away, towards the kitchen. I'd been hatching this plan all the way back from the field, and the more I thought about it, the more I was convinced it would work. Get the word out. Let the Jonestown residents know they could leave. Speak to them all, tell them, spread the good news. If they all turned up at the gate at five, hundreds of them, what could Moira possibly do?

On my way to the kitchen I passed by the hospital, so I stopped and walked over there instead, up the short flight of stairs and on to the veranda. There I stopped: the door to the staffroom was open. I edged myself along the wall until I could peek inside. A nurse sat at a table, sideways to me, preparing medicines. I flitted past the doorway and down to the end of the veranda. Alexis's door was open. I slipped inside. As usual, Alexis lay with her back to the door. So did Louisa. If I had not known the truth I could have sworn they were both fast asleep.

'Alexis!' I whispered, 'It's me, Zoe.'

I sank down on to the floor between the two beds.

'Hi!' she said, half rising on one elbow. 'What's going on?'

I told her. 'When the time comes, just get up and walk out. You and Louisa. Just walk to the gate. They can't stop you.

They wouldn't dare – Ryan's here, I'm going around telling everyone. What I want is a mass revolt.'

'That's dangerous, Zoe. Nothing infuriates Father so much as disobedience. If you start openly stirring up trouble…'

'But what can he do?' I asked. 'Not a thing! If people simply walk over to Ryan openly and say they want to leave, what the hell can Moira and Father or whatever you want to call him do? Nothing! The guards are hardly going to start shooting, watched by ten American journalists and a congressman! It's time to brazen it out.'

'It'll never work. People are too scared. It's dangerous.'

'No. Look, Ryan told me personally that anyone who wants to leave can leave, at 5 p.m. Be there at that time, with Louisa, if she wants to come. Trust me, it's going to work. Have you got a watch?'

'Of course not. But not to worry. At four thirty I get my afternoon meds; I'll come after that. I hope you're right.'

She took my hand, and I squeezed it. We hugged each other for courage, then I slipped back onto the veranda and, as stealthily as I'd arrived, out of the building.

To the east, just behind the dining hall and next to the kitchen, was a large area, covered but open-sided, where old women prepared food. Some plucked the pebbles from heaps of rice, others cut vegetables, some stamped cassava and yet others shaped out rounds of cassava bread. It was a busy place, full of people, a nice nucleus for a rebellion. I walked from one workstation to the next and delivered my little speech: 'Come to the gate at five. Everyone can leave. You can be free, today. Just come. All of you; there's strength in numbers.'

I pleaded with them, waved the flag of freedom in their faces. I put passion into my words; I begged and cajoled them to come, to rebel, to flee while they could. The only reaction was dumbfounded faces, and silence. I began to despair. Could it be that they really didn't want to leave? That in some perverse way they were really happy here, and Lucy the exception? What did those stony faces mean?

I came nearer to the answer in the kitchen itself. Here, about ten women were engaged in baking the cassava bread for the next day's breakfast: laying the flat round pancakes out on baking trays, shoving them into the stone oven, removing the finished bread and stacking the crisp warm rounds in boxes for the next day. They looked up and smiled as I entered, the same fake smile pasted on for the benefit of visitors. I tried a different tactic this time: less passion, more intimate calm, as if I knew their hearts.

'Look,' I said, 'I know many of you want to leave. Today you can. Just turn up at the gate at five. Show Ryan and the visitors the strength of your resolve. Don't worry about a thing. Don't be afraid, just turn up.'

Here too the same reaction: no answer, just blank stares and nervous glances to the left and right. 'Don't be afraid,' I repeated. 'In numbers you are stronger. You know you want to leave. You know it. And you can.'

I looked straight into the eyes of the woman nearest me, and saw, or so I thought, a brief nod and a flicker of hope in her eyes. I smiled at her to encourage her, but she did not smile back; instead, she glanced at another, older woman who stood with a tray of unbaked cassava bread in her hands. This was obviously their crew leader, for all eyes now moved from me to her.

And from her, finally, came the end result of all my afternoon's work. From her lips came the Jonestown verdict, the words every one of them no doubt thought but none expressed, because expressing them would douse the one glimmer of hope in their souls:

'Girl, you gotta be crazy.'

Those words broke the spell. A murmur of agreement rippled through the kitchen and as though at the breaking of Sleeping Beauty's spell the women began to move again, ignoring me as if I'd never spoken. I saw a few rolling eyes. I was a mirage, a false prophet; they turned from me as from a lunatic.

I drooped internally. It had all been in vain. I'd hoped to start a mass rebellion, and for my efforts I'd earned only ridicule.

I turned to walk back to my cabin. It didn't matter, I told myself. Lucy and Alexis and Louisa will surely be there at five, Lucy's child, and her grandma; if those were the only ones to leave then I'd done my bit, and I could leave too. My Jonestown episode was coming to a close. Tonight, I'd be telling Aunt and Uncle all about it. Tomorrow, I could start writing my article. It was supposed to be a scoop but even I had lost faith in my mission by now. I was exhausted, and sick of it all. I'd done my best and achieved my objective: Lucy was leaving. I could go home. If the others chose to stay, well, that was their problem.

The heat from the ovens and all that walking in the hot sun had left me thirsty, so I walked over to my cabin; I'd left my water bottle there, now more than half-empty. I drank a capful of tepid water, then removed my sweat-drenched T-shirt, put on my last clean one.

As I pulled the hem down over my jeans, the cabin door opened and closed. Someone had entered. I swung round: it was Moira.

We faced each other. All semblance of amity had vanished from her eyes, replaced by such blank loathing my blood ran cold. For the very first time I recognised that Lucy and Alexis were right: Moira was dangerous. Her eyes bored into me like steel lances; her lips were a line hardly visible. Finally, they moved. She spoke:

'So, so... Our little guest has decided to play God.'

Her voice was little more than a whisper, unemotional and calm. She could have been discussing the weather, were it not for those terrible eyes.

'Come with me.'

I had no choice. Her eyes held me as tightly as a rope round my wrists. What was it about this woman that even her voice could command obedience? I began to understand the mechanics of Jonestown. No matter how strong we think ourselves, there's always a chink in the armour; and someone of Moira's ilk has an innate instinct for those chinks, knows how to slither their way in. I followed her out of the cabin, down the steps to the walkway. Two young guards appeared from nowhere and fell into step beside me. We walked towards Jim Jones's house and for the first time since entering Jonestown, I felt afraid.

'Don't try to run,' said the guard at my left hand. As if I could possibly escape that grip.

Five minutes later, I was back in Jones's office. I stood before him a prisoner, immovable between the two guards, my wrists still held tight. Jones sat behind his desk. He said nothing, but I could almost smell the smoke of rage emanating from him. I was in the presence of a volcano about to erupt.

He nodded to the chair opposite him. The guards led me over to it and I sat down. The door behind me opened and closed and soft footsteps approached. A hand descended on my shoulder and gripped it in a talon hold. I knew that grip without looking: Moira.

Jones glowered at me from across the desk. His speechlessness only seemed to fuel the mounting wrath visible in the pulsing of a vein at his temple and in the beads of sweat along his upper lip, palpable in the throbbing air around him. I could hardly bear to look at him, yet his stare held me transfixed, drawing my eyes to his as to a magnet. I realised for the very first time the soul-draining power of his personality, the malignant force that seeped from him and wrapped itself around the minds of all those within his orbit. I felt my hastily rallied defiance wither in the sheer heat of his madness. The silence swelled, and finally exploded.

'I knew it!' he bellowed. 'I was right all along. You damned liar, you spy! Who sent you here?'

I could not answer. My throat felt like sandpaper. My brain was as empty of words as a stone. I felt Moira's fingers dig into my shoulder.

'Answer him,' she snarled.

But I could not.

'Fucking CIA spy! You fucking crazy whore, you come here as a spy full of your fucking bullshit, talking about being a journalist and shit and all you want is to spy and disrupt! We trusted you and you abused that trust!'

He picked up a paperweight from his desk – one of those glass things with a snow scene inside – and I thought he'd dash it at me. Instead he hurled it at the wall, where it bounced against the wood and fell to the floor. Sweat poured down his hairline, down his neck and under his shirt collar.

'Stand up, you!'

What was it in his voice that forced obedience? I did not even think. I stood up. Moira's hand left my shoulder and grabbed my right wrist. The woman was strong; she twisted my arm behind my back and held it there.

'You and that fool Lucy! The two of you, she's the worst traitor ever to set foot in Jonestown, another fucking whore.'

Lucy's name shocked my brain awake. So this all had to do with her. In the short time since I'd been out to her in the fields, word must have filtered down to Jones. But how? Surely there hadn't been time. His next words, though, corrected this assessment:

'You think you can trick me? Running to the US Embassy with your stories? How come you CIA spies can't trust your own people, huh? You know why? Because I'm bigger, that's why! My eyes are everywhere! Omniscient, omnipotent, that's me.'

I felt sick to my stomach. My knees felt weak, as if they

would collapse under my weight. I got it now; this had to do with my American Embassy fiasco. It had to do with Rex, and his betrayal. Perhaps he had talked some more since yesterday; perhaps he'd kept my name out of it at first and then, under pressure, he'd told the whole truth. That I was the missing link, a spy.

Jones ranted on. 'You know what we do with fucking traitors here?' he bellowed. 'We hang the men up by the nuts, that's what we do, and we teach the women a lesson they never forget. Trouble with you fucking whores, you never had a real man, that's why you do all this whoring around.'

I stared at him without reaction.

'You never had a real man, and you know how I know that? Because I'm the only real man walking this earth. All other men are fucking queers. I never have no problems with women; they know a man when they see one. I know how to tame women!'

A volley of crazed giggles broke from him. He could hardly contain himself; he doubled over his desk, convulsed with the giggling, and spittle foamed in the corners of his mouth. His hand shook with the force of his giggles. He reached for a glass of pills, shook a few into his palm, then poured himself a glass of water with shaking hands. He brought the glass to his loose and flapping lips for a sip. The water splashed about inside the glass, slopping over the edge. He leaned back and tossed half the water down his throat. Without warning, he spat into the glass and flung the remaining contents at me. The water sloshed against my face and ran down to my shoulders, where my T-shirt quickly absorbed it.

Jones looked past me to Moira.

'Take her away. Punish her. I'll deal with her later.'

CHAPTER THIRTY-SIX

Moira led the way outside. She signalled to the two guards who had escorted me here, and they closed in on me. She looked at her watch.

'Zoe, you've caused me a huge headache. This mutiny you tried to instigate – it's wasted a lot of my time, and now it's time for our esteemed visitors to leave. Perhaps you'd like to come along and watch the hordes of Jonestown residents clamouring to leave with them?'

I said nothing. The giant held me by my wrist, twisted up behind my back. Moira took the other guard aside and whispered to him. He nodded and returned to my side.

'Come along then. Let's go.'

We set off towards the main gate, single file, Moira in the lead. I walked behind her, followed by the giant. He had let go of my wrist, but I was acutely aware of the pistol hanging at his side. If I made a run for it, would he dare to shoot, with Ryan still in the compound? I'd been so sure he wouldn't, but now all bets were off. These people were crazy. There was no telling what they'd do. For the first time I realised that there was no logic to anything Jim Jones would do. The man was dangerous beyond anything I could have imagined. I did not run. I followed, meekly, my mind racing with a thousand possibilities.

We rounded the last corner. The line of vehicles stood ready to leave, each with its driver at the wheel. A farewell ceremony was in session, almost an exact replica of the welcome ceremony but in reverse. Ryan walked down the line of lieutenants, shaking hands. He smiled, they smiled; all were satisfied. Little groups of Jonestown residents stood around watching, beaming in complete joy, all ready to cheer and wave goodbye.

The journalists and relatives who had accompanied Ryan stood apart and among them I noticed a few Jonestown residents, perhaps seven in all, easily recognisable by their bedraggled clothing and the petrified expressions on their faces, guilt and relief and sheer disbelief frozen into masks, nervously twisting their fingers and shuffling on their calloused feet.

Lucy was not among them. Neither was Alexis or Louisa.

I'd imagined, hoped for, an uprising. I'd envisioned hundreds of Jonestown rebels converging on the gate at five, a congregation of deserters grown strong through numbers. I'd planned sedition. This, then, was the end result of all my efforts: a handful of frightened absconders, all reduced to jelly by their terror.

Most of all, where was Lucy, with her grandma and her boy; where was Alexis, with Louise? Bitterness filled me, as I realised: pouring courage into Lucy and Alexis had been water into sand, for in the end they'd lost their nerve.

Moira tossed me a glacial look before stepping forward, hand held out, to Ryan.

'I do hope you have enjoyed your visit here. As you can see, we are a simple group, but happy, and all we want is to be left in peace.'

'I have to say, I've been pleasantly surprised,' said Ryan. He gestured towards the waiting group. 'As you can see, a few of you have decided to leave.'

'They are welcome to do so,' Moira said. I could not see her face, for I stood behind her, but the gaiety in her voice told me that a crooked-toothed smile played on her lips. She flung out a hand to include the larger groups of Jonestownians standing around. 'In fact, everyone is free to leave. You may all go, right now. Anyone else want to go? Back to America?'

This was their chance. They could do it. En masse, they could make a stand for freedom. They had the choice; and I knew that in their secret hearts this was what they wanted. At the word 'America' a collective shudder rippled through their ranks, and a sigh of longing shivered through the dense moist air. I held my breath, waiting for the stampede.

What came was silence.

Then one of them, at the front, shook her head and smiled her broadest smile, giving the others the cue. 'No way!' murmured this brave soul, and the others took up the refrain. 'Nope, not me.' 'I ain't goin nowhere.' 'Me neither.'

'Is everyone happy to stay?' Moira's rallying cry rang out like a revivalist preacher's chant, and the resounding echo came clear and loud and carried on a rising wave of zeal: 'Ye-e-e-e-s!'

Traitors! Turncoats! Cowards! Contempt filled me, immediately transformed into rage. Among these people were women I had personally spoken to, encouraged to speak up. Women I knew wanted to go, for I had read the yearning in their eyes, the unmistakable plea of 'Take me away!' written in their faces the moment they thought themselves unwatched.

And Lucy and Alexis: still missing. They could have come forward and left with me, right now, but had obviously opted to stay. No doubt they thought I would too, and we'd stick with the original escape plan. But why on earth should I? Why stay here and help them further, if they could not be responsible for themselves? If Lucy and Alexis could not take the tiny risk of stepping forward now, then how would they cope with the far greater risk of escaping through the jungle? And why risk my own life for a bunch of chickens? I'd done my best, and it was over. I was going to leave Jonestown with Ryan, and that would be the end of the adventure.

But that decision left a bitter aftertaste. I hated failure. I'd put so much effort into this. Why, why, why? Why couldn't Lucy and Alexis and all these people just step forward now, as one, and say, 'Take me away!' loud and clear for Ryan to hear? What on earth could happen if they did?

A moment later I knew.

Ryan spotted me behind Moira and walked up, smiling.

'Zoe! I was wondering where you'd run off to. I thought you said you'd leave with us?'

My mouth opened to speak. 'I'm coming,' I wanted to say. But in the split second before I uttered a word I glanced up at Moira and caught her eye, and a dagger of pure clear ice plunged through me. Death looked out at me from those eyes. Cold, merciless death. She threw a quick and knowing glance to the guard standing right behind me.

Simultaneously, I felt the hard circle of a pistol's barrel thrust against the small of my back.

And finally, I woke up. The silence of that cold hard little ring pressing tight against my back like a finger of death spoke louder than all of Lucy's wild hysterics and Alexis's clear warnings, louder than the pleas in Gladys's eyes and the evidence of my own eyes. Louder than the guards with guns, the barbed-wire fence, the chained gate, the snarling dog, the silent giant, Alexis drugged into oblivion, and Jim Jones's mad rantings. All this, even added up, had been, up to now, a game for me, a challenge, a test of wits. I'd worn a veil: the illusion of my own role as heroine, she who would save the day, lead these poor victims out of bondage and set them free; write a dramatic story, and help to close down a cult. My veil lifted.

I'd failed, and dismally: I'd made it all worse, probably for everyone but most definitely for myself. I too was a prisoner. They could not let me go with Ryan. I knew too much. I had their secrets, and would expose them if I left.

I felt sick. In spite of the afternoon heat my skin turned to gooseflesh. I looked up, and beyond the watching throngs I glimpsed the line of guards, arms crossed, legs apart. We were encircled. And I knew for certain: one false move and whoever held that gun behind me would shoot, and shoot to kill, me first.

Not even Kuanan's skill could help me here. Kung fu – or at least, my level of training – was useless against that pistol in my back.

I also knew that once they killed me, they would kill Ryan; they'd have to. Moira's eyes told me they wouldn't hesitate to do so. And once they killed Ryan, they'd kill the rest of his group. And once they'd done that…

All of this I knew in the split second before thought, swifter than the time it takes to tell it. This was the Jonestown secret, the key to their blind obedience. This was in truth a death camp. The madman at its centre had one agenda, and that was carnage. It was only a matter of time. Mass murder, mass suicide were no empty threats but the very core of its existence. Right now, I stood in that heart of darkness, poised to make the ultimate decision.

I found my voice and finished my sentence.

'I think I'll stay just a little while longer,' I said to Congressman Ryan. 'But thank you. Have a safe journey home. My regards to Rex Bennett.'

CHAPTER THIRTY-SEVEN

The Ryan party drove off. The crowds dispersed, leaving behind Moira, at least fifteen guards, and me in the middle of them all. Moira signalled to Bruno the giant with a jerk of her chin. He lowered the gun and stepped aside. I breathed out. Every muscle in my body, which had been taut as twisted rope, relaxed.

The fifteen-odd guards closed in around Moira; Bruno stayed at my side. She was giving them some instructions. Finally, the huddle broke apart; most of them walked over to the flatbed truck parked just inside the compound gates. Only one sentry remained, and Bruno. Moira whispered a few words to Bruno; he looked at me, stepped over and gestured with his pistol: 'Walk,' that movement said. I obeyed. The second guard followed.

We marched past the pavilion to the outer ring of buildings and up to what looked like an outhouse, built, unlike the other cabins, on the ground, and windowless. The first guard opened the door; the giant shoved me inside.

I found myself in a tiny room, perfectly empty except for a trapdoor in the floor. The first guard bent over and opened it.

Beneath was a black pit. I knew what this was: the Box. A ladder, vertical against the near wall, led down into it.

'I'm not going down there!' I whispered.

But there was to be no argument. Bruno stuck his gun into its holster and before I could catch my breath, he grabbed my legs from under me. The other guard grabbed my upper body, and as I writhed and kicked and cried they wrapped their arms round me, twisted me to the ground, and pushed me down so that I sat at the hole's concrete rim. I braced my legs against the opposite wall, but Bruno leaned over and wrestled them away while the other guard, cursing, pushed my upper body forward. I screamed, and clawed at him to prevent my fall, but he grabbed both my wrists and held my arms aloft.

Bruno drew his gun and pointed it at me, then gestured to the ladder. I knew he'd shoot. I stopped fighting and climbed down.

The hole was big enough to hold a grown man standing, well over six feet deep and four feet square. Reaching up, I could just touch its upper rim.

'Please!' I cried, 'Don't!' but even as I said the words I knew how futile they were.

They hoisted up the ladder. The trapdoor banged shut. Wooden bolts scraped shut across it. My knees gave way and I sank to the slab of concrete at the bottom of the Box.

An hour or so after my incarceration in the Box, another drama was playing out not too far away. A convoy of vehicles arrived at the Port Kaituma airstrip and parked just outside the tiny office. Congressman Ryan and his party emerged from the vehicles; stiff from the long, bouncing drive through the jungle, they stretched their arms and flexed their legs. The Jonestown deserters were smiling now, relieved that their ordeal was over. A few of them approached Ryan to thank him once again.

It was time to leave. The sun slid down behind the forest roof in a blaze of tangerine sky; it would be night before they arrived in Georgetown. Ryan walked over to the waiting plane, the ragged group following him.

The flatbed truck rolled out from the jungle track. Ryan stopped, turned, looked back.

Ten men in black leapt from the truck's flat bed. They raised their rifles, aimed, and shot.

The staccato crack of gunfire tore into the jungle's evening hush. Four men fell. Others, screaming, raced towards the jungle's edge and merged into the blackness waiting there. Others ran for the nearest plane; some fell as they ran. They scrambled up the stairs and entered amid a volley of flying bullets. The plane taxied down the runway, bullets ricocheting off its fuselage. It rose up into the darkening sky.

The men in black jumped back into the truck; it turned a wide circle and disappeared back into the jungle whence it came. Five still bodies remained in the silence of the jungle night, like abandoned sacks of rice. Among them, Congressman Ryan.

In the orange sky above, a vulture circled.

PART FOUR
WHITE NIGHT

18th November 1978

CHAPTER THIRTY-EIGHT

My knees buckled and I sank to the ground, my back against the concrete wall. Blackness enclosed me in a cold, damp shroud. Only my own breathing and the hammering of my heart broke the silence, and only my own terror kept me company: that, and the acrid stench of stale excreta.

An eternity passed. I tried to keep track of time by counting my breaths, and this effort calmed me, but eventually I lost count and had to start from the beginning. *Six counts in. Six counts hold. Six counts out. Increase to eight counts in. Eight counts hold. Eight counts out...*

My heartbeat fell into the rhythm. Its wild racing slowed into a steady beat and little by little, my terror dissolved into coherent thought. Not many thoughts: just one. I had to get out of here. I stood up, stretching out my hands to feel the boundaries of my prison.

The Box was high and narrow. My hands patted nothing but rough concrete; without the ladder I would never reach the trapdoor. This was a prison with no way out.

I remembered what Lucy and Alexis had told me: people were kept in here for up to ten days. No wonder the stench was so intense. I wondered about the technicalities of feeding and excretion for someone kept prisoner here for that long; I figured there must be some exchange of slop pails and food buckets. Perhaps these were lifted in and out by ropes. The thought brought on the realisation that I could do with a slop pail myself; I'd had a pee on the way back from the fields, but that was how long ago? I had no idea. I'd have to hold it in until someone outside remembered me. How long would that be? What if they forgot me altogether? I was hungry and thirsty, too, and desperately missed my water bottle. Would they bring food and drink, and when?

Or had I been left here to die? Wild terror gripped me. *No, No! Not here! I don't want to die in here! Rex, save me, Rex!*

And then again rational thought returned to me. They couldn't. They must know that my relatives would look for me, the Guyana government would look for me. Congressman Ryan would say he'd seen me. Keeping me here too long would certainly provoke an investigation, and they must know that. No, they wouldn't let me die. But the full ten days? Or even less?

I sobbed. I could not last even a night in here. Not even an hour longer. The Box would be my own grave. I sank back to the ground and huddled there, hugging my knees, floored by despair.

I began to pray. *Help me, Lord, oh help.*

I'd never been religious, and in fact in the last three years I'd been profoundly irreligious, tragedy flinging me far away from faith. Now, lacking all means of helping myself and without hope of rescue, lacking everything except inner words and inner worlds, I floundered in the vacuum of myself, groping and grasping at fleeting thoughts. Finally, from some deep cavern within, I stumbled against long-forgotten verses drummed into me two decades ago, memorised prayers dismissed as empty formula.

Now they returned to me as if etched into my soul and laid there latent, coated with the rust of the passing years. In desperation I snatched at them, and their rust fell away, and there they were again, complete and whole, vibrant and powerful, stronger by far than my fears. The Lord's Prayer. Psalm 23. Over and over again they rang in my heart, until the words dug into my being and I clung to them as a drowning man clings to a rope. *Yea, though I walk through the valley of the shadow of death, I will fear no evil...*

Again, I lost track of time, but this time round I did not mind for I had the company of living words; even the darkness was no threat, for my eyes were closed and my heart quiet.

I relaxed and leaned back against the wall, arms loosely around my knees, head slightly bent back, my breathing calm and rhythmic, settled in myself at last.

But not for long. A moment later the screech of a siren tore into my newfound pristine peace and ripped it to shreds.

The siren's wail went on forever. There must have been a loudspeaker directly outside the Box, for it was so deafening I stuck my fingers into my ears. Even then its nerve-fraying, soul-piercing screech reverberated through me till I screamed back at it to stop, stop, STOP.

When it did stop, the silence it left seemed just as deafening, but then that too broke down in sparks of static that themselves gave way to the boom of a most familiar voice.

Children, my dearest children.

The voice was calm. After the frenzy of the siren it came as a soothing balm, and I read sadness into it, and regret, and a promise of something great to come. I held my breath and waited. After what seemed an eternity the voice returned.

Children, this is the night. It has come after all. Our final White Night. The night of our greatest triumph. I want you all to come to the pavilion immediately. Every one of you, even the old and the sick, anyone who can walk. Let us gather together one last time, let us be a family one last time, let us be strong together. Please come now, all of you. Thank you.

Stillness. Then muffled sounds rose in the darkness: excited voices, footsteps, now and then a child's cry and a mother's admonishment to stop. I knew well what was going on. I remembered from the previous assembly, only hours ago – though it felt like days. I could imagine the people streaming from the buildings, all headed towards the centre, like flies to the hub of a spider's web. That's what Jonestown is, I thought. Sick at heart. A web of lies and deceit and death, with the big fat spider of Jones at its rotten core, sitting there waiting to gobble up his prey.

And me? I thought. What about me? Have I been forgotten? I remembered to pray; it was the only thing that held my panic at bay. I imagined starving to death down here, forgotten by the world. I squeezed my eyes shut. *Help me, Lord, oh help.*

No sooner had I thought the words than a bolt grated, and a hinge squeaked; a moment later, footsteps thumped right above my head. More bolts scraped back, and the trapdoor creaked open. The blackness of my hole diffused to grey, and a beam of light shone down to me, and a ladder appeared from above, and a disembodied voice spoke down from the greyness: 'Come out of there. Quickly, now.'

I needed no urging. I climbed the ladder. When I reached the top, a strong hand closed over my wrist, and pulled me to one side, away from the trapdoor. I could see little, but I realised that there were two men in the room, one of them holding a torch, its beam trained on me.

'Don't struggle, or you go right back down there,' said the

man who held me, now at both wrists. It was guard Number Two. I did not struggle. More than anything, I loathed that Box.

Bruno stood, legs akimbo, arms crossed, waiting for me as I emerged from the Box. Number Two closed the trapdoor, then turned the beam to the wall, where in its moving spotlight I could see various tools and gadgets hanging. He found what he wanted and turned back to me. A moment later I felt a rope being bound round my wrists.

'Follow me,' said Number Two, and led me from the Box like a dog on a lead. I did not mind; every step away from the Box seemed a step away from hell. Bruno followed.

As we walked into the night I inhaled deeply. After the stench and narrow confines of the Box, fresh air felt like the ultimate luxury. I forgot the guards and the guns and the madman's voice in my ears and only cried in silence, *thank you*: for space and air and light, even the light of night.

But the moment of celebration passed with that one breath. Bruno pushed me forward and I stumbled on the edge of the walkway. He kicked at me with a heavy army boot and, when I scrambled to get up, kicked again.

Number Two handed the rope to Bruno, and he kicked me forward.

We were not the only ones on the move. All around us, people streamed forward. Old women limped along, some in twos, supporting each other. Mothers carried bawling babies – ripped from their cradles, no doubt. Some fathers carried older children on their shoulders. Still older children gripped the hands of their parents and hurried to keep up. Above them, a disembodied voice bellowed encouragement:

White Night. White Night is upon us. Everyone to the pavilion. No time to lose. Everyone to come. Come, my children, come to me.

We joined the stream of flowing humans and fell into step. A few people looked down at the rope that held me, and then at Bruno. A few frowned at the sight, looked up to meet my eyes, but quickly looked away again. I tried to read those faces but could not. Over the last day I'd seen a variety of emotions flicker across the Jonestown faces, if only for a second. But today these faces were blank, like empty picture frames. Whatever thoughts crossed the minds behind them stayed hidden from me.

We reached the pavilion. At its entrance Moira stood monitoring the orderly entry of Jonestown's thousands; as there was only the one door, congestion was inevitable, and several Inner Circle members intervened to hold some people back, allow others to enter, organise the crowd into single files that flowed smoothly forward. Moira looked up, saw me and walked up.

'Hello, Zoe! Did you enjoy yourself?' She spoke gaily, as if welcoming me back from a holiday.

I bit my lip, said nothing, and looked at her feet. She was wearing scuffed white pumps.

'I thought you'd like to know what's going on, and what your own schedule will be,' she continued, her voice still casual. 'Are you listening?'

I said nothing.

'Are you listening?' she screeched. Bruno kicked my shins. I looked up at Moira and nodded.

'Look at me when I speak to you!'

I glared at her, but she didn't like that either.

'Look at me *respectfully*!'

Quick as a whip, her hand flew out and slashed me across the cheek. She wore a ring, and it caught my lip. I tried to lift my hand to touch it, forgetting the rope round my wrists. Bruno wrapped the loose end of the rope several times around his hand and pulled my hands back down. I licked away the trickle of blood from my bottom lip and folded it into my mouth. I purged my mind of defiance and looked at Moira as artlessly as I could.

'That's better. You may now be wondering why we've let you go. We could have left you there in that Box forever, you know, let you slowly rot away in there. It'd have been a long time before anybody found your body. But we changed our minds. We have plans for you. Congratulations, Zoe: you shall live.'

At those words relief flooded through me. It was OK. I would live. I'd be free.

Moira flashed a cheery smile, like a teacher applauding a child for a well-written essay.

'We have two tasks for you this night. I don't know how much you know of the Jonestown mystique, but you are about to witness a thing of honour, unheard of in the history of mankind. You are about to witness an event that has never before taken place on earth. An oppressed people are about to make the ultimate stand against their oppressors.

'The world will never forget this night. It is the climax of Father's life on earth. Father's only disappointment, on our practice runs, is that we have no witnesses. Nobody to take note of our courage and determination, nobody to report it to the world. We have made tapes, but tapes can lie. We want a witness and, dear Zoe, that witness will be you. *Look at me!*'

I had dropped my eyes again, unable to bear the chill of her unflinching gaze. I looked up and her eyes hooked into mine in a stare stripped bare of all sensation. Hers were the eyes of a mannequin: flat and dead; only the occasional blink reminded me that they were human.

'Yes, Zoe. We all know what a talented writer you are. In fact, you tricked your way into Jonestown with that talent. You are a filthy spy, come here to disrupt and disturb the peace of the world's most advanced society. Like everyone else, you want to pull us back into your primitive dog-eat-dog way of life.

You should be severely punished. Instead, we are going to reward you. This night, dear Zoe, is going to be the scoop of your lifetime. You alone shall witness Jonestown's glory and live to tell the tale. Father wants that tale told, and he wants *you* to tell it. He wants *you* to record the incredible bravery and determination of our people and tell it to the world. Our sacrifice shall serve as a beacon to oppressed people everywhere, for all time: never be afraid! Jonestown shall live on in history, and Father will go down as the greatest leader the world has ever known. And you are our scribe. Tomorrow, they will find our bodies; but you will write of how we all faced death with courage and fortitude. You will tell the story of the greatest revolution of all time. Our revolutionary suicide is our legacy to the world.'

She paused.

'But that is not all. Father has a second privilege in store for you, a more private, personal one. It's up to you if you want to make *that* known to the world.'

I shuddered at those worlds. A cold, clammy panic filled my body and my brain. A fear of something perhaps worse, even, than the Box.

She looked at her watch.

'In about an hour's time, after you've witnessed enough of our White Night, Bruno will take you to Father. Once you are there, Father will explain what he wants you to do. Don't worry, it's something I'm sure you'll enjoy. All women do. Father has chosen you as his last female companion on earth. Don't look so shocked. It's an honour. Yes, we know you are damaged goods; Father is willing to overlook that flaw because of the important role you will be playing as our only witness. Bruno, you will take her over to Father at about...' She looked at her watch. 'At about ten o'clock. It's five past eight now. In two hours' time. Is that clear?'

Bruno grunted and nodded.

'Good. Now take her inside; everyone's there already. I'm going to call Father over so we can start.'

She nodded curtly, and strode off.

Bruno pushed me into the pavilion. The atmosphere was electric, buzzing with the sound of almost a thousand people whispering to each other in excitement. The rows of benches were filled right up to the back, with several standing. In spite of the half-open sides the air was close and malodorous from almost a thousand unwashed bodies packed together. I could hardly breathe. Inside me, the panic filled every atom of my body. I shivered with it. In my helplessness I offered up a prayer: *Help! Help me, Lord! Don't let this happen!* But it *was* happening, and all I could do was watch.

Since there was no sitting room, Bruno made me stand at the back of the room. His hand gripped my upper arm so tightly I feared he was cutting off the blood flow; my right hand began to feel numb. I flinched, but he only tightened his grasp. Jonestown inmates glanced at us, looked down at my tied wrists, and glanced away again. Nobody seemed surprised to see me a prisoner. By now, I supposed, they were used to everything. Life in Jonestown had been stripped of surprise.

All at once a *shhh* reverberated through the crowd and the buzz gave way to an expectant hush. Above the heads of the seated people five figures walked across the dais to sit down upon five empty chairs at the front. Jim Jones, assisted by Moira, took the middle chair.

The crowd broke into cheers and clapping. It lasted at least five minutes, sinking and swelling, finally dying as Jones raised a hand for silence. Still seated, he drew the microphone nearer, coughed, and spoke.

'My children. My dearest.' His voice was hoarse and rasping. He cleared his throat and began again.

'My darling children. We are all together and united at this, our greatest hour, the hour of our... of our...' He coughed, looked at Moira as if struggling for the right word. Moira's lips moved, and Jones finished. '...the hour of our greatest triumph. Congressman Ryan is a traitor. He wants to fly back to Georgetown to report us to the CIA. Now what's going to happen here in a matter of a few minutes is that one of those people on that plane is gonna – gonna shoot the pilot. I know that. I didn't plan it, but I know it's going to happen. They're gonna shoot that pilot, and down comes that plane into the jungle. And we had better not have any of our children left when it's over, because they'll parachute in here on us. I'm going to be just as plain as I know how to tell you. I've never lied to you. I never have lied to you. I know that's what's gonna happen. That's what he intends to do, and he will do it. He'll do it.'

I gasped in shock. They were going to shoot down the plane? Was he lying? My heart thumped so loudly I could hear it myself. I held my breath.

'Yes, it is true. That rat is going to lie dead on the jungle floor and so are his cronies. They are lying dead on the jungle floor even now. We have punished him. But now the United States government is going to be after us. They'll want revenge. They are going to kill us all tonight, and those they don't kill, they will take captive. Listen and you will hear them, hidden in the jungle, all around us, waiting to attack. Just listen.'

Everyone listened. Only a baby murmured somewhere among them, and somebody coughed, to be silenced with an indignant '*Shhh!*'

And then we heard it, in the distance, muffled as if absorbed by the foliage: the pop-pop-pop of distant gunfire. Jones nodded and raised his right hand; at that cue the crowd erupted into the vulgar hissing of a thousand mocking tongues.

'We will not be moved!' cried Jones, and as one voice the crowd broke into song:

'We will not, we will not be moved!'

They sang one verse, then Jones signalled them to stop. His voice rang out again:

'Long live the revolution!'

The crowd cheered.

'We will show the world that we will stand up to forces of evil even unto death!'

The crowd cheered louder.

'Long live the glory of revolutionary suicide!'

The crowd went wild.

When the cheering died down, Jones spoke again, and this time his voice was calm and assured:

'My dear children, I am so proud of you. And now I want you to come forward, one by one, and make your political statement of revolutionary suicide. This is our message to the world, our record for posterity; we also have one living enemy reporter among us who will sally forth and tell the world of our greatness. For all time we, the People's Temple, will live on in history as a community so mighty, so united, not even the greatest Satan on earth, which is the United States government with its CIA pigs, could crush it. Let the world know that we choose *death above oppression*!'

Wild cheering broke out. He'd thrown a spell over his people; they were his, completely and absolutely, one mind, one soul. On the two occasions I'd had a private audience with him the man had been obviously mentally ill, but tonight that lunacy seemed sane, legitimised through the crowd's adoration. This was charisma in action, the crowd's collective mind bent in unity with his.

'The People's Temple will be renowned for ever more!' he bellowed. 'And Jim Jones revered as a mighty leader whose people remained loyal to the end! Who will be the first to speak? Who will tell the world why we have come to this final solution to all the oppression we have been subjected to?'

Scuffling and coughing broke out near the front of the room.

Jones and Moira whispered among themselves. A man walked up on the dais and spoke into the mike, loud and confident:

'My name is Luke Templeton, and I am a member of this beautiful family of People's Temple. This night I will commit revolutionary suicide to show the world that I would rather *die* than give up the great ideals set forth by our pastor, Jim Jones.' The crowd cheered. Luke paused, waited for the cheering to die, then continued:

'...we've come to a decision that we would rather *die* than to *live* on this earth because there is nowhere else we can *go*. There is nowhere else that would *suit* the purposes of the beautiful teachings and the life that we have that we built here in Jonestown. So we would rather commit a *revolutionary* suicide, and if the world is wondering why we took our lives or our babies' or our seniors' lives, this is why.'

Amid cheering and whooping, Luke stepped down. A woman passed him on the steps. I recognised her: she was Gladys, the woman who'd sat next to me at the meeting yesterday. The mike sizzled with static as she touched it and spoke:

'My name is Gladys Harrison, and I'm happy to be here in Jonestown. But I would rather take my life than live on in this world of lies of deception and persecution. Let the world know that we have died for *freedom*!'

'Freedom! Freedom!' cheered the crowd as Gladys stepped down. A man stepped up.

'My name is Joseph Ward. I am a Marxist–Leninist and proud of it, and that's what the world don't like! We're fighting for the rights of the underdog, of the underprivileged people of the world. And we have made the decision to commit revolutionary suicide this night, and we want the world to know why. And the answer is: *freedom*!'

He punched the air with his fist and the crowd did likewise, cheering and whooping. Jones silenced them with a raised hand and said: 'I'd like to hear some of you younger ones speak up.'

More scuffling broke out, and finally, a young girl walked up to the mike.

'My name is Christa Adams, and I am eleven years old.' She stopped.

Jones prompted: 'And are you also prepared to commit revolutionary suicide, Christa?'

Christa's voice was high but clear: 'Yes, Dad. I would rather die than live on in this cruel world.'

'What about us going to another communist nation like uh, Cuba or the Soviet Union?'

'OK, it might be a problem for… for some of us to adjust to other nations like you know they might not be able to understand our ways or our life and… and um… it would… it would just be hard for us… for me to separate from… from… um… from this group, and we wouldn't know the language, and so… So I want to die with all of us together.'

'Thank you, Christa. Anyone else? Michael? What about you?'

Another man stepped up. He seemed less confident than the others, and even from my place at the back I could see that his hand shook. His voice certainly shook.

'I am Michael Kirby, and, uh, we've debated this uh, um, uh, revolutionary suicide many, many times tonight and, uh, tonight is the night, and I have made up my mind that this is the way I prefer going, because I have been in this group for uh, almost twenty years now and I have never uh, uh, and we finally came to this decision. I-I-I just… I-I think this is the best way to go.'

And so it continued, into the night. One by one, people stepped up to make their statements. After some twenty had spoken, Jones himself took the mike again. His voice rang out:

'How many in this uh, assembly, feel this by saying, and there's about a thousand people here, how many here feel it by the sounding of a *yeah*?'

The crowd stamped their feet and cheered, extended and loud:

'YEAH!'

'Peace, peace, peace. How many feel it by *nay?*'

Not even a baby whimpered into the silence.

'You're free! We shall die for socialism, for the revolution! The problem is solved! Thank you, my children.'

The crowd cheered as Jones, followed by his four lieutenants, stepped down and walked outside. People began to stand up, and near the front a small child bawled. The crowd, restless and excited, began to push towards the doors. Bruno nudged me to walk towards the door, but I couldn't because a throng had gathered before me. Finally, Moira walked up to the mike again, and an uneasy silence fell.

'Please calm down. You know the routine. Please don't push. Everyone will have their turn. You will line up at the door, mothers and children first, and walk out in an orderly fashion. Please don't cause a stampede.'

Those who could returned to their benches and sat down. A straggling line formed near the door. Bruno pushed me forward again, a firm hold on my wrists tied behind my back. I edged forward, and the ragged crowd parted to let us pass by. As we left the pavilion I breathed in thankfully. The air inside had been so stuffy I'd felt almost faint, and now the fresh air made me dizzy. My head swirled. I felt as if I were in a dream, that I would wake up in a minute and rub my eyes. But this was no dream. Not even a nightmare. *This is not happening*, I repeated to myself. But indeed, it was.

On the porch outside two trolleys had been wheeled up. On them stood enormous metal vats filled with a dark liquid. I shuddered. I knew what was in there. I recognised the women from the kitchen, who now took charge, pushing the first people into a straight line.

'Now, everybody line up nice and quiet and when I say so,

you come forward. You, Peggy, control your child, stop him crying. Marlene, where do you think you're going?'

One woman, holding a toddler, had tried to slink off into the night. A guard materialised from nowhere and pushed her back into line. She began to sob. Taking the cue from his mother, the toddler screamed.

'Disgraceful! Traitor!' The cook shook her head in amazement. She picked up a ladle and a paper cup. She poured one ladle of the purple liquid into the cup, handing it to the first person in the line, a mother with a small child about five years old.

'Give it to him first, and then you,' said the cook. 'Go on, baby, you'll like it, it's sweet. Drink the Kool-Aid.'

I watched, horrified, as the mother placed the cup to the lips of her child. The child drank. The mother held out the cup for a refill. She drank herself. She took her child by the hand and wandered off. Sickness rose up in me. I wanted to vomit, but I couldn't; my stomach was empty. There'd been no dinner tonight. The sickness turned into a dread that seeped through every cell of my body.

One by one, the women and children moved forward, took their cups, and walked off. It was agonising to watch. I longed to run away but couldn't, for Bruno's massive hand held my two wrists in a vice.

Forced to stand there, I tried to turn my eyes away, but even that was beyond me, for they were glued to the vat and the movement of the cook's ladle: into the vat, out, pouring the purple juice into a cup. In, out, in, out. The cup held to a child's lips, or a mother's. The line slowly moving forward, inching on, the victims obediently sipping their last drink, stumbling off into the night. I tried to cry out, but it came out as a croak. I leaned forward and dry-retched. Bruno yanked me upright. My knees gave way, and I sank in a half-faint. I wept inwardly.

At that moment the loudspeaker just above my head crackled. A familiar voice boomed out into the night:

Children, my beloved children. Our night of glory is upon us! Tonight, we show the world: People's Temple is triumphant! Greater than Satan! They have us surrounded! Did they think they could march in here and People's Temple would stand there with their hands up in surrender? What a joke!

A volley of giggles followed, cries of 'Right!'

And so it continued. On and on, that hysterical voice, that crazed laughter. The same recorded words, over and over again, the voice stumbling at the same places, leaving the same gaps, giggling at the same intervals, that high-pitched, frenzied cackle, grating as nails down a blackboard, and all the while his people shuffled forward to take their poison. I was stiff with horror, cold with revulsion, yet dripping wet with sweat. Transfixed by abomination, I could only watch.

...they will come here tomorrow and find us and know that we were strong, that we held together to the end, were – were united, up to the end!

Out of the night a tall, cool figure loomed: Moira. She came up to us and, ignoring me, spoke to Bruno.

'Father will see her now,' she said.

Bruno nodded and pulled me away. Moira fell into step beside me.

CHAPTER THIRTY-NINE

Bruno shoved me into Jones's bedroom, so that I landed on the floor at his feet. I looked up at him. He seemed to be waiting for me, for he sat in a chair in the middle of the room, facing the door. Compared to all the other rooms I had seen in Jonestown, this one was pure luxury, and yet it was still simple: the main piece of furniture was a double bed covered with a pure white, fluffy counterpane, jutting into the centre of the room like a shrine. In the far corner a small table was laid as if for a romantic dinner for two: plates, knives, napkins, two candles, a rose in a vase, wine glasses and a carafe of red liquid. It could be wine – or it could be the same stuff that was in the vats outside. He himself sat on a low armchair, plush red like an artefact from a brothel, pushed against the foot of the bed, one arm resting casually on the armrest, one ankle resting on the other knee. He leaned forward as I tumbled to his feet, and his rubbery lips spread in a wide grin.

'Zoe. Hello, my little darling!' he said.

Through the open window the loudspeaker bellowed:

'...deadly weapons I mean, surrounded us in the jungle, what could we do? Helpless victims! Those fascist pigs – those, fa-fascists! Hunted us down like so much prey, like animals, helpless animals! And send their spies in...

I scrambled to rise to my feet, but it was difficult with my wrists tied behind my back, and I slumped back to the ground.

'Sweetheart, would you like some help? Bruno, what are you standing there for? Help her up!'

Bruno bent down and yanked me to my feet.

'Easy now, not so rough, Bruno, this is my beloved. You know that, don't you, darling? Ever since you set eyes on me you must have known. All women lust for me. Don't fight it, darling.'

I said nothing, but stood before him, head bowed.

'Look at me!' he yelled. He jumped to his feet and stood, hardly two feet away from me. I lifted my head and looked at him with all the defiance I could gather.

'So, Zoe darling, admit your lust for me. You want me, don't you?'

I said nothing, but simply stared. His hand shot out and slapped my cheek. 'Say it! Say yes!'

'No.'

He slapped me again.

'Want me to rough she up a li'l bit, Dad?' Bruno asked. It was the first time I'd heard him speak, and I started at the West Indian lilt. I'd assumed he was American, like all the rest. I couldn't quite place the accent; maybe Jamaican.

'No, no, I want to hear the words voluntarily. She is resisting. She refuses to acknowledge her lust. I need to break down that resistance. Just a few little love-slaps will do it.'

He slapped me again, and again, till my cheek stung and tears – not of pain but of frustration – gathered in my eyes.

'See, you won't admit it even to yourself. Fucking prude!

But listen to me. *Listen,* you hear?' Another slap. 'I'm the only true lover in the world. No other man but me can ever satisfy a woman. I'm every woman's true lover. I'm the Universal Man. All other men but me are faggots. It's not your fault you don't know it yet; you come from the fascist world, you've been brainwashed like all of them. But in truth, you want me. Your sweet little pussy is hungry for me.' He cackled.

As he spoke, he paced the room like a caged tiger. His shoulders drooped, and sweat poured from his temples, and his soaked shirt clung to his body like a second skin. Outside the open window, the eerie voice boomed:

> *...tomorrow People's Temple will go down in the annals of history, a downtrodden, persecuted society who did no worse than live in peace and harmony, and the United States government, they are the ones who drove us to this...*

He circled the room, keeping close to the walls, and as he returned to where I stood, he repeated: 'You lust for me, Zoe; and your resistance is just your pride. I could take you by force but I won't, because I care for you. I love to conquer a woman, to break down her resistance, wrest the admission of hunger from her until she begs and pleads with me for more. I love to see a woman come to the truth, the truth of her lust, her overwhelming hunger for me, to hear her say the precious words: that I am her Universal Lover, the only true man she has ever known. So, Zoe darling, are you ready to admit it? *Look at me!*'

He screamed the last words, because I'd dropped my head again. He was so close that when he spoke, I smelt the putrefaction in his hot moist breath, so foul I knew his innards were rotting away, that beneath the hull of his skin decay spread through his mind and his organs. He raised his hand again, and I flinched from the coming blow; Bruno held me tightly from behind, and Jones's voice changed. It became a crooning plea:

'Zoe, my darling, the moment I set eyes on you I felt your lust. I saw it in your eyes. Pure lust, pure greed for me. But I also saw your resistance. Now you have a unique chance, the chance to be my last lover on this earth, the one I have waited for to share the moment of my greatest glory. Zoe, I have picked you out for everlasting fame. You have made me angry, but only because I hate it when a woman won't admit her lust. It's a lie. I want truth from you. Because I want you to *know*. I want you to recognise how great this moment is, the moment when you and I join in ecstasy. And then I want you to tell the world. That is your role here tonight: to tell the world of my greatness and my power. I will die and you will live; you, the last witness of my greatness. I want you to live beyond this night to tell the world what happened. I must die and you must live. It is a great privilege. I am prepared to die, die with all my children. My last wish on this earth is to hear those words from your lips: that you want me. I want your admission. I want you to want to die with me, in revolutionary suicide. I want you to confess. Zoe, tell me the words. Tell me you want me. Call me Dad. Admit it. I want to hear those words from your own lips. Say it: "I want you, Dad."'

His hands wandered all over my body. He touched my forehead, let his fingers run round my eyes, down my nose, across my lips, lightly touching. They ran down my shoulders, and to my breasts. He cupped both of them, and squeezed them.

'Ahhhhh...' he said and closed his eyes.

His fingers, stiff plump sausages, wandered down to my hips and probed upwards, under my T-shirt, wet slugs creeping over my bare skin, moving up again towards my breasts. I squirmed in mental agony. He pinched me, hard. I screamed.

'Stop that! Be quiet!' he yelled.

Through the window floated the disembodied voice:

...Our night of glory is upon us. The night of our greatest triumph against the forces of oppression. Tonight, we show the world...

His fingers dug into the soft flesh of my belly and crept further upwards, squeezing, probing. I flinched and struggled, but this time he said nothing. I tried to pull my wrists out of Bruno's hold, but he held me tightly. In fact, he now let go with one hand, pushed his body up against me from behind, and placed one arm round my shoulders. I could feel Bruno hard against me from behind, while Jones's fingers cupped my breasts and began to knead.

'Ooohh,' he moaned. He came closer. Put his arms round me. 'I really want you to want me,' he whispered. His face nudged against me, his moist rubbery lips rubbed my cheek. His voice was hoarse, his breath hot and stinking. I pulled my face away. He drew back immediately and slapped me again.

'Don't do that!' he yelled. 'Don't you know who I am? Don't you know?! I'm Jesus Christ! I'm above Jesus Christ! You fucking little whore, how dare you! I give you this... this privilege, this chance and you... you...'

He choked and staggered away in a violent attack of coughing. He stumbled over to the bedside table and with shaking hands, opened various pill bottles. Still coughing, he shook random amounts of coloured pills into one cupped hand – several fell to the floor – poured himself a glass of water from the jug, swallowed it all down. This seemed to help immediately.

He turned to me again.

'Zoe,' he said. His voice had changed again. Now it was soothing, soft. 'I think you'll be more comfortable on the bed. Bring her here, Bruno. I wish I could free you from those ropes. I don't want to force you. I want you to open your eyes, realise who I am. I want you to adore me like all the other women. I want your adoration, Zoe. I want to see you as a great big fucking she-tiger giving in to your lust for me. Come on. You don't realise... you don't understand. See over there...' He gestured to the table in the corner.

'That's for us. Our last meal. Can you smell the food? It's in the oven keeping warm. Soon, we shall enjoy that meal. Toast each other. See that wine? See those glasses? That's how we'll celebrate. It's a special wine. A very special wine. Special vintage.'

He cackled, and the hairs on the back of my neck stood up. The cackles turned to coughing. He gulped down some more water.

All this time Bruno and I were engaged in a silent struggle, he pushing forward, me backward. He was stronger and won. He pushed me right up to the bed.

'Sit down, darling. Make yourself comfortable. I really wish I could loosen those ropes. I want you to feel at ease with me. But I can't trust you yet. Oh darling, if you would only open up to me. Your mind, your heart, your legs.' Giggling uncontrollably, he lunged across the bed and grabbed my waist.

I clenched my teeth and didn't resist. All this time my thoughts were racing, desperately grabbing at mental straws. I had to be sensible. It was my only chance. If only I could play the game a little, let him believe I was willing, they might untie the rope. I'd have a better chance then. And then I had to get rid of Bruno. I looked around the room, frantic for some weapon, some gadget with which I could overpower Jones once we were alone together. My eyes fell on the fork, and the knife on the table; the wine bottle. But they were too far away. Above the metal bedstead, a dirty cord was fixed to the wall by a loose, rusty nail. Could I grab that, throttle him with it?

And across the room, the open window.

He pushed me down until I was lying beside him. His hands cupped my breasts again, and as he kneaded them, he panted into my face: 'Ooh, my sweet. My darling. Come on now, let me. I like this. I like you. I want you to love me. You will see. I won't hurt you. I'll be so gentle, so kind. You will see that I am the only true lover. I won't take you by force, that is beneath me. I want you to admit it. Admit it. Admit your whole body hungers for me as mine does for you, or do you want another slap to help you?'

He pulled me to him and nuzzled up to me, moaning into my shoulder, nibbling and kneading. I let him. Bruno had let go of me, but I knew he stood behind me, watching, pistol ready.

I have to get rid of Bruno.

I no longer resisted. My mind raced full tilt into a plan... but could I do it? Could I persuade Jones that I wanted him, that I would give myself to him once Bruno left the room? And then...

Alexis's words came back to me: *'I should've fucked the brains out of him, and then...'*

That was what I had to do. It was my only chance.

Once the ropes were off and Bruno had left the room I could pounce.

The options ticked through my mind in rapid succession. He'd be naked, which made it easier. Knock his head against the iron bedstead. Make of my hand a blade of bone aimed at his windpipe, grab it and yank it out. Stab at his eyes. Smash in his Adam's apple, claw at it, rip it out. Or that soft space just beneath the ribs. Grab him round the neck with my legs, grab his balls, twist them away. Kick his groin.

If I could get him off the bed, more options opened up. I'd have weapons. Grab the fork, or the knife, or the wine bottle. Crack the bottle over his head. The methods Kuanan had taught me, kicks and blows that could knock out a man twice my size.

Or else: Rex's three-shot combination, groin, head, neck. And all the other moves he had taught me, in those three days on the beach in Georgetown. *Rex. Rex, oh Rex, tell me what to do, show me, be with me now. I need you.* It was almost a prayer.

My knees and hands, legs and feet, and elbows: my whole body would turn into a lethal weapon loaded with the flame of my loathing. My mind raced, my heart hammered as the possibilities rose before me. There was no way to plan this, I had to play it by ear. Only the moment would tell me what to do, and I had to live totally in the moment, totally focused, totally alert, and act as the moment demanded, as Kuanan had taught me. As Rex had shown me. The moment had come to practise all I'd learned.

I didn't have to kill him. I just had to disable him long enough to make my leap for the window – before he screamed and Bruno charged in. *I must remember to grab my clothes before I go*, I thought, and almost chuckled at the notion. And run for my life.

I felt a great surge of power. I knew I could do it once I got past that first hurdle: overcome my revulsion and loathing. Because that was the worst of all, and the most difficult. I had to play the game. Relax and feign enjoyment enough to convince Jones that I wanted him, the way he believed I did.

All this ran through my mind in a matter of seconds, even as he groped me. His sweating, slimy body nudged and writhed against me, his hands beneath my shirt slid on my own sweat. I cringed and closed my eyes, gritted my teeth.

Consciously, I relaxed my body. He felt it beneath his hands, and his response was immediate.

'Oooh, my sweet darling. That's right. That's nice. Now let me see that lust in your eyes. I need it. Let me see the tiger within you. It's that I want. I can heal you. I can heal you of your resistance and your prudish shit. Open up for me. Come on, open your legs. Take off your clothes and show me. Be my little tiger. My sweet little she-tiger. We can have a perfect night and then I will die and you will live to tell the world, so that the world knows. Look, I will show you how much I trust you. Bruno, untie her.'

He rolled away from me. Obediently, Bruno twisted me round so that my back was to him. I felt him fumble at the rope. It was working!

Jones, meanwhile, stroked my face and groped at my chest under the T-shirt. I let him, gritting my teeth. A small price to pay for the freedom of my hands.

But this was just the start. My mind flailed out in rebellion against what I had to do, and a pleading, whining voice rose from within: *No, no, I can't. Don't make me. Please!*

But a second voice, stiller than the first, not my own and yet more than ever mine, subtle and powerful at once, wormed its way through my lament:

You can. You can do it. Overcome your revulsion, and do it. Tell him you lust for him. Fake that lust. Pleasure him till he falls faint. Do it until you find the right moment – then strike!

My hands fell free. I opened my eyes and looked at the pasty, sweating face, grimacing with lust, panting over me. I reached out one hand and tentatively stroked his face.

'I-I'm beginning to... feel it now,' I said. 'I really feel it, your power. Your manliness. I-I really want to. But – not with *him* watching.' I softened my eyes as I spoke these words, and gestured towards Bruno with my chin.

My hands reached for Jones's top button, nudging it out of its hole. I leaned in closer to him.

'Get rid of Bruno,' I whispered, nibbling his ear. 'Make him leave the room; I can't do it in front of him. Make him go away and I will be your tiger. That's what I really want. What I long for. Please!'

CHAPTER FORTY

Meanwhile, Liz Evans, in Georgetown for a dentist appointment, was at dinner with Patsy Boyle. Patsy, her three children, the seven members of the Jonestown basketball team, and two other women were seated around the table at Patsy's Campbellville home, eating – chow mein, Liz remembered afterwards – when a young woman named Silvia burst into the dining room.

'Patsy, Patsy, come with me to the radio room, it's urgent.'

She ran over to Patsy, bent down and whispered in her ear. Patsy stopped chewing and listened, nodding. Behind her longstanding tan her face turned pale. Around the table all conversation halted, all eyes turned to the two of them. The ticking of the clock above them was the only sound to be heard; even the frogs outside seemed to stop their croaking. It was as if the whole world listened. Seconds later, Patsy dropped her knife and fork. They clattered to the floor. No one picked them up. She audibly gulped down the half-chewed food in her mouth, washed it down with the dregs in her glass, wiped her mouth with a napkin, and stood up briskly.

'I'm going,' she said to Silvia. 'You stay here.'

'What's up, Mom?' Judith asked.

'I'll tell you in a minute, honey. You stay here and finish your meal.'

Silvia took a seat, and now all eyes shifted to her.

'Tell us!' whispered Liz.

Silvia shook her head. 'Patsy will tell us when she returns. Moira has some instructions for her.'

'But are they... are they...?'

Silvia shook her head and poured herself a glass of water. She refused to look at anyone, but Liz caught her eye for a second as she glanced away. What she saw there was blank terror. Liz looked around the table. Everyone was doing the same; not speaking, they looked at each other, into eyes that mirrored their own dread. It was Liz who finally broke the silence.

'It's happening, isn't it, Silvia?'

Silvia only shook her head. She played with the food on her plate, not eating.

'What can we do? Where can we go?' Liz whispered again, but no one answered.

Half an hour ago they had heard over the ham radio that Congressman Ryan was dead, killed by their own people. Since then, radio silence. They were as if turned to stone, waiting for news, for instructions. Nobody had dared to comment or conjecture while Patsy was among them; and now that she had left the room the panic and the questions swelled up within them and spilled out of their eyes, but still they could not talk. The only one among them with any answers kept her eyes on her plate, but something in her stooped posture told them all they needed to know, and the panic swelled but the silence was too strong to break. One of the basketball players spoke:

'It's White Night, isn't it? For real.'

Silvia broke down.

'Yes, yes, it's that. And we have to follow orders. We have to follow Dad's instructions. And I know what Dad's instructions are, Moira's telling Patsy right now.'

'I ain't followin' no orders! I'm goin' home! I ain't got nothin' to do with this! I'm goin'!'

The basketballer jumped to his feet and plunged out into the night. The others fell back into their morose silence. Silvia tried to catch Helen's eye; Helen and she had whispered together earlier and it seemed that Helen might just join her, Silvia, if she decided to make a run for it, but you never could tell. Perhaps Helen, too, was a spy. Finally, their gazes met; but Helen glanced sideways, at Judith, Patsy's eleven-year-old daughter, and pursed her lips as if to say 'hush'.

Liz understood. Judith would tell her mother all that was said; Judith could not be trusted. Everything spoken, and even unspoken signs, would get back to Patsy.

The minutes ticked by. Nobody moved. Their plates sat before them, the food untouched since Patsy had left the room. Even Patsy's youngest child, Freddy, said nothing, though he fidgeted in his chair. At last Mildred, who had cooked the meal, made a move. She began to gather up the plates, scraping the leftovers into a serving bowl. Mildred, who usually spoke non-stop, was as silent as the rest of them.

Patsy's footsteps clattered up the front stairs. The door opened, and she entered. Some people stood up. Liz spoke:

'What's going on, Patsy?'

Patsy's face was whiter than it had ever been. She ignored Liz, ignored them all, but grabbed little Freddy's hand: 'Freddy, Betty, Judith, come with me.'

Surrounded by her three children, she clattered up the stairs to the living quarters. Once again, Liz and the others could only stare at each other and wonder, and nobody said a word.

And then the screaming began. Children's voices, shrieking and yelling, pleading for mercy:

'No, Mom, no, please, no!'

And finally, silence again.

CHAPTER FORTY-ONE

Jones moaned with pleasure. 'Oh, yes, yes, my darling, I know you want me. I know. Touch me. Love me, Zoe. Be my little tiger.'

Inside me, the battle raged on. Under my fingers his face felt hot and greasy, and his writhing body half covered mine. Involuntarily I choked as repugnance washed up and flooded through me. I pulled away my hand. *No!* I screamed silently, and the wave of disgust washed over the quiet voice of reason and it drowned.

Why hadn't he sent Bruno away? As long as Bruno was in the room my hands were as tied as if the ropes still bound them.

A moment later I had the answer: I couldn't. Jones lunged fully on top of me, pressed his mouth to mine and tried to prise open my lips with his tongue. At the same time his left hand grabbed my crotch.

It was a reflex. I writhed and kicked and flung him off me; and because I'd caught him by surprise, he fell away. Bruno lunged forward and grabbed me, flinging his arms round my upper body.

'You little bitch...'

'Lemme rough she up, man.' That, of course, was Bruno.

'No, no. Let her go. She needs time. She only needs time. She was coming along nicely. It was all my fault. Let her go, Bruno. Trust me, I will win her over. My sweet Zoe, I'm so sorry. I was too rough. I know you want me to be gentle. I'll try again. Come to me, darling. Come...'

Bruno let me go and stood up again. I closed my eyes tightly, allowed Jones to touch me again, not resisting, biting my lip and praying.

'Sweetheart,' he crooned. His sticky sausage fingers moved down my face, massaging my temples. 'Darling, I know you love me. I can make you love me. This is our night of glory... this is—' His voice broke.

I saw my chance. 'I'm sorry,' I whispered. 'There's still – still some resistance. It's because – because he's watching, I can't. Please, Jim...'

I stopped, glanced at Bruno, and continued.

'Please be patient with me and understand. I'm – I'm so embarrassed. In front of him, I just can't – I'm so sorry! I have to be alone with you... Dad. Please, Dad.'

He giggled and nibbled my neck with his loose rubbery lips. I clenched my teeth in agony.

'I like that. That *Dad*. It shows you trust me, at last. Very well, I understand you're shy. I like shy little girls. I'll ask him to leave. Bruno...'

He looked up, and the room exploded. It all happened at once: a deafening bang, a scream, a shrill yell: 'Don't move, don't move!'

Bruno, who'd been standing at the bedside, slumped and fell across me, his head hitting the iron bedstead as he fell. Blood splattered over me, the bed, Jones. Blood, pulsing from a wound somewhere in Bruno's body. Jones pulled away, rolled across the bed and dropped to the ground, where he crouched. I pulled myself from under Bruno's enormous bulk, crawled to the bedhead and sat up to see.

Lucy was in the room. Right now, she was walking sideways, round the bed, both hands grasping a gun aimed at the figure crouching on the floor. Jones had grabbed a pillow as he fell, and was holding it against his face as a shield. He cowered against the wall.

'Drop that! Hands up or I shoot!' Lucy yelled.

He dropped the pillow and lifted his hands.

'Stand up!'

He stumbled to his feet. His face was ghostly white, his eyes wide open in terror, his loose bottom lip trembling. He was muttering something, too low to hear.

A second shot exploded into the night. Jones's forehead burst open in a spurt of blood. He slumped down upon the bed, and around his head a red stain crept across the fluffy white counterpane.

Immediately, Lucy dashed forward, grabbed me and pulled me off the bed.

'Come on, Zoe. Hurry,' she said. She pulled me from the room.

Still clutching my hand, Lucy ran before me into the dark hallway. We slipped out of the front door and down the stairs. At the bottom a guard lay sprawled on his back, limbs akimbo; I couldn't tell if he was dead or not, and I didn't care. I jumped as a figure peeled away from the shadows and joined us as we ran. It was Alexis. Our eyes met fleetingly; she smiled at me, but there was no time for more. In her hand she held an iron crowbar; I assumed that they had attacked the guard with it and taken his gun. Clever, brave girls! How could I ever have doubted them?

We ran, following Lucy. She led the way along the side of the house, and beyond it, not using the wooden walkways, choosing the darkest pathways, the roundabout way, slinking like a thief in the night. Hadn't she mentioned that she'd once been a thief? Well, her talents came to light now as she dashed and darted from building to building, Alexis and me close on her heels.

Once we were well clear of Jones's house Lucy stopped. Alexis and I collided with her, but it didn't matter because anyway, we were in each other's arms.

'Oh my God, oh my God,' Lucy repeated. She hugged and kissed me as if I were back from the dead, which in a way I was. I was in tears of relief. Alexis stood back, grinning.

'How did you find me?' I whispered to Lucy.

'Find you? I wasn't looking for you. I was after him, and Moira. I still am. You just happened to be there. I got a gun now!'

'But you got him, Lucy, you got him! He's dead! We're free, it's over! You saved us all!'

Lucy looked at the gun in her hand. She no longer smiled. I felt Alexis's arm round my waist.

'No, Zoe. It's not over, not by a long shot,' Alexis said.

Lucy nodded.

'It ain't over till we get Moira.'

'But...'

'You still don't get it, do you?' Alexis said. 'Dad's not the only one we need to get. He's batshit crazy, but finally, just a puppet. The real power behind the throne is Moira. She's not mad, she's bad. Really wicked.'

'Yep,' said Lucy. 'She's using his madness. It helps her keep control. But control is what she really wants. She *wants* this to happen. It fits in with her own plans.'

'Moira's evil through and through,' Alexis said. 'And if we don't get her now this madness will go on. They've got a couple hundred people down already. If we want to save the rest, we've got to get Moira.'

'But – how?'

'I gonna get guns for the two of you,' said Lucy. 'I gonna shoot two guards and get their guns.'

'Take it easy, Lucy. I don't want a gun. I never held a gun in my life, don't know how to use one. What about you, Zoe?' Alexis said.

I shook my head. 'I'd shoot my own foot by mistake but holding one would be nice.'

But Alexis was adamant. 'Lucy, no! Don't waste your bullets. Don't risk anything. Let's just go. We found Zoe, that's good enough.'

'I want Moira!' Lucy cried.

Lucy's eyes burned with frenzied passion, a wild primitive power finally unleashed and reckless in its resolve. She looked ready to dash off into the night, shooting wildly left and right, pumped up with adrenaline.

In the distance, in the floodlit area around the pavilion, we could glimpse the straggling line of people as they inched forward. We heard the screams and saw the little scurries of rebellion, easily put down. We saw the guards, their backs to us, guns ready. From the nearest loudspeaker Jones's voice rambled on:

We go without fear. This is our White Night. This is our glory. This is our final triumph. My children, do not fear. This is your father speaking. Know that I am with you.

Alexis's eyes met mine, mirroring my own thoughts: those people were in the grip of something beyond our comprehension and beyond our power to control. No matter how much we might wish to stop them, we couldn't. They were possessed, dominated by something bigger than us all, and those few who rebelled had no chance, for an outside power controlled them. Lucy might very well kill Moira and end it all, for she was fearless and passionate and determined to get her way. But if she failed, the disaster would engulf us all.

'I gotta get Moira,' Lucy repeated. 'I gotta get back over there.' She gestured towards the pavilion with her chin.

Alexis took her arm. 'Lucy,' she said gently, 'it's over. You can't stop it.'

'Who says I can't? You're just a coward, both of you!'

I had to admit that she was right – I didn't want to go back over there. Having escaped Jones by the skin of my teeth I wanted to run, to hide, to put as much distance between me and that centre of evil, that pavilion, as possible. I wanted safety, comfort, home.

Alexis seemed to be thinking my way.

'Lucy,' she said, and her voice was calm and sensible. 'Lucy, you can't stop it. This thing is greater than you and all three of us. You've got responsibilities. What about Danny, and your grandma, and the rest of them? This place is crawling with assassins. We need to save ourselves, and those who depend on us. We can't save everyone.'

Lucy's wild eyes looked at her and then me; a question flickered in them, and a doubt, but then ferocity again took over.

'Look after them for me!' she cried, then turned and leapt away, into the night.

'Lucy!' Alexis cried out and tried to grab her, but Lucy was too sleek, too agile, a wildcat already running towards the pavilion.

'The little fool,' said Alexis. 'She'll spoil everything.'

'But she rescued me,' I said.

'Pot luck. She didn't know you were there. I went with her to keep her under control, but she's tasted blood now; she wants Moira and won't give up till she's got her.'

'What can we do? We've got to help her.'

'Zoe, this may sound cowardly, but there are other people who need our help more. Come with me.'

She set off and I followed. Like Lucy, she kept away from

the walkways and slunk between the buildings, dashing through the shadowy areas between one house and the next, edging along the walls. I had no idea where we were, but she seemed to know where to go. I trusted her implicitly. She headed for the edge of the community, but just as we reached the last house she drew back and pushed me back against the wall.

'Shit!'

'What?'

'This place is crawling with guards. Take a look at that!'

I peeped round the corner of the house. Before me was the wide expanse between the edge of the community and the jungle. Three sentries strolled past. Rifles protruded over their shoulders. I was sure they also carried handguns.

'Not only that, they're searching all the houses, one by one. Systematically.'

'Where shall we go, then?'

'Just follow me.'

It took us almost half an hour, slinking along walls, seeking the shadows and running from one building to the next, to arrive at our destination. On the way we passed my own cabin. I stopped Alexis, and whispered to her: 'Just let me go in for a moment. We need my stuff.'

'OK, but be quick.'

The door was still unlocked, just as I'd left it, and my backpack and water bottle were still there. I grabbed both and returned to Alexis. We crept forward. Sometimes we saw the black shadows of guards entering or leaving houses; we heard cries coming from those houses, and, occasionally, a gunshot. Another time a baby screamed, and a woman. Two shots silenced them.

Alexis led me to a building near the edge of the compound. No more than a windowless box, it looked like a garden shed or storeroom. Alexis cautiously pushed open the door. I followed her inside, into the blackness.

As we entered, a child cried out, but the sound was quickly muffled.

'It's OK,' Alexis whispered, 'It's only us. Zoe, where's your flashlight?'

I reached into my backpack and removed my torch. I switched it on and let its circle of light wander around the room. One face after another appeared in that circle, faces wide-eyed with terror and yet pleading for help. So many faces I could not count them all. My heart sank.

All this time I'd been planning our escape in the back of my mind. It was all arranged; I'd thought out the precise details the day before. Originally, I'd planned for just me and Lucy. Later, I'd added Danny and Lucy's grandma, then Alexis, then Louisa. One by one the group had grown, until finally I'd reckoned we'd be six. That seemed the maximum I could safely get to the forest, and then hide until morning, and then lead to the boat. The canoe only had room for two!

'How many are there?' I asked Alexis.

'Ten or eleven,' she replied. She counted off on her fingers. 'Lucy's granma, Stella; Stella's friends, Kathleen and Amy. Lucy's son, Danny. Louisa. My friend Maggie, her three kids. That makes nine.'

'Counting yourself, Lucy, and me – twelve in all.'

'Guess so.'

I said nothing. Then I whispered, 'Alexis – can we go outside a moment?'

'Sure.'

When we were outside we both crouched down and kept our voices low.

'I can't do it, Alexis. I just can't. Please don't... I really can't.'

'But you have to.'

'But why? Why can't we just stay hiding here until – till it's all over?'

'Till everyone's dead? Because then we'll be dead too. You

still don't get it, Zoe. They're searching house to house. Sooner or later they'll find us. Right now, they're taking it slowly – they've got to watch the Kool-Aid guzzlers up front. But just wait. When nobody's left to watch they'll all be after us. Then I guess they'll all just shoot each other. We have to get out.'

'But – you don't understand. It's bad enough, one or two of us escaping, in the daytime. Twelve, at night! It's impossible...'

I couldn't finish the sentence. I slumped back against the wall, trembling. First, the Box, then Jones, now this. The nightmare just would not end. It couldn't be real. From the other side of the compound I could hear the faraway screams, gunshots, babies crying. Over there was bedlam, and with all my being I longed to wake up and find myself in my soft bed at home, in Georgetown.

As if she could read my thoughts, Alexis placed a hand on my shoulder and said, 'You can do it. I know you can. You'll see – once you decide to do it, you can.'

'But twelve! Old women, children!'

'I know. It won't make it easy but we couldn't just leave them. We couldn't. They're good people, Amy and Kathleen, and Maggie, and her kids – how could I?'

'I want to, I just don't think...'

'You can.'

I took a deep breath, closed my eyes. *You can*, I repeated to myself. *You can. Somewhere in there is a reservoir of strength. You can.* I spoke a silent prayer, and then said, 'We can't go without Lucy.'

Alexis squeezed my shoulder. 'That little idiot! She'll get herself killed, out there. That girl's a loose cannon. You're lucky she didn't kill you instead of Jones. That was sheer luck.'

'We'll have to wait here for her.'

'We can't – we might wait forever.'

I knew what Alexis meant, and shuddered.

Lucy's plight pumped new energy into me, overcoming

exhaustion and cowardice. She was the reason I'd come in here in the first place but there was more to it than that: Lucy had grown into more than a curious obsession; now I owed her my life.

'We'll have to find her, then.'

'We can't both go. One of us has to stay here. These folk are scared shitless, sitting here in the dark. And since I know the place, and you don't, and you're the one who can take them out if… well, if Lucy and me don't come back, it's you. Sorry, honey, it's babysitting time.'

'Alexis – please! I don't – I can't…'

'Really, really sorry. If I'm not back in half an hour, with or without Lucy, take them all and go. Go inside now. You can't stay out here.'

'Alexis, wait…'

But she was already gone, melted into the night. I waited for a while, listening to the pounding of my own heart. Of all the choices open to me, the one I longed to take was – do nothing, stay here, leaning against the shed. Sit the whole thing out. Not go back inside, because in there it was black, airless, lightless – now I didn't even have a torch. I'd be alone with a horde of terrified women and children. In pitch-darkness. Sheer panic gripped me, coursed through my veins, filled my heart, my soul, my being.

CHAPTER FORTY-TWO

Rex Bennett was sipping cocktails at the Canadian Ambassador's home in Kingston – it was the Ambassador's wife's birthday party – when an Embassy aide arrived, flashed his ID at the security guard and, spotting Rex at the bar, walked across the room and whispered in his ear.

Even as he saw him coming, Rex knew that something terrible had happened; the aide's face told him half the story.

'Oh my God!' he gasped when he heard the other half.

Five seconds later he was in his car and racing towards the Embassy. From there he spent an hour on the phone speaking to people from the State Department and the White House. Guyanese government officials had to be located and notified. He tried to reach Jonestown over the ham radio but they had changed the frequency; they did that often.

He tried other radios in the area, spoke to key persons. He organised a flight to take an Embassy delegation to the North West immediately, and a second flight for himself, but later. Then he called Patsy Boyle. The phone was busy. He made more calls, then tried Patsy's line again. It was still busy.

'Damn!' He slammed down the receiver.

Driven by a nasty premonition, he ran out to the car and in a squeal of tyres reversed out of the driveway and into the street. He raced towards Campbellville, nearly mowing down the bicycles gathered at the red traffic light at Lamaha and Camp. A donkey-cart laden with water coconuts drove right down the middle of Vlissingen Road, blocking his path, and its driver, half-asleep or drunk or simply indifferent to harassment, refused to give in to his frantic horn-blowing. He careened around the cart, narrowly missing the trench. The feeling of dread grew into an all-consuming fever.

Again and again, Zoe's face flashed across his mind. *Gotta find Zoe. Gotta find Zoe.* Though a hundred thoughts tumbled through his mind, though a hundred people had to be notified and plans made and tactics organised, though behind the dread and the horror already a strategy was sifting through and the cornerstones for action falling into place, that mantra ticked away silently as the most important strategy of all: the source of his dread. *Gotta find Zoe. Gotta find Zoe.* The practicalities for the next twenty-four hours took precedence; his job. This other thing, this anxious sickening empty-bucket feeling in the pit of his stomach – it was personal, it was quiet, but it overrode all other concerns. No letter from Zoe this week. A bad, bad feeling, like a break in communication. Patsy would know more.

In a town given to frequent power cuts and blackouts, and whose inhabitants knew to be sparing with their electricity, Patsy's house glowed like a Christmas tree. Every light in every room was on, it seemed from the outside, right down to the little radio room under the house. Rex checked that first; he knew that this was where Patsy spent most of her time, talking to her colleagues in Jonestown and in the US. But the room was empty and had an abandoned feel to it, as if someone had rushed out of it; the speaker dangled on its cord, and one of the chairs lay on its side on the floor. Rex took the front steps three at a time.

He found them in the dining room, in the living room, on the balcony, in tiny groups, some hugging each other, some individuals crying. No sign of Patsy or any of her children.

From room to room he sped, asking always the same question: 'Where's Patsy?'

He got no answers. Just blank stares, horrified and unblinking, or heads turned away, or buried in hands; Liz Evans shook her head slightly, and that was the sole acknowledgement of his presence. A house of zombies, he thought as he flew up the stairs to the upper storey.

Upstairs, there were four bedrooms. Rex raced from one to the other, peering inside to check they were empty. They were. Rex had always been a pragmatic man, not given to flights of fancy and not believing in silly New Age things such as intuition or premonition. In fact, he scoffed at such concepts as hippy hocus-pocus. This night, though, he *knew*. He knew with the same certainty that he knew tomorrow the sun would rise. He knew what was waiting for him; it was just the ghastly *how*, the details, that were missing.

He found them in the bathroom. The door was ajar and he pushed at it, but a weight behind it prevented it from opening. He pushed harder, using all his might, and the door budged and opened enough to let him in. He'd already taken in the blood on the white-tiled floor, inching forward from the crack under the door, warning of worse to come.

Rex had seen some bad stuff in his career up to now, death in many forms. He had never seen this: three children with their throats slashed open, and a woman, their murderer, lying across their bodies as if claiming them even in death, her own throat gashed open, the knife lying beside her open hand as if it had just fallen out. And everywhere blood. Rex had never seen so much of it in all his life.

'Oh my God! Oh no! Oh my God, Jesus Christ, no!'

His hand flew to his own throat; he gagged and stumbled

backwards out of the room into the hallway. There, he fell to his knees, dry-retched. Finally, he vomited. The Canadian Ambassador's wife's birthday feast spilled out half-digested on to the wooden floor, fizzling with champagne.

Back at the Embassy, the Ambassador himself was waiting, and after a quick report Rex was back on the phone. He rounded up as many members of staff as he could find, and scheduled a crisis meeting for eleven o'clock in the conference room. He organised three more planes, but no pilots were available for at least two hours. He spoke to the Prime Minister, Mr Burnham, and the Home Secretary, and the Chief of the Guyana Defence Force. The State Department again, the Head of the CIA, the White House, the President of the United States. And all the time the mantra continued unabated, silent and constant at the back of his mind: *Gotta find Zoe. Gotta find Zoe.*

At quarter to ten he found the time to radio Jonestown; again, without success. It was then that the call came through from Dr Bill Turner in the North West District.

'What's this about an American killed at the airport? Over.'

'It's true, Dr Turner. Can I speak to Zoe? Over.'

'It's really true? Oh my God! Oh Lord! I heard the rumour and couldn't believe it. Over.'

'Is Zoe with you? Are you at home or at the hospital? Over.'

'I'm at home and no, you can't speak to Zoe. Zoe's in Jonestown. Over.'

'*In Jonestown?*' Rex yelled the words and almost dropped the speaker. 'Since when's she been in Jonestown? Oh hell, oh no, oh my God!'

He leaned forward and buried his face in his hands. 'Oh my God! Oh my God, Dr Turner, can you hear me? We have to get her out. I'll be up there as soon as I can. Can you give me any more information? How long's she been there?' He waited, and when no answer came he remembered. 'Over.'

'She's been there since yesterday morning. And, Mr Bennett, something bad's going on in there. Worse than ever – the noises! Mr Bennett, you got to get up here as quick as possible. We need some armed officers, police, army, anything you can get, get soldiers up here, quick, man. Over.'

'I'll be there as soon as I can. Might be a few hours. I'll come and pick you up.' He deliberated as to whether to tell him about Patsy, but immediately dismissed the idea. No need to cultivate fear. Quite the opposite. 'Don't worry, Dr Turner, we'll get your girl out. I'll be there as soon as I can make it. Over and out.'

But it was 3 a.m. before Rex finally arrived at Jonestown, and by then the worst was over.

CHAPTER FORTY-THREE

Back in the day they'd called her Kitty-cat, and now all Lucy's skills of stealth returned to her. She'd been using them all along, of course, over the last year and a half: to steal this and that, to listen at doors, to collect the secrets that would one day, so she hoped, set her free. She should have been a spy; morphing into shadows on a wall came naturally to her, and in another, better life that might have been a legal choice. The illegal way had only landed her in trouble but tonight she would save lives. And avenge Serena. She had to find Moira. Kill Moira. It was personal. Moira had killed Serena, her darling baby, as certainly as if she'd smothered her with a pillow.

And so, now, she slunk along walls and skulked between the alleyways, kept away from the walkways, hid beneath stairs and crouched beneath houses, inching closer to the centre of madness.

Meanwhile, Dad's voice continued to reverberate but now they had changed the tape: *...that's what they get! They hunted us down like animals! The CIA! They sent their spies! Five hundred Green Berets are in that jungle out there watching us, and two hundred Black Guard soldiers from England! The whole* *country is riddled with spies, watching us, ready to move against us! What choice do we have?*

Dad... why did she call him Dad, still? Sheer habit, of course, but it was an insult to her own father, and whatever wrong he'd done in deserting them all, four kids and she the youngest, he was a saint compared to the man she'd just killed.

Funny how when you've killed once it's easy to do it again. The first time is the hardest, and she'd never come near to it before. She'd held the gun when Big Joe held up the gas station, but that was just to scare the guy; the gun wasn't loaded and he must have guessed because he drew his own gun and shot Big Joe dead and turned it towards her and she'd dropped hers, and put up her hands. She wasn't really made for a life of crime; Big Joe had dragged her into it, and that hold-up was the turning point. The shock of Big Joe's death and then police and the trial and jail, and then meeting Father, had turned her around, and then, of course, little Danny.

But now, with Moira, it was different. This time she'd shoot to kill. Killing Bruno and Dad — that was just practice, getting the feel for it. She had expected Moira to be there, too, and it would have been good to get all three, and it was Moira she was looking for and Moira she'd kill.

Bruno and Father — dead by happenstance, but well dead, all the same. Two down, one to go. Once Moira was dead, she could stop the party. She, Lucy. Half of Jonestown was still alive and she could save them. Not the kids, though. The kids were already dead. Except for Danny and the three others hiding in the shed.

All those kids, dead. And Serena. Someone had to pay, and that someone was Moira.

By now she was in full sight of the pavilion and the straggling queue of victims shuffling forward to their death. An abject, defeated bunch, resigned to die. Just from the way they held their bodies she could tell. They were all dead already.

Living in this place did that to you. It robbed you of all your will to be alive. If you looked forward and all you could see was more of the same. Day after day for the rest of your life, and no way out, no way out at all, till you finally didn't care if you lived or died, and in a way, death seemed the easiest option and that was how they felt.

That was how *she* had felt some days, but there was something in her that would not let it happen, something that had to fight back, and she did, and she had, and that something had placed her here, now, hunting down the one person who could stop this carnage.

Behind the queue she saw the bodies, countless humps, some still writhing in agony, some whimpering, some moaning. The smallest lay still, already lifeless. It was too late to save those on the ground, and those now sipping the death-brew, but what about those standing there, moving forward? She couldn't see Moira anywhere, just the guards. What if she shot the guards, and told them all to run, run for their lives? Forget about Moira?

But no. Even from here, she saw five guards. She had only four bullets left. Even if she were to kill or seriously maim four of the guards, whoever was left over would yell and more from behind would come running at the first shot.

Moira would emerge from wherever she was and hunt her, Lucy, down, and the show would go on, and anyway, she doubted she could hit four of them, much less seriously maim or kill them; not at that range. The only reason she'd got Bruno and Father was because it had been at close range. She couldn't take that risk now, and waste her bullets; and anyway, even if she did, they'd probably all still march to their deaths, because they'd made up their minds to die and nothing was going to stop them now, not even if all the guards and Moira dropped dead; but if she got Moira, she could run forward and tip over those vats of Kool-Aid. No, they'd be too heavy for her alone. They'd shoot her in the process, of course, but right now she just didn't care. She was ready to die trying. The only thing she cared about was Danny but Alexis would look after Danny, and Zoe too, bring Danny home to Mom and Mom would raise him.

...the joke's on them, my children! Our White Night is our final triumph! Think of their faces when they find us tomorrow! We go with courage, our heads high. As of today, the world will know of this new weapon of the oppressed: Revolutionary Suicide!

Dad was dead, and they didn't even know it. If they knew it, they'd want to die all the more – to follow him wherever he was. They'd think he'd gone before, to prepare a place for them. Dad had sucked them dry. He'd clung to them like a leech, he as dependent on them as they on him, until all that was left of their union was this: him with a hole in the head, and they writhing in the throes of death. Such a waste.

Tears filled Lucy's eyes. Faces appeared before her: Marjory and Jeannie and Pat and all those wonderful women she'd loved and lived with and admired. She'd eaten their cakes and their home-made jams and they were like mothers to her but they'd given up on life because life was just a never-ending travail of toil and hunger, sickness and despair and fear and there was no going back; not ever.

She might have stayed there forever, watching. The sight of her friends shambling forward to their deaths was hypnotic; she could not take her eyes away. But then a shot rang out and that woke her out of the straitjacket of horror.

Meghan Vaughn, her baby in her arms, had broken out of the queue and was running towards her. They were shooting after her, but she kept on running, and then she was out of sight, escaped, one of the guards behind her. The other two guards returned to watching the queue, but not Lucy. She'd seen enough. There was no time to lose. She had to find Moira. There were only two places Moira might be: in Dad's house, or the radio room. Lucy bet on the radio room. Moira must have already discovered Dad's body, because she'd changed the tape. She'd be radioing the news to America right now.

Lucy was right. As she approached the radio room, Moira emerged. She paused in the doorway, head raised as if sniffing the air.

Lucy crouched down, took careful aim, and pulled the trigger.

The shot was louder than it had been when she shot Dad; or so it seemed as she fell backwards. It felt like a hole blasted through her eardrums. And then she looked and she saw that Moira was still standing, not dead, apparently not even scratched; Moira, looking dazed; and then Moira running in her direction, but she could not possibly have seen her. Lucy stood transfixed, unable to run, and then a second person emerged from the radio room, a giant, and it was Bruno, Bruno who was dead, or who was supposed to be dead, but he wasn't for he was right there and he had a gun in his hand, and one arm with a white stripe – must be a bandage – and running towards her; but there was no time to think how Bruno could still be alive because Lucy too was running, running, running, away from the radio room, away from the pavilion, towards the only place of safety she knew.

CHAPTER FORTY-FOUR

I closed the door and the blackness closed me in, and right away, the voices began. First, a little child, whimpering:

'Mom, I want my mom!'

A woman's voice:

'Danny, shut up! Mom'll be back in a minute!'

'But I want her now!'

'You'll just have to wait.'

More voices:

'What's going on? When can we get out? Where's Alexis gone?' Questions, questions, and me alone to answer them.

'Shhh, everyone be quiet!' I said into the darkness. 'Lucy and Alexis will be back soon. We have to be quiet. You know why. Try and keep the children quiet. Please!'

But Danny only cried louder. 'I want my mom! I'm scared!'

Another child tuned in. 'I'm scared too, Mom! When can we leave here? It's dark!'

My nerves twisted. 'Listen, you've got to be quiet. Really!'

'Sue, you heard what the lady said. Shut up! What's your name, miss?'

'Zoe.'

'How long we got to stay here? What we doin' next?'

'As soon as Lucy and Alexis return, we're going to make a run for it. I'm taking you through the jungle.'

My nine listeners broke out in apoplexy, all at once and at the tops of their voices. We might just as well have climbed on the roof and waved a white flag to Jones's assassins.

'Lord have mercy!'

'Mom, I ain't goin' into no jungle!'

'Mom, the tigers gonna get us!'

'I not going into no jungle! It's crawling with tigers! I rather drink poison!'

'Girl, you outta your mind! That place full of tigers!'

'CIA soldiers too!'

I had no choice but to shout them down.

'Shut up, everyone, and *listen!*'

At last the clamour died down.

'OK, listen,' I said. 'There are *no tigers* in that jungle. Not one!'

'Not true! We hear them, roaring in the night! It's full of tigers. Dad said so.'

'Mummy, I don't want to go in the jungle with the tigers!'

'What you hear is jaguars but they're not usually dangerous to humans. I know this place, I've been through it a hundred times. No tigers in there. No soldiers either.'

I spoke confidently, but I did have some doubts. We'd have several small children with us. Jaguars normally did not attack adult humans, they preferred small animals, as I'd tried to tell Miranda. But children *were* small animals to a jaguar. Easy prey. To ease my own fears, I repeated:

'Jaguars don't attack humans. Only very rarely.'

'But alligators, snakes, spiders...'

They all started up again. I wished I could at least see their faces; I had a torch in my backpack but I could not use it; I could not waste the batteries. I'd need that light later. As it was, the disembodied voices hurling through the darkness frayed at my substance. Their voices came at me like whips; not one of them sounded friendly, or grateful, or even comforted by my presence. And I was supposed to save this unruly crew? If they couldn't behave in the relative safety of the hut, what would they be like out there? Four of them were small children. Three of them were old women. And I knew none of them. Never met them in my life. What if Alexis and Lucy never came back? Alexis had my torch; how would I make it even to the edge of the jungle, much less through it, to the creek? *At night?*

Creeping along the wall of a building, Alexis saw a guard emerge from one of the houses, pushing a woman with a baby in her arms. The infant bawled, the woman begged for mercy, stumbling and struggling with the guard. It was Meghan Vaughn, one of the few white girls in Jonestown. Alexis crouched and hid until they were out of sight, and steeled her heart against the guilt and the horror and the rage. There was nothing, absolutely nothing, she could do.

Somewhere out there was Lucy, with a gun.

Alexis edged along the wall, keeping to the shadows, her eyes still on the little threesome: guard, mother and baby. The baby screeched. Meg fell to her knees, begging to be saved. The guard pulled her up and shoved her forward. She stumbled, fell again; the guard pulled her to her feet and thrust her on. Alexis reached the corner of the building. She had the crowbar in her right hand; if she was fast enough, she could run out there and get the guard from behind.

Alexis, her back pressed to the wall, edged round the corner, but then she felt the hand upon her bare arm and before she could stop herself, she screamed.

But then a hand was over her mouth, muffling the scream,

and an arm round her body, and someone was throwing her to the ground; she wrestled, struggled, tried to escape but couldn't, and only then did she hear the voice and stop struggling, because the person holding her was speaking to her, whispering her name, and she knew that voice and it was Lucy.

They sat on the earth facing each other. Lucy's eyes, always so dead, so downbeat, seemed on fire and when she spoke, her voice was hoarse with excitement.

'What are you doing here? Where's Zoe?'

'Back in the shed.'

'C'mon, we have to hurry.'

'Wait, Lucy. Where's the gun?'

'There.' It lay on the ground, where Lucy had dropped it. She picked it up now. A scream made them both look up: Meg had broken free and was running in their direction. The guard fired, Meg plunged forward, the baby in her arms. The guard fired again. Lucy and Alexis scrambled to their feet, melted back into the shadows, but the guard had seen them, and a bullet whizzed past Alexis's ear.

Another shot, and Meg screamed again and stumbled, never again to rise. Alexis lunged forward. As Meg fell, she threw the screaming baby, tossed it across to Alexis, her face distorted with pain, her eyes screaming, 'Take her, take her, take my precious.'

For a moment the child, still screaming, hovered in the air. Alexis flung out her arms and caught the little girl, falling backwards herself but cushioning the baby's fall with her body.

As Alexis caught the baby, Lucy fired the gun, and this time she was right on target: the guard fell.

Lucy stepped over to Meg, who now lay still on her stomach. Around the hole at the back of her head the blonde hair was wet and dark with blood.

Lucy reached out a hand to Alexis. 'We have to hurry,' she said again. 'Moira is after me. And Bruno.'

'Bruno? I thought he was—'
'*Not* dead. And mad as hell. I think he went to get the dog.'

CHAPTER FORTY-FIVE

I said, 'Look, Danny, if you don't shut up, they'll find us and *kill* us!'

That silenced his wailing, but only for a minute. Soon he was whimpering again, and Sue with him, and a couple of women took that as a licence to chatter, and to me it sounded like bedlam. I suppressed the urge to strangle them all.

But then one of the old women began to hum 'Amazing Grace'. A minute later, other voices tuned in, muted and gentle. Danny's crying petered out. Calm settled into the hut.

After a while I found that even my own heart had stopped its erratic racing, and I began to breathe again. I even managed to hum along with the song, and it calmed my own jagged nerves. An eternity passed by, made only tolerable by the low, sweet song.

And then the waiting was over. The door flew open and Alexis's voice, low but commanding, cut into the chorus:

'OK, everybody out. Hurry.'

They scuffled and scurried to their feet and a moment later we were all outside, where Lucy waited for us. Alexis began to sort through us, pairing off the children with the adults. Danny, of course, lunged for Lucy and gripped her hand. Maggie had a baby, carried in a sling over her shoulder, plus a girl, Sue, of about four, and a boy, Dave, of about six. Alexis placed Sue's hand in Louise's and Dave's in mine, and it was only then I noticed that she herself had a baby in her arms. I wondered briefly where she'd picked it up, but there was no time now for questions.

'Let's go,' said Lucy, and we were off. Without even consulting, we fell into formation, Alexis in the lead and Lucy and me at the back. A long and ragged line, we slunk into the night.

All seemed quiet at this side of the compound. Not a guard in sight. From the pavilion we could hear the hullabaloo, muted now through distance; women crying, guards shouting, and above it all, the boom of Jones's pep talk:

...I am your father, your God, and I am telling you this is the right thing, the way to go. Do you want them to win? Do you want them to come here and capture us? We must be strong.

There was a difference, though. Up to now, Jones's talk had been accompanied by the low howling of Bruno's dog. That howling now became the furious staccato of barking. And it was in real life, not over the loudspeaker, and it was growing louder. Lucy took my arm, drew close to me and whispered, 'Bruno is alive. I managed to lead him off-track but he must have gone to get the dog. That's him. He's after us!'

But I had no time to think about Bruno and his dog. We had a problem, but only we at the back noticed. The children had been my main worry up to now, but I saw now that I'd been wrong. It wasn't the children, it was the old women.

Stella hobbled along as fast as she could, but at best it was a fast limp. Kathleen was even worse; bent almost double, she walked with a stick and even her best effort was no more than a shuffle. Amy, grey-haired and frail but able-bodied, walked between those two with her arms hooked in theirs, supporting and carrying them along. But soon this little group – the three elderly women, Lucy, myself, Danny and Dave – dropped far behind the leading group of Alexis, Louise and Maggie.

Lucy whistled. Alexis stopped, and waited for us to catch up.

'You all right?'

'Yes, but slow down. Otherwise we'll lose you.'

Alexis nodded. I knew where she was leading us – to a point just outside the reach of the floodlights. Once we crossed the wasteland between Jonestown and the forest we'd be relatively safe and could creep along the edge of the underbrush until we reached my point of entry – the two landmark coconut palms. Even from here, I could see their fronds silhouetted against the night sky, beckoning me on.

The barking seemed nearer than ever. Just round the corner.

'Now!' whispered Alexis, and we sallied out from the safety of Jonestown's shadows into the floodlit plain, actors walking onstage for the entire world to see. I could have wept with frustration: instinct urged me to race ahead, pull Dave with me to the safety of the bush, but my elbow was hooked into Stella's and hers into Amy's, who clung to Kathleen, and all we could do was creep forward in a pathetic human knot. Again, our two groups split apart.

Somehow we reached the middle of the plain.

Two things happened simultaneously.

The first shot rang out.

And Danny wailed: 'Mom! I dropped my teddy!' I held my breath, and looked behind me; there lay the teddy, about three yards behind us. Would Lucy go back for it?

'Honey, I'm sorry, you'll just have to leave it behind.'

I relaxed. She was being sensible. But Danny wasn't; he

leaned over his mother's shoulders and stretched out his hand for the bear.

'I want my teddy! Mommy, please!'

A second shot rang out, whizzing past our heads. Then shouting, dogs barking. I looked behind me, but I could as yet see no guards after us.

'Hurry, hurry,' I gasped. The old women picked up speed. They swayed back and forth in their haste, and only Amy kept them upright. It was all I could do not to run past them, leave them behind. But I didn't.

Danny wailed again: 'My teddy, Mommy!'

Lucy looked back at the teddy. She even stopped, and put Danny down on the ground, where he looked ready to dash back to get his bear. Was Lucy out of her mind? But no. She grabbed Danny's arm and pulled him to her, picked him up in her other arm and hurried forward, and the tone of her voice said the matter was at an end.

'Sorry, honey. I'll get you a new one.' She covered Danny's mouth. We hurried on.

And then we were there. We reached the shadowed forest edge, and there was Alexis, waiting for us with her people. Our two groups became one, and now I took the lead. From this point I was in charge; I alone knew the forest. Not one of them had ever been this far.

From Jonestown came commotion: shouting, and barking, and three more shots. I looked back and saw three guards in midfield, black shapes clearly outlined in the white fluorescent light. One was huge: Bruno. As I watched, Bruno bent over. A black shape leapt away from him. My heart stopped: Diablo, Bruno's vicious attack dog.

'Hurry, hurry!' I said, and almost dragged Stella forward. But Lucy stayed where she was.

'Get a move on, Lucy!'

'No, I can get him. I've got two bullets left.'

Before anyone could stop her, Lucy had pulled the gun from her waistband and fired two shots. Bruno continued his run towards us.

'You little fool!' Alexis's voice shook with fury. 'We might have needed those bullets later!'

'Never mind,' I whispered. 'Hurry!'

We crept along the bushes edging the jungle. My heart pounded so loud I could hear it, but now I was in my own territory and confidence, sadly lacking up to now, returned in bucketloads. I looked back at the field separating us from our pursuers, and my heart lifted: Diablo was not following, but running around in zigzags and circles. He could not find our scent! We had thrown them off! We had a head start; once we were in the bush Bruno and company could never find us without Diablo's help.

Five minutes later, I found the place I was looking for. The twin coconut trees loomed above me. I took one last look across the field to Jonestown and gasped with dismay.

Bruno was bending down again, taking something from Diablo. I knew exactly what it was – Danny's teddy! Diablo now had a scent, and he was after us. He lunged forward, followed by Bruno and his men.

'Quick,' I said. I fumbled in my backpack for my torch, switched it on and, following its beam, plunged into the blackness. Immediately we were swallowed by the body of sound that is the tropical rainforest after dark.

My mouth turned dry. This was not the jungle I knew. I had only been here in the day; at night it was a different beast altogether. The beam of light showed only circles of leaves or trunks or, pointed downwards, earth; I only knew whole pictures, whole scenes. Once we were safe within the bush I had planned to wait for daylight, but with the dog and Bruno behind us that was now impossible. We had to continue, through the darkness.

I shone the light downward and crouched to inspect the ground more closely. To my amazement, in the soft black earth of the jungle floor I saw the faint outline of my own shoes. I knew they were mine as I had learned to look for exactly this particular pattern. Though it seemed weeks and weeks since I had last been here, it was in fact just two days: my old tracks were still readable. I shone the light on the trees and found the first white arrow.

'Come on,' I said. My voice rang with enthusiasm. Inside I quaked, but I would not let them know it. If they knew we were doomed, they'd all give up.

I shone my light on Dave's face. 'You OK?'

Dave nodded. Thank goodness for sensible kids. He had followed me without a murmur all this time.

I patted his head. 'Brave boy!'

Danny whimpered: 'Mom! The *tigers!*'

Oh God, I said to myself, *don't let them start that again!*

'It's OK, honey. No tigers here, you gonna be OK, Mom's with you.'

The old ladies began to murmur to themselves. At first, I could not make out what they were saying, but their mutterings grew louder and finally I got the words:

'*...for Thou art with me, Thy rod and Thy staff to comfort me... Thou preparest a table before me in the presence of mine enemies...*'

I turned to Lucy, walking right behind me. 'See if you can get them to pray quietly.'

She passed on the message, and the prayer became a whisper again.

Progress was excruciatingly slow, but this time I could not blame it on the old ladies. My torchlight led the way, seeking out the white arrows on trees as well as footprints; faint indentations I would never have seen but for my training only days ago.

Only days. I could hardly believe it – it seemed more like months.

The night noises sizzled around us, as if every creature from miles around was watching and hissing at us, warning us away. The last time I'd been here I'd felt so serene, at home with nature; now none of that composure remained, and the environment reflected my own unease, for the noises were hostile, evil even, telling of danger and untold perils. A million voices chimed in an orchestra of high-pitched, frantic cheeping. In the darkness, tiny lights blinked: fireflies – or the eyes of animals. The wild cacophony outside reflected my own turmoil, the frenzy of emotions threatening to tear me apart. And progress was so excruciatingly slow.

The barking grew louder by the minute. Bruno and his dog had reached the forest entrance, hard on our track, faster than us for Diablo did not need to painstakingly follow half-deleted footprints. The dog would lead Bruno straight to us, and in a matter of minutes.

We had reached a part of the forest that I recognised. The trees here were sparsely laid out and the underbrush thicker, which gave us some measure of protection. The fact that I had passed here just a few days back meant that a path had already been cut, and not had time to grow back. I was pleased to note that I was, indeed, on the right path, and thankful for the slight protection the undergrowth gave us.

The children, those old enough to understand, whimpered. Danny sobbed aloud. Both babies cried, not knowing why but sensing adult fear and hopelessness. Only the old ladies remained calm, if not silent; they knew that sound was not our giveaway, but smell. We were already lost, had been lost ever since Diablo found the bear. Their whispered prayer grew loud and fervent:

'...yea, though I walk through the valley of the shadow of

death, I will fear no evil for Thou art with me... Thy rod and Thy staff to comfort me...'

Minutes slipped away, and in each one I expected the end, a snarling, raging Diablo to leap at us from behind and rip us all to pieces. Alexis would fall first; she brought up the rear. Ahead of her, Louise, then Maggie, all three of them with children in their arms. Then the three old ladies, then brave Dave – who up to now had not uttered a sound, and who would not budge from my heels – with me in the lead. Each one held on to the person in front, and I slashed our path forward with the crowbar. I had no choice but to lead them on. Diablo could not be more than ten yards behind us, now; I could even hear the crash of broken branches as Bruno and his little troop plunged forward behind his dog.

Then the barking stopped. Afterwards I wondered what had halted Diablo in his tracks and shut him up so suddenly. What had caught his attention, even above the thrill of the chase? I pictured him there in the darkness, one black paw raised, snout up, nostrils flared, feeling the presence of another, as animals do, listening for some audible clue, sniffing for some olfactory sign to explain the sense of danger. It seemed as if in that moment the entire forest held its breath, and everything froze, for just one second, to listen to the silence.

Diablo's one last yelp of shock and the jaguar's dull thump as it landed on the dog's back set the world spinning again. A few seconds of ferocious snarling as the two animals fought. And then even I at the front heard the clean snap as a giant paw doubled back Diablo's head and cracked his neck.

The jaguar's low growl was like the humming of a motorbike, deeply satisfied, and didn't sound at all threatening to me; but not so, apparently, to Bruno. The next thing we knew he was yelling for his life:

'*Get back, get back, run, tiger, man, tiger!*'

And then the thunder of footsteps and the crashing of

branches as Bruno and company ran for their lives, back towards Jonestown, away from us. In that moment I actually laughed out loud.

We walked on, slower now that Diablo and Bruno were no more. The undergrowth thinned out even more. I led my little group on. We weren't far from the creek; I estimated fifteen minutes if I were on my own, in daylight, but in the present circumstances it would take half an hour, forty-five minutes maximum. We had made it... almost. I began to plan the logistics of getting them all to Akinawa village. First, I would have to take the canoe, with just one passenger. I would have to go to the village, wake them up and bring help, which in this case meant more canoes. At least six two-man dugouts, or three or four larger boats.

I was just figuring out whom to take for my first trip out when Dave screamed. I whipped round to find him writhing at my feet, grasping his ankle and howling in agony.

'Something bit me!' he managed to sob, and as I crouched down to inspect the damage my blood ran cold. I knew there were many kinds of snake in this part of the jungle – the danger had been very real all along – but snakes are as shy as jaguars and I'd believed, hoped, prayed that the noise of our coming would keep them away. But tonight our luck was on a rollercoaster ride and right now, it seemed, it had once more reached rock bottom: my greatest fear was the bushmaster.

I peeled away Dave's fingers and saw the tiny red puncture marks, the flesh around them already turning hot and puffy, starting to swell. Maggie, who had been just a second behind me, was beside me on the ground.

'Honey, honey, what happened? Oh, my baby, what's the matter?'

She flung her youngest child into my arms to grab Dave's leg and inspect the wound. Dave flung his arms round her and clung to her, sobbing in pain. The little boy in my arms wailed in protest at his demotion, beating at me with his fists and flailing to get away from me.

'Something bit me, Mom! Ooow! Mommy, Mommy!'

'Oh my God, honey! What bit you? Let me see, where?'

'My leg, Mommy, owww, it hurts so bad!'

'Shhh, honey, don't scream! We don't know who else is here, looking for us!'

Dave stopped screaming immediately; biting his lip, he looked up at me, grabbed me with one hand and held tight.

'That's a brave boy,' I said. 'It's OK, Maggie, he'll be fine. My uncle's a doctor. We'll have him at the hospital in no time.'

'Aren't you supposed to suck the poison out?'

I remembered what Uncle Bill had told me once. 'No. That way, you can poison yourself as well. It's a myth. What we need is antivenom. But don't worry – we'll be at the creek soon, I've got a boat there.'

'What's the matter, Zoe?' Alexis called from the back, while Lucy, answering some profound motherly instinct, edged her way past the old women – who had, on sensing a new disaster, all begun to pray aloud once more – and took the infant from me, pushing Danny into my arms in exchange. But Danny, little brat, also rejected me, struggled against my attempts to hold him still, and called out to his mom, who handed the baby back to his mother and took him in her arms.

The first shock over, I bent down to pick up Dave. He hung limp across my arms. His mother stood up, stroking his face, now wet with sweat.

'What is it?' she sobbed. 'Is it dangerous? He's so hot...'

All snakebites here in the jungle are potentially dangerous, but I couldn't tell her that.

'My uncle's a doctor,' I said again, in as calm a voice as I could manage. 'We have to get him to hospital. Somebody has to carry him; I'd do it, but I need both hands.'

Alexis squeezed forward to join us. With one hand she supported Meg's baby, who straddled her hip.

'Let me take Dave,' she said. She held out the baby to me. 'Here, you take Tammy. She's not heavy.'

'But I need both hands!' I protested. I picked up the items I had laid down to tend to Dave, and showed her: the crowbar and the torch.

'There are five kids, and we're five adults, not counting Stella, Amy and Kathleen,' Alexis said. 'You'll have to carry one of them.'

'Here, take my sling,' said Maggie. She wriggled her way out of the knotted cotton shawl she wore across her shoulder. 'I can do without it.'

She hung the sling over my head and adjusted it, all with one hand, for she held her baby on her hip with the other. Lucy put Danny down, took Meg's baby from Alexis and slipped her into the sling. She fiddled with it until Tammy sat comfortably pressed against my side. Then Lucy picked up Danny, Alexis picked up Dave – still whimpering, but more quietly now – and we marched on in the same order as before.

By now I was on familiar territory and knew the way to the creek. The undergrowth had given way to tree trunks, well-spaced out. With no bush to hack through, I estimated we'd be there in five minutes maximum.

Ten minutes later, though, we still weren't there.

I stopped. The trees looked familiar. I knew them. I'd been here countless times. And yet there were no white arrows on them.

I walked on. A further five minutes later, I stopped again. I had reached a wall of undergrowth. This was wrong.

'Just a minute.'

I pushed past the women and children thronged behind me,

stooped down and shone my light on the ground. My heart sank. A mess of footprints, disturbed earth, leading back into the forest. Since the incident with Dave we had come full circle. And no white arrows.

I noticed another thing. I had in fact been aware of it for some time, but had tried to ignore it; after all, we were nearly there. But now I had to acknowledge the horrible truth. The light from my torch flickered; it was growing dimmer by the minute. The battery was running out.

'Come this way,' I said and led them back the way we'd come. At some point, surely, I'd find the right way again. If it was daylight it'd be so easy. But it wasn't daylight, it was pitch-dark, and the only light we had was running out.

'Mom, I'm thirsty!' That was Dave, calling from the back.

I remembered I still had some water left in my bottle. We were all thirsty. Stopping might help me find some calmness again, for by now my heart was thumping madly, and marching forward into the blackness was not helping. So I stopped, and turned.

'Let's have a pause,' I said. 'Lucy, there's a water bottle in my bag.'

Alexis edged up to me, whispered in my ear: 'We're lost, right?'

I nodded. My mouth was dry. A lump rose in my throat. I felt Alexis's fingers on my hand. She took the torch from me, switched it off, but I knew it was too late to save the battery. The last thing I saw was Dave's pale face, his eyes closed. He no longer whimpered, no longer moved. I touched his forehead: it was burning hot.

Complete blackness enclosed us. We moved into a huddle. Nobody spoke, and no child cried. They all knew I had failed them. The night noises screeched around us. Lucy passed the water bottle around, and each of us took a sip.

I knew I had to say something, reassure them in some way,

and so I said, 'It can't be long till morning. When it gets lighter, I can find my way out. Everybody keep together, hold on to each other.'

In fact, I had no idea how I would ever find the creek from where we now stood.

'But my baby, my poor Davey,' whimpered Maggie. 'We have to get him to a doctor. You can't let my Dave die!'

But what can I do? I'm as helpless as you! I screamed in silence. Aloud, I had nothing to say, for she was right: we needed antivenom.

'Well, I don't know about the rest of you but I ain't standin' around here in the dark, waitin' for mornin'!' declared one of the old women. 'I'm tired! I'm sittin' down!'

'Yeah, yeah, me too!' chorused the other two.

'But you can't... it's dangerous! Don't!' I cried into the night. We were all tired. Exhausted, in fact. Not for the first time tonight a vision of my Georgetown bed appeared to me: crisp white sheets, yellow curtains blowing in the soft Atlantic breeze and a kiskadee chirping in the mango tree outside. My entire body ached. My reservoirs of strength, drained to the utmost tonight, were empty. And it was not over yet, not by a long shot.

The old women ignored my protests completely. Our human huddle buckled as three of its members creaked to the ground.

'I'm tired too, and Dave's heavy,' said Maggie. I protested aloud and tried to grab her, but she was down. And so were two others – Louise and Lucy, I figured by a process of elimination, for Alexis reached out and clutched my hand.

'Come on, Zoe,' she whispered. 'You can't stand here for hours. Let's rest.'

And suddenly I no longer cared. We'd come this far by some miracle, and if snakes and predatory animals were to get us now, I was too tired to care. I sank to the ground.

So there we all sat on the soft moist forest floor, invisible to each other, a tangle of arms and legs, leaning against each other for support, babies and small children asleep in our laps, at the mercy of the mighty bush, waiting for the dawn, which might not come for some of us and probably would not for Dave.

I yawned, deep and long. A child whimpered in her sleep. A soft familiar murmur arose:

'Our Father, which art in heaven...'

CHAPTER FORTY-SIX

Rex Bennett made sure the drivers of the two Jeeps knew the way, and watched them roll away from Port Kaituma's airstrip, melting into the jungle darkness. Only then did he get into the third Jeep. He looked at his watch: 1.15 a.m.

The sickened dread in the pit of his stomach had warned him to keep away. He already knew what would meet him there. Patsy's bathroom had told him what horror was waiting for him.

It was what *else* might meet him there that caused his stomach to turn these somersaults, that raised the bile in his throat and caused his heart to hammer this way. And no matter what he did to calm it, nothing worked.

Stop that, he ordered himself. *You're a professional. You've seen it all before. This is just a job. If she's there, among the dead, then so what? You warned her. You warned her again and again. Leave it to us, you'd said. If she went in anyway, it was at her own risk. OK, so she's a friend. You hoped she'd be your lover. Your wife. But still – leave emotions out of this, and just do your goddamned duty.* Those last words he screamed at himself, into the silence of that dread.

You should never have gotten involved. You should have kept your own counsel, realised she was into it thick and heavy, and kept out of it. Kept feelings out of it. Why didn't you? You should have known it would end this way.

It wasn't Zoe's fault he'd fallen in love with her; in fact, she had tried to discourage him. He'd done it in spite of his common sense, in spite of knowing better. Never mix work with love had always been his motto. He should never have departed from it; but then, he hadn't considered Zoe *work*. She was a member of the public reporting an American citizen in distress; it was all done and dusted, officially, in the very first meeting. But no. He had used work to get to know her better, inviting her back for viewing the tapes, introducing her to Patsy. Just not professional. And now he was doing it again – mixing the personal with the professional. He needed a cool head for the night ahead, and instead he was almost berserk with worry. Why?

Because I'm human, and a man. And I love her.

The two beams from the Jeep's headlights coalesced into one and cut a bright wedge from the jungle blackness ahead. The sand had not yet settled from the two Jeeps' passing; it hung in the yellow glow like a fine mist, while their own wheels threw up new sand that floated through the open window and settled in his hair and the corners of his lips and the creases of his eyelids, coating the insides of his nostrils.

Damned sand. Damned jungle. Damned everything.

It was hot, so hot, a close, moist, oppressing heat that sucked the sweat from him and made him pant for air. He did not speak. Could not speak.

Suddenly he was tired. So exhausted he could lie down and sleep and not wake up till it was over. He knew all too well what waited for him at Jonestown. He expected the worst, and worse even than the worst. Zoe was in there, with them. He needed sleep. Or drink. One of the two; anything but this, bouncing along in a Jeep in the dead of night to an encounter with the mother of all nightmares. He closed his eyes. *Let it not be true.* He was not a praying man, but still he prayed.

He must have dozed off, because the next thing he knew the Jeep was slowing down, and the lights switched off. He looked at his watch: only two thirty, too early to be at Jonestown.

'What's the matter? Why're you stopping?'

'Roadblock, sah.'

The driver switched on the light briefly so he could see: ahead of him, blocking the track, were the two Jeeps he had sent off a while ago. One of his men walked towards him. He opened the door, stepped out into the night and walked to meet him: it was Jeff.

'What's up?'

Jeff unwittingly repeated the driver's words.

'Roadblock, sir.' He wiped his face with a grubby handkerchief. The night was hot and airless, his face sticky with sweat and sand.

'A flatbed truck, the one from Jonestown.'

'What the...?'

Rex was immediately wide awake. He strode towards the two Jeeps parked one behind the other and passed them. Beyond them stood the flatbed truck. He'd seen it before, even driven in it once, on one of his visits to Jonestown.

'No driver in sight, sir. We found it here, deserted, in the middle of the road. There's no room to pass by so we've been trying to clear some of the bush away to push it off-road.'

Rex saw the men with cutlasses, working to cut down the roadside bushes. They had cleared two yards of space already.

'Is it locked? Did you go inside?'

'Yep, locked, sir. We broke the window to get in. Keys missing, handbrakes on. No sign of driver or passengers.'

Rex walked around the truck, inspecting it from all sides. He peered into the cabin, and onto the loading surface. As Jeff had said, it was empty.

'Our guess is they parked it here to delay investigations, sir. To keep us out as long as possible.'

'Makes sense. How long do you need to get it off the road?'

'Ten minutes at most, sir. We're nearly finished.'

'OK, thanks. Do you have a flashlight for me?'

'Sure. Take mine.'

Rex walked around the truck again, opened the cab door, climbed in. He peered into the glove compartment. Nothing there but a dried-up banana skin and an empty Coke bottle. He shone the light under the seats and into the door compartments. Down at the bottom he saw a long, hard object. He reached in and took it out: it was a walkie-talkie, held together by a dirty and frayed strip of tape.

CHAPTER FORTY-SEVEN

I dreamed of Paul. It was our wedding day, and we were dancing the night away to the tinkle of a steel band playing 'Brown Skin Gal', me in my wedding dress and Paul in his pyjamas. The moon shone full and round, and all our guests stood around us laughing and clapping, and they were all Jonestown inmates. Paul whirled me faster and faster. I cried for him to stop but he wouldn't. We whirled and twirled in a tight embrace and then a shot rang out and Paul dropped dead at my feet in a pool of blood. I looked up and all the guests had vanished and Rex Bennett stood there with a smoking gun, and then Rex turned into a jaguar leaping towards me.

'No, no, you've got it wrong, jaguars don't attack humans!' I cried, and the jaguar vanished and Jim Jones in a white robe was walking towards me, tears streaming down his face, arms held out towards me. 'Zoe, Zoe! Please love me!' he cried.

'I don't! Don't touch me!' I screamed back at him, yet my voice came out as low as a whisper, and that's when I woke up.

'Zoe! Zoe! Zoe!'

This time, no dream. It came from far away, yet I could hear it distinctly.

'Here!' I yelled, and jumped to my feet, throwing somebody's legs from my lap. I realised that I was clutching a baby, Meg's baby Tammy. I must have taken her from the sling before I dozed off, but couldn't remember doing so. It was still pitch-dark, and yet there was a feel in the air of early morning; or perhaps the bush had a different voice at this time of night and that was what I recognised.

I did not, however, recognise the voice, which now called clearer than ever: 'Zoe! Is that you?'

'Yes!' I yelled with all my might, and it was no whisper and this was no dream. 'Here!'

Others were stirring by now. Somebody touched my legs. Fumbling hands found my shoulders, my arms, in the dark, and I too groped for support as I rose to my feet. A child cried; which one I could not tell, and it was good, this time, for the more noise we made the better.

'Over here!' I cried, and others joined in. 'We're here! Here!'

A few minutes of this later and a moving light-beam came into view, sometimes broken by the trees but stronger all the while, and finally steady and fixed on us.

At last it was right there before us.

'Who is it?' I asked cautiously. There was still a chance that by some horrible trick of fate it was a Jonestown assassin. I could hardly believe that my luck had changed, and this was indeed a friend.

'It's me,' said the holder of the torch and turned the light on himself.

'Winston!' I cried, and threw myself at him, my arms round him. Winston, not given to florid demonstrations of affection, recoiled, and I giggled and let him go. Almost hysterical with joy, I hugged the person standing next to me, who happened to be Lucy. And only then did I recall the danger we'd been in and stop laughing.

'Is everybody here? Are we all OK?' I said, and then, 'Oh my God, how's Dave?'

'Down here,' said Maggie.

'Can I have that, please?' I took the torch from Winston and shone it to the earth, seeking out Maggie and Dave. Maggie's face looked up at me, streaked with grime and contorted with distress. Dave's face was so placid he could only be in a coma, or dead. 'Is he...?'

'He's still breathing,' Maggie said, 'But he's hot. High fever.'

'What's the matter?' That was Winston.

'A snake bit him.'

Winston crouched down and inspected Dave's wound.

He looked up. 'Not bushmaster,' he said. 'Parrot snake. Baby parrot snake. Just one minute...'

And he was gone, with the light, and the darkness closed around us once more, and the children whined and the adults huddled together.

'Don't worry, he'll be back,' I told them with more confidence than I felt, but I was right, for in less than five minutes Winston was back, crouched beside Dave once more and rubbing some leaves between his fingers.

'Bush violet,' he said briefly, glancing up at me. 'Will help for now but we got to get him to doctor, fast.'

'Will he...?' That was Maggie, but Winston ignored her.

'Follow me,' he said.

'Wait.' I took the torch from him again and shone it around, highlighting each one of us and counting: five young adults, three old ones, five children.

'We're all here,' I said then, 'Let's go.'

Just ten minutes from Jonestown Rex's Jeep's tyre burst. They stopped to change it, causing a further delay and Rex to arrive almost half an hour later than his men. By now his Jeep was the first in a new convoy, for several Guyana Defence Force army trucks and Jeeps had drawn up behind his. The Jonestown gates were wide open for once, and Rex's Jeep drove right in.

Steve was waiting for him at the gate. He ran along beside the Jeep until it stopped, then leaned in through the window. His face was a mask of dismay.

'This is... it's terrible, Rex, terrible. They're dead, all of them. The whole damn lot, hundreds!'

Rex leapt from the Jeep and hurried into the compound. There he stopped and gasped in utter horror. In the grey dawn light, hundreds of bodies lay before him. Between the bodies, a slight mist lifted from the ground. Somewhere, a cock crowed, and the first birds begin to chirp at the early-morning splendour.

Rex stood rooted to the ground, but only for a second. A minute later he was his old professional self, taking charge and giving orders.

'Radio the Embassy,' he told one man, and, 'Get the bodies counted,' he told another. 'See if anyone's alive.'

He himself began to step across the bodies, and no professionalism in the world could banish the sheer dread clutching his heart right now: one of them might be Zoe.

Next to him, Guyana Defence Force soldiers spread out and stepped among the bodies too, turning some of them over, their faces masks that showed no emotion.

An aide approached Rex: 'Would you please follow me, sir.' He led Rex over to a house, a little apart and set in a garden, bigger and more elaborate than the others. The front door stood open, and they entered. Rex followed the aide into a bedroom. Jones's body lay across a luxurious white bed, flat on its back with arms sprawled out, in the middle of the forehead a bullet hole in an aureole of dried blood. Around his head the fluffy counterpane had turned to red.

. . .

Our two canoes slid up to the wooden jetty at Akinawa village. The first canoe was Winston's. Behind him sat Maggie with Dave in her arms. Several people sat on the riverbank waiting for us, and as we approached the jetty they called and waved and walked down to meet us, some bearing kerosene lamps even though the sky had turned the pale grey of first light.

I recognised two people among those welcoming us. I leapt from the canoe and a moment later, I was in Aunt Edna's arms, and then in Uncle Bill's.

The next few minutes went by in a flurry of activity. Uncle Bill, on hearing of Dave's plight, immediately gave orders to a youth, who ran back down to the jetty and paddled off downstream at a breakneck speed. Winston organised several more canoes to go in the opposite direction, and they too sped off. The rest of us followed Uncle Bill, Dave limp in his arms, up to the village.

Rex looked up at the carrion crows circling overhead, then down at the body at his feet. Young and female, face downwards. Hair just like Zoe's. He held his breath and turned it over and for the fourteenth time that morning breathed out in relief. Not Zoe. On he went, stepping over bodies.

The scene was surreal. A bucolic peace lay over Jonestown. Birds chirped gaily, swooping and sailing across the pale blue sky. An early-morning mist rose up, covering the earth in a diaphanous blanket as if to shroud the gruesome vision of death. Men, Rex's men and GDF soldiers, walked among the bodies, slowly, as if dazed, knee-deep in the mist, some bending over to peer through it to the bodies below. There was a flurry of activity at the gate and Rex walked over to see what it was.

Dr Mootoo, a Guyanese pathologist, had arrived from Georgetown, and Rex walked with him back to the bloodless battlefield, filling him in with as many details as he could spare.

The same aide as before approached Rex. His voice trembled as he spoke: 'Would you come here a minute, sir.'

He led Rex over to a small wooden hut and stood back to let him enter.

It was dark inside the hut, for closed curtains hung at the windows. It took a few seconds for Rex to get used to the light, and only then did he see her: a woman, with two children, cowering in a corner, the woman hugging the children to her. All three stared at Rex, wide-eyed and speechless.

'She won't talk, sir.'

Rex walked over to the woman and reached out a hand. She stared back at him, then at the hand, and finally she took it and let herself be pulled up. The two children clung to her skirt, pulling it tight against her legs, and scrambled to their feet.

'What's your name?' Rex asked gently.

'Gladys,' replied the woman. 'My daughter—' And she collapsed in a heap on the ground.

Rex turned to his aide. 'Go and get Dr Mootoo,' he said.

Dave writhed in pain, muttering in his sleep. Maggie held his hand, wiped the sweat from his face and looked up anxiously at Uncle Bill. 'Will he be all right?' she asked for the umpteenth time, but he only shook his head and looked concerned. Alexis, sitting at Dave's other side, leaned forward to pick up his wrist and take his pulse.

'The antivenom will be here soon,' she said, but her face told a different story, one of vanishing hope. Uncle Bill prepared a syringe, slid the needle into Dave's arm. He looked at his watch and frowned.

I sat at the foot of the bed, Tammy in my arms. She had slept all through the hubbub, but now she began to stir, and cry. She'd be hungry, as we all were.

I took her outside the hut and went in search of Aunt Edna;

she'd taken the old women to another hut and put them to bed, and then she had taken care of the children, fed them and put them to bed too. She'd help me find food for Tammy. Yet the moment I moved, Tammy fell asleep in my arms again.

As I walked through the village an approaching motorboat chugged nearer. A youth ran down to the jetty to meet it, and I followed him. The motorboat drew up. The youth grabbed the rope thrown at him and tied it to the jetty. Andy Roper stepped out of the boat, carrying a cool-box. He rushed up to the village, passing me, but as he passed he stopped for a second, and our glances met. He smiled and rushed on. I followed him into the hut.

The gasp of relief as he entered was the most beautiful sound of that morning. He waved at everyone, glanced at Dave, and opened the cool-box. He removed a small container, labelled ANTIVENOM. KEEP COOL.

I longed to watch, but Tammy stirred again and cried out in that penetrating tone of babies serious with their hunger. I left the hut.

I ran into Aunt Edna just leaving the community hut where the others slept. She found me a banana for Tammy, which would have to do till the village woke up and cooked breakfast was served. I went down to the jetty to feed her; by now she was screaming as if in the grip of a terrible torture, most distracting for those tending Dave and those asleep. I clasped her to me and rocked her and stroked her silky hair to quieten her; she was far too hysterical to eat – she missed her mum.

The horror of all that had gone before – pandemonium, death, terror, unspeakable tragedy, and the bundle of my own personal pain – all faded into the background in the present anguish of this one tiny being and her need for solace and food. I began to hum, the first song that came to mind, the gospel the old ladies had sung during our nightmare.

At once, Tammy stopped crying. She must have been about

six months old, a small, slight baby with huge, limpid eyes that now looked up at me, suddenly trusting. As I broke off bits of banana she reached for them, and I let her feed herself. We looked at each other for the longest time, both earnest, while she ate. I told her in silence that her world had changed dramatically. There'd be no more Mom for her. Did she have relatives in America, a dad, a grandma? Tears swelled in my eyes, and I bent down to kiss the top of her head.

The creek was as smooth and clear as a mirror. Not one ripple ruffled its surface, and its silver sheen reflected the treetops, a white sliver of moon and a single cloud scurrying past. The calmness settled into my soul, a healing hand upon the churning waters this terrible night had thrown up. Peace. Be still. Even the jungle song spoke to me and calmed me.

After a while Tammy fell asleep. I got up and strolled back to the house, holding her lightly pressed to me, my chin just touching the crown of her head. A sweet baby smell tickled my nostrils, conjuring up a deeply buried memory: me, aged six, holding a newborn, spellbound with wonder. Maybe in this very village.

It's a mesmerising scent, penetrating deep into the soul and playing upon it as on a harp. Emotion welled in me, soft and vulnerable and melting. A love as strong and pure as had she been my own, and yet free, not tarnished with the selfish stain of possession. A love so sweet and strong I'd run from it for years, for that sweetness, the loss of it, had been too bitter to bear.

In that night of carnage I found healing and all grief gone. My tears were not only for the dead but for the living. Tammy was all children, everywhere, and I was every mother.

I entered the *benab*, the round thatched-roof community hut. Except for Alexis, Dave and his mother, our group now slept snug in a web of hammocks lashed to the supporting poles and pillars. I found an empty hammock for Tammy, laid her in it and was about to return to Dave when an ear-splitting crash sliced the calm and a human cry tore through the night:

'You bitch! You fucking bitch! Take that! And that! And that!'

I ran towards the noise, which had come from the middle of the village. There stood Lucy, clutching an axe in both hands, chopping at the tree trunk that served as a bench. She hewed at it as if it were a living beast, hacking at it with the rage and venom of a maniac, screaming foul words and curses at it. Under her attack the log began to splinter away, and on she hacked without lag or loss of strength. I screamed at her to stop – I dared not approach, for the demented way she flung the axe behind her and flailed at the log warned me to stay away. She had lost her senses; anything before her would feel that blade.

The noise drew others from their huts, and within minutes a sizeable crowd of villagers had gathered around. Oblivious to her audience, Lucy hacked away, still screaming at the log.

'Bitch! Murderess! Take that! And that! Die, you bitch, die!'

And then, as suddenly as it had started, it was over. She flung the axe from her and collapsed in a heap on the ground, sobbing as if her heart would break. I walked up, knelt beside her and laid a hand on her heaving back.

'Lucy... Lucy, it's all right. It's over. We're safe. We're alive and safe. Moira's dead. It's all over.'

She sat up at those words and looked at me as if about to grab the axe and start her attack all over again, on me. In her eyes burned a fury so hot I flinched away.

'You don't get it, right? You still don't get it. Moira ain't dead. That fucking murdering bitch who killed my baby and all my friends ain't dead. She was never gonna kill herself, you crazy? She's gone. She planned this whole thing and she's gone. I bet she's in Venezuela by now, with that monster and the money. They won. You get it now? The fucking bitch won!'

. . .

He'd lost count of the bodies. He'd not missed one, but none of them was Zoe. His men must think him mad, walking through the ranks of corpses, turning the females on to their backs, making sure. He did not explain his actions – he could not.

Negative. Negative. Negative. Negative identification. He repeated the official designation to himself with each corpse that was not Zoe. How often he'd used those words in the course of duty. How many times an American body had turned up somewhere in the world, and he'd had to ask relatives for a *positive identification.* How soulless those words. Yet *negative identification* were the only words that kept him from yelling and falling to the ground and hammering it with his fists, the only words that gave him hope. Each time he said them he rejoiced even as he tottered on the brink of desolation.

He had to return to Georgetown; they were waiting for him. Personal issues were getting in the way of duty. But to hell with duty! To hell with the mind-numbing, soul-destroying reduction of people to ciphers and statistics, of playing with life and death as if humans were pawns on the chessboard of foreign policy. If he found Zoe alive and well, he would whisk her away to a tropical island somewhere far away from here. Bali or Tahiti or some such place. But it was a very big *if,* and with every corpse that was not her, dread mingled with hope; for if she were not here, dead, then she might be somewhere else dead, and that was worse, as *somewhere else* was infinite.

Another female corpse was missing: Moira's. And yet another corpse, that of the brute they called Bruno.

He remembered the flatbed truck in the middle of the road, and the walkie-talkie he knew was Moira's because on his last visit she had been carrying it around. There was a connection between the abandoned truck and the missing persons. Perhaps the two had fled and taken Zoe with them as a hostage; and when she was no longer needed they'd kill her and fling away her corpse. Toss it into the river, where Amerindians would find it floating, black and bloated, in a few days' time, while Moira and Bruno escaped to Venezuela. That was why he almost preferred to find the corpse now, here, rather than face the uncertainty of not knowing. And yet, not knowing left hope, something to cling to.

I led Lucy down to the creek and she told me the whole story. She had calmed down by now, the fire in her eyes extinguished. Her face was dull and flat, as if all will to live had left it.

'Moira never intended to die,' she told me. Her voice was monotonous, almost bored. 'She *wanted* this whole thing to happen. At best, she *let* it happen. Moira ain't suicidal. She ain't mad, like Dad. She ain't nothing but a plain old murderer. A mass murderer. Jones would never have succeeded without her. She and Bruno, they won.'

'But *why?* What's the point?'

'Of allowing a thousand innocents to die? Well, I guess now it's money. We had a hundred thousand dollars in cash in Jonestown, and a couple million more in number accounts all over the world. She's a signatory. And Bruno. All they gotta do now is go and get the loot.'

The morning's chill crept into my bones. Moira's icy eyes arose in my vision, and now I knew what it was that made them so different to all the other Jonestownians. That *lost-ness* was missing from them. Behind the steely fanaticism I'd seen in the eyes of all the diehards I'd met there had always been that abysmal despair, a bottomless chasm of it. Even, ultimately, in Jones's eyes. Not in Moira's. Lucy was right: she wasn't suicidal.

'But that doesn't make sense,' I said. 'If they were both signatories, and could get at the money, and were friends, why didn't they just leave Jonestown, together, months ago?'

'Because Dad would've hunted them down. They'd never have been safe nowhere in the world. Dad's got contacts, spies, even CIA people, everywhere. You've only seen the mad version of him; I knew him before he went crazy, and he was no fool. Wherever she went, he'd hunt her down, if he was alive. No, Dad had to die first. Moira knows that.'

'But why everyone else? Why couldn't she just kill him and get away with the loot? Why this whole crazy thing with mass suicide? Was that all her idea?'

Lucy shook her head.

'No. That was all the madness of Jim Jones. Moira just sat it out. Moira was never a true believer. She didn't join People's Temple for the same reason we did. We were idealists; we wanted a better world, we dreamed of a perfect society, of love and peace and harmony. Not Moira. At first, all she wanted was power. She gets her kicks from being on top, watching others cringing at her feet. She killed my Serena! She hasn't been with Jones for very long – not more than five years – but from the moment she joined, she was a leader. And a sadist. She gets a kick from hurting others. She encouraged Dad, goaded him on. At first the power was all his, but the more he drifted into insanity, the more she was able to take over. See, she'd never have been able to build up such a huge following on her own. Moira ain't got no charisma, people shrink from her. The charisma was all Dad's.'

'So, he was just her puppet? She used his charisma to get what she wanted?'

'Yes. When Dad began to talk of mass suicide she saw that as her chance. We were doomed. But we were always doomed. Jonestown just wasn't working, and where else could we go? We were trapped. So I guess she got Bruno over on to her side – that was easy enough; he's so dumb.'

'If he's stupid, how come he's a signatory?'

'Exactly for that reason! Dad didn't want too many intelligent people in charge of the funds. One person clever enough to talk to the bank people, and one stupid one devoted to him. Two people who would never get along. That's the two of them. He knew Moira hates Blacks.'

'She does?'

'Of course. You should hear her when she gets one of us alone. She's got a foul mouth, that bitch. Hitler would have been proud of her; but it wasn't Jews she wanted eliminated, it was us. Until that day she wanted power over us.'

'So how did she get Bruno on her side?'

Lucy chuckled. 'The way women have done it since the beginning of time. Alexis told me. They did it right next door to her room, in the pharmacy, the room where they kept the poison. There ain't many places for privacy in Jonestown, and that's one of them. She thought Alexis was drugged; but no, she heard it all. Grunt, grunt, grunt.' Lucy snorted to imitate copulating pigs, and made a lewd gesture.

'So, once they were all dead, she and Bruno would scoot. To Venezuela. And nobody in the world would know, cos everyone who knew 'bout the money was dead. They'd get the money, and then she'd get rid of him.'

I could say nothing to that. A new sense of horror crept through me. Mass suicide was bad enough, but this was worse – the sheer evil it would take to pull through such a thing was beyond my understanding. I was speechless. Lucy too seemed to have run out of words, and we simply sat there on the creek bank. Almost an hour had passed, and morning was approaching. A soft grey mist was rising from the earth and the sky above the eastern riverbank glowed with the first morning rays.

Someone tapped me on the shoulder from behind. I swung round: it was Andy. I looked up at him.

'How's Dave?'

But I knew before he spoke; for his eyes smiled.

'He's going to make it.'

Relief swept through me. Lucy and I looked at each other, and for the first time since her chopping fit, she smiled. We hugged each other in relief. I longed to bawl. *He'll make it. Brave Dave will make it. He's not going to die.* It was the best thing in this night of horror, a miracle.

I pulled myself together and looked up at Andy, who was speaking again.

'Your uncle's taking him to hospital in the motorboat. He'll order a chopper to take him from there to Georgetown.'

'I'll go with them,' Lucy said firmly. 'Me and Danny and Granma. His mom's my best friend, she needs me.'

Alexis walked up. I opened my arms and she flung herself on me. Then Lucy too nudged in between us and we all wept together. None of us shed tears. We couldn't. Dry-eyed, we clung to each other. We wailed out our agony, the three of us, and our relief. We moaned in grief, we choked in release. We'd made it. But so many hadn't... This clinging to each other was all the comfort we had left. We had no tears; our wails were dry croaks. Then we pulled apart.

Andy still stood there, and he was crying too, and he had tears. But he wiped them away with the back of his hand as we turned to him.

'Let's go,' he said.

We walked down to the jetty and that's where the four of us sat for the next hour, talking quietly. That's where Dora found us, with a breakfast of hot bakes and mashed pumpkin and steaming cups of coffee. That's where we watched the world turn golden and heard the sheer delight of early-morning birdsong. Amerindians in their canoes slid past and waved, and the world woke up on the morning of the first day of the rest of my life, cut clean away by a night of utter devastation.

Then the motorboat came and some of us left, and the rest of us got into the canoes and rowing boats that would take us back to civilisation. And, in my case, back to Rex.

. . .

It was the longest half-hour of his life. Everything in him soared, and everything in him was an outpouring of gratitude to whichever power had brought about the miracle. She was alive! He'd known she would come, sooner or later. He'd waited.

At first it was just a very faint humming, hardly discernible above the birdsong. But it grew louder by the minute, and finally, he made it out to be human voices, singing, and he even recognised the tune, and finally made out the words:

Michael row the boat ashore, Alleluia!

A canoe rounded the corner and slid nearer. Rex stood up to watch. He could see four heads.

River is deep and the river is wide, alleluia! Milk and honey on the other side! Alleluia!

As it drew up to the jetty, Rex's heart sank. No Zoe in there; just an Amerindian rowing and three old women singing. He sat down again, but shot back up immediately: a second boat.

This one was a rowing boat. He could see the backs of the rowers, a man and a woman. Facing them – and him – at the prow of the boat, two women. One was – Zoe! His heart lurched; he waved, with both hands. She waved back, with one hand, less enthusiastically than he'd hoped, but as the boat drew nearer, he saw that she had a baby on her lap and that explained it.

The boat drew up and he was there, reaching out for the rope. One of the rowers, the man, stood up and handed him the rope. Rex pulled the boat in. Their eyes met, and something passed between them; Rex felt it to be an instant dislike, mistrust, hostility, totally uncalled for since the man had an agreeable face and a friendly smile, eyes that held laughter beneath a surface of sorrow and fatigue.

Rex grimaced; what was this man doing here? Who was he? What was his connection to Zoe? Why was he in the boat with her?

'Hi, I'm Andy,' said the man. He leapt on to the jetty, thanked Rex and took the rope. Simultaneously, the two men leaned forward, both offering Zoe, now standing up in the boat, a helping hand. She hesitated, looked from one to the other. Then slowly, she held out the baby and passed it to Andy, and took Rex's hand.

Rex could only gulp aloud as he pulled her to him. She fell into his arms and to his great shock and relief and joy burst into tears, heaving and choking as if the flood of water held back for years now burst through a dam and convulsed her body in sobs so violent he thought she would fall. He held her so she wouldn't, rubbing her back and whispering in her ear the words he'd been meaning to tell her for weeks, but hadn't.

CHAPTER FORTY-EIGHT

Alexis said, 'And still she got away with it.'

Rex frowned. 'Who?'

'Moira, of course. You still don't get it, do you? Moira's role in the whole drama.'

The four of us, Alexis, Andy, Rex and I, sat on the hospital canteen's veranda enjoying a second breakfast of fried eggs on toast and yet more coffee. I'd been dreaming of bed for hours but knew I could never sleep, and anyway, the men showed no inclination of leaving us. Between us, Alexis and I had been piecing together the plot of last night's story for Rex's benefit, and Andy's.

'It's true,' Rex said. 'Moira's body wasn't there. She's gone.'

'And I bet Bruno's body was missing too?'

'That's right. I specifically looked for the two of them, because they're the only two, apart from Jones himself, whom I'd be able to identify. How did you know?'

Alexis said: 'They'll be in Venezuela by now; they won.'

Rex looked up. 'What do you mean? You make it sound as if...'

Alexis nodded, and told Rex the rest. About Moira and Bruno, and the money, and Moira's diabolical plan.

'Once the suicides were well under way they must have taken the flatbed truck and scooted,' she concluded. 'They planned—'

Rex reached out and put his hand on her arm.

'Wait a minute. They took the flatbed truck?'

'Must have done. And gone to some guy named... I forget the name. A Portuguese guy with a boat.'

I shot: 'Pereira? Vinnie Pereira?' I looked at Andy, and he nodded. It seemed so long ago now, the two of us at Vinnie's buying chicken wire. I had not yet heard this part of the story, the details of Moira's flight. Now I knew instinctively: that sparkling new launch we'd seen at Vinnie's, so out of place in the ramshackle boathouse, belonged to Moira.

'That's the one. She'd bought a boat and moored it with Vinnie. She and Bruno must have driven off with the flatbed truck, must have driven it straight to Vinnie, taken the boat. By now they'll be in Venezuela.'

'Except,' Rex said slowly, 'except that the flatbed truck is nowhere near Vinnie's. It was in the middle of the road when we came up last night. Miles from Port Kaituma. I found a walkie-talkie in it, Moira's. I recognised it by the tape holding it together.'

'They must have had engine trouble. Or they ran out of gas.'

Rex nodded. 'And had to walk to Vinnie's, through the bush, beside the road. That would take hours.'

He was already on his feet. He looked at his watch, then at Andy. 'We might still catch them. You coming?'

Andy nodded, stood up and looked from me to Alexis. 'See you later.'

But Alexis looked at me, and I nodded. We both got up. She spoke for me.

'We're coming too.'

. . .

Vinnie's Hardware looked deserted; the shop's door was closed, and the only sign of life was a scrawny cat meandering through the trees at the edge of the clearing. But then, it had been deserted the last time I was here as well. Vinnie, I remembered, had been in the boathouse. That sparkling new launch must be Moira's.

'You girls stay here,' said Rex. A gun had materialised into his hand and, beckoning to Andy, he crept up to the main door. A moment later, he was inside the shop, Andy behind him.

Another moment later, all hell broke loose.

The Jeep door at my side flew open and a giant's arm was flung round me, tearing me from my seat. And then I was in that giant's grip, clutched to his chest as he dragged me, writhing and screaming, towards the shop. Alexis, still in the Jeep, cried out and I heard her scrambling behind me. A shot rang out; I looked behind me and saw Alexis on the ground, grasping a bleeding leg.

Simultaneously, a woman's voice called: 'Bennett, come out of there.'

I looked around, and there she was: Moira; and she too held a gun, aimed straight at the door.

'Bennett!'

But Rex had heard the first time. He appeared at the door. The moment he saw me, held against Bruno, helpless as a rag doll, he turned as white as a ghost.

'Hands up and come out here,' Moira said. 'And tell your friend to come too. Otherwise we shoot these ladies.'

But Andy had already emerged from the shop. 'Hands up. Both of you. Come away from that door.'

Rex and Andy, hands in the air, edged towards the Jeep. Simultaneously, Moira and Bruno sidled towards the shop, with me as their hostage. Bruno lifted me over his shoulder and carried me through the shop as if I were a rag-doll, while Moira walked backwards after us, protecting us with her gun. Down the rickety steps to the boathouse.

Vinnie Pereira's body lay sprawled on the boathouse floor in a pool of blood. Bruno stumbled over it and almost fell, but caught himself in time and threw me into the launch.

A moment later, Moira, still walking backwards, had joined us. She handed Bruno the gun and moved to the boat's bow. It growled into action. Another moment, and the three of us, me, Moira and Bruno, were speeding away down the Kaituma River, headed for the coast, the Atlantic Ocean, and Venezuela, just a few miles north.

Except, as I knew without a doubt, I'd never make it that far.

Bruno stood at the helm, me as a shield before him, his gun aimed at the boathouse. Sure enough, only a few seconds later the motorboat raced out, Rex and Andy in it, heading straight towards us, Andy at the helm and Rex at the bow, his own gun in his hand. But he did not shoot. How could he? I was a perfect shield for Bruno.

Bruno, on the other hand, did shoot. He fired three times. Rex ducked, and he missed.

'Bruno! Don't fire all the bullets!' cried Moira.

'Right, ma'am.'

Bruno fired two more shots, then stopped. I knew who he was saving the last bullet for.

The distance between the two boats widened. I stared out at the motorboat, and as it diminished, so did the last tendril of my hope. I was alone with two murderers in the middle of the river. The boat slowed.

'OK, Bruno, get rid of her.'

I squeezed my eyes together and held my breath as Bruno loosened his grip and aimed the pistol at my forehead. A few last thoughts. Would I feel the explosion, in the seconds before my head burst open, or would death come simultaneously? I waited.

A click. That was it. No explosion. No bang. No death.

Moira turned.

'What's the matter?'

'Bullets use up, ma'am.'

'You idiot! I *told* you not to fire them all!'

'I didn't, ma'am. Only five I fire.'

Bruno held up the gun and looked at it as if puzzled at its failure to perform.

'Moronic nigger! You should have fired four! Four! Can't you count? You used one on Pereira! Throw her out of the boat!'

A moment later, I was underwater, thrashing for the surface. The launch sped off, towards Venezuela, freedom, and Moira's new beginning. And I was alive.

I swam towards the approaching motorboat.

CHAPTER FORTY-NINE

THREE MONTHS LATER

I cut through the creek in a lazy crawl, eyes closed, back towards the Parrot Creek jetty. The water was alternately icy cold and warm, patched by sunlight and shadow, stained deep amber from centuries of decaying leaves, and as I grabbed the ladder and hoisted myself up it sloshed away from me with a deeply satisfying splatter.

I saw Rex right away, sitting on the jetty near my heap of clothes, arms round his knees, grinning like the cat that got the cream. As I walked towards him he stood up and threw me the roll of towel. I patted my face with it and wrapped it round my waist. We embraced.

'That was quick! I wasn't expecting you for another two weeks!'

'I came as soon as I got your summons.'

'Not a summons – just an invitation.'

'Let's just call it an excuse to get the first flight out of Washington, and a charter plane up here.'

After White Night, Rex had returned to the US with the last bodies flown out of Jonestown. He'd thought it would only be for a few days, but then he sent a telegram saying he'd be away much longer, six weeks or so. Those six weeks had turned into three months. He'd written; I'd replied. And then I told him to come. That was a week ago.

'When did you get in? How long are you staying?'

'Last night. As long as you want me to?'

I pulled a T-shirt over my wet swimsuit, wrapped the towel round my head.

'If you want, we can go swimming again.'

'No – I've had enough. Let's go up.'

We walked up the wooden slats to the farm, me leading the way, Rex chatting as we went.

'I hadn't realised how much this country has gotten under my skin. I really missed it... it's good to be back.'

'Guyana's like that. It's got a homey feel to it. I thought it affected just us Guyanese, but foreigners have told me the same.'

'Yes – homey, that's the word. Anyway, I'm here now. How's Alexis doing? She recovered OK?'

I nodded. The gunshot wound on her thigh had not been deep – enough to disable her at that last showdown, but in Andy's hands it had healed up well enough. 'She couldn't stick it out around here. She's back in America.'

'And Lucy?'

'Also back home, back with her mom. She writes; she needs time but she'll be OK, and her boy, and her grandma. She's applying to college, wants to start a new life, put all this behind her. Like all of us.'

Our eyes met; he smiled and nodded, as if he knew what I meant, but he didn't, so I didn't smile back, and doubt flitted across his eyes. He tried to take my hand, but I managed to discreetly move it away.

We reached my hut. I led the way inside.

'You get my best chair!' I said, pulling out my only one for him. 'Would you like a drink? What'll it be, Campari and orange, or pure warm water?'

He chuckled, and I poured him a glass without waiting for an answer. Far from reassuring him, my weak attempts at jokes seemed to be making him nervous. He wiped his face with a handkerchief, but immediately more beads of sweat broke out along his temples. I felt sorry for him. He looked around the room.

'So this is where you live!'

'Yep. My little castle. Some fruit?'

Again, not waiting for an answer, I grabbed a plate, a knife and a bowl of mangoes, which I set on the bed. I sat down crosslegged and began to peel and slice the plumpest mango.

'You said – we had to talk?'

'That's right. But it wasn't *that* urgent.'

'Sure it was, for me. Zoe, I've told you how I feel.'

I decided not to dither. To plunge right in.

'Rex, I can't marry you. I wish I could, but I can't.'

'But why? It was all so clear when I left. I thought you—'

'Things have changed.' I shook my head.

He spoke again. 'What do you mean? What's changed?'

I bent my head and concentrated on the mango. I arranged the peeled slices nicely on the plate, got up and threw away the skins, trying to delay the moment. This was harder than I'd thought. I handed him the plate of sliced mango.

'A couple of things. Actually, it's one thing, and I've known it a long time. Rex – it's been there all along. I guess you can call it a lack of trust. I know your feelings for me are genuine and deep but there are just some issues I can't get over.'

'Like what?'

'Like, why did you betray me to Moira, or whoever you spoke to at Jonestown?'

'No idea what you're talking about.'

'Come on, you know what I mean. After my visit to Georgetown. You got straight on the radio and told them about Lucy. OK, I know that's not really betraying me, but I'd told you about Lucy in confidence and as a result they put her in the Box for ten days! That wasn't very nice. I trusted you!'

Rex broke out in smiles. 'Ah, so that's what it is! Thank God!'

'What do you mean?'

'Zoe, that wasn't me! Lucy was right, we *did* have a spy in the Embassy who told tales back to Jonestown, but it wasn't any of us Americans – it was Sita, Sita Singh. My secretary! It all came out during the initial investigation – we'd always suspected there was a Jonestown spy in our midst. Sita listened at doors. She was supposed to tell them of anyone from Jonestown who wanted to escape... a simple case of bribery. She confessed. She did it for the money, and now she's gone.'

'Oh!'

'So it's OK. I'm innocent! Pure as the driven snow!'

'Not quite.'

His face fell. 'What do you mean?'

'That's peanuts. The other thing is huge. And you know what it is.'

He said nothing.

'I've been doing some more research. Collecting information, gathering data. I've got a friend in Georgetown helping; she's got access to people who – well, let's say they tell her stuff the public doesn't get to know. She sent me some – documents. Look.'

I got up and picked up a large cardboard box from the floor. I took the lid off it, and ruffled through the heap of papers inside.

'I got copies of all kinds of official reports. Like this, about the body count. There's a huge discrepancy between the number originally given out; that said three hundred dead. Far less than the *final* body count, which was over nine hundred.

Why, Rex? The Americans said the Guyanese didn't count properly. Did that assessment come from you?'

No answer.

'There's talk of seven hundred people fleeing into the bush – seven hundred! We know that didn't happen, Rex, and that must be how you got the three-hundred count. It's all a mess, and those who know the truth aren't talking. Or are you, Rex?'

Silence. I shuffled some more among the papers, then raised my hands in despair.

'At first it all seemed so straightforward. It isn't. Why were no autopsies performed on the bodies? Why did the US take so long to fly them out? Why did some of the bodies have injection marks, just below the shoulder blades? Dr Mootoo confirmed this. Everything contradicts everything else, Rex. People who know won't speak, or tell lies. The further I dig, the more of an unholy mess I find.'

I burrowed some more. 'Ah, here it is. The only thing that makes sense – copies of letters they found in Jonestown, written by Lucy, sort of a secret journal she was keeping. But that's irrelevant right now.'

I put Lucy's journal aside, and dug out something else. 'Look at this, for instance. The first news that the massacre had taken place came from the CIA, at 2 a.m. What was the CIA doing up there that night? And how come you were there so early? How come, Rex? And why *you*?'

No answer. I brought out my *pièce de résistance*. It was in a manila envelope.

'This is a transcript of a tape made in Jonestown. Jones and co really loved making tapes; according to Alexis, as a legacy for when they were no more. He absolutely believed in the historical significance of White Night, believed that he himself would go down in history as a great revolutionary and martyr, à la Che Guevara. I've got piles and piles of transcripts. But I like this one best. It's a conversation between Jones and Patsy Boyle; it took place just a few days before Ryan's visit. It seems Patsy made one last quick visit to Jonestown at that time, soon after you and I had visited her. A bit of this is about me. She's trying to persuade Jones to invite me into Jonestown – Patsy really believed in me. But look at this bit.'

I passed the page to Rex. He took the transcript and read. I knew it by heart: the typical Jones rant about CIA spies and FBI traitors. Patsy trying to convince him to invite me. More by Patsy, apparently indecipherable. Patsy must have been sitting a bit too far from the mike. Then, from Jones, excited: 'Really? Really?'

More from Patsy: according to the transcript, 'indecipherable'.

Another rant on the CIA from Jones. CIA spies, CIA fascists, CIA murderers. Another sentence from Patsy: 'indecipherable'.

And then:

It's bent! It's bent! (Excited, shouting.)
Patsy: (indecipherable.)
Jones: Switch off that tape.

I could almost hear the final click.

Rex handed me back the page, and I placed it in its envelope. Sweat poured down his temples.

'At first I was puzzled,' I said. 'I just didn't get it. Those words, "it's bent", really irritated me. What bent thing could have excited him this much? I thought and thought – what can you *bend*? A spoon, maybe, if you're a psychic. A road bends. You can bend the truth.'

I looked up, and our eyes met. He looked away.

'The truth.' I snapped my fingers. 'Click! The transcribers got it wrong. Not "bent", but "Bennett". You. The CIA. Jones was right. They were deep into Jonestown, weren't they? They knew a lot more than anybody else. *You* knew a lot more. *You* were deep into Jonestown. And you really scared Jones, didn't you? And *you* were chief of operations, or whatever you spy guys call it, weren't you?'

Rex kept his silence. His head was lowered. So was my voice.

'Once that clicked, I did some thinking. I tried to figure it out. I thought and thought about it, and the more I thought, the more things fell into place. And I have a theory. I really want to tell you. Is that OK?'

Rex shrugged, a tacit go-ahead.

'OK, what I think is this. You were watching Jonestown, that's clear. You even admitted that much to me, when we first met. But I think you were doing more than watching. I think you were planning something. I think you knew exactly what Jones was planning. Of course you did. You knew about White Night, and you took it seriously. How couldn't you? When Katy Harris escaped, she told you in plain words. You knew very well. That's why you tried to keep me out, right, Rex? You knew how bad it was. You knew – because you had a spy in there, didn't you?'

Rex said nothing. His head was lowered, and I knew it was because of what his eyes might give away.

I whispered. 'It was Moira, wasn't it? She was your spy.'

Rex ran his fingers through his hair and said nothing.

'It had to be her, the only one who never intended to die. Moira confirmed Katy's story about White Night. You and Moira had an arrangement. Moira would let you know when the real White Night was about to happen. Then you, the CIA, could move in and catch Jones at it, in flagrante, all the inmates lined up, the guards shooting the people who ran away. Then he could be arrested for murder, tried and hanged. Right? Only thing – Moira didn't warn you, because Moira had an agenda of her own, and her very own plan of escape, and never intended to play your game. You weren't prepared for Ryan's shooting, and you weren't ready for White Night. You didn't have enough troops out there to move in on time. It all went horribly wrong. Didn't it?'

Rex looked at me now, and gave me a half-smile and even, I thought, the ghost of a nod. But I wasn't finished.

'That's what I figured, and that's the more generous interpretation, the one I want to believe. But I discussed it with Alexis, and she has a totally different theory. The opposite, in fact. She thinks you *deliberately* drove Jones to do what he did. You knew how unstable he was, and you knew how to scare him even more. I assumed those gunshots from the bush were Jones scaring his own people, but what if they were really CIA? What if Jones's paranoia had a basis in truth? Alexis thinks so. Alexis thinks you – you plural, that is, the CIA, the USA – *wanted* this to happen, that you wanted to push Jones to the edge and over it. You wanted to scare him, and you knew the consequences very well, because of what Moira and Katy were saying, but you – you, plural – thought the deaths of a thousand poor Black women and children would be expendable, a small price to pay, a means to a greater end, which would be to show the danger of communism and what it leads to. And if that was the plan, you succeeded very well.'

A deathly silence fell between us. Rex looked straight at me this time, but even his eyes said nothing.

'So those are the two theories, mine and Alexis's. I prefer mine, because I want to believe the prettier, kinder, version. But, Rex, it's all right. Even if it's the other one, the ugly, callous, one, I don't think that it's *your* idea or *your* plan or *your* policy.'

Rex was trembling. I felt truly sorry for him. I reached out and placed a hand on his shoulder. I made my voice as kind as I could, because that was how I felt.

'I don't blame you for anything, Rex. You had a job, you did it, and I'm giving you the benefit of the doubt. I don't know what your role was in this and I don't want to know. Because, because...'

I paused, and our eyes met again, and in his hope he reached out to me, begging for clemency.

'Because I care about you.'

He took my hand, but I eased mine away from him. 'But, don't you see the irony of you and me, married?' I chuckled, but not in mirth. 'Me, the wife of a CIA agent. I don't think so. I've raged against the CIA most of my adult life. They helped bring down the one honest government we had in this country, our one good leader, Cheddi Jagan. It's personal, Rex.'

He looked up, started to speak, but I interrupted.

'But it's not just that. Think about it. If we were to marry, this would be between us all our lives. So much would be between us, big things, things we could never talk about because they're confidential. I'm after the truth of Jonestown, and you have most of it, and you won't ever be able to tell me. That kills me, Rex. It does!'

My voice trembled. This was harder than I'd imagined. I really cared for him; I did. He heard the break in my voice and looked up, took my hand. His eyes were moist, and looked into mine, and there was nothing covert in his, not one speck of a lie.

'Zoe, I love you and that's all that matters.'

'I know you do. And I want to, I think I could, love you too, if only... Rex, this was the biggest thing in my whole life and I just can't face seeing you every day and wondering what really happened and dying to know and knowing you know and wondering what you really did, and thinking of Patsy and how she ended up, and...'

Rex got up and marched to the wall, where he gazed out beyond the wire mesh. Then suddenly he swung round.

'Zoe, I'm leaving the CIA. I've already handed in my resignation. I've got to go back to Washington for a last debriefing and then I'll be free. I can wipe the slate clean, and you can too. We could put this horror entirely behind us. I know we could. I know I can. I know you could.'

I shook my head. 'I don't know. Maybe. Maybe some day.'

'I'll wait. As long as you like. Till you're ready.'

Right then I wanted to reach out, touch him. Pull him to me, tell him I was ready, now, that the gap between us wasn't real; that love was all it took to bridge it. But I heard my own voice speak, and I knew the decision stood, and it was right.

'Rex – I'm going away. Far from here. I can't stay here, where all this happened.'

'Where are you going to?'

'Back to India.'

'India! What for?'

I smiled wryly, aware of the irony. 'For peace and quiet, maybe? Just like you said, putting this all behind me. And finishing off what I started here.'

'What do you mean, finishing it off? It's all over.'

'No, Rex, it's not all over. Not for me. Take a look at this.'

There was only one way to get beyond this thing, this monster that had stepped into my life and broken it in two. It had gnawed its way into my being, and I had to let it out. Rex was right: I had to wipe the slate clean, and for me there was only one way.

I walked over to the table, where my typewriter still stood the way I'd left it earlier that morning.

I pulled the single sheet out of the carriage. I glanced at it before handing it to him.

White Night
By
Zoe Quint

A LETTER FROM SHARON

Dear Readers,

Thank you so much for reading *A Home for the Lost*. I do hope you enjoyed it; that would be my greatest reward! If you did enjoy it, perhaps you would like to share your pleasure with other readers through social media, or by writing a review? And if you'd like to keep up to date with my latest releases, please do sign up at the following link. Your email address will always be confidential and you can unsubscribe at any time.

www.bookouture.com/sharon-maas

In the meantime, I'd love to hear from you; you can use the contact form on my website, or else find me on the social media links below.

Sharon

www.sharonmaas.com

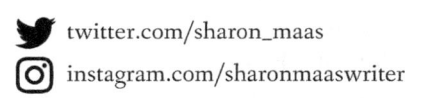

twitter.com/sharon_maas
instagram.com/sharonmaaswriter

BACKGROUND HISTORY AND ACKNOWLEDGMENTS

Before the late 70s, if you told an outside stranger you were from Guyana they'd either ask 'Where's that?' or else their eyes would light up in supposed recognition: Ghana! Yes! In Africa!

In 1978, that changed forever, and not in a good way. Now they'll say in sympathy, 'Ah, yes. Jonestown. Mass suicide. Terrible, terrible.'

Jonestown brought notoriety to Guyana; undeservedly so, as the tragedy really had nothing to do with the country in which it happened. The People's Temple could very well have settled in the jungles of Venezuela, Brazil or Colombia. But Guyana was politically convenient, and it is an English-speaking country, and that's where Jim Jones chose to bring his people. And so the words Jonestown and Guyana have ever since been irreversibly linked, to the discomfort of Guyanese everywhere.

Many of us are quick to deny the link. 'It has nothing to do with Guyana!' some of us say, or 'That was an American thing. Keep Guyana out of it!' With this book, I did the opposite; I set it squarely in Guyana, with Guyanese interacting with the Americans, and at the same time I made sure that readers understood that it was an alien thing, a stifled foreign body stuck in the middle of wholesome breathing nature: a force for disruption that never belonged.

My reasons for writing it were quite personal. In the early 70s, during my anti-establishment phase, I had settled with some friends on a farm not too far away from what would later be the Jonestown site. Intending to go off-grid, we tried to wrestle our own little piece of heaven from virgin land, and I lived there for several months. I was a freelance journalist at the time, but later, once I'd found my calling as a novelist, the inevitable happened: that niggling question *what if?* that is the launching pad of many a novel. What if, I thought, our own farm had been a neighbour of Jonestown and we had heard those noises, met some of the people there? What if I'd been curious enough to investigate? And so this story was born.

It has taken a few decades, but here is that book, in your hands. And you are probably wondering how much of this story is true and how much is embellished, and my answer is quite straightforward: the bones of the story are fact, but the flesh I've put on those bones is entirely fiction. And so Zoe and her friends and family are invented: Edna, Moira, Lucy, Rex, Andy, Bruno and Donna are all fictional. Everything pertaining to them, every word they speak, is a product of my overactive imagination.

Jim Jones and Congressman Ryan are, of course, real people, and what they did and what happened to them, except when they interact with made-up characters, is true. Ryan was killed as described, and Jones died of a gunshot wound to the head, one of only two people to die in Jonestown of a bullet. No one knows who shot Jones.

Patsy Boyd is based on a real character and so are her children, and their horrifying end is mostly accurate. There was indeed an Inner Circle in Jonestown, but nothing like the one in this book. Out of respect for their surviving family members, I've kept other real people out of the story; two real Jonestown people referenced have had a name change, while references to two well-known Guyanese have kept their real names.

From the beginning of my research into the Jonestown tragedy I've been supported mainly by one person: Fielding (Mac) McGehee, editor and research director of the Jonestown

Institute. McGehee is married to Rebecca Moore, who lost her two sisters and a nephew in the Jonestown tragedy. He and Rebecca spent decades recovering the People's Temple's tapes, documents and lost footage. They sometimes fought long battles with the FBI and other government agencies in their efforts to archive everything so as to preserve the temple's history, and to humanise those who died in Jonestown. Through their work we can all have a better understanding of what happened behind the scenes, and this is preserved on the website http://jonestown.sdsu.edu.

It is also Mac who transcribed the Jonestown tapes; most of the direct quotes and announcements ascribed to Jones in this book are his actual words. So are many of the statements made by Jonestown residents on the last night, in which they confirm their decision to commit 'revolutionary suicide', though the names have been changed. These quotes can be found in the immense body of work contained on the above website. All of them are in the public domain.

I have been in touch with Mac from from the very start, and he has encouraged and supported me in the writing of this, answered questions and asked some of his own; he knows that I've taken creative license with the facts, and supports that as well.

And so first of all, immense thanks go out to him; without him this book would never have been possible.

My thanks also to the wonderful staff at Bookouture, editors, copyeditors, and proofreaders, who helped to bring this project to life after so many decades.